The Heart of Rome by F. Marion Crawford

I0690391

A Tale of the 'Lost Water'

Francis Marion Crawford was born on August 2nd, 1854 at Bagni di Lucca, Italy. An only son and a nephew to Julia Ward Howe, the American poet and writer of 'The Battle Hymn of the Republic'.

His education began at St Paul's School, Concord, New Hampshire, then to Cambridge University; University of Heidelberg; and the University of Rome.

In 1879 Crawford went to India, to study Sanskrit and then edited The Indian Herald. In 1881 he returned to America to continue his Sanskrit studies at Harvard University.

At this time in Boston he lived at his Aunt Julia house and in the company of his Uncle, Sam Ward. His family was concerned about his employment prospects. After a singing career as a baritone was ruled out, he was encouraged to write.

In December 1882 his first novel, 'Mr Isaacs', was an immediate hit which was amplified by 'Dr Claudius' in 1883.

In October 1884 he married Elizabeth Berdan. They went on to have two sons and two daughters.

Encouraged by his excellent start to a literary career he returned to Italy with Elizabeth to make a permanent home, principally in Sant' Agnello, where he bought the Villa Renzi that then became Villa Crawford.

1

In the late 1890s, he began to write his historical works: 'Ave Roma Immortalis' (1898), 'Rulers of the South' (1900) and 'Gleanings from Venetian History' (1905). The Saracinesca series is perhaps his best work. 'Saracinesca' was followed by 'Sant' Ilario' in 1889, 'Don Orsino' in 1892 and 'Corleone' in 1897, that being the first major treatment of the Mafia in literature.

Francis Marion Crawford died at Sorrento on Good Friday 1909 at Villa Crawford of a heart attack.

Index of Contents

Chapter XXV
F. Marion Crawford – A Short Biography
F. Marion Crawford – A Concise Bibliography

CHAPTER I

The Baroness Volterra drove to the Palazzo Conti in the heart of Rome at nine o'clock in the morning, to be sure of finding Donna Clementina at home. She had tried twice to telephone, on the previous afternoon, but the central office had answered that "the communication was interrupted." She was very anxious to see Clementina at once, in order to get her support for a new and complicated charity. She only wanted the name, and expected nothing else, for the Conti had very little ready money, though they still lived as if they were rich. This did not matter to their friends, but was a source of constant anxiety to their creditors, and to the good Pompeo Sassi, the steward of the ruined estate. He alone knew what the Conti owed, for none of them knew much about it themselves, though he had done his best to make the state of things clear to them.

The big porter of the palace was sweeping the pavement of the great entrance, as the cab drove in. He wore his working clothes of grey linen with silver buttons bearing the ancient arms of his masters, and his third best gold-laced cap. There was nothing surprising in this, at such an early hour, and as he was a grave man with a long grey beard that made him look very important, the lady who drove up in the open cab did not notice that he was even more solemn than usual. When she appeared, he gave one more glance at the spot he had been sweeping, and then grounded his broom like a musket, folded his hands on the end of the broomstick and looked at her as if he wondered what on earth had brought her to the palace at that moment, and wished that she would take herself off again as soon as possible.

He did not even lift his cap to her, yet there was nothing rude in his manner. He behaved like a man upon whom some one intrudes when he is in great trouble.

The Baroness was rather more exigent in requiring respect from servants than most princesses of the Holy Roman Empire, for her position in the aristocratic scale was not very well defined.

She was not pleased, and spoke with excessive coldness when she asked if Donna Clementina was at home. The porter stood motionless beside the cab, leaning on his broom. After a pause he said in a rather strange voice that Donna Clementina was certainly in, but that he could not tell whether she were awake or not.

"Please find out," answered the Baroness, with impatience. "I am waiting," she added with an indescribable accent of annoyance and surprise, as if she had never been kept waiting before, in all the fifty years of her more or less fashionable life.

There were speaking-tubes in the porter's lodge, communicating with each floor of the great Conti palace, but the porter did not move.

"I cannot go upstairs and leave the door," he said.

"You can speak to the servant through the tube, I suppose!"

The porter slowly shook his massive head, and his long grey beard wagged from side to side.

"There are no servants upstairs," he said. "There is only the family."

"No servants? Are you crazy?"

"Oh, no!" answered the man meditatively. "I do not think I am mad. The servants all went away last night after dinner, with their belongings. There were only sixteen left, men and women, for I counted them."

"Do you mean to say—" The Baroness stopped in the middle of her question, staring in amazement.

The porter now nodded, as solemnly as he had before shaken his head.

"Yes. This is the end of the house of Conti."

Then he looked at her as if he wished to be questioned, for he knew that she was not really a great lady, and guessed that in spite of her magnificent superiority and coldness she was not above talking to a servant about her friends.

"But they must have somebody," she said. "They must eat, I suppose! Somebody must cook for them. They cannot starve!"

"Who knows? Who knows? Perhaps they will starve."

The porter evidently took a gloomy view of the case.

"But why did the servants go away in a body?" asked the Baroness, descending from her social perch by the inviting ladder of curiosity.

"They never were paid. None of us ever got our wages. For some time the family has paid nobody. The day before yesterday, the telephone company sent a man to take away the instrument. Then the electric light was cut off. When that happens, it is all over."

The man had heard of the phenomenon from a colleague.

"And there is nobody? They have nobody at all?"

The Baroness had always been rich, and was really trying to guess what would happen to people who had no servants.

"There is my wife," said the porter. "But she is old," he added apologetically, "and the palace is big. Can she sweep out three hundred rooms, cook for two families of masters and dress the Princess's hair? She cannot do it."

This was stated with gloomy gravity. The Baroness also shook her head in sympathy.

"There were sixteen servants in the house yesterday," continued the porter. "I remember when there were thirty, in the times of the old Prince."

"There would be still, if the family had been wise," said the Baroness severely. "Is your wife upstairs?"

"Who knows where she is?" enquired the porter by way of answer, and with the air of a man who fears that he may never see his wife again. "There are three hundred rooms. Who knows where she is?"

The Baroness was a practical woman by nature and by force of circumstances; she made up her mind to go upstairs and see for herself how matters stood. The name of Donna Clementina might not just now carry much weight beside those of the patronesses of a complicated charitable organization; in fact the poor lady must be in a position to need charity herself rather than to dispense it to others. But the Baroness had a deep-rooted prejudice in favour of the old aristocracy, and guessed that it would afterwards be counted to her for righteousness if she could be the first to offer boundless sympathy and limited help to the distressed family.

It would be thought distinctly smart, for instance, if she should take the Princess, or even one of the unmarried daughters, to her own house for a few days, as a refuge from the sordid atmosphere of debt and ruin, and beyond the reach of vulgar creditors, one of whom, by the way, she knew to be her own excellent husband. The Princess was probably not aware of that fact, for she had always lived in sublime ignorance of everything connected with money, even since her husband's death; and when good Pompeo Sassi tried to explain things, telling her that she was quite ruined, she never listened to what he said. If the family had debts, why did he not borrow money and pay them? That was what he was paid for doing, after all. It was true that he had not been paid for a year or two, but that was a wretched detail. Economy? Had not the Princess given up her second maid, as an extravagance? What more did the man expect?

The Baroness knew all this and reflected upon what she knew, as she deliberately got out of her cab at the foot of the grand staircase.

"I will go upstairs myself," she said.

"Padrona," observed the porter, standing aside with his broom.

He explained in a single word that she was at liberty to go upstairs if she chose, that it was not of the least use to go, and that he would not be responsible for any disappointment if she were afterwards not pleased. There is no language in the world which can say more in one word than the Italian, or less in ten thousand, according to the humour of the speaker.

The Baroness took no notice as she went up the stairs. She was not very tall, and was growing slowly and surely stout, but she carried her rather large head high and had cultivated importance, as a fine art, with some success. She moved steadily, with a muffled sound as of voluminous invisible silk bellows that opened and shut at each step; her outer dress was sombre, but fashionable, and she wore a long gold chain of curious and fine workmanship to carry her hand-glass, for she was near-sighted. Her thick hair was iron-grey, her small round eyes were vaguely dark with greenish lights, her complexion was like weak coffee and milk, sallow, but smooth, even and healthy. She was a strong woman of fifty years, well used to the world and its ways; acquisitive, inquisitive and socially progressive; not knowing how to wish back anything from the past, so long as there was anything in the future to wish for; a good wife for an ambitious man.

The magnificent marble staircase already looked neglected; there were deep shadows of dust in corners that should have been polished, there was a coat of grey dust on the head and shoulders of the colossal marble statue of Commodus in the niche on the first landing; in the great window over the next, the armorial crowned eagle of the Conti, cheeky, argent and sable, had a dejected look, as if he were moulting.

It was in March, and though the sun was shining brightly outside, and the old porter wore his linen jacket, as if it were already spring, there was a cold draught down the staircase, and the Baroness instinctively made haste up the steps, and was glad when she reached the big swinging door covered with red baize and studded with smart brass nails, which gave access to the grand apartment.

By force of habit, she opened it and went in. There used to be always two men in the outer hall, all day long, and sometimes four, ready to announce visitors or to answer questions, as the case might be. It was deserted now, a great, dismal, paved hall, already dingy with dust. One of the box-benches was open, and the tail of a footman's livery greatcoat which had been thrown in carelessly, hung over the edge and dragged on the marble floor.

The Baroness realized that the porter had spoken the truth and that all the servants had left the house, as the rats leave a sinking ship. One must really have seen an old ship sink in harbour to know how the rats look, black and grey, fat and thin, old and young, their tiny beads of eyes glittering with fright as they scurry up the hatches and make for every deck port and scupper, scrambling and tumbling over each other till they flop into the water and swim away, racing for safety, each making a long forked wake on the smooth surface, with a steady quick ripple like the tearing of thin paper into strips.

The strong middle-aged woman who stood alone in the empty hall knew nothing of sinking vessels or the ways of rats, but she had known incidentally of more than one catastrophe like this, in the course of her husband's ascendant career, and somehow he had always been mysteriously connected with each one. An evil-speaking old diplomatist had once said that he remembered Baron Volterra as a pawn-broking dealer in antiquities, in Florence, thirty years earlier; there was probably no truth in the story, but after Volterra was elected a Senator of the Kingdom, a member of the opposition had alluded to it with piquant irony and the result had been the exchange of several bullets at forty paces, whereby honour was satisfied without bloodshed. The seconds, who were well disposed to both parties, alone knew how much or how little powder there was in the pistols, and they were discreet men, who kept the secret.

The door leading to the antechamber was wide open, and the Baroness went on deliberately, looking about through her hand-glass, in the half light, for the shutters were not all open. Dust everywhere, the dust that falls silently at night from the ancient wooden ceilings and painted beams of Roman palaces, the dust of centuries accumulated above and sifting for ever to the floors below. It was on the yellow marble pier tables, on the dim mirrors in their eighteenth century frames, on the high canopy draped with silver and black beneath which the effigy of another big cheeky eagle seemed to be silently moulting under his antique crown, the emblem of a race that had lived almost on the same spot for eight hundred years, through good and bad repute, but in nearly uninterrupted prosperity. The Baroness, who hankered after greatness, felt that the gloom was a twilight of gods. She stood still

9

before the canopy, the symbol of princely rank and privilege, the invisible silk bellows were silent for a few seconds, and she wondered whether there were any procurable sum which she and her husband would grudge in exchange for the acknowledged right to display a crowned eagle, cheeky, argent and sable, in their hall, under a canopy draped with their own colours. She sighed, since no one could hear her, and she went on. The sigh was not only for the hopelessness of ever reaching such social greatness; it was in part the outward show of a real regret that it should have come to an untimely end. Her admiration of princes was as sincere as her longing to be one of them; she had at least the melancholy satisfaction of sympathizing with them in their downfall. It brought her a little nearer to them in imagination if not in fact.

The evolution of the snob has been going on quickly of late, and quicker than ever since vast wealth has given so many of the species the balance of at least one sort of power in society. His thoughts are still the same, but his outward shape approaches strangely near to that of the human being. There are snobs now, who behave almost as nicely in the privacy of their homes as in the presence of a duchess. They are much more particular as to the way in which others shall behave to them. That is a test, by the bye. The snob thinks most of the treatment he receives from the world; the gentleman thinks first how he shall act courteously to others.

The Baroness went on and entered the outer reception room, and looking before her she could see through the open doors of the succeeding drawing-rooms, where the windows had been opened or perhaps not closed on the previous evening. It was all vast, stately and deserted. Only ten days earlier she had been in the same place at a great reception, brilliant with beautiful women and handsome men, alive with the flashing of jewels and decorations in the vivid light, full of the discreet noise of society in good-humour, full of faces she knew, and voices familiar, and of the moonlight of priceless pearls and the sunlight of historic diamonds; all of which manifestations she dearly loved.

Her husband had perhaps known what was coming, and how soon, but she had not. There was something awful in the contrast. As she went through one of the rooms a mouse ran from under the fringe of a velvet curtain and took refuge under an armchair. She had sat in that very chair ten days ago and the Russian ambassador had talked to her; she remembered how he had tried to extract information from her about the new issue of three and a half per cent national bonds, because her husband was one of the financiers who were expected to "manipulate" the loan.

A portrait of a Conti in black velvet, by Velasquez, looked down, coldly supercilious, at the empty armchair under which the mouse was hiding. It could make no difference, great or small, to him, whether the Baroness Volterra ever sat there again to talk with an ambassador; he had sat where he pleased, undisturbed in his own house, to the end of his days, and no one can take the past from the dead, except a modern German historian.

Not a sound broke the stillness, except the steady plash of the water falling into the fountain in the wide court, heard distinctly through the closed windows. The Baroness wondered if any one were awake except the old porter downstairs. She knew the house tolerably well. Only the Princess and her two unmarried daughters slept in the apartment she had entered, far off, at the very end, in rooms at the corner overlooking the small square and the narrow street. The rest of the old palace was surrounded by dark and narrow streets, but the court was wide and full of sunshine. The only son of the house, though he was now the Prince, lived on the floor above, with his young wife and their only child, in what had been a separate establishment, after the old Roman custom.

The Baroness went to one of the embrasures of the great drawing-room and looked through the panes at the windows of the upper story. All that she could see were shut; there was not a sign of life in the huge building. Ruin had closed in upon it and all it held, softly, without noise and without pity.

It was their own fault, of course, but the Baroness was sorry for them, for she was not quite heartless, in spite of her hard face. The gloomiest landscape must have a ray of light in it, somewhere. It was all their own fault; they should have known better; they should have counted what they had instead of spending what they had not. But their fall was great, as everything had been in their prosperity, and it was interesting to be connected with it. She faintly hoped Volterra would keep the palace now that they could certainly never pay any more interest on the mortgage, and it was barely possible that she might some day live in it herself, though she understood that it would be in very bad taste to occupy it at once. But this was unlikely, for her husband had a predilection for a new house, in the new part of the city, full of new furniture and modern French pictures. He had a pronounced dislike for old things, including old pictures and old jewellery, though he knew much about both. Possibly they reminded him of that absurd story, and of his duel at forty paces.

Volterra would sell the palace to the Vatican, with everything in it, and would look about for another lucrative investment. The Vatican bought all the palaces in the market for religious institutions, and when there were not enough "it" built the finest buildings in Rome for its own purposes. Volterra was mildly anti-clerical in politics, but he was particularly fond of dealing with the Vatican for real estate. The Vatican was a most admirable house of business, in his estimation, keen, punctual and always solvent; it was good for a financier to be associated with such an institution. It drove a hard bargain, but there was never any hesitation about fulfilling its obligations to the last farthing. Dreaming over one of his enormous Havanas after a perfect dinner, Baron Volterra, Senator of the Kingdom of Italy, often wondered whether the prosperity of the whole world would not be vastly increased if the Vatican would consent to be the general financial agent for the European nations.

Such stability as there would be, such order! Above all, such guarantees of good faith! Besides all that, there were its cordial relations with the United States, that is to say, with the chief source of the world's future wealth! The Senator's strongly-marked face grew sweetly thoughtful as he followed his own visions in the air, and when his wife spoke of living in an antiquated Roman palace and buying an estate with an old title attached to it, which the King might graciously be pleased to ratify, he playfully tapped his wife's sallow cheek with two fat fingers and smiled in a way that showed how superior he was to such weakness. It was not even worth while to say anything.

Once more the Baroness sighed as she turned from the window. She meant to have her own way in the end, but it was hard to wait so long. She turned from the window, glanced at a beautiful holy family by Bonifazio which hung on the opposite wall above an alabaster table, estimated its value instinctively and went on into the next drawing-room.

As she passed through the door, a low cry of pain made her start and hesitate, and she stood still. The degree of her acquaintance with the members of the family was just such that she would not quite dare to intrude upon them if they had given way to an expression of pardonable weakness under their final misfortune, whereas if they were bearing it with reasonable fortitude she could allow herself to offer her sympathy and even some judicious help.

She stood still and the sound was repeated, the pitiful little tearless complaint of a young thing suffering alone. It was somewhere in the big room, hidden amongst the furniture; which was less stiffly arranged here than in the outer apartments. There were books and newspapers on the table, the fireplace was half-full of the ashes of a burnt-out fire, there were faded flowers in a tall vase near the window, there was the undefinable presence of life in the heavier and warmer air. At first the Baroness had thought that the cry came from some small animal, hurt and forgotten there in the great

13

catastrophe; a moment later she was sure that there was some one in the room.

She moved cautiously forward in the direction whence the sound had come. Then she saw the edge of a fawn-coloured cloth skirt on the red carpet by an armchair. She went on, hesitating no longer. She had seen the frock only a day or two ago, and it belonged to Sabina Conti.

A very fair young girl was kneeling in the shadow, crouching over something on the floor. Her hair was like the pale mist in the morning, tinged with gold. She was very slight, and as she bent down, her slender neck was dazzling white above the collar of her frock. She was trembling a little.

"My dear Sabina, what has happened?" asked the Baroness Volterra, leaning over her with an audible crack in the region of the waist.

At the words the girl turned up her pale face, without the least start of surprise.

"It is dead," she said, in a very low voice.

The Baroness looked down, and saw a small bunch of yellow feathers lying on the floor at the girl's knees; the poor little head with its colourless beak lay quite still on the red carpet, turned upon one side, as if it were resting.

"A canary," observed the Baroness, who had never had a pet in her life, and had always wondered how any one could care for such stupid things.

But the violet eyes gazed up to hers reproachfully and wonderingly.

"It is dead."

That should explain everything; surely the woman must understand. Yet there was no response. The Baroness stood upright again, grasping her parasol and looking down with a sort of respectful indifference. Sabina said nothing, but took up the dead bird very tenderly, as if it could still feel that she loved it, and she pressed it softly to her breast, bending her head to it, and then kissing the yellow feathers. When it was alive it used to nestle there, almost as it lay now. It had been very tame.

"I suppose a cat killed it," said the Baroness, wishing to say something.

Sabina shook her head. She had found it lying there, not wounded, its feathers not torn—just dead. It was of no use to answer. She rose to her feet, still holding the tiny body against her bosom, and she looked at the Baroness, mutely asking what had brought her there, and wishing that she would go away.

"I came to see your sister," said the elder woman, with something like apology in the tone.

Sabina was still very pale, and her delicate lips were pressed together, but there were no tears in her eyes, as she waited for the Baroness to say more.

"Then I heard the bad news," the latter continued. "I heard it from the porter."

Sabina looked at her quietly. If she had heard the bad news, why had she not gone away? The Baroness began to feel uncomfortable. She almost quailed before the pale girl of seventeen, slender as a birch sapling in her light frock.

"It occurred to me," she continued nervously, "that I might be of use."

"You are very kind," Sabina answered, with the faintest air of surprise, "but I really do not see that you could do anything."

"Perhaps your mother would allow you to spend a few days with me—until things are more settled," suggested the Baroness.

"Thank you very much. I do not think she would like that. She would not wish me to be away from her just now, I am sure. Why should I leave her?"

The Baroness Volterra did not like to point out that the Princess Conti might soon be literally homeless.

"May I ask your mother?" she enquired. "Should you like to come to me for a few days?"

"If my mother wishes it."

"But should you like to come?" persisted the elder woman.

"If my mother thinks it is best," answered Sabina, avoiding the Baroness's eyes, as she resolutely avoided answering the direct question.

But the Baroness was determined if possible to take in one of the family, and it had occurred to her that Sabina would really be less trouble than her mother or elder sister. Clementina was the eldest and was already looked upon as an old maid. She was intensely devout, and that was always troublesome, for it meant that she would insist upon going to church at impossibly early hours, and must have fish-dinners on Fridays. But it would certainly be conferring a favour on the Princess to take Sabina off her hands at such a time. The devout Clementina could take care of herself. With her face, the Baroness reflected, she would be safe among

Cossacks; besides, she could go into a retreat, and stay there, if necessary. Sabina was quite different.

The Princess thought so too, as it turned out. Sabina took the visitor to her mother's door, knocked, opened and then went away, still pressing her dead canary to her bosom, and infinitely glad to be alone with it at last.

There was confusion in the Princess Conti's bedroom, the amazing confusion which boils up about an utterly careless woman of the great world, if she be accidentally left without a maid for twenty-four hours. It seemed as if everything the Princess possessed in the way of clothes, necessary and unnecessary, had been torn from wardrobes and chests of drawers by a cyclone and scattered in every direction, till there was not space to move or sit down in a room which was thirty feet square.

Princess Conti was a very stout woman of about the same age as her visitor, but not resembling her in the least. She had been beautiful, and still kept the dazzling complexion and magnificent eyes for which she had been famous. It was her boast that she slept eight hours every night, without waking, whatever happened, and she always advised everybody to do the same, with an airy indifference to possibilities which would have done credit to a doctor.

She was dressed, or rather wrapped, in a magnificent purple velvet dressing-gown, trimmed with sable, and tied round her ample waist with a silver cord; her rather scanty grey hair stood out about her head like a cloud in a high wind; and her plump hands were encased in a pair of old white gloves, which looked oddly out of place. She was standing in the middle of the room, and she smiled calmly as the Baroness entered. On a beautiful inlaid table beside her stood a battered brass tray with an almost shapeless little brass coffee-pot, a common earthenware cup, chipped at the edges, and three pieces of doubtful-looking sugar in a tiny saucer, also of brass. The whole

17

had evidently been brought from a small cafe near by, which had long been frequented by the servants from the palace.

Judging from her smile, the Princess seemed to think total ruin rather an amusing incident. She had always complained that the Romans were very dull; for she was not a Roman herself, but came of a very great old Polish family, the members of which had been distinguished for divers forms of amiable eccentricity during a couple of centuries.

She looked at the Baroness, and smiled pleasantly, showing her still perfect teeth.

"I always said that this would happen," she observed. "I always told my poor husband so."

As the Prince had been dead ten years, the Baroness thought that he might not be wholly responsible for the ruin of his estate, but she discreetly avoided the suggestion. She began to make a little apology for her visit.

"But I am delighted to see you!" cried the Princess. "You can help me to pack. You know I have not a single maid, not a woman in the house, nor a man either. Those ridiculous servants fled last night as if we had the plague!"

"So you are going out of town?" enquired the Baroness, laying down her parasol.

"Of course. Clementina has decided to be a nun, and is going to the convent this morning. So sensible of her, poor dear! It is true that she has made up her mind to do it three or four times before now, but the circumstances were different, and I hope this will be final. She will be much happier."

The Princess stirred the muddy coffee in the chipped earthenware cup, and then sipped it thoughtfully, sipped it again, and made a face.

"You see my breakfast," she said, and then laughed, as if the shabby brass tray were a part of the train of amusing circumstances. "The porter's wife went and got it at some dirty little cafe," she added.

"How dreadful!" exclaimed the Baroness, with more real sympathy in her voice than she had yet shown.

"I assure you," the Princess answered serenely, "that I am glad to have any coffee at all. I always told poor dear Paolo that it would come to this."

She swallowed the rest of the coffee with a grimace, and set down the cup. Then, with the most natural gesture in the world, she pushed the tray a little way across the inlaid table, towards the Baroness, as she would have pushed it towards her maid, and as if she wished the thing taken away. She did it merely from force of habit, no doubt.

Baroness Volterra understood well enough, and for a moment she affected not to see. The Princess had the blood of Polish kings in her veins, mingled with that of several mediatized princes, but that was no reason why she should treat a friend like a servant; especially as the friend's husband practically owned the palace and its contents, and had lent the money with which the high and mighty lady and her son had finally ruined themselves. Yet so overpowering is the moral domination of the born aristocrat over the born snob, that the Baroness changed her mind, and humbly took the obnoxious tray away and set it down on another table near the door.

"Thank you so much," said the Princess graciously. "It smells, you know."

"Of course," answered the Baroness. "It is not coffee at all! It is made of chicory and acorns."

"I do not know what it is made of," said the Princess, without interest, "but it has an atrociously bad smell, and it has made a green stain on my handkerchief."

She looked at the bit of transparently fine linen with which she had touched her lips, and threw it under the table.

"And Sabina?" began the Baroness. "What shall you do with her?"

"I wish I knew! You see, my daughter-in-law has a little place somewhere in the Maremma. It is an awful hole, I believe, and very unhealthy, but we shall have to stay there for a few days. Then I shall go to Poland and see my brother. I am sure he can arrange everything at once, and we shall come back to Rome in the autumn, of course, just as usual. Sassi told me only last week that two or three millions would be enough. And what is that? My brother is so rich!"

The stout Princess shrugged her shoulders carelessly, as if a few millions of francs more or less could really not be such a great matter. Somebody had always found money for her to spend, and there was no reason why obliging persons should not continue to do the same. The Baroness showed no surprise, but wondered whether the Princess might not have to lunch, and dine too, on some nauseous little mess brought to her on a battered brass tray. It was quite possible that she might not find five francs in her purse; it was equally possible that she might find five thousand; the only thing quite sure was that she had not taken the trouble to look, and did not care a straw.

"Can I be of any immediate use?" asked the Baroness with unnecessary timidity. "Do you need ready money?"

"Ready money?" echoed the Princess with alacrity. "Of course I do! I told you, Sassi says that two or three millions would be enough to go on with."

"I did not mean that. I am afraid—"

"Oh!" ejaculated the Princess with a little disappointment. "Nothing else would be of any use. Of course I have money for any little thing I need. There is my purse. Do you mind looking? I know I had two or three thousand francs the other day. There must be something left. Please count it. I never can count right, you know."

The Baroness took up the mauve morocco pocket-book to which the Princess pointed. It had a clasp in which a pretty sapphire was set; she opened it and took out a few notes and silver coins, which she counted.

"There are fifty-seven francs," she said.

"Is that all?" asked the Princess with supreme indifference. "How very odd!"

"You can hardly leave Rome with so little," observed the Baroness. "Will you not allow me to lend you five hundred? I happen to have a five hundred franc note in my purse, for I was going to pay a bill on my way home."

"Thanks," said the Princess. "That will save me the trouble of sending for Sassi. He always bores me dreadfully with his figures. Thank you very much."

"Not at all, dear friend," the Baroness answered. "It is a pleasure, I assure you. But I had thought of asking if you would let Sabina come and stay with me for a little while, until your affairs are more settled."

"Oh, would you do that?" asked the Princess with something like enthusiasm. "I really do not know what to do with the girl. Of course, I could take her to Poland and marry her there, but she is so peculiar, such a strange child, not at all like me. It really would be immensely kind of you to take her, if your husband does not object."

"He will be delighted."

"Yes," acquiesced the Princess calmly. "You see," she continued in a meditative tone, "if I sent her to stay with any of our cousins here, I am sure they would ask her all sorts of questions about our affairs, and she is so silly that she would blurt out everything she fancied she knew, whether it were true or not—about my son and his wife, you know, and then, the money questions. Poor Sabina! she has not a particle of tact! It really would be good of you to take her. I shall be so grateful."

"I will bring my maid to pack her things," suggested the Baroness.

"Yes. If she could only help me to pack mine too! Do you think she would?"

"Of course!"

"You are really the kindest person in the world," said the Princess. "I was quite in despair, when you came. Just look at those things!"

She pointed to the chairs and sofas, covered with clothes and dresses.

"But your boxes, where are they?" asked the Baroness.

"I have not the least idea! I sent the porter's wife to try and find them, but she has never come back. She is so stupid, poor old thing!"

"I think I had better bring a couple of men-servants," said the Baroness. "They may be of use. Should you like my carriage to take you to the station? Anything I can do—"

The Princess stared, as if quite puzzled.

"Thanks, but we have plenty of horses," she said.

"Yes, but you said that all your servants had left last night. I supposed the coachman and grooms were gone too."

"I daresay they are!" The Princess laughed. "Then we will go in cabs. It will be very amusing. By the bye, I wonder whether those brutes of men thought of leaving the poor horses anything to eat, and water! I must really go and see. Poor beasts! They will be starving. Will you come with me?"

She moved towards the door, really very much concerned, for she loved horses.

"Will you go down like that?" asked the Baroness aghast, glancing at the purple velvet dressing-gown, and noticing, as the Princess moved, that her feet, on which she wore small kid slippers, were stockingless.

"Why not? I shall not catch cold. I never do."

The Baroness would have given anything to be above caring whether any one should ever see her, or not, on the stairs of her house in a purple dressing-gown, without stockings and with her hair standing on end; and she pondered on the ways of the aristocracy she adored, especially as represented by her Excellency Marie-Sophie-Hedwige-Zenaide-Honorine-Pia Rubomirska, Dowager Princess Conti. Ever afterwards she associated purple velvet and bare feet with the idea of financial catastrophe, knowing in her heart that even ruin would seem bearable if it could bring her such magnificent indifference to the details of commonplace existence.

At that moment, however, she felt that she was in the position of a heaven-sent protectress to the Princess.

"No," she said firmly. "I will go myself to the stables, and the porter shall feed the horses if there is no groom. You really must not go downstairs looking like that!"

"Why not?" asked the Princess, surprised. "But of course, if you will be so kind as to see whether the horses need anything, it is quite useless for me to go myself. You will promise? I am sure they are starving by this time."

The Baroness promised solemnly, and said that she would come back within an hour, with her servants, to take away Sabina and to help the Princess's preparations. In consideration of all she was doing the Princess kissed her on both her sallow cheeks as she took her leave. The Princess attached no importance at all to this mark of affectionate esteem, but it pleased the Baroness very much.

Just as the latter was going away, the door opened suddenly, and a weak-looking young man put in his head.

"Mamma! Mamma!" he cried, in a thin tone of distress, almost as if he were going to cry.

He was nearly thirty years old, though he looked younger. He was thin, and pale, with a muddy and spotted complexion, and his scanty black hair grew far back on his poorly developed forehead. His eyes had a look that was half startled, half false. Though he was carefully dressed he had not shaved, because he could not shave himself and his valet had departed with the rest of the servants. He was the Princess's only son, himself the present Prince, and the heir of all the Conti since the year eleven hundred.

"Mamma!"

"What is the matter, sweetheart?" asked the Princess, with ready sympathy. "Your hands are quite cold! Are you ill?"

"The child! Something has happened to it—we do not know—it looks so strange—its eyes are turned in and it is such a dreadful colour—do come—"

But the Princess was already on her way, and he spoke the last words as he ran after her. She turned her head as she went on.

"For heaven's sake send a doctor!" she cried to the Baroness, and in a moment she was gone, with the weak young man close at her side.

The Baroness nodded quickly, and when all three reached the door she left the two to go upstairs and ran down, with a tremendous puffing of the invisible silk bellows.

"The Prince's little girl is very ill," she said, as she passed the porter, who was now polishing the panes of glass in the door of his lodge, because he had done the same thing every morning for twenty years.

He almost dropped the dingy leather he was using, but before he could answer, the cab passed out, bearing the Baroness on her errand.

CHAPTER II

Signor Pompeo Sassi sat in his dingy office and tore his hair, in the good old literal Italian sense. His elbows rested on the shabby black oilcloth glued to the table, and his long knotted fingers twisted his few remaining locks, on each side of his head, in a way that was painful to see. From time to time he desisted for an instant, and held up his open hands, the fingers quivering with emotion, and his watery eyes were turned upwards, too, as if directing an unspoken prayer to the dusty rafters of the ceiling. The furrows had deepened of late in his respectable, trust-inspiring face, and he was as thin as a skeleton in leather.

His heart was broken. On the big sheet of thick hand-made paper, that lay on the desk, scribbled over with rough calculations in violet ink, there were a number of trial impressions of the old stamp he had once been so proud to use. It bore a rough representation of the Conti eagle, encircled by the legend: "Eccellentissima Casa Conti." When his eyes fell upon it, they filled with tears. The Most Excellent House of Conti had come to a pitiful end, and it had been Pompeo Sassi's unhappy fate to see its fall. Judging from his looks, he was not to survive the catastrophe very long.

He loved the family, and yet he disliked every member of it personally except Sabina. He loved the "Eccellentissima Casa," the checky eagle, the Velasquez portraits and his dingy office, but he never had spoken with the Princess, her son, his wife, or his sister Clementina, without a distinct feeling of disapproving aversion. The old Prince had been different. In him Sassi had still been able to respect those traditional Ciceronian virtues which were inculcated with terrific severity in the Roman youth of fifty years ago. But the Prince had died prematurely at the age of fifty, and with him the Ciceronian traditions had ended in Casa Conti, and their place had been taken by the caprices of the big, healthy, indolent, extravagant Polish woman, by the miserable weaknesses of a degenerate heir, and the fanatic religious practices of Donna Clementina.

Sassi was sure that they all three hated him or despised him, or both; yet they could not spare him. For different reasons, they all needed money, and they had long been used to believing that no one but Sassi could get it for them, since no one else knew how deeply the family was involved. He always made difficulties, he protested, he wrung his hands, he warned, he implored; but caprice, vice and devotion always overcame his objections, and year after year the exhausted estate was squeezed and pressed and mortgaged and sold, till it had yielded the uttermost farthing.

Then, one day, the whole organization of Casa Conti stood still; the unpaid servants fled, the unpaid tradesmen refused to trust any longer, the unpaid holders of mortgages foreclosed, the Princess departed to Poland, the Prince slunk away to live on what was left of his wife's small estate, Donna Clementina buried herself in a convent to which she had given immense sums, the Conti palace was for sale, and Pompeo Sassi sat alone in his office, tearing his hair, while the old porter sat in his lodge downstairs peeling potatoes.

It was not for himself that the old steward of the estate was in danger of being totally bald. He had done for himself what others would not allow him to do for them, a proceeding which affords some virtuous people boundless satisfaction, though it procured him none at all. He was provided for in his old age. During more than thirty years he had saved and scraped and invested and added to the little sum of money left him by his father, an honest old notary of the old school, until he possessed what was a very comfortable competence for a childless old man. He had a small house of his own near the Pantheon, in which he occupied two rooms, letting the rest, and he had a hundred thousand francs in government bonds, besides a few acres of vineyard on the slope of Monte Mario.

More than once, in the sincerity of his devotion to the family he served, he had thought of sacrificing all he possessed in an attempt to stave off final ruin; but a very little reflection had convinced him that all he had would be a mere drop in the flood of extravagance, and would forthwith disappear with the rest into the bottomless pit of debt.

Even that generous temptation was gone now. The house having collapsed, its members appeared to him only in their true natures, a good-for-nothing young man, tainted with a mortal disease, a foolish mother, a devout spinster threatened with religious mania, and the last descendant of the great old race, one little girl-child not likely to live, and perhaps better dead. In their several ways they had treated him as the contemptible instrument of their inclinations; they were gone from his life and he was glad of it, when he thought of each one separately. Yet, collectively, he wished them all in the palace again, even a month ago, even on the day before the exodus; good, bad, indifferent, no matter what, they had been Casa Conti still, to the end, the family he had served faithfully, honestly and hopelessly for upwards of a third of a century. That might seem to be inconsistent, but it was the only consistency he had ever known, and it was loyalty, of a kind.

But there was one whom he wished back for her own sake; there was Donna Sabina. When he thought of her, his hands fell from his head at last, and folded themselves over the scrawled figures on the big sheet of paper, and he looked long and steadily at them, without seeing them at all.

He wondered what would become of her. He had seen her on the last day and he should never forget it. Before going away with the Baroness Volterra she had found her way to his dark office, and had stood a few moments before the shabby old table, with a small package in her hand. He could see the slight figure still, when he closed his eyes, and her misty hair against the cold light of the window. She had come to ask him if he would bury her dead canary, somewhere under the sky where there was grass and it would not be disturbed. Where could she bury it, down in the heart of Rome? She had wrapped it in a bit of pink satin and had laid it in a little brown cardboard box which had been full of chocolates from Ronzi and Singer's in Piazza Colonna. She pushed back the lid a finger's breadth and he saw the pink satin for a second. She laid the box before him. Would he please do what she asked? Very timidly she slipped a simple little ring off her finger, one of those gold ones with the sacred monogram which foreigners insist upon calling "Pax." She said she had bought it with her own money, and could give it away. She wished to give it to him. He protested, refused, but the fathomless violet eyes gazed into his very reproachfully. He had always been so kind to her, she said; would he not keep the little ring to remember her by?

So he had taken it, and that same day he had gone all the way to his lonely vineyard on Monte Mario carrying the chocolate box in his hands, and he had buried it under the chestnut-tree at the upper end, where there was some grass; and the breeze always blew there on summer afternoons. Then he had sat on the roots of the tree for a while, looking towards Rome.

He would have plenty of time to go to the vineyard now, for in a little while he should have nothing to do, as the palace was going to be sold. When he got home, he wrote a formal letter to Donna Sabina, informing her that he had fulfilled the commands she had deigned to give him, and ventured to subscribe himself her Excellency's most devoted, humble and grateful servant, as indeed he was, from the bottom of his heart. In twenty-four hours he received a note from her, written in a delicate tall hand, not without character, on paper bearing the address of Baron Volterra's house in Via Ludovisi. She thanked him in few words, warmly and simply. He read the note several times and then put it away in an old-fashioned brass-bound secretary, of which he always kept the key in his pocket. It was the only word of thanks he had received from any living member of the Conti family.

A month had passed since then, but as he sat at his desk it was all as vivid as if it had happened yesterday.

He was in his office to-day because he had received notice that some one was coming to look at the palace with a view to buying it, and he considered it his duty to show it to possible purchasers. Baron Volterra had sent him word in the morning, and he had come early. Then, as he sat in his old place, the ruin of the great house had enacted itself again before his eyes, so vividly that the pain had been almost physical. And then, he had fallen to thinking of Sabina, and wondering what was to become of her. That was the history of one half-hour in his life, on a May afternoon; but the whole man was in it, what he had been thirty years earlier, and a month ago, what he was to-day and what he would be to the end of his life.

CHAPTER III

If Sabina had known what was before her when she got into the Baroness Volterra's carriage and was driven up to the Via Ludovisi, followed by a cab with her luggage, she would probably have begged leave to go with her elder sister to the convent. Her mother would most likely have refused the permission, and she would have been obliged to accept the Volterras' hospitality after all, but she would have had the satisfaction of having made an effort to keep her freedom before entering into what she soon looked upon as slavery.

Her mother would have considered this another evidence of the folly inherent in all the Conti family. Sabina lived in a luxurious house, she was treated with consideration, she saw her friends, and desirable young men saw her. What more could she wish?

All this was true. The Baroness was at great pains to make much of her, and the Baron's manner to her was at once flattering, respectful and paternal. During the first few days she had discovered that if she accidentally expressed the smallest wish it was instantly fulfilled, and this was so embarrassing that she had since taken endless pains never to express any wish at all. Moreover not the slightest allusion to the misfortunes of her family was ever made before her, and if she was in total ignorance of the state of affairs, she was at least spared the humiliation of hearing that the palace was for sale, and might be sold any day, to any one who would pay the price asked.

From time to time the Baroness said she hoped that Sabina had good news of her mother, but showed no curiosity in the matter, and the girl always answered that she believed her mother to be quite well. Indeed she did believe it, for she supposed that if the Princess were ill some one would let her know. She wrote stiff little letters herself, every Sunday morning, and addressed them to her uncle's place in Poland; but no one ever took the least notice of these conscientious communications, and she wondered why she sent them, after all. It was a remnant of the sense of duty to her parents instilled into her in the convent, and she could not help clinging to it still, from habit.

She had a few friends of her own age, and they came to see her now and then. They were mostly companions of her recent convent days, and they asked her many questions, to most of which she had no answer. She noticed that they looked surprised, but they were well brought up girls, and kept their reflections to themselves, until they were at home.

The Conti had fewer near relations than most Roman families, for of late they had not been numerous. The Prince's only sister had died childless, the dowager Princess was a Pole, and her daughter-in-law was a Tuscan. Sabina and her generation had therefore no first cousins; and those who were one degree or more removed were glad that they had not been asked to take charge of the girl after the catastrophe. It would have been all very well merely to give her a room and a place at table, but the older ones shook their heads, and said that before long the Baroness Volterra would have to dress her too, and give her pocket-money. Her good-for-nothing brother would not do anything for her, if he could, and the Princess, who was amusing herself in Poland, if not in Paris, was capable of forgetting her existence for a year at a time.

All these things greatly enhanced the outward and visible merit of the Volterra couple, but made Sabina's position daily less endurable. So the Baroness laid up treasures in heaven while Sabina unwillingly stored trouble on earth.

She was proud, to begin with. It was bad enough to have been ordered by her mother to accept the hospitality of people she did not like, but it was almost unbearable to realize by degrees that she was living on their effusive charity. If she had been as vain as she was proud, she would probably have left their house to take refuge in her sister's convent, for her vanity could not have borne the certainty that all society knew what her position was. The foundation of pride is the wish to respect oneself, whatever others may think; the mainspring of vanity is the craving for the admiration of others, no matter at what cost to one's self-respect. In the Conti family these qualities and defects were unevenly distributed, for while pride seemed to have been left out in the character of Sabina's brother, who was vain and arrogant, she herself was as unspoilt by vanity as she was plentifully supplied with the characteristic which is said to have caused Lucifer's fall, but which has been the mainstay of many a greatly-tempted man and woman. Perhaps what is a fault in angels may seem to be almost a virtue in humanity, compared with the meanness of worse failings.

Sabina was not suspicious, yet she could not help wondering why the Baroness had been so very anxious to take her in, and sometimes she thought that the object might be to marry her to one of Volterra's two sons. One was in a cavalry regiment stationed in Turin, the other was in the diplomacy and was now in Washington. They were both doing very well in their careers and their father and mother often talked of them.

The Baron was inclined to be playful now and then.

"Ah, my dear young lady," he would cry, shaking one fat finger at Sabina across the dinner table, "take care, take care! You will lose your heart to both my boys and sow discord in my family!"

At this he never failed to laugh, and his wife responded with a smile of motherly pride, followed by a discreet side glance at Sabina's delicate face. Then the finely-pencilled eyebrows were just the least bit more arched for a second, and the slender neck grew slightly straighter, but that was all, and the Baron did not even see the change. Sometimes Sabina said nothing, but sometimes she asked if the sons were coming home on leave. No, they were not coming at present. In the spring Volterra and his wife generally spent a few weeks in Turin, to see the elder son, on their way to Aix and Paris, but his brother could hardly expect to come home for another year. Then the couple would talk about both the young men, until Sabina's attention wandered, and she no longer heard what they were saying.

She did not believe that they really thought of trying to marry her to one of the sons. In her own opinion they could gain nothing by it; she had no dowry now, and her mother had always talked of marriage as a business transaction. It did not occur to her that they could care to be allied with a ruined family, and that her mere name could be worth anything in their scale of values. They were millionaires, of course, and even the dowry which she might formerly have expected would have been nothing compared with their fortune; but her mother had always said that rich people were the very people who cared the most for money. That was the reason why they were rich. This explanation was so logical that Sabina had accepted it as the true one.

Her knowledge of the world was really limited to what she had learned from her mother, after she had come back from the convent six months before the crash, and it was an odd mixture of limitations and exaggerations. When the Princess was in a good humour she believed in everybody; when she was not, which was when she had no money to throw away, she attributed the basest motives to all mankind. According to her moods, she had encouraged Sabina to look forward to a life of perpetual pleasure, or had assured her with energy that all men were liars, and that the world was a wretched place after all. It was true that the Princess entertained the cheerful view more often than not, which was perhaps fortunate for her daughter; but in her heart the young girl felt that she would have to rely on her own common sense to form any opinion of life, and as her position became more difficult, while the future did not grow more defined, she tried to think connectedly about it all, and to reach some useful conclusion.

It was not easy. In her native city, living under the roof of people who held a strong position in the society to which she belonged, though they had not been born to it, she was as completely isolated as if she had been suddenly taken away and set down amongst strangers in Australia. She was as lonely as she could have been on a desert island.

The Volterra couple were radically, constitutionally, congenitally different from the men and women she had seen in her mother's house. She could not have told exactly where the difference lay, for she was too young, and perhaps too simple. She did not instinctively like them, but she had never really felt any affection for her mother either, and her own brother and sister had always repelled her. Her mother had sometimes treated her like a toy, but more often as a nuisance and a hindrance in life, to be kept out of the way as much, as possible, and married off on the first opportunity. Yet Sabina knew that far down in her nature there was a mysterious tie of some sort, an intuition that often told her what her mother would say or do, though she herself would have spoken and acted otherwise. She had felt it even with her brother and sister, but she could not feel it at all with the Baron or his wife. She never could guess what they might do or say under the most ordinary circumstances, nor what things they would like and dislike, nor how they would regard anything she said or did; least of all could she understand why they were so anxious to keep her with them.

It was all a mystery, but life itself was mysterious, and she was little more than a child in years though she had never had what one calls a real childhood.

She often used to sit by her window, the sliding blinds partly drawn together, but leaving a space through which she could look down at the city, with a glimpse of Saint Peter's in the distance against the warm haze of the low Campagna. Rome seemed as far from her then as if she saw it in a vision a thousand miles away, and the very faint sounds from the distance were like voices in a dream. Then, if she closed her eyes a moment, she could see the dark streets about the Palazzo Conti, and the one open corner of the palace, high up in the sunlight; she could smell the acrid air that used to come up to her in the early morning when the panes were opened, damp and laden with odours not sweet but familiar in the heart of Rome; odours compounded of cabbages, stables, cheese and mud, and occasionally varied by the fumes of roasting coffee, or the sour vapours from a wine cart that was unloading stained casks, all wet with red juice, at the door of the wine shop far below, a dark little wine shop with a dry bush stuck out through a smoky little grated window, and a humble sign displaying the prices of drink in roughly painted blue and red figures. For her room had looked upon the narrowest and darkest of the streets, though it had been stately enough within, and luxuriously furnished, besides containing some objects of value and beauty over which there would be much bidding and squabbling of amateurs and experts when the great sale took place.

It had been gloomy and silent and loveless, the life down there; and yet she would have gone back to it if she could, from the sunshine of the Via Ludovisi, and from the overpowering freshness of the

35

Volterra house, where everything was modern, and polished, and varnished, and in perfect condition, suggesting that things had been just paid for. She had not liked the old life, but she liked her present surroundings even less, and at times she felt a furious longing to leave them suddenly, without warning; to go out when no one would notice her, and never to come back; to go she knew not where, out into the world, risking she knew not what, a high-born, penniless, fair-haired girl not yet eighteen.

What would happen, if she did? She rarely laughed, but she would laugh at that, when she thought of the consternation her flight would produce. How puzzled the fat Baron would look, how the Baroness's thin mouth would be drawn down at the corners! How the invisible silk bellows would puff as she ran up and down stairs, searching the house for Sabina!

There was more than one strain of wild blood in the delicate girl's veins, and the spring had come suddenly, with a bursting out of blossom and life and colour, and a twittering of nesting birds in the old gardens, and a rush of strange longings in her heart.

Then Sabina told herself that there was nothing to keep her where she was, but her own will, and that no one would really care what became of her in the wide world; certainly not her mother, who had never written her so much as a line, nor sent her a message, since they had parted on the day of the catastrophe; certainly not her brother; probably not even her sister, whose whole being was absorbed in the tyrannical government of what she called her soul. Sabina, in her thoughts, irreverently compared Clementina's soul to a race-horse, and her sister to a jockey, riding it cruelly with whip and spur to the goal of salvation, whether it liked it or not.

Sabina rose from her seat by the window, when she thought of liberty, and she walked up and down her room, driven by something she could not understand, and yet withheld by something she understood even less. For it was not fear, nor reflection, nor even common sense nor the thought of giving pain to any one that hindered her from leaving the house at such moments. It was not even the memory of the one human being who had hitherto loved her, and for whom she had felt affection and gratitude,—one of the nuns at the convent school, a brave, quiet little lady who made her believe in good. She meant to do no harm if she were free, and the nun would not really blame her, if she knew the truth.

It was not that. It was the secret conviction that there was harm in the world from which mere courage could not protect her; it was the sort of instinct that warns young animals not to eat plants that are poisonous; it was the maiden intuition of a strange and unknown danger.

She sat down again disconsolately. It was absurd, of course, and she could not run away. Where could she go? She had no money, and she would have to starve or beg before one day was out. She would be homeless, she would be driven to some house of charity, for a meal and a place to sleep, or else to sleep out under the sky. That would be delightful for once. She had always longed to sleep out of doors, to feel the breeze playing with her feathery hair in the dark, to watch the constellations turning slowly westwards, to listen to the night sounds, to the low rhythmical piping of the tree toad, the sorrowful cry of the little southern owl and the tolling of the hour in a far-off belfry.

But it might rain. At the idea, Sabina laughed again. It would be very unpleasant to be caught in a shower while napping on a bench in a public garden. Besides, if the policemen found her there, an extremely young lady, extremely well dressed but apparently belonging to no one, they would in all likelihood ask her name, and she would have to tell them who she was; and then she would be brought back to Baron Volterra's house, unless they thought it more prudent to take her to a lunatic asylum.

At that stage in her imaginings it was generally time to go out with the Baroness for the daily drive, which began with the leaving of cards and notes, then led to the country or one of the villas, and generally ended in a turn or two through the Corso before coming home. The worst part of the daily round was dinner when the Baron was at home. It was then that she felt most strongly the temptation to slip out of the house and never to come back. Often, however, he and his wife dined out, and then Sabina was served alone by two solemn men-servants, so extremely correct that they reminded her a little of her old home. These were the pleasantest evenings she spent during that spring, for when dinner was over she was free to go to her own room and curl herself up in a big armchair with a book, and read or dream till bedtime, as she pleased.

When she was alone, her life seemed less objectless, less inexplicably empty, less stupidly incomprehensible, less lonely than in the company of those excellent people with whom she had nothing in common, but to whom she felt that she was under a great obligation. In their company, it was as if her life had stopped suddenly at the beginning and was never to go on again, as if she had stuck fast like a fly in a drop of amber, as if nothing of interest could ever happen to her though she might live a hundred years.

She could hardly remember anything which had given her great pleasure. She did not remember to have been ever radiantly happy, though she could not recall much unhappiness since she had left the convent school. The last thing that had really hurt her had been the death of her pet canary, and she had kept her feelings to herself as well as she could, with the old aristocratic instinct of hiding pain.

It was all idle and strangely empty, and yet hard to understand. She would have been much surprised if she could have guessed how much its emptiness interested other people in Rome; how the dowagers chattered about her over their tea, abusing her mother and all her relations for abandoning her like a waif; how the men reasoned about Baron Volterra's deep-laid schemes, trying to make out that his semi-adoption of Sabina, as they called it, must certainly bode ruin to some one, since he had never in his life done anything without a financial object; how the young girls unanimously declared that the Baroness wanted Sabina for one of her sons, because she was such a dreadful snob; how Cardinal Della Crusca shook his wise old head knowingly, as he, who knew so much, always did on the rare occasions when he knew nothing about the matter in hand; how a romantic young English secretary of Embassy christened her the Princess in the Tower; and how old Pompeo Sassi went up to his vineyard on Monte Mario every Sunday and Thursday and sat almost all the afternoon under the chestnut-tree thinking about her and making unpractical plans of his own.

CHAPTER IV

If Baron Volterra did not choose to sell the Palazzo Conti to the first comer, he doubtless knew his own business best, and he was not answerable to every one for his opinion that the fine old building was worth a good deal more than the highest offer he had yet received. Everybody knew that the palace was for sale, and some of the attempts made to buy it were openly discussed. A speculator had offered four hundred thousand francs for it, a rich South American had offered half a million; it was rumoured that the Vatican would give five hundred and fifty thousand, provided that the timbers of the carved ceilings were in good condition, but Volterra steadily refused to allow any of the carvings to be disturbed in order to examine the beams. During several days a snuffy little man with a clever face poked about with a light in dark places between floors, trying to find out whether the wood were sound or rotten, and asking all sorts of questions of the old porter, and of two workmen who went with him, and who had been employed in repairs in the palace, as their fathers had been before them, perhaps for generations. But their answers were never quite satisfactory, and the snuffy man disappeared to the mysterious regions beyond the Tiber, and did not come back.

Some people, knowing the ways of the Romans, might have inferred that the two workmen, a mason and a carpenter, had not been treated by Baron Volterra in such a way as to make them give a favourable report; and as he seemed perfectly indifferent about the result this is quite possible. At all events the carpenter made out that he could not get at the beams in question, without moving the decorations which covered them, and the mason affirmed that it was quite impossible to get a view of the foundations of the north-west corner of the palace, which were said to be weak, without knocking a hole through a wall upon which depended such solidity as there was. It was useless, he said. The snuffy gentleman could ask the Baron, if he pleased, and the Baron could do what he liked since the property now belonged to him: but he, the mason, would not lay hand to pick or crowbar without the Baron's express authorization. The Baron was a Senator of the Kingdom, said the mason, and could therefore of course send him to penal servitude in the galleys for life, if he pleased. That is the average Roman workman's idea of justice. The snuffy expert, who looked very much like a poor priest in plain clothes, though he evidently knew his business, made no reply, nor any attempt to help the mason's conscience with money.

But he stood a little while by the wall, with his lantern in his hands, and presently put his ear to the damp stones, and listened.

"There is running water somewhere not far off," he said, looking keenly at the workman.

"It is certainly not wine," answered the man, with a rough laugh, for he thought it a very good joke.

"Are there any 'lost waters' under the palace?" asked the expert.

40

"I do not know," replied the mason, looking away from the lantern towards the gloom of the cellars.

"I believe," said the snuffy gentleman, setting down his lantern, and taking a large pinch from a battered silver snuff-box, on which the arms of Pius Ninth were still distinguishable, "I believe that the nearest 'lost water' to this place is somewhere under the Vicolo del Soldati."

"I do not know."

The expert skilfully inserted the brown dust into his nostrils with his right thumb, scarcely wasting a grain in the operation.

"You do not seem to know much," he observed thoughtfully, and took up his lantern again.

"I know what I have been taught," replied the mason without resentment.

The expert glanced at him quickly, but said nothing more. His inspection was finished, and he led the way out of the intricate cellars as if he knew them by heart, though he had only passed through them once, and he left the palace on foot when he had brushed some of the dust from his shabby clothes.

The porter looked enquiringly at the two men, as they filled little clay pipes that had cane stems, standing under the deep entrance.

"Not even the price of half a litre of wine," said the mason in answer to the mute question.

"Church stuff," observed the carpenter discontentedly.

The porter nodded gravely, and the men nodded to him as they went out into the street. They had nothing more to do that day, and they turned into the dark little wine shop, where the withered bush stuck out of the blackened grating. They sat down opposite each other, with the end of the grimy board of the table between them, and the carpenter made a sign. The host brought a litre measure of thin red wine and set it down between them with two tumblers. He was ghastly pale, flabby and sullen, with a quarter of an inch of stubbly black beard on his unhealthy face.

The carpenter poured a few drops of wine into one of the tumblers, shook it about, turned it into the other, shook it again, and finally poured it on the unctuous stone floor beside him. Then he filled both glasses to the brim, and both men drank in silence.

They repeated the operation, and after the second glass there was not much left in the measure. The flabby host had retired to the gloomy vaults within, where he played cards with a crony by the light of a small smoking lamp with a cracked chimney.

"That was the very place, was it not?" asked the carpenter at last, in a low tone, and almost without moving his lips.

The mason said nothing, but shrugged his shoulders, in a sort of enigmatic assent. Both drank again, and after a long time the carpenter smiled faintly.

"He was looking for the 'lost water,'" he said, in a tone of contempt.

The faint smile slowly reflected itself in the mason's face. The two finished their wine, lit their pipes again, left the price of their drink on the table without disturbing the host and went away.

So far as any outsider could have judged, the expert's curiosity and the few words exchanged by the workmen referred to the so-called "lost water," which might be somewhere under the north-west corner of the Palazzo Conti, and no one unacquainted with subterranean Rome could possibly have understood what any of the three meant.

The "lost waters" of Rome are very mysterious. Here and there, under old streets and far down amongst the foundations of ancient palaces, there are channels of running water which have no apparent connection with any of the aqueducts now restored and in use. It is a water that comes no one knows whence and finds its way to the Tiber, no one knows how. It is generally clear and very cold, and in the days when the aqueducts were all broken and most people drank of the river, the "lost water" was highly prized. It appears in the most unexpected places, sometimes in great quantities and seriously interfering with any attempt to lay the foundations of a new building, sometimes black and silent, under a huge flagstone in an old courtyard, sometimes running with an audible rush through hidden passages deeper than the deepest cellars. It has puzzled archaeologists, hydraulic engineers and architects for generations, its presence has never been satisfactorily explained, there seems not to be any plan of the city which shows its whereabouts, and the modern improvements of the Tiber's banks do not appear to have affected its occult courses. By tradition handed down from father to son, certain workmen, chiefly masons and always genuine Romans, claim to know more about it than other people; but that is as much as can be said. It is known as the "lost water," and it rises and falls, and seeks different levels in unaccountable ways, as water will when it is confined under the earth but is here and there confronted by the pressure of the air.

But though the old-fashioned Roman workman still looks upon all traditional information about his trade as secret and never to be revealed, that fact alone might seem insufficient to account for the behaviour of Gigi the carpenter and of Toto the mason under the particular circumstances here narrated, still less for the contempt they showed for the snuffy expert who was apparently looking for the "lost water." An invisible witness would have gathered that they had something of more importance to conceal. To the expert, their conduct and answers must have been thoroughly unsatisfactory, for the Vatican was even said to have refused to pay the additional fifty thousand francs, On the ground that the state of the foundations was doubtful and that the timbers of the upper story were not sound.

Baron Volterra's equanimity was not in the least disturbed by this. On the contrary, instead of setting the price lower, he frankly told all applicants, through his agent, that he was in no hurry to sell, as he had reason to believe that the land about the Palazzo Conti would soon rise in value. He had settled with the representatives of the Conti family, and it was said that he had behaved generously. The family had nothing left after the crash, which might partially account for such an exhibition of generosity; but it was hinted that Baron Volterra had given them the option of buying back the palace and some other property upon which he had foreclosed, if they should be able to pay for it in ten years.

Soon after the visit of the snuffy expert, Volterra's agent informed the porter that a gentleman had taken the small apartment on the intermediate story, which had formerly been occupied by a chaplain but had been disused for years. It had been part of the Conti's folly that they had steadily refused to let any part of the vast building since the old Prince's death.

On the following day, the new-comer moved in, with his belongings, consisting of a small quantity of new furniture, barely sufficient for himself and his one servant, and a number of very heavy cases, which turned out to be full of books. Gigi, the carpenter, was at once sent for to put up plain shelves for these, and he took stock of the lodger while the latter was explaining what he wanted.

"He is a gentleman," said Gigi to Toto, that very evening, as they stood filling their pipes at the corner of the Vicolo del Soldati. "His name is Malipieri. He is as black as the horses at a funeral of the first-class, and he is not a Roman."

"Who knows what race of animal this may be?" Toto was not in a good humour.

"He is of the race of gentlemen," asserted Gigi confidently.

"Then he will end badly," observed Toto. "Let us go and drink. It is better."

"Let us go and drink," repeated Gigi. "You have a sensible thought sometimes. I think this man is an engineer, or an architect. He wants a draughtsman's table."

"Evil befall his little dead ones, whatever he is," returned the other, by way of welcome to the young man who had moved into the palace.

"He advanced me ten francs to buy wood for the shelves," said Gigi, who was by far the more cheerful of the two.

"Come and drink," returned Toto, relevantly or irrelevantly. "That is much better."

So they turned into the wine shop.

CHAPTER V

Baron Volterra introduced Marino Malipieri to the two ladies. The guest had come punctually, for the Baron had looked at his watch a moment before he was announced, and it was precisely eight o'clock.

Malipieri bowed to the Baroness, who held out her hand cordially, and then to Sabina.

"Donna Sabina Conti," said the Baron with extreme distinctness, in order that his guest should be quite sure of the young girl's identity.

Sabina looked down modestly, as the nuns had told her to do when a young man was introduced to her. At the same moment Malipieri's eyes turned quietly and quickly to the Baron, and a look of intelligence passed between the two men. Malipieri understood that Sabina was one of the family in whose former palace he was living. Then he glanced again at the young girl for one moment, before making a commonplace remark to the Baroness, and after that Sabina felt that she was at liberty to look at him.

She saw a very dark man of average height, with short black hair that grew rather far back from his very white forehead, and wearing a closely clipped black beard and moustache which did not by any means hide the firm lines of the mouth and chin. From the strongly marked eyebrows downward his face was almost of the colour of newly cast bronze, and the dusky hue contrasted oddly with the clear whiteness of his forehead. He was evidently a man who had lately been living much out of doors under a burning sun. Sabina thought that his very bright black eyes and boldly curved features suggested a young hawk, and he had a look of compact strength and a way of moving which betrayed both great energy and extreme quickness.

But there was something more, which Sabina recognized at the first glance. She felt instantly that he was not like the Baron and his wife; that he belonged in some way to the same variety of humanity as herself; that she would understand him when he spoke, that she would often feel intuitively what he was going to say next, and that he would understand her.

She listened while he talked to the Baroness. He had a slight Venetian accent, but his voice had not the soft Venetian ring. It was a little veiled, and though not at all loud it was somewhat harsh.

Sabina did not dislike the manly tone, though it was not musical, nor the Venetian pronunciation, although that was unfamiliar. In countries like Italy and Germany, which have had many centres and many historical capital cities, almost all educated people speak with the accents of their several origins, and are rather tenacious of the habit than anxious to get rid of it, generally maintaining that their own pronunciation is the right one.

"Signor Malipieri," said the Baron to Sabina, as they went in to dinner, "is the celebrated archaeologist."

"Yes," Sabina answered, as if she knew all about him, though she had never heard him mentioned.

Malipieri probably overheard the Baron's speech, but he took no notice of it. At dinner, he seemed inclined to be silent. The Baron asked him questions about his discoveries, to which he gave rather short answers, but Sabina gathered that he had found something extraordinary in Carthage. She did not know where Carthage was, and did not like to ask, but she remembered that Marius had sat there among some ruins. Perhaps Malipieri had found his bones, for no one had ever told her that Marius did not continue to sit among the ruins to his dying day. She connected him vaguely with AEneas and another person called Regulus. It was all rather uncertain.

What she saw clearly was that the Baron wished to make Malipieri feel at his ease, but that Malipieri's idea of being at his ease was certainly not founded on a wish to talk about himself. So the conversation languished for some time.

The Baroness, who knew about as much about Carthage as Sabina, made a few disconnected remarks, interspersed with laudatory allusions to the young man's immense learning, for she wished to please her husband, though she had not the slightest idea why Malipieri was asked to dinner. Finding that he was not perceptibly flattered by what she said, she began to talk about the Venetian aristocracy, for she knew that his name was historical, and she recognized in him at once the characteristics of the nobility she worshipped. Malipieri smiled politely, and in answer to a direct question admitted that his mother had been a Gradenigo.

The Baroness was delighted at this information.

"To think," she said, "that by a mere accident you and Donna Sabina should meet here, the descendants of two of the oldest families of the Italian aristocracy!"

"I am a republican," observed Malipieri quietly.

"You!" cried the Baroness in amazement. "You, the offspring of such races as the Malipieri and the Gradenigo a republican, a socialist, an anarchist!"

"There is a difference," said Malipieri with a smile. "A republican is not an anarchist!"

"I can never believe it," answered the Baroness solemnly.

She ate a few green peas and shook her head.

"I went to Carthage because I was condemned to three years' confinement in prison," replied Malipieri with calm.

"Prison!" exclaimed the Baroness in horror, and she looked at her husband, mutely asking why in the world he had brought a convict to their table.

The Baron smiled benignly, as he disposed of an ample mouthful of green peas, before he spoke.

"Signor Malipieri," he said, when he had swallowed the last one, "founded and edited a republican newspaper in the north of Italy."

"And you were sent to prison for that?" asked Sabina with indignation.

"It is one thing to send a man to prison," said Malipieri. "It is another to make him go there. I escaped to Switzerland, and I came back to Italy quite lately, after the amnesty."

"I am amazed!" The Baroness looked at the servants timidly, as if she expected the butler and the footman to express their disapprobation of the guest.

"I have left politics for the present," Malipieri replied, looking at Sabina and smiling.

"Of course!" cried the Baroness. "But—" she stopped short.

"My wife," said the financier with a grin, "is afraid you have dynamite about you."

"How absurd!" The Baroness felt that she was ridiculous. "But I do not understand how you can be friends," she added, glancing from her husband to Malipieri.

"We are at least on good terms of acquaintance," said the younger man a little markedly.

Sabina liked the speech and the way in which it was spoken.

"We have a common ground for it in our interest in antiquities. Is it not true, Signer Malipieri?"

The Baron looked at him and smiled again, as if there were a secret between them, and Malipieri glanced at Sabina.

"It is quite true," he said gravely. "The Baron has read all I have written about Carthage."

Volterra possessed a sort of rough social tact, together with the native astuteness and great knowledge of men which had made him rich and a Senator. He suddenly became voluble and led the conversation in a new direction, which it followed till the end of dinner.

Several people came in afterwards, as often happened, before the coffee was taken away. They were chiefly men in politics, and two of them brought their wives with them. They were not the sort of guests whom the Baroness preferred, for they were not by any means all noble Romans, but they were of importance to her husband and she took great pains to make them welcome. To one she offered his favourite liqueur, which happened to be a Sicilian ratafia; for another she made the Baron send for some of those horribly coarse black cigars known as Tuscans, which some Italians prefer to anything else; for a third, she ordered fresh coffee to be especially made. She took endless trouble.

Malipieri seemed to know none of the guests, and he took advantage of the Baroness's preoccupation for their comforts to sit down by Sabina. He did not look at her, and she thought he looked bored, as he sat a moment in silence. Then a thin deputy with a magnificent forehead and thick grey hair began to hold forth on the subject of a projected divorce law and the guests gathered round him. Sabina had never heard of Sydney Smith, but she had a suspicion that nobody could be as great as the speaker looked. While she was thinking of this, Malipieri spoke to her in a low voice.

"I suppose that you are stopping in the house," he said.

"Yes."

Sabina turned her eyes a little, but did not look straight at him. She saw, however, that he was still watching the people in the room, and still looked bored, and she was quite unprepared for what followed.

"Are the affairs of your family finally settled?" he enquired, without changing his tone.

Sabina was so much surprised that she waited a moment before answering. Her first instinct was to ask him stiffly why he put such a question, and she would have replied to it in that way if it had come from any other guest in the room; but she changed her mind almost instantly.

"No one has told me anything," she said simply, in a low voice. Malipieri turned his head a little with a quick movement, and clasped his brown hands over one knee.

"You know nothing?" he asked. "Nothing whatever about the matter?"

"Nothing."

He bit his lip as if he were indignant, and were repressing an exclamation.

"No one has written to me—for a long time," Sabina said, after a moment.

She had been on the point of saying that she had never received a line from any member of her family since the crash, but that seemed to sound like a confidence, and what she really said was quite true.

"Has not the Senator told you anything either?" Malipieri asked.

"No. I suppose he does not like to speak about our misfortunes before me."

"Have you, I mean you yourself, any interest in the Palazzo Conti now? Can you tell me that?"

"I know nothing—nothing!" Sabina repeated the word with a slight tremor, for just then she felt her position more keenly than ever before. "Why do you ask?"

She could not help putting the question which rose to her lips the second time, but there was no coldness in her voice. She was very lonely, and she felt that Malipieri was speaking from some honourable motive.

"I am living in the palace," Malipieri answered.

Sabina looked up quickly, with an expression of interest in her pale young face. The thought that the man beside her was living in her old home was like a bond of acquaintance.

"Really?" she cried. "In which part of the house?"

"Do not seem interested, please," said Malipieri, suddenly looking very bored again. "If you do, we shall not be allowed to talk. I am living in the little apartment on the intermediate story. They tell me that a chaplain once lived there."

"I know where it is," answered Sabina, "but I was never in the rooms. They used to be shut up, I think."

The deputy who was haranguing on the subject of divorce seemed to be approaching his peroration. His great voice filled the large room with incessant noise, and everybody seemed anxiously waiting for a chance to contradict him. Malipieri was in no danger of being overheard.

"If it happens," he said, "that I wish to communicate with you on a matter of importance, how can I reach you best?"

He asked the question quite naturally, as if he had known Sabina all his life. At first she was so much surprised that she could hardly speak.

"I—I do not know," she stammered.

She had never received letters from any one but her own family or her school friends, and a very faint colour rose in her pale cheek. Malipieri looked more bored and weary than ever.

"It may be absolutely necessary for me to write to you before long," he said. "Shall I write by post?"

Sabina hesitated.

"Is there no one in all Rome whom you can trust to bring a note and give it to you when you are alone?"

"There is Signor Sassi," Sabina answered almost instinctively. "But really, why should you—"

"How can I find Sassi?" asked Malipieri, interrupting the question. "Who is he?"

"He was our agent. Is he gone? The old porter will know where to find him. I think he lived near the palace. But perhaps the porter has been sent away too."

"He is still there. Have you been made to sign any papers since you have been here?"

"No."

"Will you promise me something?"

Sabina could not understand how it was that a man who had been a stranger two hours earlier was speaking to her almost as if he were an intimate friend, still less why she no longer felt that she ought to check him and assert her dignity.

"If it is right, I will promise it," she answered quietly, and looking down.

"It is right," he said. "If the Senator, or any one else asks you to sign a paper, will you promise to consult me before doing so?"

"But I hardly know you!" she laughed, a little shyly.

"It is of no use to waste time and trouble on social conventions," said Malipieri. "If you do not trust me, can you trust this Sassi?"

"Oh yes!"

"Then consult him. I will make him consult me, and it will be the same—and ten times more conventional and proper."

He smiled.

"Will you promise that?" he asked.

"Yes. I promise. But I wish you would tell me more."

"I wish I could. But I hardly know you!" He smiled again, as he repeated her own words.

"Never mind that! Tell me!"

"No. I cannot. If there is trouble I will tell you everything—through Sassi, of course."

Sabina laughed, and all at once she felt as if she had known him for years.

At that moment the deputy finished his speech, and all who had anything to say in answer said it at once, in order to lose no time, while the speaker relighted his villainous black cigar, puffing tremendously.

The Baroness suddenly remembered Sabina and Malipieri in the corner, and after screaming out several incoherent phrases, which might have been taken for applause or dissent and were almost lost in the general din, she moved across the room.

"It is atrocious!" she cried, as she reached Sabina. "I hope you have not heard a word he said!"

"When a man has such a voice as that, it is impossible not to hear him," said Malipieri, rising and answering before Sabina had time to speak.

Sabina rose, too, rather reluctantly.

"And of course you agreed with everything he said," the Baroness replied. "All anarchists do!"

"I beg your pardon. I do not agree with him at all, and I am really not an anarchist."

He smiled politely, and Sabina noticed with an unaccountable little thrill of satisfaction that the smile was quite different from the one she had seen in his face more than once while they had been talking together. As for the deputy's discourse, she had not heard a word of it.

The Baroness sat down on the sofa, and Sabina slipped away. She was not supposed to be in society yet, as she was not quite eighteen, and there was certainly no reason why she should stay in the drawing-room that evening, while there were many reasons why she should go away. The Baroness breathed an audible sigh of relief when she was gone, for it was never possible to predict what some excited politician might say before her in the heat of argument.

In the silence of her own room she sat down to think over the unexpected events of the evening. Very young girls love to look forward to the moment when they shall be able to "think" of what has happened, after they have met men they are inclined to like, and who interest them. But when the time really comes they hardly ever think at all. They see pictures, they hear voices, they feel again what they have felt, they laugh, they shed tears all alone, and they believe they are thinking, or even reasoning. Their little joys come back to them, the little triumphs of their vanity, and also all the little hurts their sensitiveness has suffered, and which men do not often guess and still more rarely understand.

There must be some original reason why all boys call girls silly, and all girls think boys stupid. It must be part of the first manifestation of that enormous difference which exists between the point of view of men and women in after life.

Women are, in a sense, the embodiment of practice, while men are the representatives of theory. In practice, in a race for life, the runner who jumps everything in his way is always right, unless he breaks his neck. In theory, he is as likely to break his neck at the first jump as at the second, and the chances of his coming to grief increase quickly, always in theory, as he grows tired. So theory says that it is safer never to jump at all, but to go round through the gates, or wade ignominiously through the water. Women jump; men go round. The difference is everything. Women believe in what often succeeds in practice, and they take all risks and sometimes come down with a crash. Men theorize about danger, make elaborate calculations to avoid it and occasionally stick in the mud. When women fall at a stone wall they scream, when men are stuck in a bog they swear. The difference is fundamental. In nine cases out of ten it is the woman who enjoys the ecstatic delight of saying "I told you so," and there are plenty of women who would ask no greater joy in paradise than to say so to their husbands for ever and ever. Indeed, eternal reward and punishment could thus be at once combined and distributed in a simple manner.

Sabina took her first fence that evening, for when she put out her candle she was sure that Malipieri was already her friend, and that she could trust him in any emergency. Moreover, though she would not have acknowledged it, she inwardly hoped that some emergency might not be far in the future.

But Malipieri walked all the way from the Via Ludovisi to the Palazzo Conti, which is more than a mile, without noticing that he had forgotten to light the cigar he had taken out on leaving Volterra's house.

CHAPTER VI

Malipieri had the Palazzo Conti to himself. The main entrance was always shut now, and only a small postern, cut in one side of the great door, was left ajar. The porter loafed about in the great court with his broom and his pipe; in the morning his wife went upstairs and opened a few windows, merely as a formality, and late in the afternoon she shut them again. Malipieri's man generally went out twice every day, carrying a military dinner-pail, made in three sections, which he brought back half an hour later. Malipieri sometimes was not seen for several days, but frequently he went out in the morning and did not come back till dark. Now and then,

57

things were delivered for him at the door,—a tin of oil for his lamps, a large box of candles, packages of odd shapes, sometimes very heavy, and which the porter was told to handle with care.

The old man tried to make acquaintance with Malipieri's man, but found it less easy than he had expected. In the first place, Masin came from some outlandish part of Italy where an abominable dialect was spoken, and though he could speak school Italian when he pleased, he chose to talk to the porter in his native jargon, when he talked at all. He might just as well have spoken Greek. Secondly, he refused the porter's repeated offers of a litre at the wine shop, always saying something which sounded like a reference to his delicate health. As he was evidently as strong as an ox, and as healthy as a savage or a street dog, the excuse carried no conviction. He was a big, quiet fellow, with china-blue eyes and a reddish moustache. The porter was not used to such people, nor to servants who wore moustaches, and was inclined to distrust the man. On the other hand, though Masin would not drink, he often gave the porter a cigar, with a friendly smile.

One day, in the morning, Baron Volterra came to see Malipieri, and stayed over an hour, a part of which time the two men spent in the courtyard, walking up and down in the north-west corner, and then taking some measurements with a long tape which Malipieri produced from his pocket. When the Baron went away he stopped and spoke with the porter. First he gave him five francs; then he informed him that his wages would be raised in future by that amount; and finally he told him that Signor Malipieri was an architect and would superintend the repairs necessary to the foundations at the north-west corner, that while the work was going on even the little postern door was to be kept shut all day, and no one was to be admitted on any condition without Signor Malipieri's express permission. The fat Baron fixed his eyes on the porter's with an oddly hard look, and said that he himself might come at any moment to see how the work was going on, and that if he found anybody inside the gate without Signor Malipieri's authority, it would be bad for the porter. During this conversation, Malipieri stood listening, and when it ended he nodded, as if he were satisfied, and after shaking hands with the Baron he went up the grand staircase without a word.

It was all very mysterious, and the porter shook his head as he turned into his lodge after fastening the postern; but he said nothing to his wife about what had passed.

From what he had been told, he now naturally expected that a number of masons would come in a day or two in order to begin the work of strengthening the foundations; but no one came, and everything went on as usual, except that the postern was kept shut. He supposed that Malipieri was not ready, but he wisely abstained from asking questions. Then Malipieri asked him for the address of Pompeo Sassi, and wrote it down in his pocket-book, and went out. That was on the morning after he had dined at the Baron's house, for it was not his habit to waste time when he wanted information.

Sassi received Malipieri in a little sitting-room furnished with a heterogeneous collection of utterly useless objects, all of which the old agent treasured with jealous affection, and daily recommended to the care of the elderly woman who was his only servant. The sofa and chairs had been new forty years ago, and though the hideous red-and-green stuffs with which they were covered were still tolerably vivid in colours the legs did not look safe, and Malipieri kept his feet well under him and sat down cautiously. Two rickety but well-dusted tables were loaded with ancient nicknacks, dating from the early part of the second French Empire, with impossibly ugly little figures carved out of cheap alabaster, small decayed photograph albums, and ingeniously bad wax flowers under glass shades. On the walls hung bad lithographs of Pius Ninth, Napoleon Third and Metternich, with a large faded photograph of old Prince Conti as a young man. Malipieri looked at it curiously, for he guessed that it represented Sabina's father. The face was clean-shaven, thin and sad, with deep eyes and fair hair that looked almost white now, as if the photograph had grown old with the man, while he had lived.

Sassi sat down opposite his visitor. He wore a black cloth cap with a green tassel, and rubbed his hands slowly while he waited for Malipieri to speak. The latter hesitated a moment and then went to the point at once.

"You were the agent of the Conti estate for many years," he said. "I know the Senator Volterra and have met Donna Sabina. I understand that her mother has left her under the charge of the Senator's wife, and seems to have forgotten her existence. The young lady is apparently without resources of her own, and it is not clear what would become of her if the Volterra couple should not find it convenient to keep her with them. Is that the state of affairs?"

Sassi nodded gravely. Then he looked keenly at the young man, and asked him a question.

"May I enquire why you take an interest in Donna Sabina Conti?"

Malipieri returned the other's gaze quietly.

"I am an architect, called in by the Senator to superintend some work on the palace. The Senator, as you know, took over the building when he foreclosed the mortgage, and he has not yet sold it, though he has refused several good offers. I have an idea that he believes it to be very valuable property. If this should turn out to be true, and if he should have made a very profitable transaction, he ought in honour, if not in law, to make over a part of the profits to Donna Sabina, who has practically been cheated of her share in her father's estate. Her mother, and her brother and sister, spent everything they could lay hands on, whereas she never had anything. Is that true?"

"Quite true, quite true," repeated Sassi sadly.

"And if Donna Sabina were to call them to account, I fancy the law would take a rather unpleasant view of what they did. I have heard that sort of thing called stealing when the persons who did it were not princes and princesses, but plain people like you and me. Do you happen to think of any better word?"

Sassi was silent. He had eaten the bread of the Conti all his life. He glanced at the faded photograph of the Prince, as if to explain, and Malipieri understood.

"You are an honorable man," he said. "I can no more tell you why I wish to help Donna Sabina to her rights, if she has any, than I can explain a great many things I have done in my life. When I see a dog kicked, I always kick the man, if I can, and I do not remember to have regretted any momentary unpleasantness that has followed in such cases. I have only seen Donna Sabina once, but I mean to help her if possible. Now tell me this. Has she any legal claim in the value of the palace or not?"

"I am afraid not," Sassi answered.

"Do you know whether she was ever induced to sign any release of her guardians?"

"She never did."

"That might be bad for them. That is all I wished to know. Thank you."

Malipieri rose to take his leave.

"If anything of importance happens, can you communicate with Donna Sabina?" he asked.

"I can write to her," Sassi answered. "I suppose she would receive me if I went to the house."

"That would be better."

"Excuse me," said the old man, before opening the door to let his visitor out, "am I right in supposing that the work the Baron wishes done is connected with the foundations?"

"Yes."

"At the north-west corner within the courtyard?"

"Yes," answered Malipieri, looking at him attentively. "Do you happen to know anything about the condition of that part of the palace?"

"Most people," Sassi replied, "have now forgotten that a good deal of work was done there long ago, under Pope Gregory Sixteenth."

"Indeed? I did not know that. What was the result?"

"The workmen came across the 'lost water.' It rose suddenly one day and one of them was drowned. I believe his body was never recovered. Everything was filled in again after that. For my own part I do not think the building is in any danger."

"Perhaps not," said Malipieri, suddenly looking bored. "I only carry out the Senator's wishes," he added, as if with an afterthought. "It is my business to find out whether there is danger or not."

He took his leave and went away, convinced that the old agent knew about other things besides Sabina's friendless condition, but unwilling to question him just then. The information Sassi had volunteered was interesting but not useful. Malipieri thought he himself knew well enough where the "lost water" was, under the Palazzo Conti.

It was not far from Sassi's house to the palace, but he walked very slowly through the narrow streets, and stopped more than once, deliberately looking back, as if he were trying to keep the exact direction of some point in his mind, and he seemed interested in the gutters, and in the walls, at their base, just above the pavement. At the corner of the Vicolo dei Soldati he saw a little marble tablet let into the masonry and yellow with age. He stopped a moment and read the inscription. Then he turned away with a look of annoyance, for it set forth that "by order of the most Eminent Vicar all persons were warned not to empty garbage there, on pain of a fine." It was a forgotten document of the old papal administration, as he could have told without reading it if he had known Rome better. From the corner he counted his paces and then stopped again and examined the wall and the pavement minutely.

There was nothing to be seen at all different from the pavement and the wall for many yards further on and further back, and Malipieri apparently abandoned the search, for he now walked on quickly till he reached the entrance of the palace, on the other side, and went in.

From the low door of the wine shop, Toto, the mason, had seen him, and stood watching him till he was out of sight.

"He does not know where it is," Toto said, sitting down again opposite Gigi.

"Engineers know everything," retorted the carpenter.

"If this one knew anything, he would not have stood there looking at the stones. I do not suppose the municipality is going to put up a monument to my grandfather, whom may the Lord preserve in glory!"

At this Gigi laughed, for he knew that Toto's grandfather had been drowned in the "lost water" somewhere deep down under that spot, and had never been found. The two men drank in silence. After a long time Toto spoke again.

"A woman," he said, with a shrug of the shoulders.

"A woman drowned him?" asked Gigi. "How could a woman do it?"

"A man did it. But it was for jealousy of a woman."

"The man was a mason, I suppose," suggested Gigi.

"Of course. He was working with the others in the morning, and he knew where they would be after dinner. He did not come back with them, and half an hour after they had gone down the water came. How many times have I told you that?"

"It is always a new tale," answered Gigi. "It gives me pleasure to hear it. Your father was a young man then, was he not?"

"Eighteen." Toto lighted his pipe.

"And the man who did it died soon afterwards?" Gigi said.

"Of course," said Toto. "What else could my father do? He killed him. It was the least he could have done. My father is also in Paradise."

"Requiescat!" ejaculated the carpenter devoutly.

"Amen," answered Toto. "He killed him with a mattock."

"It was well done," observed Gigi with satisfaction. "I suppose," he continued after a pause, "that if anybody went down there now, you could let in the water."

"Why should I? I do not care what they do. If they send for me, I may serve them. If they think they can do without me, let them try. I do not care a cabbage!"

"Perhaps not," Gigi answered thoughtfully. "But it must be a fine satisfaction to know that you can drown them all, like rats in a hole."

"Yes," said Toto, "it is a fine satisfaction."

"And even to know that you can make the water come before they begin, so that they can never do anything without you."

"That too," assented the mason.

"They would pay you a great deal to help them, if they could not pump the water out. There is no one else in Rome who knows how to turn it off."

Gigi made the remark tentatively, but Toto did not answer.

"You will need some one to help you," suggested the carpenter in an insinuating tone.

"I can do it alone."

"It is somewhere in the cellars of number thirteen, is it not?" asked Gigi.

He would have given all he had to know what Toto knew, and the bargain would have been a very profitable one, no doubt. But though the mason was his closest friend there were secrets of the trade which Toto would not reveal to him.

"The numbers in the street were all changed ten years ago," Toto answered.

He rose from his seat by the grimy table, and Gigi followed his example with a sigh of disappointment. They were moderate men, and hardly ever drank more than their litre of their wine. Toto smelt of mortar and his fustian clothes and hairy arms were generally splashed with it. Gigi smelt of glue and sawdust, and there were plentiful marks of his calling on his shiny old cloth trousers and his coarse linen shirt. Toto's face was square, stony and impenetrable; Gigi's was sharp as a bill and alive with curiosity. Gigi wore a square paper cap; Toto wore a battered felt hat of no shape at all. On Sundays and holidays they both shaved and turned out in immaculate white shirts, well brushed broadcloth and decent hats, recognizable to each other but not to their employers.

Malipieri was accosted by a stranger at the gate of the palace. The porter, faithfully obedient to his orders, was standing inside the open postern, completely blocking it with his bulk, and when Malipieri came up the visitor was still parleying with him.

"This gentleman is asking for you, sir," said the old man.

The individual bowed politely and stepped back a little. He had a singularly worthy appearance, Malipieri thought, and he would have inspired confidence if employed in a bank; his thick grey hair was parted in the middle, and at first sight Malipieri felt perfectly sure that it was parted down the back. His brown eyes were very wide open, and steady, his slightly grizzled moustache was neither twisted straight up at the ends in the imperial German manner, nor straight out like a cat's whiskers, nor waxed to fine points in the old French fashion. It grew naturally and was rather short, but it hid his mouth almost completely. The man was extremely well dressed in half-mourning, wore dark grey gloves and carried a plain black stick. He spoke quietly and Malipieri thought he recognized the Genoese accent.

"Signor Marino Malipieri?"

"Yes," answered the architect, in a tone that asked the visitor's name in return.

"My name is Vittorio Bruni. May I have a few words with you?"

"Certainly," Malipieri answered, with considerable coolness.

"Thank you. I have been much interested by your discoveries in Carthage, and if you would allow me to ask you one or two questions—"

"Pray come in."

"Thanks. After you."

"After you," insisted Malipieri, standing aside.

They went in. Before shutting the postern, the porter looked out into the street. It was almost deserted. Two men were standing together near the corner, apparently arguing some question, and stopping in their walk in order to talk more at their ease, as Romans often do. The porter shut the little door with a clang, and went back to his lodge. Malipieri and his visitor were already on the stairs.

Malipieri let himself in with a small latch-key, for he had ordered a modern patent lock to be put on his door as soon as he moved into the house. Masin appeared almost at once, however, and stood waiting for his master at the door of the sitting-room, like a large, placid mastiff. Malipieri nodded to him, and went in with Signor Bruni.

They sat down by the open window and Signor Bruni began to talk. In a few minutes it became evident that whether the man knew anything of the subject or not he had read everything that Malipieri had written, and remembered most of it by heart. He spoke fluently and asked intelligent questions. He had never been to Carthage, he said, but he thought of making the trip to Tunis during the following winter. Yes, he was a man of leisure, though he had formerly been in business; he had a taste for archaeology, and did not think it was too late to cultivate it, in a modest way, for his own pleasure. Of course, he could never hope to accomplish anything of importance, still less to become famous like Malipieri. It was merely a taste, and was better than nothing as an interest in life.

Malipieri protested that he was not famous, but agreed with Signor Bruni about other matters. It was better to follow a serious pursuit than to do nothing with one's life.

"Or to dash into politics," suggested Bruni carelessly, as if he had thought of trying that.

Perhaps he had heard of Malipieri's republican newspaper, but if he had thought of drawing the young man into conversation about it, he was disappointed. Malipieri continued to agree with him, listening attentively to all he said without once looking bored.

"And now," continued Bruni presently, "if it is not indiscreet, may I ask whether you have any new field of discovery in view?"

The phrases ran along as if they had been all prepared beforehand. The accent was now decidedly Genoese, and Malipieri, who was a Venetian, disliked it.

"Not at present," he said. "I have undertaken a little professional work in Rome, and I am trying to learn more about the Phoenician language."

"That is beyond me!" Bruni smiled pleasantly.

Malipieri looked at him a moment.

"If you are going to look into Carthaginian antiquities," he said, with much gravity, "I strongly advise you to study Phoenician."

"Dear me!" exclaimed Bruni with a sigh of regret, "I had hoped it might not be necessary."

He rose to take his leave, but as if seeing the bookshelves for the first time, asked permission to look at their contents. Malipieri saw that his glance ran sharply along the titles of the volumes, and that he was reading them as quickly as he could.

"I suppose you live here quite alone," he said.

"Yes. I have a servant."

"Of course. They tell me that Baron Volterra has not decided what he will do with the palace, and will not give a lease of it to any one."

"I do not know what he means to do," answered Malipieri, looking at the straight part down the back of his worthy visitor's hair, as the latter bent to look at the books.

"I suppose he lends you this apartment, as a friend," said Bruni.

"No. I pay rent for it."

Signor Bruni was becoming distinctly inquisitive, thought Malipieri, who answered coldly. Possibly the visitor perceived the hint, for he now finally took his leave. In spite of his protestations Malipieri went all the way downstairs with him, and let him out himself, just as the porter came out of his lodge at the sound of their footsteps.

Signor Bruni bowed a last time, and then walked briskly away. By force of habit, the porter looked up and down the street before shutting the door after him, and he was somewhat surprised to see that the two men whom he had noticed half an hour earlier had only just finished their argument and turned to go on as Signor Bruni passed them. Then the porter watched them all three till they disappeared round the corner. At the same moment, from the opposite direction, Toto reached the door of the palace, and greeted the porter with a rough good-evening.

"I have forgotten the name of this palace," he added, by way of a joke, meaning that he had not been called to do any work for a long time. "Perhaps you can tell me what it is called."

"It used to be a madhouse," returned the porter in the same strain. "Now that the madmen are gone, a mole lives here. I kept the door open for the lunatics, and they all got out. I keep it shut for the mole, when he does not shut it himself."

"I will come in and smoke a pipe with you," said Toto. "We will talk of old times."

The porter shook his head, and blocked the way.

"Not if you were the blessed soul of my father come back from the dead," he said. "The Baron's instructions are to let no one in without the mole's orders."

"But I am an old friend," objected Toto.

"Not if you were my mother, and the Holy Father, and Saint Peter, and all the souls of Purgatory at once," answered the porter.

"May an apoplexy seize you!" observed Toto pleasantly, and he went off, his pipe in his mouth.

The porter shrugged his shoulders at the imprecation, shut the door reluctantly, and went in to supper. Upstairs, Malipieri stood at his open window, smoking and watching the old fountain in the court. It was evening, and a deep violet light filled the air and was reflected in the young man's bronzed face. He was very thoughtful now, and was not aware that he heard the irregular splash of the water in the dark basin at the feet of the statue of Hercules, and the eager little scream of the swallows as they shot past him, upward to the high old eaves, where their young were, and downwards almost to the gravel of the court, and in wide circles and madly sudden curves. The violet light faded softly, and the dusk drank the last drop of it, and the last swallow disappeared under the eaves; but still Malipieri leaned upon the stone window-sill, looking down.

For a long time he thought of Signor Bruni. He wondered whether he had ever seen the man before, or whether the face only seemed familiar because it was the type of a class of faces all more or less alike, all intensely respectable and not without refinement, expressing a grave reticence that did not agree with the fluent speech, and a polite reserve at odds with the inquisitive nature that revealed itself.

Malipieri was inclined to think he had never met Bruni, but somehow the latter recalled the hot times in Milan, and his short political career, and the association was not to the man's advantage. He could not recall the name at all. It was like any other, and rather especially unobtrusive. Anybody might be called Vittorio Bruni, and Vittorio Bruni might be anybody, from a senator to a shoemaker; but if he had been a senator, or any political personage, Malipieri would have heard of him.

There was something very odd, too, about his knowledge of Carthaginian antiquities, which was entirely limited to the contents of Malipieri's own pamphlets. He knew nothing of the Egyptians and very little about the Greeks, beyond what Malipieri had necessarily written about both. He had talked much as a man does who has read up an unfamiliar subject in order to make a speech about it, and though the speech is skilful, an expert can easily detect the shallowness of attainment behind it.

There could be only one reason why any one should take so much trouble; the object was evidently to make Malipieri's acquaintance, in the absence of an ordinary introduction. And yet Signor Bruni had quite forgotten to give his card with his address, as almost any Italian would have done under the circumstances, whether he expected the meeting to be followed by another or not. Malipieri spent most of his time in his rooms, but he knew very well that he might go about Rome for weeks and not come across the man again.

He recalled the whole conversation. He had in the first place expected that Bruni would be inquisitive about the palace, and perhaps ask to be shown over it, but it was only at the last that he had put one or two questions which suggested an interest in the building, and then he had at once taken the hint given him by Malipieri's cold tone, and had not persisted. On the other hand he had looked carefully at the titles of the books on the shelves, as if in search of something.

Then Malipieri was conscious again of the association, in his own mind, between the man's personality and his own political experiences, and he suddenly laughed aloud.

"What a precious fool I am!" he thought. "The man is nothing but a detective!"

The echo of his laugh came back to him from across the dusky court in rather a ghostly way.

The evening air was all at once chilly, and he shut his window and called for Masin, who instantly appeared with a lamp. Masin was always ready, and, indeed, possessed many qualities excellent in a faithful servant, among which gratitude to Malipieri held a high place.

He had something to be grateful for, which is not, however, always a cause of gratitude in the receiver of favours and mercies. He had been a convict, and had served a term of several years in penal servitude. The sentence had been passed upon him for having stabbed a man in the back, in a drunken brawl, but Masin had steadily denied the charge, and the evidence against him had been merely circumstantial. It had happened in Rome, where Masin had worked as a mason during the construction of the new Courts of Justice. He was from the far north of Italy, and was, of course, hated by his companions, as only Italians of different parts of the country can hate one another. To shield one of themselves, they unanimously gave evidence against Masin; the jury was chiefly composed of Romans, the judge was a Sicilian, and Masin had no chance. Fortunately for him, the man lived, though much injured; if he had died, Masin would have got a life sentence. It was an old story; false witnesses, a prejudiced jury, and a judge who, though willing to put his prejudices aside, had little choice but to convict.

Masin had been sent to Elba to the penitentiary, had been a "good-behaviour man" from first to last, and his term had been slightly abridged in consequence. When he was discharged, he went back to the north. Malipieri had found him working as a mason when some repairs were being made in the cathedral of Milan, and had taken a fancy to him. Masin had told his story simply and frankly, explaining that he found it hard to get a living at all since he had been a convict, and that he was trying to save enough money to emigrate to New York. Malipieri had thought over the matter for a week, speaking to him now and then, and watching him, and had at last proposed to take him into his own service. Later, Masin had helped Malipieri to escape, had followed him into exile, and had been of the greatest use to him during the excavations in Carthage, where he had acted as body-servant, foreman, and often as a trusted friend.

He was certainly not an accomplished valet, but Malipieri did not care for that. He was sober, he was honest, he was trustworthy, he was cool in danger, and he was very strong. Moreover, he was an excellent and experienced mason, a fact of little or no use in the scientific treatment of shoes, trousers, silk hats, hair-brushes and coffee, but which had more than once been valuable to Malipieri during the last few years. Finally, his gratitude to the man who had believed in his innocence was deep and lasting. Masin would really have given his life to save Malipieri's, and would have been glad to give it.

He set the lamp down on the table, and waited for orders, his blue eyes quietly fixed on his master.

"I never saw that gentleman before," said Malipieri, setting some papers in order, under the bright light, but still standing. "Did you look at his face?"

"Yes, sir," answered Masin, and waited.

"What sort of man should you take him to be?"

"A spy, sir," replied Masin promptly.

"I think you are right," Malipieri answered. "We will begin work to-morrow morning."

"Yes, sir."

Malipieri ate his supper without noticing what Masin brought him, and then installed himself with his shaded lamp at his work-table. He took from the drawer a number of sketches of plans and studied them attentively, by a rather odd process.

He had drawn only one plan on heavy paper, in strong black lines. An architect would have seen at once that it represented a part of the foundations of a very large building; and two or three persons then living in Rome might have recognized the plan of the cellars under the north-west corner of the Palazzo Conti—certainly not more than two or three, one of whom was the snuffy expert who had come from beyond the Tiber, and another was Baron Volterra. Toto, the mason, could have threaded the intricate ways in the dark, but could assuredly have made nothing of the drawings. On the other hand, the persons who were acquainted with them did not know what Toto knew, and he was not at all inclined to impart his knowledge to any one, for reasons best known to himself.

Furthermore, an architect would have understood at a glance that the plan was incomplete, and that there was some reason why it could not be completed. A part of it was quite blank, but in one place the probable continuation of a main wall not explored, or altogether inaccessible, was indicated by dotted lines.

Besides this main drawing, Malipieri had several others made on tracing paper to the same scale, which he laid over the first, and moved about, trying to make the one fit the other, and in each of these the part which was blank in the one underneath was filled in according to different imaginary plans. Lastly, he had a large transparent sheet on which were accurately laid out the walls and doors of the ground floor of the palace at the north-west corner, and in this there was marked a square piece of masonry, shaded as if to represent a solid pilaster, and which came over the unexplored part of the cellars. Sometimes Malipieri placed this drawing over the first, and then one of the others on both, trying to make the three agree. It was like an odd puzzle, and there was not a word written on any of the plans to explain what they meant. On most of the thin ones there were blue lines, indicating water, or at least its possible course.

The imaginary architect, if he could have watched the real one, would have understood before long that the latter was theorizing about the probable construction of what was hitherto inaccessible, and about the probable position of certain channels through which water flowed, or might be expected to flow. He would also have gathered that Malipieri could reach no definite conclusion unless he could break through one of two walls in the cellar, or descend through an opening in the floor above, which would be by far the easiest way. He might even have wondered why Malipieri did not at once adopt the latter expedient. It is not a serious matter to make an aperture through a vault, large enough to allow the passage of a man's body, and it could not be attended with any danger to the building. It would be much less safe and far more difficult to cut a hole through one of the main foundation walls, which might be many feet thick and yet not wholly secure. Nevertheless the movements made by the point of Malipieri's pencil showed that he was contemplating that method of gaining an entrance.

CHAPTER VII

Sabina had been more than two months in Baron Volterra's house, when she at last received a line from her mother. The short letter was characteristic and was, after all, what the girl had expected, neither more nor less. The Princess told her that for the present she must stay with the "kind friends" who had offered her a home; that everything would be right before long; that if she needed any advice she had better send for Sassi, who had always served the family faithfully; that gowns were going to be short next year, which would be becoming to Sabina when she "came out," because she had small feet and admirable ankles; and that the weather was heavenly. The Princess added that she would send her some pocket-money before long, and that she was trying to find the best way of sending it.

76

In spite of her position Sabina smiled at the last sentence. It was so like her mother to promise what she would never perform, that it amused her. She sat still for some time with the letter in her hand and then took it to the Baroness, for she felt that it was time to speak out and that the interview could not be put off any longer. The Baroness was writing in her boudoir. She wrote her letters on large sheets of an especial paper, stamped with her initials, over which appeared a very minute Italian baron's coronet, with seven points; it was so small that one might easily have thought that it had nine, like a count's, but it was undeniably smart and suggested an assured position in the aristocracy. No one quite remembered why the late King had made Volterra a baron, but he undoubtedly had done so, and no one disputed Volterra's right to use the title.

Sabina read her letter aloud, and the Baroness listened attentively, with a grave expression.

"Your dear mother—" she began in a soothing tone.

"She is not my 'dear mother' at all," said Sabina, interrupting her. "She is not any more 'dear' to me than I am to her."

"Oh!" exclaimed the Baroness, affecting to be shocked by the girl's heartlessness.

"If it were not for my 'dear mother,' I should not be a beggar," said Sabina.

"A beggar! What a word!"

"There is no other, that I know of. I am living on your charity."

"For heaven's sake, do not say such things!" cried the Baroness.

"There is nothing else to say. If you had not taken me in and lodged me and fed me, I should like to know where I should be now. I am quite sure that my 'dear mother' would not care, but I cannot help wondering what is to become of me. Are you surprised?"

"Are you not provided for here?" The question was put in a tone almost of deprecation.

"Provided for! I am surrounded with every sort of luxury, when I ought to be working for my living."

"Working!" The Baroness was filled with horror. "You, my dear, the daughter of a Roman Prince! You, working for your living! You, a Conti!"

Sabina smiled and looked down at her delicate hands.

"I cannot see what my name has to do with it," she said. "It is not much to be proud of, considering how my relatives behave."

"It is a great name," said the Baroness solemnly and emphatically.

"It was once," Sabina answered, leaning back in the low chair she had taken, and looking at the ceiling. "My mother and my brother have not added lustre to it, and I would much rather be called Signorina Emilia Moscetti and be a governess, than be Sabina Conti and live on charity. I have no right to what I do not possess and cannot earn."

"My dear child! This is rank socialism! I am afraid you talked too long with Malipieri the other night."

"There is a man who works, though he has what you call a great name," observed Sabina. "I admire that. He was poor, I suppose— perhaps not so poor as I am—and he made up his mind to earn his living and a reputation."

"You are quite mistaken," said the Baroness drily.

Sabina looked at her in surprise.

"I thought he was a distinguished architect and engineer," she answered.

"Yes. But he was never poor, and he will be very rich some day."

"Indeed!" Sabina seemed rather disappointed at the information.

There was a little pause, and the Baroness looted at her unfinished letter as if she wished that Sabina would go away. She had foreseen that before long the girl would make some protest against her position as a perpetual guest in the house, but had no clear idea of how to meet it. Sabina seemed so very decided.

"We have done our best to make you feel at home, like one of the family," the Baroness said presently, in a rather injured tone.

Sabina did not wish to be one of the family at all, but she knew that she was under great obligations to her hosts, and she did not wish to be thought ungrateful.

"You have been more than kind," she answered gently, "and I shall never forget it. You have taken more trouble with me in two or three months than my mother in all my life. Please do not imagine that I am not thankful for all you have done."

The words were spoken sincerely, and when Sabina was very much in earnest there was something at once convincing and touching in her voice. The Baroness's sallow cheek actually flushed with pleasure, and she was impelled to leave her seat and kiss Sabina affectionately. She was restrained by a reasonable doubt as to the consequences of such demonstrative familiarity, though she would not have hesitated to kiss the girl's mother under like circumstances.

"It was the least we could do," she said, knowing very well that the phrase meant nothing.

"Excuse me," Sabina objected, "but there was no reason in the world why you should do anything at all for me! In the natural course of things I should either have been sent to the country with my sister-in-law, or to the convent with Clementina."

"You would have been very unhappy, my dear child."

"I do not know which would have been worse," said Sabina frankly. "They both hate me, and I hate them."

"Dear me!" exclaimed the Baroness, shocked again, or pretending to be.

"In our family," Sabina answered calmly, "we all hate each other."

"I am sure your sister Clementina is far too religious to feel hatred for any one."

"You do not know her!" Sabina laughed, and looked at the ceiling. "She hates 'the wicked' with a mortal hatred!"

"Perhaps you mean that she hates wickedness, my dear," suggested the Baroness in a moralizing tone.

"Not at all!" laughed the young girl. "She would like to destroy everybody who is not like her, and she would begin with her own family. She used to tell me that I was doomed to eternal flames because I loved my canary better than I loved her. I did. It was quite true. As for my brother, she said he was wicked, too. I quite believe he is, but she had a friendly understanding with him, because they used to make Signor Sassi get money for them both. In the end they got so much that there was nothing left. Her share all went to convents and extraordinary charities, and his went heaven knows where!"

"And yours?" asked the Baroness, to see what she would say.

"I suppose it went to them too, like everything else, and to my mother, who spent a great deal of money. At all events, none of us have anything now. That is why I want to work."

"It is an honourable impulse, no doubt," the Baroness said, in a tone of meditative disapproval.

Sabina leaned forward, her chin on her hand.

"You think I am too young," she said. "And I really know nothing, except bad French and dancing. I cannot even sew, at least, not very well, and I cannot cook." She laughed. "I once made some very good toast," she added thoughtfully.

"You must marry," said the Baroness. "You must make a good marriage."

"No one will marry me, because I have no dowry," answered Sabina with perfect simplicity.

"Some men marry girls who have none. You are very pretty, you know."

"So my mother used to tell me when she was in a good humour. But Clementina always said I was hideous, that my eyes were like a little pig's, quite inside my head, and that my hair was grey, like an old woman's, and that I was as thin as a grasshopper."

"You are very pretty," the Baroness repeated with conviction; "and I am sure you would make a good wife."

"I am afraid not!" Sabina laughed. "We are none of us good, you know. Why should I be?"

The Baroness disapproved.

"That is a flippant speech," she said severely.

"I do not feel flippant at all. I am very serious. I wish to earn my living."

"But you cannot—"

"But I wish to," answered Sabina, as if that settled the question.

"Have you always done what you wished?" asked the Baroness wisely.

"No, never. That is why I mean to begin at once. I am sure I can learn to be a maid, or to make hats, or feed babies with bottles. Many girls of eighteen can."

The Baroness shrugged her shoulders in a decidedly plebeian way. Sabina's talk seemed very silly to her, no doubt, but she felt slightly foolish herself just then. At close quarters and in the relative intimacy that had grown up between them, the descendant of all the Conti had turned out to be very different from what the financier's wife had expected, and it was not easy to understand her. Sometimes the girl talked like a woman of the world, and sometimes like a child. Her character seemed to be a compound of cynicism and simplicity, indifference and daring, gentleness, hardness and pride, all wonderfully amalgamated under a perfectly self-possessed manner, and pervaded by the most undeniable charm. It was no wonder that the poor Baroness was as puzzled as a hen that has hatched a swan.

Sabina had behaved perfectly, so far; the Baroness admitted this, and it had added considerably to her growing social importance to be regarded as the girl's temporary guardian. Even royalty had expressed its approval of her conduct and its appreciation of her generosity, and it was one of the Baroness's chief ambitions to be noticed by royalty. She had shown a good deal of tact, too, for she was woman enough to guess what the girl must feel, and how hard it must be to accept so much without any prospect of being able to make a return. So far, however, matters had gone very well, and she had really begun to look forward to the glory of presenting Sabina in society during the following winter, and of steering her to a rich marriage, penniless though she was.

But this morning she had received a new impression which disturbed her. It was not that she attached much importance to Sabina's wild talk about working for a living, for that was absurd, on the face of it; but there was something daring in the tone, something in the little careless laugh which made her feel that the delicate girl might be capable of doing very unexpected and dangerous things. The sudden conviction came upon her that Sabina was of the kind that run away and make love matches, and otherwise break through social conventions in a manner quite irreparable. And if Sabina did anything of that sort, the Baroness would not only lose all the glory she had gained, but would of course be severely blamed by Roman society, which would be an awful calamity if it did not amount to a social fall. She alone knew how hard she had worked to build up her position, and she guessed how easily an accident might destroy it. Her husband had his politics and his finance to interest him, but what would be left to his wife if she once lost her hold upon the aristocracy? Even the smile of royalty would not make up for that, and royalty would certainly not smile if Sabina, being in her charge, did anything very startlingly unconventional.

Sabina was quite conscious that the Baroness did not understand; indeed, she had not really expected to be understood, and when she saw the shrug of the shoulders that answered her last speech she rose quietly and went to the window. The blinds were drawn together, for it was now late in May, but she could see down to the street, and as she looked she started a little.

"There is Signor Malipieri!" she cried, and it was clear that she was glad.

The Baroness uttered an exclamation of surprise.

"Are you sure?" she asked.

Yes, Sabina was quite sure. He had just driven up to the door in a cab. Now he was paying the cabman, too, instead of making him wait. The Baroness glanced at the showy little clock set in turquoises, which stood on her writing-table, and she put away her unfinished letter.

"We will ask him to stay to luncheon," she said, in a decided tone.

After sending up to ask if he would be received, Malipieri entered the room with an apology. He said that he had hoped to find the Baron in, and had been told that he might come at any moment. The Baroness thereupon asked the visitor to stay to luncheon, and Malipieri accepted, and sat down.

It had always amused Sabina to watch how the Baroness's manner changed when any one appeared whom she did not know very well. Her mouth assumed a stereotyped smile, she held her head a little forward and on one side, and she spoke in quite another tone. But just now Sabina did not notice these things. She was renewing her impression of Malipieri, whom she had only seen once and in evening dress. She liked him even better now, she thought, and it would have pleased her to look at him longer.

Their eyes met in a glance as he told the Baroness that he had come to see Volterra on a matter of business. He did not explain what the business was, and at once began to talk of other things, as if to escape possible questions. Sabina thought he was paler than before, or less sunburnt, perhaps; at all events, the contrast between his very white forehead and his bronzed face was less strong. She could see his eyes more distinctly, too, than she had seen them in the evening, and she liked their expression better, for he did not look at all bored now. She liked his voice, too, for the slight harshness that seemed always ready to command. She liked the man altogether, and was conscious of the fact, and wished she could talk with him again, as she had talked that evening on the sofa in the corner, without fear of interruption.

That was impossible, and she listened to what he said. It was merely the small talk of a man of the world who knows that he is expected to say something not altogether dull, and takes pains to be agreeable, but Sabina felt all through it a sort of sympathy which she missed very much in the Volterra household, the certainty of fellowship which people who have been brought up in similar surroundings feel when they meet in an atmosphere not their own.

A few minutes after he had come, a servant opened the door and said that the Baron wished to speak to the Baroness at the telephone. She rose, hesitated a moment and went out, leaving the two young people together.

"I have seen Sassi," said Malipieri in a low voice, as soon as the door was shut.

"Yes," answered Sabina, with a little interrogation.

She was very much surprised to hear a slight tremor in her own voice as she uttered the one word.

"I like him very much," Malipieri continued. "He is a good friend to you. He said that if anything of importance happened he would come and see you."

"I shall be glad," Sabina said.

"Something is happening, which may bring him. Be sure to see him alone, when he comes."

"Yes, but what is it? What can possibly happen that can make a difference?"

Malipieri glanced at the door, fearing that the Baroness might enter suddenly.

"Can you keep a secret?" he asked quickly.

"Of course! Tell me!" She leaned forward with eager interest, expecting his next words.

"Did you ever hear that something very valuable is said to be hidden somewhere under the palace?"

Sabina's face fell and the eagerness faded from her eyes instantly. She had often heard the story from her nurses when she had been a little girl, and she did not believe a word of it, any more than she believed that the marble statue of Cardinal Conti in the library really came down from its pedestal on the eve of All Souls' and walked through the state apartments, or the myth about the armour of Francesco Conti, of which the nurses used to tell her that on the anniversary of the night of his murder his eyes could be seen through the bars of the helmet, glowing with the infernal fire. As for any hidden treasure, she was quite positive that if it existed her brother and sister would have got at it long ago. Malipieri sank in her estimation as soon as he mentioned it. He was only a Venetian, of course, and could not be expected to know much about Rome, but he must be very weak-minded if he could be imposed upon by such nonsense. Her delicate lip curled with a little contempt.

"Is that the great secret?" she asked. "I thought you were in earnest."

"The Senator is," observed Malipieri drily.

"If the old gentleman has made you believe that he is, he must have some very deep scheme. He does not like to seem foolish."

Malipieri did not answer at once, but he betrayed no annoyance. In the short silence, he could hear the Baroness's powerful voice yelling at the telephone. It ceased suddenly, and he guessed that she was coming back.

"If I find anything, I wish you to see it before any one else does," he said quickly.

"That would be very amusing!" Sabina laughed incredulously, just as the door opened.

The Baroness heard the light laughter, and stood still with her hand on the latch, as if she had forgotten something. She was not a woman of sudden intuitions nor much given to acting on impulses, and when a new idea crossed her mind she almost always paused to think it over, no matter what she chanced to be doing. It was as if she had accidentally run against something which stunned her a little.

"What is it?" asked Sabina, very naturally.

The Baroness beckoned silently to her, and she rose.

"Only one moment, Signor Malipieri," said the Baroness, apologizing for leaving him alone.

When she and Sabina were out of the room, she shut the door and went on a few paces before speaking.

"My husband has telephoned that he cannot leave the Senate," she said.

"Well?" Sabina did not understand.

"But Malipieri has come expressly to see him."

"He can see him at the Senate," suggested Sabina.

"But I have asked Malipieri to stay to luncheon. If I tell him that my husband is not coming, perhaps he will not stay after all."

"Perhaps not," echoed Sabina with great calmness.

"You do not seem to care," said the Baroness.

"Why should I?"

"I thought you liked him. I thought it would amuse you if he lunched with us."

Sabina looked at her with some curiosity.

"Did you tell the Baron that Signor Malipieri is here?" she asked carelessly.

"No," answered the Baroness, looking away. "As my husband said he could not come to luncheon, it seemed useless."

Sabina understood now, and smiled. This was the direct consequence of the talk which had preceded Malipieri's coming; the

Baroness had at once conceived the idea of marrying her to Malipieri.

"What shall we do?" asked the Baroness.

"Whatever you think best," answered Sabina, with sudden meekness. "I think you ought at least to tell Signor Malipieri that the Baron is not coming. He may be in a hurry, you know. He may be wasting time."

The Baroness smiled incredulously.

"My dear," she said, "if he had been so very anxious to see my husband, he would have gone to the Senate first. It is near the palace."

She said no more, but led the way back to the morning room, while Sabina reflected upon the possible truth of the last suggestion, and wondered whether Malipieri had really made his visit for the sake of exchanging a few words with her rather than in order to see Volterra. The Baroness spoke to him as she opened the door.

"My husband has not come yet," she said. "We will not wait for him."

She rang the bell to order luncheon, and Malipieri glanced at Sabina's face, wondering what the Baroness had said to her, for it was not reasonable to suppose that the two had left the room in order to consult in secret upon the question of waiting for Volterra. But Sabina did not meet his look, and her pale young face was impenetrably calm, for she was thinking about what she had just discovered. She was as certain that she knew what had passed in the Baroness's thoughts, as if the latter had spoken aloud. The knowledge, for it amounted to that, momentarily chased away the recollection of what Malipieri had said.

It was rather amusing to be looked upon as marriageable, and to a man she already knew. Her mother had often talked to her with cynical frankness, telling her that she was to make the best match that could be obtained for her, naming numbers of young men she had never seen and assuring her that likes and dislikes had nothing to do with matrimony. They came afterwards, the Princess said, and it generally pleased Providence to send a mild form of aversion as the permanent condition of the bond. But Sabina had never believed her mother, who had cheated her when she was a child, as many foolish and heartless women do, promising rewards which were never given, and excursions which were always put off and little joys which always turned to sorrows less little by far.

Moreover, her sister Clementina had told her that there was only one way to treat the world, and that was to leave it with the contempt it deserved; and she had heard her brother tell his wife in one of his miserable fits of weakly brutal anger that marriage was hell, and nothing else; to which the young princess had coldly replied that he was only where he deserved to be. Sabina had not been brought up with the traditional pious and proper views about matrimony, and if she did not think even worse of it, the merit was due to her own nature, in which there was much good and hardly any real evil.

But she could not escape from a little inherited and acquired cynicism either, and while Malipieri chatted quietly during luncheon, an explanation of the whole matter occurred to her which was not pleasant to contemplate. The story about the treasure might or might not be true, but he believed in it, and so did Volterra. The Baron was therefore employing him to discover the prize. But Malipieri showed plainly that he wished her to possess it, if it were ever found, and perhaps he meant it to be her dowry, in which case it would come into his own hands if he could marry her. This was ingenious, if it was nothing else, and though Sabina felt that there was something mean about it, she resented the idea that he should expect her to think him a model of generosity when she hardly knew him.

She was therefore very quiet, and looked at him rather coldly when he spoke to her, but the Baroness put this down to her admirably correct manners, and was already beginning to consider how she could approach Malipieri on the subject of his marrying Sabina. She was quite in ignorance of the business which had brought him and her husband together, as Sabina now knew from many remarks she remembered. Volterra was accustomed to tell his wife what he had been doing when the matter was settled, and she had long ago given up trying to make him talk of his affairs when he chose to be silent.

On the whole, so far as Sabina was concerned, the circumstances were not at first very favourable to the Baroness's newly formed plan on this occasion, though she did not know it. On the other hand, Malipieri discovered before luncheon was over, that Sabina interested him very much, that she was much prettier than he had realized at his first meeting with her, and that he had unconsciously thought about her a good deal in the interval.

CHAPTER VIII

Malipieri was convinced before long that his doings interested some one who was able to employ men to watch him, and he connected the fact with Bruni's visit. He was not much disturbed by it, however, and was careful not to show that he noticed it at all. Naturally enough, he supposed that his short career as a promoter of republican ideas had caused him to be remembered as a dangerous person, and that a careful ministry was anxious to know why he lived alone in a vast palace, in the heart of Rome, knowing very few people and seeing hardly any one except Volterra. The Baron himself was apparently quite indifferent to any risk in the matter, and yet, as a staunch monarchist and supporter of the ministry then in office, it might have been expected that he would not openly associate with the monarchy's professed enemies. That was his affair, as Malipieri had frankly told him at the beginning. For the rest, the young architect smiled as he thought of the time and money the government was wasting on the supposition that he was plotting against it, but it annoyed him to find that certain faces of men in the streets were becoming familiar to him, quiet, blank faces of respectable middle-aged men, who always avoided meeting his eyes, and were very polite in standing aside to let him pass them on the pavement. There were now three whom he knew by sight, and he saw one of them every time he went out of the house. He knew what that meant. He had not the smallest doubt but that all three reported what they saw of his movements to Signor Vittorio Bruni, every day, in some particularly quiet little office in one of the government buildings connected with the Ministry of the Interior. It troubled him very little, since he was quite innocent of any political machinations for the present.

He had determined from the first not to employ any workmen to help him unless it should be absolutely necessary. He was strong and his practical experience in Carthage had taught him the use of pick and crowbar. Masin was equal to two ordinary men for such work, and could be trusted to hold his tongue.

Malipieri told the porter that he was exploring the foundations before attempting to strengthen them, and from time to time he gave him a little money. At first the old man offered to call Toto, who had always served the house, he said; but Malipieri answered that no help was needed in a mere preliminary exploration, and that another man would only be in the way. He made no secret of the fact that he was working with his own hands, however. Every morning, he and his servant went down into the north-west cellars by a winding staircase that was entered from a passage between the disused stables and the empty coach-house. Like every large Roman palace, the Palazzo Conti had two arched entrances, one of which had never been opened except on important occasions, when the carriages that drove in on the one side drove out at the other after their owner had alighted. This second gate was at the west end of the court, not far from the coach-house. To reach their work Malipieri and Masin had to go down the grand staircase and pass the porter's lodge. Masin wore the rough clothes of a working mason and Malipieri appeared in overalls and a heavy canvas jacket. Very soon the garments of both were so effectually stained with mud, green mould and water that the two men could hardly have been distinguished from ordinary day labourers, even in broad daylight.

They began work on the very spot at which the snuffy little expert had stopped to listen to the water. It was evidently out of the question to break through the wall at the level of the cellar floor, for the water could be heard running steadily through its hidden channel, and if this were opened the cellars might be completely flooded. Besides, Malipieri knew that the water might rise unexpectedly to a considerable height.

It was therefore best to make the opening as high as possible, under the vault, which at that point was not more than ten feet from the ground. The simplest plan would have been to put up a small scaffolding on which to work, but there was no timber suitable for the purpose in the cellar, and Malipieri did not wish to endanger the secrecy of his operations by having any brought down. He therefore set to work to excavate an inclined aperture, like a tunnel, which began at a height of about five feet and was intended to slope upwards so as to reach the interior chamber at the highest point practicable.

It was very hard work at first, and it was not unattended by danger. Masin declared at the outset that it was impracticable without blasting. The wall appeared to be built of solid blocks of travertine stone, rough hewn on the face but neatly fitted together. It would take two men several days to loosen a single one of these blocks, and if they finally succeeded in moving it, it must fall to the ground at once, for their united strength would not have sufficed to lower it gently.

"The facing is stone," said Malipieri, "but we shall find bricks behind it. If we do not, we must try to get in by some other way."

In order to get any leverage at all, it was necessary to chisel out a space between the first block to be moved and those that touched it, an operation which occupied two whole days. Masin worked doggedly and systematically, and Malipieri imitated him as well as he could, but more than once nearly blinded himself with the flying chips of stone, and though he was strong his hands ached and trembled at the end of the day, so that he could hardly hold a pen. To Masin it was easy enough, and was merely a question of time and patience. He begged Malipieri to let him do it alone, but the architect would not hear of that, since there was room for two to use their tools at the same time, at opposite ends of the block. He was in haste to get over the first obstacle, which he believed to be by far the most difficult, and he was not the kind of man to sit idly watching another at work without trying to help him.

On the third day they made an attempt to use a crowbar. They had two very heavy ones, but they did not try to use both, and united their strength upon one only. They might as well have tried to move the whole palace, and it looked as if they would be obliged to cut the block itself away with hammer and chisel, a labour of a fortnight, perhaps, considering the awkward position in which they had to work.

"One dynamite cartridge would do it!" laughed Malipieri, as he looked at the huge stone.

"Thank you, sir," answered Masin, taking the suggestion seriously. "I have been in the galleys seven years, and that is enough for a lifetime. We must try and split it with wedges."

"There is no other way."

They had all the tools necessary for the old-fashioned operation; three drilling irons, of different sizes, and a small sledge-hammer, and they went to work without delay. Malipieri held the iron horizontally against the stone with both hands, turning it a little after Masin had struck it with the sledge. It was very exhausting after a time, as the whole weight of the tool was at first carried by Malipieri's uplifted hands. Moreover, if he forgot to grasp it very firmly, the vibration of the blow made the palms of his hands sting till they were numb. At regular intervals the men changed places, Masin held the drill and Malipieri took the hammer. Every now and then they raked out the dust from the deepening hole with a little round scoop made for the purpose and riveted to the end of a light iron rod a yard long.

Hour after hour they toiled thus together, far down under the palace, in the damp, close air, that was cold and yet stifling to breathe. The hole was now over two feet deep.

Suddenly, as Masin delivered a heavy blow, the drill ran in an inch instead of recoiling in Malipieri's tight hold.

"Bricks," said Masin, resting on the haft of the long hammer.

Malipieri removed the drill, took the scoop and drew out the dust and minute chips. Hitherto the stuff had been grey, but now, as he held his hand under the round hole to catch what came, a little bit of dark red brick fell into his palm. He picked it out carefully and held it close to the bright unshaded lamp.

"Roman brick," he said, after a moment.

"We are not in Milan," observed Masin, by way of telling his master that he did not understand.

"Ancient Roman brick," said Malipieri. "It is just what I expected. This is part of the wall of an old Roman building, built of bricks and faced with travertine. If we can get this block out, the worst will be over."

"It is easier to drill holes in stone than in water," said Masin, who had put his ear to the hole. "I can hear it much louder now."

"Of course you can," answered Malipieri. "We are wasting time," he added, picking up the drill and holding it against the block at a point six inches higher than before.

Masin took his sledge again and hammered away with dogged regularity. So the work went on all that day, and all the next. And after that they took another tool and widened the holes, and then a third till they were two inches in diameter.

Masin suggested that they might drive an iron on through the brickwork, and find out how much of it there was beyond the stone, but Malipieri pointed out that if the "lost water" should rise it would pour out through the hole and stop their operations effectually. The entrance must incline upwards, he said.

They made long round plugs of soft pine to fit the holes exactly, each one scored with a channel a quarter of an inch deep, which was on the upper side when they had driven the plugs into their places, and was intended to lead the water along the wood, so as to wet it more thoroughly. To do this Malipieri poked long cotton wicks into each channel with a wire, as far as possible. He made Masin buy half-a-dozen coarse sponges and tied one upon the upper end of each projecting plug. Finally he wet all the sponges thoroughly and wound coarse cloths loosely round them to keep in as much of the water as possible. By pouring on water from time to time the soft wood was to be ultimately wet through, the wicks leading the moisture constantly inward, and in the end the great block must inevitably be split into halves. It is the prehistoric method, and there never was any other way of cleaving very hard stone until gunpowder first brought in blasting. It is slow, but it is quite sure.

The place where the two men had been working was many feet below the level of the courtyard, but the porter could now and then hear the sound of blows echoing underground through the vast empty cellars, even when he stood near the great entrance.

Toto heard the noise too, one day, as he was standing still to light his pipe in the Vicolo dei Soldati. When it struck his ear he let the match burn out till it singed his horny fingers. His expression became even more blank than usual, but he looked up and down the street, to see if he were alone, and upward at the windows of the house opposite. Nobody was in sight, but in order to place his ear close to the wall and listen, he made a pretence of fastening his shoe-string. The sound came to him from very far beneath, regular as the panting of an engine. He knew his trade, and recognized the steady hammering on the end of a stone drill, very unlike the irregular blows of a pickaxe or a crowbar. The "moles" were at work, and knew their business; sooner or later they would break through. But Toto could not guess that the work was being actually done by Malipieri and his servant, without help. One man alone could not do it, and the profound contempt of the artisan for any outsider who attempts his trade, made Toto feel quite sure that one or more masons had been called in to make a breach in the foundation wall. As he stood up and lighted his pipe at last, he grinned all alone, and then slouched on, his heart full of very evil designs. Had he not always been the mason of the Palazzo Conti? And his father before him? And his grandfather, who had lost his life down there, where the moles were working? And now that he was turned out, and others were called in to do a particularly confidential job, should he not be revenged? He bit his pipe and thrust his rough hands deep into the pockets of his fustian trousers, and instead of turning into the wine shop to meet Gigi, he went off for a walk by himself through all the narrow and winding streets that lie between the Palazzo Conti and Monte Giordano.

He came to no immediate conclusion, and moreover there was no great hurry. He knew well enough that it would take time to pierce the wall, after the drilling was over, and he could easily tell when that point was reached by listening every day in the Vicolo dei Soldati. It would still be soon enough to play tricks with the water, if he chose that form of vengeance, and he grinned again as he thought of the vast expense he could force upon Volterra in order to save the palace. But he might do something else. Instead of flooding the cellars and possibly drowning the masons who had ousted him, he could turn informer and defeat the schemes of Volterra and Malipieri, for he never doubted but that if they found anything of value they meant to keep the whole profit of it to themselves.

He had the most vague notions of what the treasure might be. When the fatal accident had happened his grandfather had been the only man who had actually penetrated into the innermost hiding-place; the rest had fled when the water rose and had left him to drown. They had seen nothing, and their story had been handed down as a mere record of the catastrophe. Toto knew at least that the vaults had then been entered from above, which was by far the easier way, but a new pavement had long ago covered all traces of the aperture.

There was probably gold down there, gold of the ancients, in earthen jars. That was Toto's belief, and he also believed that when it was found it would belong to the government, because the government took everything, but that somehow, in real justice, it should belong to the Pope. For Toto was not only a genuine Roman of the people, but had always regarded himself as a sort of hereditary retainer of an ancient house.

His mind worked slowly. A day passed, and he heard the steady hammering still, and after a second night he reached a final conclusion. The Pope must have the treasure, whatever it might be.

That, he decided, was the only truly moral view, and the only one which satisfied his conscience. It would doubtless be very amusing to be revenged on the masons by drowning them in a cellar, with the absolute certainty of never being suspected of the deed. The plan had great attractions. The masons themselves should have known better than to accept a job which belonged by right to him, and they undoubtedly deserved to be drowned. Yet Toto somehow felt that as there was no woman in the case he might some day, in his far old age, be sorry for having killed several men in cold blood. It was really not strictly moral, after all, especially as his grandfather's death had been properly avenged by the death of the murderer.

As for allowing the government to have a share in the profits of the discovery, that was not to be thought of. He was a Roman, and the Italian government was his natural enemy. If he could have turned all the "lost water" in the city upon the whole government collectively, in the cellars of the Palazzo Conti, he would have felt that it was strictly moral to do so. The government had stolen more than two years of his life by making him serve in the army, and he was not going to return good for evil. With beautiful simplicity of reasoning he cursed the souls of the government's dead daily, as if it had been a family of his acquaintance.

But the Pope was quite another personage. There had always been popes, and there always would be till the last judgment, and everything connected with the Vatican would last as long as the world itself. Toto was a conservative. His work had always kept him among lasting things of brick and stone, and he was proud of never having taken a day's wages for helping to put up the modern new-fangled buildings he despised. The most lasting of all buildings in the world was the Vatican, and the most permanent institution conceivable was the Pope. Gigi, who made wretched, perishable objects of wood and nails and glue, such as doors and windows, sometimes launched into modern ideas. Toto would have liked to know how many times the doors and windows of the Palazzo Conti had been renewed since the walls had been built! He pitied Gigi always, and sometimes he despised him, though they were good friends enough in the ordinary sense.

The Pope should have the treasure. That was settled, and the only question remaining concerned the means of transferring it to him when it was discovered.

CHAPTER IX

One evening it chanced that the Volterra couple were dining out, and that Sabina, having gone up to her room to spend the evening, had forgotten the book she was reading and came downstairs half-an-hour later to get it. She opened the drawing-room door and went straight to the table on which she had left the volume. As she turned to go back she started and uttered a little cry, almost of terror.

Malipieri was standing before the mantelpiece, looking at her.

"I am afraid I frightened you," he said quietly. "Pray forgive me."

"Not at all," Sabina answered, resting the book she held in her hand upon the edge of the table. "I did not know any one was here."

"I said I would wait till the Senator came home," Malipieri said.

"Yes." Sabina hesitated a moment and then sat down.

She smiled, perhaps at herself. In her mother's house it would have been thought extremely improper for her to be left alone with a young man during ten minutes, but she knew that the Baroness held much more modern views, and would probably be delighted that she and Malipieri should spend an hour together. He had been asked to luncheon again, but had declined on the ground of being too busy, much to the Baroness's annoyance.

Malipieri seated himself on a small chair at a discreet distance.

"I happened to know that they were going out," he said, "so I came."

Sabina looked at him in surprise. It was an odd way to begin a conversation.

"I wanted to see you alone," he explained. "I thought perhaps you would come down."

"It was an accident," Sabina answered. "I had left my book here. No one told me that you had come."

"Of course not. I took the chance that a lucky accident might happen. It has, but I hope you are not displeased. If you are, you can turn me out."

"I could go back to my room." Sabina laughed. "Why should I be displeased?"

"I have not the least idea whether you like me or not," answered Malipieri.

Sabina wondered whether all men talked like this, or whether it were not more usual to begin with a few generalities. She was really quite sure that she liked Malipieri, but it was a little embarrassing to be called upon to tell him so at once.

"If I wanted you to go away, I should not sit down," she said, still smiling.

"I hate conventions," answered Malipieri, "and I fancy that you do, too. We were both brought up in them, and I suppose we think alike about them."

"Perhaps."

Sabina turned over the book she still held, and looked at the back of it.

"Exactly," continued Malipieri. "But I do not mean that what we are doing now is so dreadfully unconventional after all. Thank heaven, manners have changed since I was a boy, and even in Italy we may be allowed to talk together a few minutes without being suspected of planning a runaway marriage. I wanted to see you alone because I wish you to do something very much more 'improper,' as society calls it."

Sabina looked up with innocent and inquiring eyes, but said nothing in answer.

"I have found something," he said. "I should like you to see it."

"There is nothing so very terrible in that," replied Sabina, looking at him steadily.

"The world would think differently. But if you will trust me the world need never know anything about it. You will have to come alone. That is the difficulty."

"Alone?" Sabina repeated the word, and instinctively drew herself up a little.

"Yes."

A short silence followed, and Malipieri waited for her to speak, but she hesitated. In years, she was but lately out of childhood, but the evil of the world had long been near her in her mother's house, and she knew well enough that if she did what he asked, and if it were known, her reputation would be gone. She was a little indignant at first, and was on the point of showing it, but as she met his eyes once more she felt certain that he meant no offence to her.

"You must have a very good reason for asking me to do such a dangerous thing," she said at last.

"The reasons are complicated," answered Malipieri.

"Perhaps I could understand, if you explained them."

"Yes, I am sure you can. I will try. In the first place, you know of the story about a treasure being concealed in the palace. I spoke of it the other day, and you laughed at it. When I began, I was not inclined to believe it myself, for it seems never to have been anything more than a tradition. One or two old chronicles speak of it. A Venetian ambassador wrote about it in the sixteenth century in one of his reports to his government, suggesting that the Republic should buy the palace if it were ever sold. I daresay you have heard that."

"No. It does not matter. You say you have found something—that is the important point."

"Yes; and the next thing is to keep the secret for the present, because so many people would like to know it. The third point of importance is that you should see the treasure before it is moved, before I can move it myself, or even see all of it."

"What is this treasure?" asked Sabina, with a little impatience, for she was really interested.

"All I have seen of it is the hand of what must be a colossal statue, of gilt bronze. On one of the fingers there is a ring with a stone which I believe to be a ruby. If it is, it is worth a great deal, perhaps as much as the statue itself."

Sabina's eyes had opened very wide in her surprise, for she had never really believed the tale, and even when he had told her that he had found something she had not thought it could be anything very valuable.

"Are you quite sure you have seen it?" she asked with childlike wonder.

"Yes. I lowered a light into the place, but I did not go down. There may be other things. They belong to you."

"To me? Why?" asked Sabina in surprise.

"For a good many reasons which may or may not be good in law but which are good enough for me. You were robbed of your dowry—forgive the expression. I cannot think of another word. The Senator got possession of the palace for much less than its market value, let alone what I have found. He sent for me because I have been fortunate in finding things, and he believed it just possible that there might be something hidden in the foundations. Your family spent long ago what he lent them on the mortgage, and Sassi assures me that you never had a penny of it. I mean you to have your share now. That is all."

Sabina listened quietly enough to the end.

"Thank you, very much," she said gravely, when he had finished.

Then there was another pause. To her imagination the possibilities of wealth seemed fabulous, and even Malipieri thought them large; but Sabina was not thinking of a fortune for its own sake. Of late none of her family had cared for money except to spend it without counting. What struck her first was that she would be free to leave the Volterras' house, that she would be independent, and that there would be an end of the almost unbearable situation in which she had lived since the crash.

"If the Senator can keep it all for himself, he will," Malipieri observed, "and his wife will help him."

"Do you think this had anything to do with their anxiety to have me stay with them?" asked Sabina, and as the thought occurred to her the expression of her eyes changed.

"The Baroness knows nothing at all about the matter," answered Malipieri. "I fancy she only wanted the social glory of taking charge of you when your people came to grief. But her husband will take advantage of the obligation you are under. I suspect that he will ask you to sign a paper of some sort, very vaguely drawn up, but legally binding, by which you will make over to him all claim whatever on your father's estate."

"But I have none, have I?"

"If the facts were known to-morrow, your brother might at once begin an action to recover, on the equitable ground that by an extraordinary chain of circumstances the property has turned out to be worth much more than any one could have expected. Do you understand?"

"Yes. Go on."

"Very well. The Senator knows that in all probability the court would decide against your brother, who has the reputation of a spendthrift, unless your claim is pushed; but that any honest judge, if it were legally possible, would do his best to award you something. If you had made over your claim to Volterra, that would be impossible, and would only strengthen his case."

"I see," said Sabina. "It is very complicated."

"Of course it is. And there are many other sides to it. The Senator, on his part, is as anxious to keep the whole matter a secret as I am, for your sake. He has no idea that there is a colossal statue in the vaults. He probably hopes to find gold and jewels which could be taken away quietly and disposed of without the knowledge of the government."

"What has the government to do with it?"

"It has all sorts of claims on such discoveries, and especially on works of art. It reserves the right to buy them from the owners at a valuation, if they are sold at all."

"Then the government will buy this statue, I suppose."

"In the end, unless it allows the Vatican to buy it."

"I do not see what is going to happen," said Sabina, growing bewildered.

"The Senator must make everything over to you before it is sold," answered Malipieri calmly.

"How can he be made to do that?"

"I do not know, but he shall."

"Do you mean that the law can force him to?"

"The law might, perhaps, but I shall find some much shorter way."

Sabina was silent for a moment.

"But he employs you on this work," she said suddenly.

"Not exactly." Malipieri smiled. "I would not let Volterra pay me to grub underground for his benefit, any more than I would live in his house without paying him rent."

Sabina bit her lip and turned her face away suddenly, for the thoughtless words had hurt her.

"I agreed to make the search merely because I am interested in archaeology," he continued. "Until I met you I did not care what might become of anything we found in the palace."

"Why should you care now?"

The question rose to her lips before she knew what she was saying, for what had gone before had disturbed her a little. It had been a very cruel speech, though he had not meant it. He looked at her thoughtfully.

"I am not quite sure why I care," he answered, "but I do."

Neither spoke for some time.

"I suppose you pity me," Sabina observed at last, rather resentfully.

He said nothing.

"You probably felt sorry for me as soon as you saw me," she continued, leaning back in her chair and speaking almost coldly. "I am an object of pity, of course!"

Malipieri laughed a little at the very girlish speech.

"No," he answered. "I had not thought of you in that light. I liked you, the first time I saw you. That is much simpler than pitying."

He laughed again, but it was at himself.

"You treat me like a child," Sabina said with a little petulance. "You have no right to!"

"Shall I treat you like a woman, Donna Sabina?" he said, suddenly serious.

"Yes. I am sure I am old enough."

"If you were not, I should certainly not feel as I do towards you."

"What do you mean?"

"If you are a woman, you probably guess."

"No."

"You may be offended," suggested Malipieri.

"Not unless you are rude—or pity me." She smiled now.

"Is it very rude to like a person?" he asked. "If you think it is, I will not go on."

"I am not sure," said Sabina demurely, and she looked down.

"In that case it is wiser not to run the risk of offending you past forgiveness!"

It was very amusing to hear him talk, for no man had ever talked to her in this way before. She knew that he was thought immensely clever, but he did not seem at all superior now, and she was glad of it. She should have felt very foolish if he had discoursed to her learnedly about Carthage and antiquities. Instead, he was simple and natural, and she liked him very much; and the little devil that enters into every woman about the age of sixteen and is not often cast out before fifty, even by prayer and fasting, suddenly possessed her.

"Rudeness is not always past forgiveness," she said, with a sweet smile.

Malipieri looked at her gravely and wondered whether he had any right to take up the challenge. He had never been in love with a young girl in his life, and somehow it did not seem fair to speak as he had been speaking. It was very odd that his sense of honour should assert itself just then. It might have been due to the artificial traditions of generations without end, before him. At the same time, he knew something of women, and in her last speech he recognized the womanly cooing, the call of the mate, that has drawn men to happiness or destruction ever since the world began. She was a mere girl, of course, but since he had said so much, she could not help tempting him to go to the end and tell her he loved her.

Though Malipieri did not pretend to be a model of all the virtues, he was thoroughly fair in all his dealings, according to his lights, and just then he would have thought it the contrary of fair to say what she seemed to expect. He knew instinctively that no one had ever said it to her before, which was a good reason for not saying it lightly; and he was sure that he could not say it quite seriously, and almost certain also that she had not even begun to be really in love herself, though he felt that she liked him. On the other hand—for in the flash of a second he argued the case—he did not feel that she was the hypothetical defenceless maiden, helpless to resist the wiles of an equally hypothetical wicked young man. She had been brought up by a worldly mother since she had left the convent where she had associated with other girls, most of whom also had worldly mothers; and some of the wildest blood in Europe ran in her veins.

On the whole, he thought it would be justifiable to tell her exactly what he felt, and she might do as she pleased about answering him.

"I think I shall fall in love with you before long," he said, with almost unnecessary calmness.

Sabina had not expected that the first declaration she received in her life would take this mild form, but it affected her much more strongly than she could understand. Her hand tightened suddenly on the book she held, and she noticed a little fluttering at her heart and in her throat, and at the same time she was conscious of a tremendous determination not to show that she felt anything at all, but to act as if she had heard just such things before, and more also.

"Indeed!" she said, with admirable indifference.

Malipieri looked at her in surprise. An experienced flirt of thirty could not have uttered the single word more effectively.

"I wonder whether you will ever like me better than you do now," he said, by way of answer.

She was wondering, too, but it was not likely that she would admit it.

"I am very fickle," she replied, with a perfectly self-possessed little laugh.

"So am I," Malipieri answered, following her lead. "My most desperate love affairs have never lasted more than a month or two."

"You have had a great many, I daresay," Sabina observed, with no show of interest. She was amazed and delighted to find how easy it was to act her new part.

"And you," he asked, laughing, "how often have you been in love already?"

"Let me see!"

She turned her eyes to his, without turning her head, and letting the book lie in her lap she pretended to count on her fingers. He watched her gravely, and nodded as she touched each finger, as if he were counting with her. Suddenly she dropped both hands and laughed gaily.

"How childish you are!" she exclaimed.

"How deliciously frank you are!" he retorted, laughing with her.

It was mere banter, and not witty at that, but they were growing intimate in it, much faster than either of them realized, for it was the first time they had been able to talk together quite without constraint, and it was the very first time Sabina had ever had a chance of talking as she pleased to a man whom she really thought young.

Moreover they were quite modern young people, and therefore entirely devoid of all the sentimentality and "world-sorrow" which made youth so delightfully gloomy and desperately cynical, without the least real cynicism, in the middle of the nineteenth century. In those days no young man who showed a ray of belief in anything had a chance with a woman, and no woman had a chance with men unless she had a hidden sorrow. Women used to construct themselves a secret and romantic grief in those times, with as much skill as they bestowed on their figure and face, and there were men who spent hours in reading Schopenhauer in order to pick out and treasure up a few terribly telling phrases; and love-making turned upon the myth that life was not worth living.

We have changed all that now; whether for better or worse, the social historians of the future will decide for us after we are dead, so we need not trouble our heads about the decision unless we set up to be moralists ourselves. The enormous tidal wave of hypocrisy is retiring, and if the shore discovered by the receding waves is here and there horribly devastated and hopelessly bare, it is at least dry land.

The wave covered everything for a long time, from religion to manners, from science to furniture, and we who are old enough to remember, and not old enough to regret, are rubbing our eyes and looking about us, as on a new world, amazed at having submitted so long to what we so heartily despised, glad to be able to speak our minds at last about many things, and astounded that people should at last be allowed to be good and suffered to be bad, without the affectation of seeming one or the other, in a certain accepted manner governed by fashion, and imposed by a civilized and perfectly intolerant society.

While progress advances, it really looks as if humanity were reverting to its types, with an honest effort at simplicity. There is a revival of the moral individuality of the middle ages. The despot proudly says, like Alexander, or Montrose in love, that he will reign, and he will reign alone; and he does. The financier plunders mankind and does not pretend that he is a long-lost type of philanthropist. The anarchist proclaims that it is virtuous to kill kings, and he kills them. The wicked do not even make a pretence of going to church on Sundays. If this goes on, we shall have saints before long.

Hypocrisy has disappeared even from literature, since no one who now writes books fit to read can be supposed to do so out of respect for public opinion, still less from any such base motive as a desire for gain.

Malipieri and Sabina both felt that they had been drawn much nearer together by what had sounded like idle chatter, and yet neither of them was inclined to continue talking in the same way. Moreover time was passing quickly, and there was a matter to be decided before they parted. Malipieri returned to the subject of his discovery, and his desire that Sabina should see it.

"But I cannot possibly come to the palace alone," she objected. "It is quite out of the question. Even if—" she stopped.

"What?" he asked.

"Even if I were willing to do it—" she hesitated again.

"You are not afraid, are you?" There was a slight intonation of irony in his question.

"No, I am not afraid." She paused a moment. "I suppose that if I saw a way of coming, I would come," she said, then. "But I see no way. I cannot go out alone. Every one would know it. There would be a terrible fuss about it!"

The idea evidently amused her.

"Could you come with Sassi?" asked Malipieri presently. "He is respectable enough for anything."

"Even that would be thought very strange," answered Sabina. "I have no good reason to give for going out alone with him."

"You would not give any reason till afterwards, and when it is over there cannot really be anything to be said about it. The Baroness goes out every afternoon. You can make an excuse for staying at home to-morrow, and then you will be alone in the house. Sassi will call for you in a closed cab and bring you to the palace, and I will be at the door to receive you. The chances are that you will be at home again before the Baroness comes in, and she will never know that you have been out. Does that look very hard?"

"No, it looks easy."

"What time shall Sassi call for you to-morrow?" asked Malipieri, who wished to settle the matter at once.

"At five o'clock," answered Sabina, after a moment's thought.

"At five to-morrow, then. You had better not wear anything very new. The place where the statue lies is not a drawing-room, you know, and your frock may be spoilt."

"Very well."

She glanced at the clock, looked at Malipieri as if hesitating, and then rose.

"I shall go back to my room now," she said.

"Yes. It is better. They may come in at any moment." He had risen also.

Their eyes met again, and they smiled at each other, as they realized what they were doing, that they had been nearly an hour together, unknown to any one, and had arranged something very like a clandestine meeting for the next day. Sabina put out her hand.

"At five o'clock," she said again. "Good-night."

He felt her touch for the first time since they had met. It was light and elastic as the pressure of a very delicate spring, perfectly balanced and controlled. But she, on her side, looked down suddenly and uttered an exclamation of surprise.

"Oh! How rough your hand is!"

He laughed, and held out his palm, which was callous as a day-labourer's.

"My man and I have done all the work ourselves," he said, "and it has not been play."

"It must be delightful!" answered Sabina with admiration. "I wish I were a man! We could have done it together."

She went to the door, and she turned to smile at him again as she laid her hand on the knob. He remembered her afterwards as she stood there a single moment with the light on her misty hair and white cheeks, and the little shadow round her small bare throat. He remembered that he would have given anything to bring her back to the place where she had sat. There was much less doubt in his mind as to what he felt then than there had been a few minutes earlier.

Half an hour after Sabina had disappeared Malipieri and Volterra were seated in deep armchairs in the smoking-room, the Baron having sent his wife to bed a few minutes after they had come in. She obeyed meekly as she always did, for she had early discovered that although she was a very energetic woman, Volterra was her master and that it was hopeless to oppose his slightest wish. It is true that in return for the most absolute obedience the fat financier gave her the strictest fidelity and all the affection of which he was capable. Like more than one of the great modern freebooters, the

Baron's private life was very exemplary, yet his wife would have been willing to forgive him something if she might occasionally have had her own way.

This evening he was not in good-humour, as Malipieri found out as soon as they were alone together. He chewed the end of the enormous Havana he had lighted, he stuck his feet out straight in front of him, resting his heels on the floor and turning his shining patent leather toes straight up, he folded his hands upon the magnificent curve of his white waistcoat, and leaning his head well back he looked steadily at the ceiling. All these were very bad signs, as his wife could have told Malipieri if she had stayed in the room.

Malipieri smoked in silence for some time, entirely forgetting him and thinking of Sabina.

"Well, Mr. Archaeologist," the Baron said at last, allowing his big cigar to settle well into one corner of his mouth, "there is the devil to pay."

He spoke as if the trouble were Malipieri's fault. The younger man eyed him coldly.

"What is the matter?" he enquired, without the least show of interest.

"You are being watched," answered Volterra, still looking at the ceiling. "You are now one of those interesting people whose movements are recorded like the weather, every twelve hours."

"Yes," said Malipieri. "I have known that for some time."

"The next time you know anything so interesting I wish you would inform me," replied Volterra.

His voice and his way of speaking irritated Malipieri. The Baroness had been better educated than her husband from the first; she was more adaptable and she had really learned the ways of the society she loved, but the Baron was never far from the verge of vulgarity, and he often overstepped it.

"When you asked me to help you," Malipieri said, "you knew perfectly well what my political career had been. I believe you voted for the bill which drove me out of the country."

"Did I?" The Baron watched the smoke of his cigar curling upwards.

"I think you did. Not that I bear you the least malice. I only mean that you might very naturally expect that I should be thought a suspicious person, and that detectives would follow me about."

"Nobody cares a straw for your politics," retorted Volterra rudely.

"Then I shall be the more free to think as I please," Malipieri answered with calm.

"Perfectly so. In the meantime it is not the Ministry of the Interior that is watching you. The present Ministry does not waste time and money on such nonsense. You are being watched because you are suspected of trying to get some statues or pictures out of Italy, in defiance of the Pacca law."

"Oh!" Malipieri blew a whiff of smoke out with the ejaculation, for he was surprised.

"I have it from one of the cabinet," Volterra continued. "He told me the facts confidentially after dinner. You see, as you are living in my house, the suspicion is reflected on me."

"In your house?"

"The Palazzo Conti is my house," answered the Baron, taking his cigar from his mouth for the first time since he had lighted it, and holding it out at arm's length with a possessive sweep while he leaned back and looked at the ceiling again. "It all belongs to me," he said. "I took it for the mortgage, with everything in it."

"By the bye," said Malipieri, "what became of that Velasquez, and those other pictures?"

"Was there a Velasquez?" enquired the Baron carelessly, without changing his attitude.

"Yes. It was famous all over Europe. It was a family portrait."

"I remember! It turned out to be a copy after all."

"A copy!" repeated Malipieri incredulously.

"Yes, the original is in Madrid," answered the Baron with imperturbable self-possession.

"And all those other pictures turned out to be copies, too, I daresay," suggested Malipieri.

"Every one of them. It was a worthless collection."

"In that case it was hardly worth while to take so much trouble in getting them out of the country secretly." Malipieri smiled.

"That was the dealer's affair," answered Volterra without the least hesitation. "Dealers are such fools! They always make a mystery of everything."

Malipieri could not help admiring the proportions and qualities of the Baron's lies. The financier was well aware that Malipieri knew the pictures to be genuine beyond all doubt. The disposal of them had been well managed, for when Malipieri moved into the palace there was not a painting of value left on the walls, yet there had been no mention of them in the newspapers, nor any gossip about them, and the public at large believed them to be still in their places. As a matter of fact most of them were already in France and England, and the Velasquez was in Saint Petersburg.

"I understand why you are anxious that the Palazzo Conti should not be watched just now," Malipieri said. "For my part, as I do not believe in your government, I cannot be expected to believe in its laws. It is not my business whether you respect them yourselves or not."

"Who is breaking the law?" asked the Baron roughly. "It is absurd to talk in that way. But as the government has taken it into its head to suspect that you do, it is not advisable for me, who am a staunch supporter of the government, to see too much of you. I am sure you must understand that—it is so simple."

"In other words?" Malipieri looked at him coldly, waiting for an explanation.

"I cannot afford to have it said that you are living in the palace for the purpose of helping dealers to smuggle objects of art out of the country. That is what I mean."

"I see. But what objects of art do you mean, since you have already sent away everything there was?"

"It is believed that you had something to do with that ridiculous affair of the copies," said Volterra, his voice suddenly becoming oily.

"They were gone when I moved in."

"I daresay they were. But it would be hard to prove, and of course the people who bought the pictures from the dealer insist that they are genuine, so that there may be trouble some day, and you may be annoyed about the things if you stay here any longer."

"You mean that you advise me to leave Rome. Is that it?" Malipieri now spoke with the utmost indifference, and glanced carelessly at the end of his cigar as he knocked the ash into the gold cup at his side.

"You certainly cannot stay any longer in the palace," Volterra said, in an advisory and deprecatory tone.

"You seem to be badly frightened," observed Malipieri. "I really cannot see why I should change my quarters until we have finished what we are doing."

"I am afraid you will have to go. You are looked upon as very 'suspicious.' It would not be so bad, if your servant had not been a convict."

"How do you know that?" Malipieri asked with sudden sternness.

"Everything of that sort is known to the police," answered Volterra, whose manner had become very mild. "Of course you have your own reasons for employing such a person."

"He is an innocent man, who was unjustly convicted."

"Oh, indeed! Poor fellow! Those things happen sometimes, I know. It is more than kind of you to employ him. Nevertheless, you cannot help seeing that the association of ideas is unfortunate and gives a bad impression. The man was never proved to be innocent, and when he had served his term, he was involved as your servant in your political escapade. You do not mind my speaking of that matter lightly? It is the safest way to look at it, is it not? Yes. The trouble is that you and your man are both on the black book, and since the affair has come to the notice of the government my colleagues are naturally surprised that you should both be living in a house that belongs to me."

"You can explain to your colleagues that you have let the apartment in the palace to me, and that as I pay my rent regularly you cannot turn me out without notice." Malipieri smiled indifferently.

"Surely," said the Baron, affecting some surprise, "if I ask you, as a favour, to move somewhere else, you will do so!"

To tell the truth, he was not prepared for Malipieri's extreme forbearance, for he had expected an outbreak of temper, at the least, and he still feared a positive refusal. Instead, the young man did not seem to care a straw.

"Of course," he said, "if you ask it as a favour, I cannot refuse. When should you like me to go?"

"You are really too kind!" The Baron was genuinely delighted and almost grateful—as near to feeling gratitude, perhaps, as he had ever been in his life. "I should hate to hurry you," he continued. "But really, since you are so very good, I think the sooner you can make it convenient to move, the better it will be for every one."

"I could not manage to pack my books and drawings so soon as to-morrow," said Malipieri.

"Oh, no! certainly not! By all means take a couple of days about it. I could not think of putting you to any inconvenience."

"Thanks." Malipieri smiled pleasantly. "If I cannot get off by the day after to-morrow, I shall certainly move the day after that."

"I am infinitely obliged. And now that this unpleasant matter is settled, owing to your wonderful amiability, do tell me how the work is proceeding."

"Fairly well," Malipieri answered. "You had better come and see for yourself before I go. Let me see. To-morrow I shall have to look about for a lodging. Could you come the day after to-morrow? Then we can go down together."

"How far have you got?" asked Volterra, with a little less interest than might have been expected.

"I am positively sure that there is an inner chamber, where I expected to find it," Malipieri answered, with perfect truth. "Perhaps we can get into it when you come."

"I hope so," said the Baron, watching the other's face from the corner of his eye.

"I have made a curious discovery in the course of the excavation," Malipieri continued. "The pillar of masonry which you showed me is hollow after all. It was the shaft of an oubliette which must have opened somewhere in the upper part of the house. There is a well under it."

"Full of water?"

"No. It is dry. We shall have to pass through it to get to the inner chamber. You shall see for yourself—a very singular construction."

"Was there nothing in it?"

"Several skeletons," answered Malipieri indifferently. "One of the skulls has a rusty knife driven through it."

"Dear me!" exclaimed the Baron, shaking his fat head. "Those Conti were terrible people! We must not tell the Baroness these dreadful stories. They would upset her nerves."

Malipieri had not supposed Volterra's wife to be intensely sensitive. He moved, as if he meant to take his leave presently.

"By the bye," he said, "whereabouts should you recommend me to look for a lodging?"

The Baron reflected a moment.

"If I were you," he said, "I would go to a hotel. In fact, I think you would be wiser to leave Rome for a time, until all these absurd stories are forgotten. The least I can do is to warn you that you may be exposed to a good deal of annoyance if you stay here. The minister with whom I was talking this evening told me as much in a friendly way."

"Really? That was very kind of him. But what do you mean by the word 'annoyance'? It is rather vague. It is one thing to suspect a man of trying to evade the Pacca law; it is quite another matter to issue a warrant of arrest against him."

"Oh, quite," answered Volterra readily. "I did not mean that, of course, though when one has once been arrested for anything, innocent or not, our police always like to repeat the operation as soon as possible, just as a matter of principle."

"In other words, if a man has once been suspected, even unjustly, he had better leave his country for ever."

The Baron shrugged his big round shoulders, and drew a final puff from his cigar before throwing the end away.

"Injustice is only what the majority thinks of the minority," he observed. "If you do not happen to be a man of genius, the first step towards success in life is to join the majority."

Malipieri laughed as he rose to his feet, reflecting that in delivering himself of this piece of worldly wisdom the Baron had probably spoken the truth for the first time since they had been talking.

"Shall we say day after to-morrow, about five o'clock?" asked Malipieri before going.

"By all means. And let me thank you again for meeting my views so very obligingly."

"Not at all."

So Malipieri went home to think matters over, and the Baron sat a long time in his chair, looking much pleased with himself and apparently admiring a magnificent diamond which he wore on one of his thick fingers.

CHAPTER X

Malipieri was convinced that Volterra not only knew exactly how far the work under the palace had proceeded, but was also acquainted with the general nature of the objects found in the inner chamber, beyond the well shaft. The apparent impossibility of such a thing was of no importance. The Baron would never have been so anxious to get rid of Malipieri unless he had been sure that the difficult part of the work was finished and that the things discovered were of such dimensions as to make it impossible to remove them secretly. Malipieri knew the man and guessed that if he could not pocket the value of everything found in the excavations by disposing of the discoveries secretly, he would take the government into his confidence at once, as the surest means of preventing any one else from getting a share.

What was hard to understand was that Volterra should know how far the work had gone before Malipieri had told him anything about it. That he did know, could hardly be doubted. He had practically betrayed the fact by the mistake he had made in assuring himself that Malipieri was willing to leave the house, before even questioning him as to the progress made since they had last met. He had been a little too eager to get rid of the helper he no longer needed. It did not even occur to Malipieri that Masin could have betrayed him, yet so far as it was possible to judge, Masin was the only living man who had looked into the underground chamber. As he walked home, he recalled the conversation from beginning to end, and his conviction was confirmed. Volterra had been in a bad temper, nervous, a little afraid of the result and therefore inclined to talk in a rough and bullying tone. As soon as he had ascertained that Malipieri was not going to oppose him, he had become oily to obsequiousness.

On his part Malipieri had accepted everything Volterra proposed, for two reasons. In the first place he would not for the world have had the financier think that he wanted a share of the treasure, or any remuneration for what he had done. Secondly, he knew that possession is nine points of the law, and that if anything could ever be obtained for Sabina it would not be got by making a show of violent opposition to the Baron's wishes. If Malipieri had refused to leave his lodging in the palace, Volterra could have answered by filling the house with people in his own employ, or by calling in government architects, archaeologists and engineers, and taking the whole matter out of Malipieri's hands.

The first thing to be ascertained was, who had entered the vaults and reported the state of the work to Volterra. Malipieri might have suspected the porter himself, for it was possible that there might be another key to the outer entrance of the cellar; but there was a second door further in, to which Masin had put a patent padlock, and even Masin had not the key to that. The little flat bit of steel, with its irregular indentations, was always in Malipieri's pocket. As he walked, he felt for it, and it was in its place, with his silver pencil-case and the small penknife he always carried for sharpening pencils.

The porter could not possibly have picked that lock; indeed, scarcely any one could have done so without injuring it, and Malipieri had locked it himself at about seven o'clock that evening. Even if the porter could have got in by any means, Malipieri doubted whether he could have reached the inner chamber of the vaults. There was some climbing to be done, and the man was old and stiff in the joints. The place was not so easy to find as might have been supposed, either, after the first breach in the Roman wall was past. Malipieri intended to improve the passage the next morning, in order to make it more practicable for Sabina.

He racked his brains for an explanation of the mystery, and when he reached the door of the palace, after eleven o'clock, he had come to the conclusion that in spite of appearances there must be some entrance to the vaults of which he knew nothing, and it was all-important to find it. He regretted the quixotic impulse which had restrained him from exploring everything at once. It would have been far better to go to the end of his discovery, and he wondered why he had not done go. He would not have insulted himself by supposing that Sabina could believe him capable of taking the gem from the ring of the statue, in other words, of stealing, since whoever the rightful owner might be, nothing in the vault could possibly belong to him, and he regarded it all as her property, though he doubted whether he could ever obtain for her a tenth part of the value it represented. He had acted on an impulse, which was strengthened until it looked plausible by the thought of the intense pleasure he would take in showing her the wonderful discovery, and in leading her safely through the mysterious intricacies of the strange place. It had been a very selfish impulse after all, and if he really let her come the next day, there might even be a little danger to her.

He let himself in and locked the postern door behind him. The porter and his wife were asleep and the glass window of the lodge door was quite dark. Malipieri lighted a wax taper and went upstairs.

Masin was waiting, and opened when he heard his master's footsteps on the landing. As a rule, he went to bed, if Malipieri went out in the evening; both men were usually tired out by their day's work.

"What is the matter?" Malipieri asked.

"There is somebody in the vaults," Masin answered. "I had left my pipe on a stone close to the padlocked door and when you were gone I took a lantern and went down to get it. When I came near the door I was sure I heard some one trying it gently from the other side. I stopped to listen and I distinctly heard footsteps going away. I ran forward and tried to find a crack, to see if there were a light, but the door is swollen with the dampness and fits tightly. Besides, by the time I had reached it the person inside must have got well away."

"What time was it?" asked Malipieri, slipping off his light overcoat.

"You went out at nine o'clock, sir. It could not have been more than half an hour later."

"Light both lanterns. We must go down at once. See that there is plenty of oil in them."

In five minutes both men were ready.

"You had better take your revolver, sir," suggested Masin.

Malipieri laughed.

"I have had that revolver since I was eighteen," he said, "and I have never needed it yet. Our tools are there, and they are better than firearms."

They went down the staircase quietly, fearing to wake the porter, and kept close to the north wall till they reached the further end of the courtyard. When they had passed the outer door at the head of the winding staircase, Malipieri told Masin to lock it after them.

"We cannot padlock the other door from the inside," he explained, "for there are no hasps. If the man managed to pass us he might get out this way."

He led the way down, making as little noise as possible. Masin held up his lantern, peering into the gloom over Malipieri's shoulder.

"No one could pass the other door without breaking it down," Malipieri said.

They reached the floor of the cellars, which extended in both directions from the foot of the staircase, far to the left by low, dark vaults like railway tunnels, and a short distance to the right, where they ended at the north-west corner. The two men turned that way, but after walking a dozen yards, they turned to the left and entered a damp passage barely wide enough for them both abreast. It ended at the padlocked door, and before unlocking the latter Malipieri laid his ear to the rough panel and listened attentively. Not a sound broke the stillness. He turned the key, and took off the padlock and slipped it into his pocket before going on. Without it the door could not be fastened.

The passage widened suddenly beyond, in another short tunnel ending at the outer foundation wall of the palace. In this tunnel, on the right-hand side, was the breach the two men had first made in order to gain access to the unexplored region. Now that there was an aperture, the running water on the other side could be heard very distinctly, like a little brook in a rocky channel, but more steady. Both men examined the damp floor carefully with their lanterns, in the hope of finding some trace of footsteps; but the surface was hard and almost black, and where there had been a little slime their own feet had rubbed it off, as they came and went during many days. The stones and rubbish they had taken from the wall had been piled up and hardened to form an inclined causeway by which to reach the irregular hole. This was now just big enough to allow a man to walk through it, bending almost double. Masin lighted one of the lamps, which they generally left at that place, and set it on a stone.

Malipieri began to go up, his stick in his right hand, the lantern in his left.

"Let me go first, sir," said Masin, trying to pass him.

"Nonsense!" Malipieri answered sharply, and went on.

Masin kept as close to him as possible. He had picked up the lightest of the drilling irons for a weapon. It must have weighed at least ten pounds and it was a yard long. In such a hand as Masin's a blow from it would have broken a man's bones like pipe stems.

The wall was about eight feet thick, and when Malipieri got to the other end of the hole he stopped and looked down, holding out his lantern at arm's length. He could see nothing unusual, and he heard no sound, except the gurgle of the little black stream that ran ten feet below him. He began to descend. The masonry was very irregular, and sloped outwards towards the ground, so that some of the irregularities made rough steps here and there, which he knew by heart. Below, several large fragments of Roman brick and cement lay here and there, where they had fallen in the destruction of the original building. It was not hard to get down, and the space was not large. It was bounded by the old wall on one side, and most of the other was taken up by a part of a rectangular mass of masonry, of rough mediaeval construction, which projected inward.

The place was familiar, but Malipieri looked about him carefully, while Masin was climbing down. Along the base of the straight wall there was a channel about two feet wide, through which the dark water flowed rapidly. It entered from the right-hand corner, by a low, arched aperture, through which it seemed out of the question that a man could crawl, or even an ordinary boy of twelve. When they had first come to this place Masin had succeeded in poking in a long stick with a bit of lighted wax taper fastened to it, and both men had seen that the channel ran on as far as it could be seen, with no widening. At the other end of the chamber it ran out again by a similar conduit. What had at first surprised Malipieri had been that the water did not enter from the side of the foundations near the Vicolo dei Soldati, but ran out that way. He had also been astonished at the quantity and speed of the current. A channel a foot deep and two feet wide carries a large quantity of water if the velocity be great, and Malipieri had made a calculation which had convinced him that if the outflow were suddenly closed, the small space in which he now stood would in a few minutes be full up to within three or four feet of the vault. He would have given much to know whence the water came and whither it went, and what devilry had made it rise suddenly and drown a man when the excavations had been made under Gregory Sixteenth.

From below, the place where an entrance had then been opened was clearly visible. The vault had been broken into and had afterwards been rebuilt from above. The bits of timber which had been used for the frame during the operation were still there, a rotting and mouldy nest for hideous spiders and noisome creatures that haunt the dark.

The air was very cold, and was laden with the indescribable smell of dried slime which belongs to deep wells which have long been almost quite dry. It was clearly a long time since the little stream had overflowed its channel, but at the first examination he had made Malipieri had understood that in former times the water had risen to within three feet of the vault. Up to that height there was a thin coating of the dry mud, which peeled off in irregular scales if lightly touched. The large fragments of masonry that half covered the floor were all coated in the same way with what had once been a film of slime.

The air, though cold, could be breathed easily, and the lights did not grow dim in it as they do in subterranean places where the atmosphere is foul. The stream of water, flowing swiftly in its deep channel from under the little arch, brought plentiful ventilation into it. Above, there was no aperture in the vaulting, but there was one in the mediaeval masonry that projected into the chamber. There, on the side towards the right, where the water flowed in, Malipieri had found a narrow slit, barely wide enough to admit a man's open hand and wrist, but nearly five feet high, evidently a passage intended for letting the water flow into the interior of the construction when it overflowed its channel and rose above the floor of the chamber.

At first Malipieri had supposed that this aperture communicated with some ancient and long-forgotten drain by which the water could escape to the Tiber; it was not until he had gained an entrance to the hollow mass of masonry that he understood the hideous use to which it had been applied.

It had not been hard to enlarge it. Any one who has worked among ruins in Italy could tell, even blindfold, the difference between the work done in ancient times and that of the middle ages. Roman brickwork is quite as compact as solid sandstone, but mediaeval masonry was almost invariably built in a hurry by bad workmen, of all sorts of fragments embedded in poorly mingled cement, and it breaks up with tolerable ease under a heavy pickaxe.

In half a day Malipieri and Masin had widened the slit to a convenient passage, but as soon as it had been possible to squeeze through, the architect had gone in. He never forgot what he felt when he first looked about him. Masin could not follow him until many blows of the pick had widened the way for his bulkier frame.

Malipieri stopped at the entrance now, holding his lantern close to the ground, and looking for traces of footsteps. He found none, but as he was about to move forward he uttered an exclamation of surprise, and picked up a tiny object which he held close to the light. It was only a wax match, of which the head had been broken off when it had been struck, so that it had not been lighted. That was all, but neither he nor Masin carried wax matches in the vaults, because the dampness soon made them useless. They took common sulphur matches in tin match-boxes. Besides, this was an English wax light, as any one could tell at a glance, for it was thicker, and stiffer, and longer than the cheaper Italian ones.

Malipieri drew back and showed it to his man, who examined it, understood, and put it into his pocket without a word. Then they both went in through the aperture in the wall.

The masonry outside was rectangular, as far as it could be seen. Inside, it was built like a small circular cistern, smoothly cemented, and contracting above in a dome, that opened by a square hole to the well-shaft above. Like the stones in the outer chamber, the cement was coated with scales of dried mud. The shaft was now certainly closed at the top, for in the daytime not a ray of light penetrated into its blackness.

The lanterns illuminated the place completely, and the two men looked about, searching for some new trace of a living being. The yellow light fell only on the remains of men dead long ago. Some of the bones lay as they had lain since then, when the drowned bodies had gently reached the floor as the "lost water" subsided. Malipieri had not touched them, nor Masin either. Two skeletons lay at full length, face downwards, as a drowned body always sinks at last, when decay has done its loathsome work. A third lay on its side, in a frightfully natural attitude, the skull a little raised up and resting against the cemented wall, the arms stretched out together, the hands still clutching a rusty crowbar. This one was near the entrance, and if, in breaking their way in, Malipieri and Masin had not necessarily destroyed the cement on each side of the slit, they would have found the marks where the dead man's crowbar had worked desperately for a few minutes before he had been drowned. Malipieri had immediately reflected that the unfortunate wretch, who was evidently the mason of whom Sassi had told him, had certainly not entered through the aperture formerly made from above in the outer chamber, since the narrow slit afforded no possible passage to the well. That doubtless belonged to some other attempt to find the treasure, and the fact that the mason's skeleton lay inside would alone have shown that he had got in from above, most likely through a low opening just where the dome began to curve inward. A further search had discovered some bits of wood, almost rotted to powder, which had apparently once been a ladder.

A much less practised eye than the architect's would have understood at a glance that if a living man were let down through the shaft in the centre of the dome, and left on the floor, he could not possibly get up even as far as the other hole, since the smooth cement offered not the slightest hold; and that if the outflow of the stream from the first chamber were arrested, the water would immediately fill it and rise simultaneously in the well, to drown the victim, or to strip his bones by its action, if he had been allowed to die of hunger or thirst. It was clear, too, that if the latter form of death were chosen, he must have suffered to the last minute of his life the agony of hearing the stream flowing outside, not three paces from him, beyond the slit. Human imagination could hardly invent a more hideously cruel death-trap, nor one more ingeniously secret from the world without.

The unhappy mason's ladder had perhaps broken with his weight, or his light had gone out, and he had then been unable to find the horizontal aperture, but he had probably entered through the latter, when he had met his fate. The fact was, as Malipieri afterwards guessed, that the hole through the vault outside had been made hastily after the accident, in the hope of recovering the man's body, but that it had been at once closed again because it appeared to open over a deep pit full of still water.

A stout rope ladder now dangled from the lateral aperture in the dome, which Malipieri had immediately understood to have been made to allow the water to overflow when the well was full. He had also felt tolerably sure that the well itself had not been originally constructed for the deadly use to which it had evidently been put in later times, but for the purpose of confining the water in a reservoir that could be easily cleaned, since it could be easily emptied, and in which the supply could be kept at a permanent level, convenient for drawing it from above. In the days when all the ancient aqueducts of Rome were broken, a well of the "lost water" was a valuable possession in houses that were turned into fortresses at a moment's notice and were sometimes exposed to long and desperate sieges.

In order to reach the horizontal opening, Malipieri had climbed upon Masin's sturdy shoulders, steadying himself as well as he might till he had laid his hands on the edge of the orifice. As he hung there, Masin had held up the handle of a pickaxe as high as he could reach against the smooth wall, as a crossbar on which Malipieri had succeeded in getting a slight foothold, enough for a man who was not heavy and was extraordinarily active. A moment later he had drawn himself up and inward. At the imminent risk of his life, as he afterwards found, he had crawled on in total darkness till the way widened enough for him to turn round and get back. He had then lowered a string he had with him, and had drawn up a lantern first, then the end of a coil of rope, then the tools for carrying on the exploration. The rest had been easy. Masin had climbed up by the rope, after making knots in it and when Malipieri had called out, from the inner place to which he had retired with the end, that it was made fast. But the light showed the architect that in turning round, he had narrowly escaped falling into an open shaft, of which he could not see the bottom, but which was evidently meant for the final escape of the overflowing water.

There was room to pass this danger, however, and they had since laid a couple of stout boards over it, weighted with stones to keep them in place. Beyond, the passage rose till it was high enough for a man to walk upright. Judging from the elevation now reached this passage was hollowed in the thickness of one of the main walls of the palace, and it was clear that the water could not reach it. A few yards from the chasm, it inclined quickly downwards, and at the end there were half a dozen steps, which evidently descended to a greater depth than the floor of the first outer chamber.

So far as it had hitherto been possible to judge, there was no way of getting to these last steps, except that opened by the two men, and leading through the dry well. In former times, there might have been an entrance through the wall at the highest level, but if it had ever existed it had been so carefully closed that no trace of it could now be found.

This tedious explanation of a rather complicated construction has been necessary to explain what afterwards happened. Reducing it to its simplest terms, it becomes clear that if the water rose, a person in the passage, or anywhere beyond the overflow shaft, could not possibly get back through the well, though he would apparently be safe from drowning if he stayed where he was; and to the best of Malipieri's knowledge there was no other way out. Any one caught there would have to wait till the water subsided, and if that did not happen he would starve to death.

The two men stood still and listened. They could still distinguish the faint gurgling of the water, very far off, but that was all.

"I believe you heard a rat," said Malipieri, discontentedly, after a long pause.

"Rats do not carry English wax matches," observed Masin.

"They eat them when they can find them," answered Malipieri. "They carry them off, and hide them, and drop them, too. And a big rat running away makes a noise very like a man's footsteps."

"That is true," assented Masin. "There were many of them in the prison, and I sometimes thought they were the keepers when I heard them at night." "At all events, we will go to the end," said Malipieri, beginning to walk down the inclined way, and carrying his lantern low, so as not to be dazzled by the light.

Masin followed closely, grasping his drilling-iron, and still expecting to use it. The end of the passage had once been walled up, but they had found the fragments of brick and mortar lying much as they had fallen when knocked away. It was impossible to tell from which side the obstacle had been destroyed.

Going further, they stepped upon the curve of a tunnel vault, and were obliged to stoop low to avoid striking against another overhead. The two vaults had been carefully constructed, one outside the other, leaving a space of about five feet between them. The one under their feet covered the inner chamber in which Malipieri had seen the bronze statue. He and Masin had made a hole a little on one side of the middle, in order not to disturb the keystones, working very carefully lest any heavy fragments should fall through; for they had at once been sure that if any thing was to be found, it must be concealed in that place. Before making the opening, they had thoroughly explored the dark curved space from end to end and from side to side, but could discover no aperture. The inner vault had never been opened since it had been built.

Malipieri, reconstructing the circumstances of the accident in the last century, came to the conclusion that the mason who had been drowned had been already between the vaults, when some of the men behind had discovered that the water was rising in the well, and that they had somehow got out in time, but that their unfortunate companion had come back too late, or had perished while trying to break his way out by the slit, through which the water must have been rushing in. How they had originally entered the place was a mystery. Possibly they had been lowered from above, down the well-shaft, but it was all very hard to explain. The only thing that seemed certain was that the treasure had never been seen by any one since it had been closed in under the vault, ages ago. Malipieri had not yet found time to make a careful plan of all the places through which he had passed. There were so many turns and changes of level, that it would be impossible to get an accurate drawing without using a theodolite or some similar instrument of precision. From the measurements he had taken, however, and the rough sketches he had made, he believed that the double vault was not under the palace itself, but under the open courtyard, at the depth of about forty feet, and therefore below the level of the Tiber at average high water.

Both men now knelt by the hole, and Masin thrust his lantern down to the full length of his arm. The light shone upon the vast hand of the statue, and made a deep reflection in the great ruby of the ring, as if the gem was not a stone, but a little gold cup filled with rich wine. The hand itself, the wrist and the great muscles of the chest on which it lay, seemed of pure gold. But Malipieri's eyes fixed themselves on something else. There were marks on the bright surface of the metal which had not been there when he had looked at it in the afternoon; there were patches of dust, and there were several small scratches, which might have been made by the nails of heavy shoes.

"You were right after all," said Malipieri, withdrawing the lantern and setting it down beside him. "The man is here."

Masin's china-blue eyes brightened at the thought of a possible fight, and his hold tightened again on his drill.

"What shall we do with him?" he asked, looking down into the hole.

Cunning, as the Italian peasant is by nature, Masin made a sign to his master that the man, if he were really below, could hear all that was said.

"Shall I go down and kill him, sir?" Masin enquired with a quiet grin and raising his voice a little.

"I am not sure," Malipieri answered, at once entering into his man's scheme. "He is caught in his own trap. It is not midnight yet, and there is plenty of time to consider the matter. Let us sit here and talk about it."

He now turned himself and sat beside the hole, placing his lantern near the edge. He took out a cigar and lit it carefully. Masin sat on the other side, his drill in his hand.

"If he tries to get out while we are talking," he said, "I can break his skull with a touch of this."

"Yes," Malipieri answered, puffing at his cigar. "There is no hurry. Keep your iron ready."

"Yes, sir." Masin made the heavy drill ring on the stones of the vault.

A pause followed.

"Have you got your pipe with you?" asked Malipieri presently. "We must talk over this quietly."

"Yes, sir. Will you hold the iron while I get a light? He might try to jump out, and he may have firearms. Thank you, sir."

Masin produced a short black pipe, filled it and lighted it.

"I was thinking, sir," he said, as he threw away the wooden match, "that if we kill him here we may have trouble in disposing of his body. Thank you, sir," he added as he took over the drill again and made it clang on the stones.

"There will be no trouble about that," Malipieri answered, speaking over the hole. "We can drop him down the overflow shaft in the passage."

"Where do you think the shaft leads, sir?" asked Masin, grinning with delight.

"To some old drain and then to the Tiber, of course. The body will be found in a week or two, jammed against the pier of some bridge, probably at the island of Saint Bartholomew."

"Yes, sir. But the drain is dry now. The body will lie at the bottom of the shaft, where we drop it, and in a few days the cellars will be perfumed."

He laughed roughly at his horrible joke, which was certainly calculated to affect the nerves of the intruder who was meant to hear it. Malipieri began to wonder when the man would give a sign of life.

"We can fill the well by plugging the arch in the outer chamber," he suggested. "Then the water will pour down the shaft and wash the body away."

"Yes, sir," assented Masin. "That is a good idea. Shall I go down and kill him now, sir?"

"Not yet," Malipieri answered, knocking the ash from his cigar. "We have not finished smoking, and there is no hurry. Besides, it occurs to me that if we drive anything into the hole when the water runs out, we shall not be able to get the plug away afterwards. Then we ourselves could never get here again."

A long silence followed. From time to time Masin made a little noise with the drill.

"Perhaps the fellow is asleep," he observed pleasantly at last. "So much the better, he will wake in Paradise!"

"It is of no use to run any risks," said Malipieri. "If we go down to kill him he may kill one of us first, especially if he has a revolver. There is no hurry, I tell you. Do you happen to know how long it takes to starve a man to death?"

"Without water, a man cannot live a week, sir. That is the best idea you have had yet."

"Yes. We will wall him up in the vault. That is easy enough. Those boards that are over the shaft will do to make a little frame, and the stones are all here, just as we got them out. We can fasten up the frame with ends of rope."

"We have no mortar, sir."

"Mud will do as well for such a small job," answered Malipieri. "We can easily make enough. Give me your iron, in case he tries to get out, and go and get the boards and the rope."

Masin began to rise.

"In a week we can come and take him out," he remarked in a matter-of-fact way. "By that time he will be dead, and we can have his grave ready."

He laughed again, as he thought of the sensations his cheerful talk must produce in the mind of the man below.

"Yes," said Malipieri. "We may as well do it at once and go to bed. It is of no use to sit up all night talking about the fellow's body. Go and get the rope and the boards."

Masin was now on his feet and his heavy shoes made a grinding noise on the stones. At that moment a sound was heard from below, and Malipieri held up a finger and listened. Somebody was moving in the vault.

"You had better stay where you are," said Malipieri, speaking down. "If you show yourself I will drop a stone on your head."

A hollow voice answered him from the depths.

"Are you Christians," it asked, "to wall a man up alive?"

"That is what we are going to do," Malipieri answered coolly. "Have you anything to say? It will not take us long to do the job, so you had better speak at once. How did you get in?"

"If I am to die without getting out, why should I tell you?" enquired the voice.

Malipieri looked at Masin.

"There is a certain sense in what the man says, sir," Masin said thoughtfully.

"My good man," said Malipieri, speaking down, "we do not want anybody to know the way to this place for a few days, and as you evidently know it better than we do, we intend to keep you quiet."

"If you will let me out, I can serve you," answered the man below. "There is nobody in Rome who can serve you as I can."

"Who are you?" asked Malipieri.

"Are you going to let me out, Signor Malipieri?" enquired the man. "If you are, I will tell you."

"Oh, you know my name, do you?"

"Perfectly. You are the engineer engaged by the Senator Volterra to find the treasure."

"Yes. Quite right. What of that?"

"You have found it," answered the other. "Of what use will it be to kill me? I cannot take that statue away in my waistcoat pocket, if you let me out, can I?"

"You had better not make too many jokes, my man, or we will put the boards over this hole in five minutes. If you can really be of use to me, I will let you out. What is your name?"

"Toto," answered the voice sullenly.

"Yes. That means Theodore, I suppose. Now make haste, for I am tired of waiting. What are you, and how did you get in?"

"I was the mason of the palace, until the devil flew away with the people who lived in it. I know all the secrets of the house. I can be very useful to you."

"That changes matters, my friend. I have no doubt you can be useful if you like, though we have managed to find one of the secrets without you. It happens to be the only one we wanted to know."

"No," answered Toto. "There are two others. You do not know how I got in, and you do not know how to manage the 'lost water.'"

"That is true," said Malipieri. "But if I let you out you may do me harm, by talking before it is time. The government is not to know of this discovery until I am ready."

"The government!" exclaimed Toto contemptuously, from his hiding-place. "May an apoplexy seize it! Do you take me for a spy? I am a Christian."

"I begin to think he is, sir," put in Masin, knocking the ash from his pipe.

"I think so, too," said Malipieri. "Throw away that iron, Masin. He shall show himself, at all events, and if we like his face we can talk to him here."

Masin dropped the drill with a clang. Toto's hairy hand appeared, grasping the golden wrist of the statue, as he raised himself to approach the hole.

"He is a mason, as he says," said Masin, catching sight of the rough fingers.

"Did you take me for a coachman?" enquired Toto, thrusting his shaggy head forward cautiously, and looking up through the aperture.

"Before you come up here," Malipieri answered, "tell me how you got in."

"You seem to know so much about the overflow shaft that I should think you might have guessed. If you do not believe that I came that way, look at my clothes!"

He now crawled upon the body of the statue, and Malipieri saw that he was covered with half-dried mud and ooze.

"You got through some old drain, I suppose, and found your way up."

"It seems so," answered Toto, shaking his shoulders, as if he were stiff.

"Are you going to let him go free, sir?" asked Masin, standing ready. "If you do, he will be down the shaft, before you can catch him. These men know their way underground like moles."

"Moles, yourselves!" answered Toto in a growl, putting his head up above the level of the vault.

Masin measured him with his eye, and saw that he was a strong man, probably much more active than he looked in his heavy, mud-plastered clothes.

"Get up here," said Malipieri.

Toto obeyed, and in a moment he sat on the edge of the hole, his legs dangling down into it.

"Not so bad," he said, settling himself with a grunt of satisfaction.

"I like you, Master Toto," said Malipieri. "You might have thought that we really meant to kill you, but you did not seem much frightened."

"There is no woman in the affair," answered Toto. "Why should you kill me? And I can help you."

"How am I to know that you will?" asked Malipieri.

"I am a man of honour," Toto replied, turning his stony face to the light of the lanterns.

"I have not a doubt of it, my friend," returned Malipieri, without conviction. "Just now, the only help I need of you, is that you should hold your tongue. How can I be sure that you will do that? Does any one else know the way in through the drain?"

"No. I only found it to-night. If there is a day's rain in the mountains, and the Tiber rises even a little, nobody can pass through it. The lower part is barely above the level of the river now."

"How did you guess that you could get here by that way?"

"We know many secrets in our trade, from father to son," answered Toto gruffly.

"You must have lifted the boards, with the stones on them, to get out of the shaft. Why did you put them back in their place?"

"You seem to think I am a fool! I did not mean to let you know that I had been here, so I put them back, of course. I supposed that I could get out through the cellars, but you have put a padlock on the inner door."

"Is there any way of turning water into that shaft?"

"Only by filling the well, I think. If the Tiber rises, the water will back up the shaft through the drain. That is why the ancients who built the well made another way for the water to run off. When the river is swollen in a flood it must be much higher in the shaft than the bottom of the well, and if the 'lost water' were running in all the time, the air would probably make it back, so that the shaft would be useless and the well would be soiled with the river water."

"You evidently know your trade, Master Toto," said Masin, with some admiration for his fellow-craftsman's clear understanding.

"You know yours," retorted Toto, who was seldom at a loss, "for just now you talked of killing like a professional assassin."

This pleasing banter delighted Masin, who laughed heartily, and patted Toto on the back.

"We shall be good friends," he said.

"In this world one never knows," Toto answered philosophically. "What are you going to do?"

"You must come back with as to my apartment," said Malipieri, who had been considering the matter, "You must stay there a couple of days, without going out. I will pay you for your time, and give you a handsome present, and plenty to eat and drink. After that you will be free to go where you please and say what you like, for the secret will be out."

"Thank you," answered Toto without enthusiasm. "Are you going to tell the government about the treasure?"

"The Senator will certainly inform the government, which has a right to buy it."

To this Toto said nothing, but he lifted his legs out of the hole and stood up, ready to go. Malipieri and Masin took up their lanterns.

CHAPTER XI

Masin led the way back, Toto followed and Malipieri went last, so that the mason was between his two captors. They did not quite trust him, and Masin was careful not to walk too fast where the way was so familiar to him, while Malipieri was equally careful not to lag behind. In this order they reached the mouth of the overflow shaft, covered with the loaded boards. Masin bent down and examined them, for he wished to convince himself that the stones had been moved since he had himself placed them there. A glance showed that this was the case, and he was about to go on, when he bent down again suddenly and listened, holding up his hand.

"There is water," he said, and began to lift off the stones, one by one.

Toto helped him quickly. There were only three or four, and they were not heavy. When the mouth of the shaft was uncovered all three knelt down and listened, instinctively lowering their lanterns into the blackness below. The shaft was not wider than a good-sized old-fashioned chimney, like those in Roman palaces, up and down which sweeps can just manage to climb.

The three men listened, and distinctly heard the steady falling of a small stream of water upon the stones at the bottom.

"It is raining," Toto said confidently, but he was evidently as much surprised by the sound as the others. "There must be some communication with the gutters in the courtyard," he added.

"There is probably a thunderstorm," answered Malipieri. "We can hear nothing down here."

"If I had gone down again, I should have been drowned," Toto said, shaking his head. "Do you hear? Half the water from the courtyard must be running down there!"

The sound of the falling stream increased to a hollow roar.

"Do you think the water can rise in the shaft?" asked Malipieri.

"Not unless the river rises and backs into it," replied Toto. "The drain is large below."

"That cannot be 'lost water,' can it?"

"No. That is impossible."

"Put the boards in their place again," Malipieri said. "It is growing late."

It was done in a few moments, but now the dismal roar of the water came up very distinctly through the covering. Malipieri had been in many excavations, and in mines, too, but did not remember that he had ever felt so strongly the vague sense of apprehension that filled him now. There is something especially gloomy and mysterious about the noise of unexplained water heard at a great depth under the earth and coming out of darkness. Even the rough men with him felt that.

"It is bad to hear," observed Masin, putting one more stone upon the boards, as if the weight could keep the sound down.

"You may say that!" answered Toto. "And in this tomb, too!"

They went on, in the same order as before. The passage to the dry well had been so much enlarged that by bending down they could walk to the top of the rope ladder. Malipieri went down first, with his lantern. Toto followed, and while Masin was descending, stood looking at the bones of the dead mason, and at the skull that grinned horribly in the uncertain yellow glare.

He took a half-burnt candle from his pocket, and some sulphur matches, and made a light for himself, with which he carefully examined the bones. Malipieri watched him.

"The man who was drowned over sixty years ago," said the architect.

"This," answered Toto, with more feeling than accuracy, "is the blessed soul of my grandfather."

"He shall have Christian burial in a few days," Malipieri said gravely.

Toto shrugged his shoulders, not irreverently, but as if to say that when a dead man has been without Christian burial sixty years, it cannot make any difference whether he gets it after all or not. "The crowbar is still good," Toto said, stooping down to disengage it from the skeleton's grasp. But Malipieri laid a hand on his shoulder, for it occurred to him that the mason, armed with an iron bar, might be a dangerous adversary if he tried to escape.

"You do not need that just now," said the architect.

Toto glanced at Malipieri furtively and saw that he was understood. He stood upright, affecting indifference. They went on, through the breach to which the slit had been widened. Toto moved slowly, and held his candle down to the running water in the channel.

"There is plenty of it," he observed.

"Where does it come from?" asked Malipieri, suddenly, in the hope of an unguarded answer.

"From heaven," answered Toto without hesitation; "and everything that falls from heaven is good," he added, quoting an ancient proverb.

"What would happen if we closed the entrance, so that it could not get in at all?"

"The book of wisdom," Toto replied, "is buried under Pasquino. How should I know what would happen?"

"You know a good many things, my friend."

Malipieri understood that the man would not say more, and led the way out.

"Good-bye, grandpapa," growled Toto, waving his hairy hand towards the well. "Who knows whether we shall meet again?"

They went on, and in due time emerged into the upper air. It was raining heavily, as Toto had guessed, and before they had reached the other end of the courtyard they were drenched. But it was a relief to be out of doors, and Malipieri breathed the fresh air with keen delight, as a thirsty man drinks. The rain poured down steadily and ran in rivers along the paved gutters, and roared into the openings that carried it off. Malipieri could not help thinking how it must be roaring now, far down at the bottom of the old shaft, led thither through deep-buried and long-forgotten channels.

Upstairs, Masin was inclined to be friendly with his fellow-craftsman, and gave him dry clothes to sleep in, and bread and cheese and wine in his own room. In spite of his experiences, Masin had never known how to be suspicious. But as Malipieri looked once more at the man's stony face and indistinguishable eyes, he thought differently of his prisoner. He locked the outer door and took the key of the patent lock with him when he went to bed at last.

It does not often rain heavily in Rome, late in the spring, for any long time, but when Malipieri looked out the next morning, it was still pouring steadily, and the sky over the courtyard was uniformly grey. It is apparently a law of nature that exceptions should come when least wanted.

In spite of the weather Malipieri went out, however, and did not even send for a cab. The porter was in a particularly bad humour and eyed him distrustfully, for he had been put to the trouble of cleaning the stairs where the three men had left plentiful mud in their track during the night. Malipieri nodded to the old man as usual, and was about to go out, but turned back and gave him five francs. Thus mollified the porter at once made a remark about the atrocious weather and proceeded to ask how the work was progressing.

"I have explored a good deal," answered Malipieri. "The Senator is coming to-morrow, and you had better sweep carefully. He looks at everything, you know."

He went out into the pouring rain, keeping a sharp lookout from under the edge of the umbrella he held low over his head. He had grown cautious of late. As he expected, he came upon one of the respectable men he now met so often, before he had turned into the Piazza Agonale. The respectable man was also carrying his umbrella low, and looking about him as he walked along at a leisurely pace. Malipieri hailed a cab.

Even in wet weather there are no closed cabs in that part of Rome. One is protected from the wet, more or less, by the hood and by a high leathern apron which is hooked to it inside. The cabman,

151

seated under a huge standing umbrella, bends over and unhooks it on one side for you to get in and out.

Malipieri employed the usual means of eluding pursuit. He gave an address and told the man to drive fast, got out quickly on reaching the house, enquired for an imaginary person with a foreign name, who, he was of course told, did not live there, got in again and had himself driven to Sassi's door, sure of losing his pursuer, if the detective followed him in another cab. Then he paid the man two fares, to save time, and went in. He had never taken the trouble to do such a thing since his political adventures, but he was now very anxious not to let it be known that he had any dealings with the former agent of the Conti family.

The matter was settled easily enough and to his satisfaction. Old Sassi worshipped Sabina, and was already fully persuaded that whatever could be found under the palace should belong to her, as also that she had a right to see what was discovered before Volterra did, and before anything was moved. He was at least as quixotic in his crabbed fashion as Malipieri himself; and besides, he really could not see that there was the least harm or danger in the scheme. It certainly would have been improper for Malipieri to go and fetch the young lady himself, but it was absurd to suppose that a man over sixty could be blamed for accompanying a girl of eighteen on a visit to her old home, in her own interest, especially when the man had been all his life employed by her family in a position of trust and confidence. Finally, Sassi hated Volterra with all his heart, as the faithful adherents of ruined gentlefolks often hate those who have profited by their ruin.

Sassi, as an old Roman, predicted that the weather would improve in the afternoon. Malipieri advised him nevertheless to keep the hood of his cab raised when he brought Sabina to the palace. To this Sassi answered that he should of course get a closed carriage from a livery stable, and an argument followed which took some time. In the opinion of the excellent old agent, it would be almost an affront to fetch the very noble Donna Sabina in a vehicle so plebeian as a cab, and it was with the greatest difficulty that Malipieri made him understand that a cab was much safer on such an occasion.

What was important was that the weather should be fine, for otherwise the Baroness might not go out, and the whole scheme would fail. In that case, it must be arranged for the following day, and Malipieri would find an excuse for putting off Volterra's visit.

He left the house on foot. So far, he had not allowed himself to think too much of the future, and had found little time for such reflection. He was a man who put all his energy into what he was doing, and was inclined to let consequences take care of themselves rather than waste thought in providing for them. He believed he was doing what was just and honourable, and if there was a spice of adventure and romance in it, that only made it the more easy to do. The only danger he could think of was that Sabina might slip in one of the difficult passages and hurt her foot a little, or might catch cold in the damp vaults. Nothing else could happen.

He congratulated himself on having got Toto in his power, since Toto was the only man who understood the ways of the "lost water." If he had before suspected that there was any one at large in Rome who knew as much he would have hesitated. But he had made the discovery of the man and had taken him prisoner at the same moment, and all danger in that quarter seemed to be removed.

As for the material difficulty, he and Masin could smooth the way very much in two or three hours, and could substitute a solid wooden ladder for the one of rope in the well. Sabina was young, slight, and probably active, and with a little help she would have no difficulty in reaching the inner chamber. It might be well to cover the skeletons. Young girls were supposed to be sensitive about such things, and Malipieri had no experience of their ways. Nevertheless he had an inward conviction that Sabina would not go into hysterics at the sight.

Old Sassi might not be able to get up the ladder, but once beyond the reach of social observation, he would trust Sabina to Malipieri and Masin for a quarter of an hour, and he could wait in the outer cellar. Malipieri had prepared him for this, and he had made no objection, only saying that he should like to see the treasure himself if it could possibly be managed. In his heart, Malipieri hoped that it would prove too much for the old man and that he might have the pleasure of showing Sabina what he had found without having the old agent at his elbow. Toto would be locked in, upstairs, for the day. He could not get out by the door, and he would not risk breaking his legs by jumping from the window. The intermediate story of the Palazzo Conti was far too high for that.

Malipieri calculated that if Sassi were punctual, Sabina would be at the door of the palace at a quarter-past five. At five minutes past, he came down, and sent the porter on an errand which would occupy at least half an hour even if executed with despatch. Masin would keep the door, he said. The old man was delighted to have an excuse for going out, and promised himself to spend a comfortable hour in a wine shop if he could find a friend. His wife, as there was so little to do, had found some employment in a laundry, to which she went in the morning and which kept her out all day. No one would see Sabina and Sassi enter, and if it seemed advisable they could be got out in the same way. No one but Masin and Malipieri himself need ever know that they had been in the palace that afternoon.

It was all very well prepared, by a man well accustomed to emergencies, and it was not easy to see how anything could go wrong. Even allowing more time than was necessary, Sabina's visit to the vaults could not possibly occupy much more than an hour.

CHAPTER XII

Malipieri was beginning to realize that his work in the vaults had been watched with much more interest than he had supposed possible, and that in some way or other news of his progress had reached various quarters. In the first place, his reputation was much wider than he knew, and many scholars and archaeologists throughout Europe had been profoundly impressed both by what he had discovered and by the learning he had shown in discussing his discoveries. It followed that many were curious to see what he would do next, and there were paragraphs about him in grave reviews, and flattering references to him in speeches made at learned conventions. He had friends whose names he had never heard, and enemies, too, ready to attack him on the one side and to defend him on the other. Some praised his modesty, and others called it affectation. His experience of the wider world was short, so far, and he did not understand that it had taken people a year to appreciate his success. He had hoped for immediate recognition of his great services to archaeology, and had been somewhat disappointed because that recognition had not been instantaneous. Like most men of superior talent, in the same situation, when praise came in due time and abundantly, he did not care for it because he was already interested in new work. To the man of genius the past is always insignificant as compared with the future. When Goethe, dying, asked for "more light," he may or may not have merely meant that he wished the window opened because the room seemed dark to his failing eyes; the higher interpretation which has been put upon his last words remains the true one, in the spirit, if not in the letter. He died, as he had lived, the man of genius looking forward, not backward, to the last, crying for light, more light, thinking not of dying and ending, but of living, hoping, doing, winning.

Besides the general body of students and archaeologists, the Italian government was exceedingly interested in Malipieri's explorations.

The government is rightly jealous in such matters, and does its very best to keep all artistic objects of real value in the country. It is right that this should be so. The law relating to the matter was framed by Cardinal Pacca, under the papal administration many years ago, and the modern rulers have had the intelligence to maintain it and enforce it. Like other laws it is frequently broken. In this it resembles the Ten Commandments and most other rules framed by divine or human intelligence for the good of mankind and the advancement of civilization. The most sanguine lovers of their fellow-men have always admitted the existence of a certain number of flagitious persons who obstinately object to being good. David, who was hasty, included a large proportion of humanity amongst "the wicked"; Monsieur Drumont limited the number to David's descendants; and Professor Lombroso, whatever he may really mean, conveys the impression that men of genius, criminals and lunatics are different manifestations of the same thing; as diamonds, charcoal and ham fat are all carbon and nothing else. We should be thankful for the small favours of providence in excepting us from the gifted minority of madmen, murderers and poets and making us just plain human beings, like other people.

There is no international law forbidding a man from making digressions when he is telling a story.

Malipieri was watched by the government, as Volterra had told him, because it was feared in high quarters that if he found anything of value under the palace, he would try to get it out of the country. He had always hated the government and had got himself into trouble by attacking the monarchy. Besides, it was known in high quarters that Senator Baron Volterra held singular views about the authenticity of works of art. It would be inconvenient to have a scandal in the Senate about the Velasquez and the other pictures; on the other hand, if anything more of the same sort should happen, it would be very convenient indeed to catch a pair of culprits in the shape of Malipieri, a pardoned political offender, and his ex-convict servant.

Then, too, in quite another direction, the Vatican was very anxious to buy any really good work of art which might be discovered, and would pay quite as much for it as the government itself. Therefore the Vatican was profoundly interested in Malipieri on its own account.

As if this were not enough, Sabina's brother, the ruined Prince Conti, had got wind of the excavations and scented some possible advantage to himself, with the vague chance of more money to throw away on automobiles, at Monte Carlo, and in the company of a cosmopolitan young person of semi-Oriental extraction whose varied accomplishments had made her the talk of Europe.

Lastly, the Russian embassy was on the alert, for the dowager Princess had heard from her maid, who had heard it from her sister in Rome, who had learned it from the washerwoman, who had been told the secret by the porter's wife, that the celebrated Malipieri was exploring the north-west foundations of the palace. The Princess had repeated the story, and the legend which accounted for it, to her brother Prince Rubomirsky, who was a very great personage in his own country. And the Prince, though good-natured, foresaw that he might in time grow tired of giving his sister unlimited money; and it occurred to him that something might turn up under the palace, after all, to which she might have some claim. So he had used his influence in Saint Petersburg with the Minister of Foreign Affairs, and the latter had instructed the Russian Ambassador in Rome to find out what he could about the excavations, without attracting attention; and Russian diplomatists have ways of finding out things without attracting attention, which are extremely great and wonderful. Also, if Russia puts her paw upon anything and declares that it is the property of a Russian subject, it often happens that smaller people take their paws away hastily.

It follows that there must have been a good deal of quiet talk, in Rome, not overheard in society, about what Malipieri was doing in the Palazzo Conti, and as the people who occupied themselves with his affairs were particularly anxious that he should not know what they said, he was in ignorance of it. But Volterra was not. He had valuable friends, because his influence was of value, and he was informed of much that was going on. If he was anxious to get rid of the architect, it was not so much because he wanted for himself the whole price which the statue or statues might bring, as because he feared lest the government should suddenly descend upon Malipieri and make an enquiry which would involve also the question of the pictures. So far, Volterra had created the impression that the young man had been concerned with a dealer in smuggling them out of the country; but in case of an investigation it could easily be proved that they were gone before Malipieri had arrived in Rome in answer to Volterra's invitation. Besides, the Senator had discovered that the young archaeologist was much more celebrated than was convenient. In private affairs there is nothing so tiresome and inconvenient as the presence of a celebrity. Burglars, when exercising their professional functions, are not accompanied by a brass band.

Toto was very docile and quiet all that day. Masin thought him philosophical, and continued to like him, after his fashion, providing him with a plentiful supply of tobacco, a good meal at noon, and a bottle of wine. The man's stony face was almost placid. At rare intervals he made a remark. After eating he looked out of the window and said rather regretfully that he thought the rain was over for the day.

Masin took this to mean that he wished he might go out, and offered him more wine by way of consolation. But Toto refused. He was a moderate man. Then he asked Masin how many rooms Malipieri occupied, and learned that the whole of the little apartment was rented by the architect. The information did not seem to interest him much.

In the morning, when Malipieri had come back from his visit to Sassi, he had given Masin the keys of the vaults, and had told him to buy a stout ladder and take it into the dry well. But Toto said that this was a useless expense.

"There is a strong ladder about the right length, lying along the wall at the other end of the west cellar," he said. "You had better take that."

Malipieri looked at him and smiled.

"For a prisoner, you are very obliging," he said, and he gave him a five-franc note, which Toto took with a grunt of thanks.

Masin was gone an hour, during which time Malipieri busied himself in the next room, leaving the door open. He went out when Masin came back. When the two men were together Toto produced the five francs.

"Can you change?" he enquired.

"Why?" asked Masin with some surprise.

"Half is two francs fifty," answered Toto. "That is your share."

Masin laughed and shook his head.

"No," he said. "What is given to you is not given to me. Why should I share with you?"

"It is our custom," Toto replied. "Take your half."

Masin refused stoutly, but Toto insisted and grew angry at last. So Masin changed the note and kept two francs and fifty centimes for himself, reflecting that he could give the money back to Malipieri, since he had no sort of right to it. Toto was at once pacified.

When Malipieri returned, Masin went out and got dinner for all three, bringing it as usual in the three tin cases strapped one above the other.

Toto supposed that he was not to be left alone in the apartment that day; but at half-past four Malipieri entered the room, with a padlock and a couple of screw-eyes in his hand.

"You would not think it worth while to risk jumping out," he said in a good-humoured tone. "But you might take it into your head to open the window, and the porter might be there, and you might talk to him. Masin and I shall be out together for a little while."

Masin shut the tall window, screwed the stout little eye-bolts into the frame and ran the bolt of the padlock through both. He gave the key to Malipieri. Toto watched the operation indifferently.

"If you please," he said, "I am accustomed to have a little wine about half-past five every day. I will pay for it."

He held out half a franc to Masin and nodded.

"Nonsense!" interposed Malipieri, laughing. "You are my guest, Master Toto." Masin brought a bottle and a glass, and a couple of cigars.

"Thank you, sir," said Toto politely. "I shall be very comfortable till you come back."

"You will find the time quite as profitable as if you were working," said Malipieri.

He nodded and went out followed by Masin, and Toto heard the key turned twice in the solid old lock. The door was strong, and they would probably lock the front door of the apartment too. Toto listened quietly till he heard it shut after them in the distance. Then he rose and flattened his face against the window pane.

He waited some time. He could see one half of the great arched entrance, but the projecting stone jamb of the window hindered him from seeing more. It was very quiet, and he could hear footsteps below, on the gravel of the courtyard, if any one passed.

At the end of ten minutes he heard a man's heavy tread, and knew that it was Masin's. Masin must have come out of the great archway on the side of it which Toto could not see. The steps went on steadily along the gravel. Masin was going to the vaults.

Toto waited ten minutes, and began to think that no one else was coming, and that Malipieri had left the palace, though he had been convinced that the architect and his man meant to go down to the vaults together. Just as he was beginning to give up the idea, he saw Sassi under the archway, in a tall hat, a black coat and gloves, and Malipieri was just visible for a moment as he came out too. He was unmistakably speaking to some one on his right, who was hidden from Toto's view by the projecting stonework. His manner was also distinctly deferential. The third person was probably Baron Volterra.

The footsteps took a longer time to reach the other end of the court than Masin had occupied. After all was silent, Toto listened breathlessly for five minutes more. There was not a sound.

He looked about him, then took up a chair, thrust one of the legs between the bolt and the body of the padlock and quietly applied his strength. The wood of the frames was old, and the heavy strain drew the screw-eyes straight out.

Toto opened the window noiselessly and looked out with caution. No one was in sight. By this time the three were in the vaults, with Masin.

Toto knew every inch of the palace by heart, inside and out, and he knew that one of the cast-iron leaders that carried the rain from the roof to the ground was within reach of that particular window, on the left side. He looked out once more, up and down the courtyard, and then, in an instant, he was kneeling on the stone sill, he had grasped the iron leader with one hand, then with the other, swinging himself to it and clutching it below with his rough boots. A few moments later he was on the ground, running for the great entrance. No one was there, no one saw him.

He let himself out quietly, shut the postern door after him, and slouched away towards the Vicolo dei Soldati.

CHAPTER XIII

Sabina had the delightful sensation of doing something she ought not to do, but which was perfectly innocent; she had moreover the rarer pleasure, quite new to her, of committing the little social misdeed in the company of the first man she had ever liked in her life. She knew very well that old Sassi would not be able to reach the inner chamber of the excavation, and she inwardly hoped that Malipieri's servant would discreetly wait outside of it, so that she might be alone with Malipieri when she first set eyes on the wonderful statue. It was amusing to think how the nuns would have scolded her for the mere wish, and how her pious sister would have condemned her to eternal flames for entertaining the temptation.

Malipieri had told her to put on an old frock, as she might spoil her clothes in spite of the efforts he had made to enlarge and smooth the way for her to pass. Her mother had a way of calling everything old which she had possessed three months, and for once Sabina was of her mother's opinion. She had a very smart cloth costume, with a rather short skirt, which had come home in February, and which she had worn only four times because the spring had been warm. It was undoubtedly "old" for she could not wear it in summer, and next winter the fashion would change; and it had rained all the morning, so that the air was damp and cold. Besides, the costume fitted her slender figure to perfection—it was such a pity that it was old already, for she might never have another as smart. The least she could do was to try and wear it out when she had the chance. It was of a delicate fawn colour; it had no pocket and it was fastened in a mysterious way. The skirt was particularly successful, and, as has been said, it was short, which was a great advantage in scrambling about a damp cellar. In order to show that she was in earnest, she put on russet leather shoes. Her hat was large, because that was the fashion, but nothing could have been simpler; it matched the frock in colour, and no colour was so becoming to her clear girlish pallor and misty hair as light fawn.

Malipieri had carried out his intention of getting rid of the porter, and was waiting inside the open postern when the cab drove up. Hitherto he had only seen Sabina indoors, at luncheon and in the evening, and when he saw her now he received an altogether new impression. Somehow, in her walking dress, she seemed more womanly, more "grown up" as she herself would have called it. As she got out of the wretched little cab, and came forward to greet him, her grace stirred his blood. It was final; he was in love.

Her intuition told her the truth, of course. There was something in his look and voice which had not quite been in either on the previous evening. He had been glad, last night, because she had come to the drawing-room, as he had hoped that she would; but to-day he was more than glad, he was happy, merely because he saw her. There never was a woman yet that could not tell that difference at a glance.

She was proud of being loved by him, and as he walked by her side, she looked up at the blue sky above the courtyard, and was glad that the clouds had passed away, for it must be sweeter to be loved when there was sunshine overhead than when it rained; but all the time, she saw his face, without looking at it, and it was after her own heart, and much to her liking. Besides, he was not only a manly man, and strong, and, of course, brave; he was already famous, and might be great some day; and she knew that he loved her, which was much to his advantage. As for being madly, wildly, desperately in love with him herself, she was not that yet; it was simply a very delicious sensation of being adored by somebody very sympathetic. Some women never get nearer to love than that, in all their lives, and are quite satisfied, and as they grow older they realize how much more convenient it is to be adored than to adore, and are careful to keep their likings within very manageable limits, while encouraging the men who love them to behave like lunatics.

Sabina was not of that kind; she was only very young, which, as Pitt pointed out, is a disadvantage but not a real crime.

They walked side by side, almost touching as they moved; they were drawn one to another, as all nature draws together those pairs of helpless atoms that are destined to one end.

Old Sassi went gravely with them. To him, it was a sad thing to see Sabina come to the palace in a way almost clandestine, as if she had no right there, and he shook his head again and again, silently grieving over the departed glory of the Conti, and wishing that he could express his sympathy to the young girl in dignified yet tender language. But Sabina was not in need of sympathy just then. Life in the Volterra establishment had been distinctly more bearable since Malipieri's appearance on the scene, and her old existence in the palace had been almost as really gloomy as it now seemed to her to have been. Moreover, she was intensely interested in what Malipieri was going to shew her.

Masin was waiting at the head of the winding stair with lanterns already lighted. When they had all entered, he turned the key. Sassi asked why he did this, and as they began to go down Malipieri explained that it was a measure of safety against the old porter's curiosity.

Sabina stepped carefully on the damp steps, while Malipieri held his lantern very low so that she could see them.

"I am sure-footed," she said, with a little laugh.

"This is the easiest part," he answered. "There are places where you will have to be careful."

"Then you will help me."

She thought it would, be pleasant to rest her hand on his arm, where the way was not easy, and she knew instinctively that he hoped she would do so. They reached the floor of the cellar, and Masin walked in front, lighting the way. Sassi looked about him; he had been in the cellars two or three times before.

"They did not get in by this way when the first attempt was made," he said.

"No," answered Malipieri. "I cannot find out how they made an entrance."

"There used to be a story of an oubliette that was supposed to be somewhere in the house," said Sabina.

"I have found it. You will see it in a moment, for we have to pass through the bottom of it."

"How amusing! I never saw one."

They came to the first breach in the cellar wall. A small lamp had been placed on a stone in a position to illuminate the entrance, and was burning brightly. Masin had lighted two others, further on, and had covered the bones in the dry well with pieces of sacking. Malipieri went up the causeway first. At first he held out his hand to Sabina, but she shook her head and smiled. There would be no satisfaction in being helped over an easy place; she should like him to help her where it would need some strength and skill to do so. She drew her skirt round her and walked up unaided, and followed by Sassi, leaning on his stick with one hand and on Masin with the other.

The descent into the first chamber was less easy. Standing at the top, Sabina looked down at Malipieri, who held his lantern to her feet. She felt a delicious little uneasiness now, and listened to the ghostly gurgle from the channel in the dark.

"What is that?" she asked, and her voice was a little awed by the darkness and strangeness of the place.

"The 'lost water.' It runs through here."

She listened a moment longer, and began to descend, placing her feet on the stones upon which Malipieri laid his hand, one after another, to show her the way.

"Perhaps you might help me a little here," she said.

"If you will let me put your feet on the right step, it will be easier," he answered.

"Yes. Do that, please. Show me the place first."

"There. Do you see? Now!"

He laid his hand firmly upon her small russet shoe, guided the little foot to a safe position and steadied it there a moment.

"So," he said. "Now the next. There are only four or five more."

She was rather sorry that there were so few, for they seemed delightfully safe, or just dangerous enough to be amusing; she was not quite sure which. Women never analyze the present, unless it is utterly dull.

At the bottom of the descent, both looked up, and saw at a glance that poor old Sassi could never get down, even with assistance. He seemed unable to put his foot down without slipping, in spite of Masin's help.

"I think you had better not try it," said Malipieri quietly. "In a few days I am sure that the Senator will have a way broken through from above, and then it will be easy enough."

"Yes," answered the old man regretfully. "I will go back again to the other side and wait for you."

"I am so sorry," said Sabina untruthfully, but looking up with sympathy.

"Take Signor Sassi back to the cellar," said Malipieri to Masin. "Then you can follow us."

Sassi and Masin disappeared through the breach. Malipieri led the way into the dry well, where there was another light. In her haste to reach the end, Sabina did not even glance at the sacking that covered the skeletons.

"Can you climb a ladder?" asked Malipieri.

"Of course!" Such a question was almost a slight.

Malipieri went up nimbly with his lantern, and knelt on the masonry to hold the top of the ladder. Sabina mounted almost as quickly as he had done, till she reached the last few steps and could no longer hold by the uprights. Then she put out her hands; he grasped then both and slid backwards on his knees as she landed safely on the edge. She had not felt that she could possibly fall, even if her feet slipped, and she now knew that he was strong, and that it was good to lean on him.

"You will have to stoop very low for a few steps," he said, taking up his lantern, and he kept his hold on one of her hands as he led her on. "It is not far, now," he added encouragingly, "and the rest is easy."

He guided her past the boards and stones that covered the overflow shaft, and down the inclined passage and the steps to the space between the vaults. A third lamp was burning here, close to the hole beneath which the statue lay. Malipieri lowered his lantern for her to see it.

She uttered an exclamation of surprise and delight. The pure gold that covered the bronze was as bright as if it had not lain in the vault for many centuries, twelve, fourteen, fifteen, no one could tell yet. The light fell into the huge ruby as into a tiny cup of wine.

"Can one get down?" asked Sabina breathlessly, after a moment's silence.

"Certainly. I have not gone down myself yet, but it is easy. I wanted you to be the first to see it all. You will have to sit on the edge and step upon the wrist of the statue."

Sabina gathered her skirt neatly round her, and with a little help she seated herself as he directed.

"Are you sure it will not hurt it, to step on it?" she asked, looking up.

"Quite sure." Malipieri smiled, as he thought of Toto's hobnailed shoes. "When you are standing firmly, I will get down too, if there is room."

"It is not a very big hole," observed Sabina, letting herself down till her feet rested on the smooth surface. She did not quite wish to be as near him as that; at least, not yet.

"I will creep down over the arm," she said, "and then you can follow me. I hope there are no beasts," she added. "I hate spiders."

Malipieri lowered his lantern beside her, and she crept along towards the statue's head. In a few moments he was beside her, bringing both the lantern and the lamp with him. They had both forgotten Masin's existence, as he had not yet appeared. Sabina looked about for spiders, but there were none in sight. The vault was perfectly dry, and there was hardly any dust clinging to the rough mortar that covered the stones. It was clear that the framework must have been carefully removed, and the place thoroughly cleaned, before the statue had been drawn into the vault from one end.

"He is perfectly hideous," said Sabina, as they reached the huge face. "But it is magnificent," she added, passing her gloved hand over the great golden features. "I wonder who it is meant for."

"A Roman emperor as Hercules, I think," Malipieri answered. "It may be Commodus. We are so near that it is hard to know how the head would look if the statue were set up."

He was thinking very little of the statue just then, as he knelt on its colossal chest beside Sabina, and watched the play of the yellow light on her delicate face. There was just room for them to kneel there, side by side.

It was magnificent, as Sabina had said, the great glittering thing, lying all alone in the depths of the earth, an enormous golden demigod in his tomb.

"You are wonderful!" exclaimed Sabina, suddenly turning her face to Malipieri.

"Why?"

"To have found it," she explained.

"I wish I had found something more practical," he answered. "In my opinion this thing belongs to you, and I suppose it represents a small fortune. But the only way for you to get even a share of it will be by bringing a suit against Volterra. Half a dozen rubies like the one in the ring would have been enough for you, and you could have taken them home with you in your pocket."

"I am afraid I have none!" Sabina laughed.

"This one will be safe in mine," Malipieri answered.

"You are not going to take it?" cried Sabina, a little frightened.

"Yes. I am going to take it for you. I daresay it is worth a good deal of money."

"But—is it yours?"

"No. It is yours."

"I wonder whether I have any right to it." Sabina was perhaps justly doubtful about the proceeding.

"I do not care a straw for the government, or the laws, or Volterra, where you are concerned. You shall have what is yours. Shall we get down to the ground and see if there is anything else in the vault?"

He let himself slide over the left shoulder, and the lion's skin that was modelled over it, and Sabina followed him cautiously. By bending their heads they could now stand and walk, and there was a space fully five feet wide, between the statue and the perpendicular masonry from which the vault sprang.

Malipieri stopped short, with both lights in his hand, and uttered an exclamation.

"What is it?" asked Sabina. "Oh!" she cried, as she saw what he had come upon.

For some moments neither spoke, and they stood side by side, pressed against each other in the narrow way and gazing down, for before them lay the most beautiful marble statue Sabina had ever seen. In the yellow light it was like a living woman asleep rather than a marble goddess, hewn and chipped, smoothed and polished into shape ages ago, by men's hands.

She lay a little turned to one side and away; the arm that was undermost was raised, so that the head seemed to be resting against it, though it was not; the other lying along and across the body, its perfect hand just gathering up a delicately futile drapery. The figure was whole and unbroken, of cream-like marble, that made soft living shadows in each dimple and hollow and seemed to quiver along the lines of beauty, the shoulder just edging forwards, the bent arm, the marvellous sweep of the limbs from hip to heel.

"It is a Venus, is it not?" asked Sabina with an odd little timidity.

"Aphrodite," answered Malipieri, almost unconsciously.

It was not the plump, thick-ankled, doubtfully decent Venus which the late Greeks made for their Roman masters; it was not that at all. It was their own Aphrodite, delicate, tender and deadly as the foam of the sea whence she came to them.

Sabina would scarcely have wondered if she had turned and smiled, there on the ground, to brush the shadows of ages from her opening eyes, and to say "I must have slept," like a woman waked by her lover from a dream of kisses. That would have seemed natural.

Malipieri felt that he was holding his breath. Sabina was so close to him that it was as if he could feel her heart beating near his own, and as fast; and for a moment he felt one of those strong impulses which strong men know when to resist, but to resist which is like wrestling against iron hands. He longed, as he had never longed for anything in his life, to draw her yet closer to him and to press his lips hard upon hers, without a word.

Instead, he edged away from her, and held the lights low beside the wonderful statue so that she might see it better; and Aphrodite's longing mouth, that had kissed gods, was curved with a little scorn for men.

The air was still and dry, and Sabina felt a strange little thrill in her hair and just at the back of her neck. Perhaps, in the unknown ways of fruitful nature, the girl was dimly aware of the tremendous manly impulse of possession, so near her in that narrow and silent place. Something sent a faint blush to her cheek, and she was glad there was not much light, and she did not wish to speak for a little while.

"I hate to think that she has lain so long beside that gilded Roman monster," said Malipieri presently.

The vast brutality of the herculean emperor had not disgusted him at first; it had merely displeased his taste. Now, it became suddenly an atrocious contrast to the secret loveliness of unveiled beauty. That was a manly instinct in him, too, and Sabina felt it.

"Yes," she said softly. "And she seems almost alive."

"The gods and goddesses live for ever," Malipieri answered, smiling and looking at her, in spite of himself.

Her eyes met his at once, and did not turn away. He fancied that they grew darker in the shadow, and in the short silence.

"I suppose we ought to be going," she said, still looking at him. "Poor old Sassi is waiting in the cellar."

"We have not been all round the vault yet," he answered. "There may be something more."

"No, she has been alone with the monster, all these centuries. I am sure of it. There cannot be anything else."

"We had better look, nevertheless," said Malipieri. "I want you to see everything there is, and you cannot come here again—not in this way."

"Well, let us go round." Sabina moved.

"Besides," continued Malipieri, going slowly forward and lighting the way, "I am going to leave the palace the day after to-morrow."

"Why?" asked Sabina, in surprise.

"Because Volterra has requested me to go. I may have to leave Rome altogether."

"Leave Rome?"

Her own voice sounded harsh to her as she spoke the words. She had been so sure that he was in love with her, she had begun to know that she would soon love him; and he was going away already.

"Perhaps," he answered, going on. "I am not sure."

"But—" Sabina checked herself and bit her lip.

"What?"

"Nothing. Go on, please. It must be getting late."

There was nothing more in the vault. They went all round the gilt statue without speaking, came back to the feet of the Aphrodite from the further side and stopped to look again. Still neither spoke for a long time. Malipieri held the lights in several positions, trying to find the best.

"Why must you leave Rome?" Sabina asked, at last, without turning her face to him.

"I am not sure that I must. I said I might, that was all."

Sabina tapped the ground impatiently with her foot.

"Why 'may' you have to go, then?" she asked a little sharply.

"Volterra may be able to drive me away. He will try, because he is afraid I may wish to get a share in the discovery."

"Oh! Then you will not leave Rome, unless you are driven away?"

Malipieri tried to see her eyes, but she looked steadily down at the statue.

"No," he said. "Certainly not."

Sabina said nothing, but her expression changed and softened at once. He could see that, even in the play of the shadows. She raised her head, glanced at him, and moved to go on. After making a few steps in the direction of the aperture she stopped suddenly as if listening. Malipieri held his breath, and then he heard, too.

It was the unmistakable sound of water trickling faster and faster over stones. For an instant his blood stood still. Then he set the lamp down, grasped Sabina's wrist and hurried her along, carrying only the lantern.

"Come as fast as you can," he said, controlling his voice.

She understood that there was danger and obeyed without losing her head. As he helped her up through the hole in the vault, she felt herself very light in his hands. In a moment he was beside her, and they were hurrying towards the inclined passage, bending low.

CHAPTER XIV

A broad stream of water was pouring down, and spreading on each side in the space between the vaults. In a flash, Malipieri understood. The dry well had filled, but the overflow shaft was covered with the weighted boards, and only a little water could get down through the cracks. The rest was pouring down the passage, and would soon fill the vault, which was at a much lower level.

"Stay here! Do not move!"

Sabina stood still, but she trembled a little, as he dashed up through the swift, shallow stream, not ankle deep, but steady as fate. In a moment he had disappeared from her sight, and she was all alone in the dismal place, in darkness, save for a little light that forced its way up from below through the hole. It seemed five minutes before his plashing footsteps stopped, up there in the passage; then came instantly the noise of stones thrown aside into the water, and of heavy pieces of board grating and bumping, as they floated for a moment. Almost instantly a loud roar came from the same direction, as the inflowing stream from the well thundered down the shaft. Sabina heard Malipieri's voice calling to her, and his approaching footsteps.

"The water cannot reach you now!" he cried.

It had already stopped running down the passage, when Malipieri emerged, dripping and holding out the lantern in front of him, as his feet slipped on the wet stones. Sabina was very pale, but quite quiet.

"What has happened?" she asked mechanically.

"The water has risen suddenly," he said, paler than she, for he knew the whole danger. "We cannot get out till it goes down."

"How soon will that be?" Sabina asked steadily.

"I do not know."

They looked at each other, and neither spoke for a moment.

"Do you think it may be several hours?" asked Sabina.

"Yes, perhaps several hours."

Something in his tone told her that matters might be worse than that.

"Tell me the truth," she said. "It may be days before the water goes down. We may die here. Is that what you mean?"

"Unless I can make another way out, that is what may happen. We may starve here."

"You will find the other way out," Sabina said quietly. "I know you will."

She would rather have died that moment than have let him think her a coward; and she was really brave, and was vaguely conscious that she was, and that she could trust her nerves, as long as her bodily strength lasted. But it would be very horrible to die of hunger, and in such a place. It was better not to think of it. He stood before her, with his lantern, a pale, courageous, strong man, whom she could not help trusting; he would find that other way.

"You had better get down again," he said, after a little reflection. "It is dry below, and the lamp is there."

"I can help you."

Malipieri looked at the slight figure and the little gloved hands and smiled.

"I am very strong," Sabina said, "much stronger than you think. Besides, I could not sit all alone down there while you are groping about. The water might come down and drown me, you know."

"It cannot run down, now. If it could, I should be drowned first."

"That would not exactly be a consolation," answered Sabina. "What are you going to do? I suppose we cannot break through the roof where we are, can we?"

"There must be ten or fifteen feet of earth above it. We are under the courtyard here."

Sabina's slight shoulders shuddered a little, for the first time, as she realized that she was perhaps buried alive, far beyond the possibility of being heard by any human being.

"The water must have risen very soon after we came down," Malipieri said thoughtfully. "That is why my man could not get to us. He could not get into the well."

"At all events he is not here," Sabina answered, "so it makes no difference where he is."

"He will try to help us from without. That is what I am thinking of. The first thing to be done is to put out that lamp, for we must not waste light. I had forgotten that."

Sabina had not thought of it either, and she waited while he went down again and brought the lamp up. He extinguished it at once and set it down.

"Only three ways are possible," he said, "and two are out of the question. We cannot get up the old shaft above the well. It is of no use to think of that. We cannot get down the overflow and out by the drains because the water is pouring down there, and besides, the Tiber must have risen with the rain."

"Which is the third way?"

"To break an opening through the wall in the highest part of the passage. It may take a long time, for I have no idea how thick the

178

wall may be, and the passage is narrow. But we must try it, and perhaps Masin will go to work nearly at the same spot, for he knows as much about this place as I do, and we have often talked about it. I have some tools down here. Will you come? We must not waste time."

"I can hold the lantern," said Sabina. "That may be of some use."

Malipieri gave her the lantern and took up the crowbar and pickaxe which lay near the hole in the vault.

"You will wet your feet, I am afraid," he said, as they went up the passage, and he was obliged to speak in a louder tone to be heard above the steady roar of the water.

He had marked the spot where he had expected that a breach would have to be made to admit visitors conveniently, and he had no trouble in finding it. He set the stones he had taken off the boards in a proper position, laid one of the wet boards upon them, and then took off his coat and folded it for a cushion, more or less dry. He made Sabina sit down with the lantern, though she protested.

"I cannot work with my coat on," he answered, "so you may as well sit on it."

He set to work, and said no more. The first thing to be done was to sound the thickness of the wall, if possible, by making a small hole through the bricks. If this could be done, and if Masin was on the other side, a communication could be established. He knew well enough that even with help from without, many hours might be necessary in order to make a way big enough for Sabina to get out; it was most important to make an opening through which food could be passed in for her. He had to begin by using his pick-axe because the passage was so narrow that he could not get his crowbar across it, much less use it with any effect. It was very slow work at first, but he did it systematically and with steady energy.

Sabina watched him in silence for a long time, vaguely wondering when he would be tired and would be obliged to stop and rest. Somehow, it was impossible to feel that the situation was really horrible, while such a man was toiling before her eyes to set her free. From the first, she was perfectly sure that he would succeed, but she had not at all understood what the actual labour must be.

He had used his pickaxe for more than half an hour, and had made a hollow about a foot and a half deep, when he rested on the shaft of the tool, and listened attentively. If the wall were not enormously thick, and if any one were working on the other side, he was sure that he could hear the blows, even above the roar of the water. But he could distinguish no sound.

The water came in steadily from the full well, a stream filling the passage beyond the dark chasm into which it was falling, and at least six inches deep. It sent back the light of the lantern in broken reflections and shivered gleams. Sabina did not like to look that way.

She was cold, now, and she felt that her clothes were damp, and a strange drowsiness came over her, brought on by the monotonous tone of the water. Malipieri had taken up his crowbar.

"I wonder what time it is," Sabina said, before he struck the wall again.

He looked at his watch.

"It is six o'clock," he answered, trying to speak cheerfully. "It is not at all late yet. Are you hungry?"

"Oh, no! We never dine till eight."

"But you are cold?"

"A little. It is no matter."

"If you will get up I will put my waistcoat on the board for you to sit upon, and then you can put my coat over your shoulders. I am too hot."

"Thank you."

She obeyed, and he made her as comfortable as he could, a forlorn little figure in her fawn-coloured hat, wrapped in his grey tweed coat, that looked utterly shapeless on her.

"Courage," he said, as he picked up his crowbar.

"I am not afraid," she answered.

"Most women would be."

He went to work again, with the end of the heavy bar, striking regularly at the deepest part of the hollow, and working the iron round and round, to loosen the brick wherever that was possible. But he made slow progress, horribly slow, as Sabina realized when nearly half an hour had passed again, and he paused to listen. He was much more alarmed than he would allow her to guess, for he was now quite convinced that Masin was not working on the other side; he knew that his strength would never be equal to breaking through, unless the crowbar ran suddenly into an open space beyond, within the next half-hour. The wall might be of any thickness, perhaps as much as six or seven feet, and the bricks were very hard and were well cemented. Perhaps, too, he had made a mistake in his rough calculations and was not working at the right spot after all. He was possibly hammering away at the end of a cross wall, following it in its length. That risk had to be taken, however, for there was at least as good a chance of breaking through at this point as at any other. He believed that by resting now and then for a short time, he could use his tools for sixteen or eighteen hours, after which, if he were without food, his strength would begin to give way. There was nothing to be done but to go on patiently, doing his best not to waste time, and yet not overtaxing his energy so as to break down before he had done the utmost possible.

He would not think of what must come after that, if he failed, and if the water did not subside.

Sabina understood very imperfectly what had happened, and there had been no time to explain. He could not work and yet talk to her so as to be heard above the roaring of the water and the noise of the iron bar striking against the bricks. She knew that, and she expected nothing of him beyond what he was doing, which was all a man could do.

She drew his coat closely round her and leaned back against the damp wall; and with half-closed eyes she watched the moving shadows of his arms cast on the wall opposite by the lantern. He worked as steadily as a machine, except when he withdrew the bar for a moment, in order to clear out the broken brick and mortar with his hand; then again the bar struck the solid stuff, and recoiled in his grasp and struck again, regularly as the swinging of a pendulum.

But no echo came back from an emptiness beyond. Ignorant as Sabina was of all such things, her instinct told her that the masonry was enormously thick; and yet her faith in him made him sure that he had chosen the only spot where there was a chance at all.

Sometimes she almost forgot the danger for a little while. It pleased her to watch him, and to follow the rhythmic movements of his strong and graceful body. It is a good sight to see an athletic man exerting every nerve and muscle wisely and skilfully in a very long-continued effort; and the woman who has seen a man do that to save her own life is not likely to forget it.

And then, again, the drowsiness came over her, and she was almost asleep, and woke with a shiver, feeling cold. He had given her his watch to hold, when he had made her sit on his waistcoat, and she had squeezed it under her glove into the palm of her hand. It was a plain silver watch with no chain. She got it out and looked at it.

Eight o'clock, now. The time had passed quickly, and she must have really been asleep. The Baron and his wife were just going to sit down to dinner, unless her disappearance had produced confusion in the house. But they would not be frightened, though they might be angry. The servants would have told them that Signor Sassi, whose card was there to prove his coming, had asked for Donna Sabina, and that she had gone out with him in a cab, dressed for walking. Signor Sassi was a highly respectable person, and though it might be a little eccentric, according to the Baroness's view, for Sabina to go out with him in a cab, especially in the afternoon, there could really be no great harm in it. The Baroness would be angry because she had stayed out so late. The Baroness would be much angrier by and by, when she knew what had really happened, and it must all be known, of course. When Sassi was sure that Masin could not get the two out of the vault himself, or with such ordinary help as he could procure, he would have to go to the Baron, who would instantly inform the authorities, and bring an engineer and a crowd of masons to break a way. There was some comfort in that, after all. It was quite impossible that she and Malipieri should be left to starve to death.

Besides, she was not at all hungry, though it was dinner time. She was only cold and sleepy. She wished she could take the crowbar from Malipieri's hands and use it for a few minutes, just to warm herself. He had said that he was too hot, and by the uncertain light she fancied she could see a little moisture on his white forehead.

183

She was right in that, for he was growing tired and knew that before long he must rest for at least a quarter of an hour. The hole was now three feet deep or more, yet no hollow sound came back from, the blows he dealt. His arms were beginning to ache, and he began to count the strokes. He would strike a hundred more, and then he would rest. He kept up the effort steadily to the end, and then laid down the bar and passed his handkerchief over his forehead. Sabina watched him and looked up into his face when he turned to her.

"You are tired," she said, rising and standing beside him, so as to speak more easily.

"I shall be quite rested in a few minutes," he answered, "and then I will go on."

"You must be very strong," said Sabina.

Then she told him what she had been thinking of, and how it was certain that the Baron would bring a large force of men to set them free. Malipieri listened to the end, and nodded thoughtfully. She was right, supposing that nothing had happened to Sassi and Masin; but he knew his own man, and judged that he must have made some desperate attempt to stop the inflowing water in the outer chamber, and it was not impossible that poor old Sassi, in his devotion to Sabina, had made a mad effort to help Masin, and that they had both lost their lives together. If that had happened, there was no one to tell Volterra where Sabina was. Enquiries at Sassi's house would be useless; all that could be known would be that he had gone out between four and five o'clock, that he had called at the house in the Via Ludovisi, and that he and Sabina had driven away together. No doubt, in time, the police could find the cab they had taken, and the cabman would remember that they had paid him at the Palazzo Conti. But all that would take a long time. The porter knew nothing of their coming, and being used to Malipieri's ways would not think of ringing at his door. In time Toto would doubtless break out, but he had not seen Sabina, for Malipieri had been very careful to make her walk close to the wall. He did not tell Sabina these things, as it was better that she should look forward to being set free in a few hours, but he had very grave doubts about the likelihood of any such good fortune.

"You must sit down," said Sabina. "You cannot rest unless you sit down. I will stand for a while."

"There is room for us both," Malipieri answered.

They sat down side by side on the board with the lantern at their feet, and they were very close together.

"But you will catch cold, now that you have stopped, working," Sabina said suddenly. "How stupid of me!"

As she spoke she pulled his coat off her shoulders, and tried to throw it over his, but he resisted, saying that he could not possibly have time to catch cold, if he went back to work in a few minutes. Yet he already felt the horrible dampness that came up out of the overflow shaft and settled on everything in glistening beads. It only made him understand how cold she must be, after sitting idle for two hours.

"Do you think we shall get out to-night?" Sabina asked suddenly, with the coat in her hand.

"I hope so," he answered.

She stood up, and looked at the cavity he had made in the wall.

"Where will that lead to?" she enquired.

He had risen, too.

"It ought to lead into the coach-house, so far as I can judge."

Instinctively, he went forward to examine the hole, and at that moment Sabina cleverly threw the coat over his shoulders and held it round his neck with both her hands.

"There!" she cried. "You are caught now!" And she laughed as lightly as if there were no such thing as danger.

Malipieri wondered whether she realized the gravity of the situation, or whether she were only pretending to be gay in order to make it easier for him. In either case she was perfectly brave.

"You must not!" he answered, gently trying to free himself. "You need it more than I."

"I wonder if it is big enough to cover us both," Sabina said, as the idea struck her. "Come! Sit down beside me and we will try."

He smiled and sat down beside her, and they managed to hold the coat so that it just covered their shoulders.

"Paul and Virginia," said Malipieri, and they both laughed a little.

But as their laughter died away, Sabina's teeth chattered, and she drew in her breath. At the slight sound Malipieri looked anxiously into her face, and saw that her lips were blue.

"This is folly," he said. "You will fall ill if you stay here any longer. It is quite dry in the vault, and warm by comparison with this place. You must go down there, while I stay here and work."

He got up, and in spite of a little resistance he made her put her arms into the sleeves of the coat, and turned the cuffs back, and fastened the buttons. She was shivering from head to foot.

186

"What a miserable little thing I am!" she cried impatiently.

"You are not a miserable little thing, and you are much braver than most men," said Malipieri. "But it will be of very little use to get you out of the vault alive if you are to die of a fever in a day or two."

She said nothing and he led her carefully down the inclined passage and the steps, away from the gloomy overflow, and the roaring water and the fearful dampness. He helped her down into the vault very gently, over the glittering chest of the great imperial statue. The air felt warm and dry, now that she was so badly chilled, and her lips looked a little less blue.

"I will light the lamp, and turn it very low," said Malipieri.

"I am not afraid of the dark," Sabina answered. "You said that we must not waste our light."

"Shall you really not be nervous?" Malipieri supposed that all women were afraid to be in the dark alone.

"Of course not. Why should I? There are no spiders, and I do not believe in ghosts. Besides, I shall hear you hammering at the wall."

"You had better sit on the body of the Venus. I think the marble is warmer than the bronze. But there is the board—I forgot. Wait a minute."

He was not gone long, and came back bringing the board and his waistcoat. To his surprise, he found her sitting on the ground, propping herself with one hand.

"I felt a little dizzy in the dark," she explained, "so I sat down, for fear of falling."

He glanced at her face, and his own was grave, as he placed the board on the ground, and laid the waistcoat over the curving waist of the Aphrodite, so that she could lean against it. She got up quickly when it was ready and seated herself, drawing up her knees and pulling her skirt closely round her damp shoes to keep her feet warm, if possible. He set the lamp beside her and gave her a little silver box of matches, so that she could get a light if she felt nervous. He looked at her face thoughtfully as he stood with his lantern in his hand, ready to go.

"But you have nothing to put on, if you have to rest again!" she said, rather feebly.

"I will come and rest here, about once an hour," he answered.

Her face brightened a little, and she nodded, looking up into his eyes.

"Yes. Come and rest beside me," she said.

He went away, climbing over the statue and out through the hole in the vault. Just before he disappeared, he held up his lantern and looked towards her. She was watching him.

"Good-night," he said. "Try to sleep a little."

"Come back soon," she answered faintly, and smiled.

Presently he was at work again, steadily driving the bar against the hard bricks, steadily chipping away a little at a time, steadily making progress against the enormous obstacle. The only question was whether his strength would last, for if he had been able to get food, it would have been merely a matter of time. A crowbar does not wear down much on bricks.

At first, perfectly mechanical work helps a man to think, as walking generally does; but little by little it dulls the faculties and makes thought almost impossible. Senseless words begin to repeat themselves with the movement, fragments of tunes fit themselves to the words, and play a monotonous and exasperating music in the brain, till a man has the sensation of having a hurdy-gurdy in his head, though he may be working for his life, as Malipieri was. Yet the unchanging repetition makes the work easier, as a sailor's chanty helps at the topsail halliards.

"We must get out before we starve, we must get out before we starve," sang the regular blows of the bar to a queer little tune which Malipieri had never heard.

When he stopped to clear out the chips, the song stopped too, and he thought of Sabina sitting alone in the vault, propped against the Aphrodite; and he hoped that she might be asleep. But when he swung the bar back into position and heard it strike the bricks, the tune and the words came back with the pendulum rhythm; and went on and on, till they were almost maddening, though there no longer seemed to be any sense in them. They made the time pass.

Sabina heard the dull blows, too, though not very loud. It was a comfort to hear anything in the total darkness, and she tried to amuse herself by counting the strokes up to a hundred and then checking the hundreds by turning in one finger after another. It would be something to tell him when he came back. She wondered whether there would be a thousand, and then, as she was wondering, she lost the count, and by way of a change she tried to reckon how many seconds there were in an hour. But she got into trouble with the ciphers when she tried to multiply sixty by sixty in her head, and she began counting the strokes again. They always stopped for a few seconds somewhere between thirty and forty.

She wished he would come back soon, for she was beginning to feel very cold again, so cold that presently she got upon her feet and walked a dozen steps, feeling her way along the great bronze statue. It was better than sitting still. She had heard of prisoners who had kept themselves sane in a dark dungeon by throwing away a few pins they had, and finding them again. It was a famous prisoner who did that. It was the prisoner of Quillon—no, "quillon" had something to do with a sword—no, it was Chillon. Then she felt dizzy again, and steadied herself against the statue, and presently groped her way back to her seat. She almost fell, when she sat down, but saved herself and at last succeeded in getting to her original position. It was not that she was faint from hunger yet; her dizziness was probably the result of cold and weariness and discomfort, and most of all, of the unaccustomed darkness.

She was ashamed of being so weak, when she listened to the steady strokes, far off, and thought of the strength and endurance it must need to do what Malipieri seemed to be doing so easily. But she was very cold indeed, chilled to the bone and shivering, and she could not think of any way of getting warm. She rose again, and struck one of the matches he had given her, and by its feeble light she walked a few seconds without feeling dizzy, and then sat down just as the little taper was going to burn her fingers.

A few minutes later she heard footsteps overhead, and saw a faint light through the hole. He was coming at last, and she smiled happily before she saw him.

He came down and asked how she was, and he sat on the Aphrodite beside her.

"If I could only get warm!" she answered.

"Perhaps you can warm your hands a little on the sides of the lantern," he said.

She tried that and felt a momentary sensation of comfort, and asked him what progress he was making.

"Very slow," he replied. "I cannot hear the least sound from the other side yet. Masin is not there."

She did not expect any other answer, and said nothing, as she sat shivering beside him.

"You are very brave," he said presently.

A long pause followed. She had bent her head low, so that her face almost touched her knees.

"Signor Malipieri—" she began, at last, in rather a trembling tone.

"Yes? What is it?" He bent down to her, but she did not look up.

"I—I—hardly know how to say it," she faltered. "Shall you think very, very badly of me if I ask you to do something—something that—" She stopped.

"There is nothing in heaven or earth I will not do for you," he answered. "And I shall certainly not think anything very dreadful." He tried to speak cheerfully.

"I think I shall die of the cold," she said. "There might be a way—"

"Yes? Anything!"

Then she spoke very low.

"Do you think you could just put your arms round me for a minute or two?" she asked.

Piteously cold though she was, the blood rushed to her face as she uttered the words; but Malipieri felt it in his throat and eyes.

"Certainly," he answered, as if she had asked the most natural thing in the world. "Sit upon my knees, and I will hold my arms round you, till you are warm."

He settled himself on the marble limbs of the Aphrodite, and the frail young girl seated herself on his knees, and nestled to him for warmth, while he held her close to him, covering her with his arms as much as he could. They went quite round her, one above the other, and she hid her face against his shoulder. He could feel her trembling with the cold like a leaf, under the coat he had made her put on.

Suddenly she started a little, but not as if she wished to go; it was more like a sob than anything else.

"What is the matter?" he asked, steadying his voice with difficulty.

"I am so ashamed of myself!" she answered, and she buried her face against his shoulder again.

"There is nothing to be ashamed of," he said gently. "Are you a little warmer now?"

"Oh, much, much! Let me stay just a little longer."

"As long as you will," he answered, pressing her to him quietly.

He wondered if she could hear his heart, which was beating like a hammer, and whether she noticed anything strange in his voice. If she did, she would not understand. She was only a child after all. He told himself that he was old enough to be her father, though he was not; he tried not to think of her at all. But that was of no use. He would have given his body, his freedom, his soul and the life to come, to kiss her as she lay helpless in his arms; he would have given anything the world held, or heaven, if it had been his; anything, except his honour. But that he would not give. His heart might beat itself to pieces, his brain might whirl, the little fires might flash furiously in his closed eyes, his throat might be as parched as the rich man's in hell—she had trusted herself to him like a child, in sheer despair and misery, and safe as a child she should lie on his breast. She should die there, if they were to die.

"I am warm now," she said at last, "really quite warm again, if you want to go back."

He did not wonder. He felt as if he were on fire from his head to his feet. At her words he relaxed his arms at once, and she stood up.

"You are so good to me," she said, with an impulse of gratitude for safety which she herself did not understand. "What makes you so good to me?"

He shook his head, as if he could not answer then, and smiled a little sadly.

"Now that you are warm, I must not lose time," he said, a moment later, taking up his lantern.

She sat down in her old place, and gathered her skirt to her feet and watched him as he climbed out and the last rays of light disappeared. Then the pounding at the wall began again, far off, and she tried to count the strokes, as she had done before; but she wished him back, and whether she felt cold or not, she wished herself again quietly folded in his arms, and though she was alone and it was quite dark she blushed at the thought. It seemed to her that the blows were struck in quicker succession now than before. Was he willing to tire himself out a little sooner, so as to earn the right to come back to her?

That was not it. He was growing desperate, and could not control the speed of his hands so perfectly as before. The night was advancing, he knew, though he had not looked at the watch, which was still in Sabina's glove. It was growing late, and he could distinguish no sound but that of the blows he struck at the bricks and the steady roar of the water. The conviction grew on him that Masin was drowned, and perhaps old Sassi too, and that their bodies lay at the bottom of the outer chamber, between the well and the wall of the cellar. If Masin had been able to get into the well, before the water was too high, he would have risen with it, for he was a good swimmer.

So was Malipieri, and more than once he thought of making an attempt to reach the widened slit in the wall by diving. That he could find the opening he was sure, but he was almost equally sure that he could never get through it alive and up to the surface on the other side. If he were drowned too, Sabina would be left to die alone, or perhaps to go mad with horror before she was found. He had heard of such things.

It was no wonder that he unconsciously struck faster as he worked, and at first he felt himself stronger than before, as men do when they are almost despairing. The sweat stood out on his forehead, and his hands tingled, when he drew back the iron to clear away the chips. He worked harder and harder.

The queer little tune did not ring in his head now, for he could think of nothing but Sabina and of what was to become of her, even if he succeeded in saving her life. It was almost impossible that such a strange adventure should remain a secret, and, being once known, the injury to the girl might be irreparable. He hated himself for having brought her to the place. Yet, as he thought it over, he knew that he would have done it again.

It had seemed perfectly safe. Any one could have seen that the water had not risen in the well for many years. Day after day, for a long time, he and Masin had worked in the vaults in perfect safety. The way to the statues had been made so easy that only a timid old man like Sassi could have found it impassable. There had been absolutely no cause to fear that after fifty or sixty years the course of the water should be affected, and the chances against such an accident happening during that single hour of Sabina's visit were as many millions to one. His motive in bringing her had been quixotic, no doubt, but good and just, and so far as Sabina's reputation was concerned, Sassi's presence had constituted a sufficient social protection.

He hammered away at the bricks furiously, and the cavity grew deeper and wider. Surely he had made a mistake at first in wishing to husband his strength too carefully. If he had worked from the beginning as he was working now, he would have made the breach by this time.

Unless that were impossible; unless, after all, he had struck the end of a cross wall and was working through the length of it instead of through its thickness. The fear of such a misfortune took possession of him, and he laid down his crowbar to examine the wall carefully. There was one way of finding out the truth, if he could only get light enough; no mason that ever lived would lay his bricks in any way except lengthwise along each course. If he had struck into a cross wall, he must be demolishing the bricks from their ends instead of across them, and he could find out which way they lay at the end of the cavity, if he could make the light of the lantern shine in as far as that. The depth was more than five feet now, and his experience told him that even in the construction of a mediaeval palace the walls above the level of the ground were very rarely as thick as that, when built of good brick and cement like this one.

When he took up his lantern, he was amazed at what he had done in less than four hours; if he had been told that an ordinary man had accomplished anything approaching to it in that time, he would have been incredulous. He had hardly realized that he had made a hole big enough for him to work in, kneeling on one knee, and bracing himself with the other foot.

But the end was narrow, of course, and when he held the light before it, he could not see past the body of the lantern. He opened the latter, took out the little oil lamp carefully and thrust it into the hole. He could see now, as he carefully examined the bricks; and he was easily convinced that he had not entered a cross wall. Nevertheless, when he had been working with the bar, he had not detected any change in the sound, as he thought he must have done, if he had been near the further side. Was the wall ten feet thick? He looked again. It was not a vaulting, that was clear; and it could not be anything but a wall. There was some comfort in that. He drew back a little, put the lamp into the lantern again and got out backwards. The passage was bright; he looked up quickly and started.

Sabina was standing beside him, holding the large lamp. Her big hat had fallen back and her hair made a fair cloud between it and her white face.

"I thought something had happened to you," she said, "so I brought the lamp. You stopped working for such a long time," she explained, "I thought you must have hurt yourself, or fainted."

"No," answered Malipieri. "There is nothing the matter with me. I was looking at the bricks."

"You must need rest, for it is past ten o'clock. I looked at the watch."

"I will rest when I get through the wall. There is no time to be lost. Are you very hungry?"

"No. I am a little thirsty." She looked at the black water, pouring down the overflow shaft.

"That water is not good to drink," said Malipieri, thinking of what was at the bottom of the well. "We had better not drink it unless we are absolutely forced to. I hope to get you out in two hours."

He stood leaning on his crowbar, his dark hair covered with dust, his white shirt damp and clinging to him, and all stained from rubbing against the broken masonry.

"It would be better to rest for a few minutes," she said, not moving.

He knew she was right, but he went with her reluctantly, and presently he was sitting beside her on the marble limbs of the Aphrodite. She turned her face to him a little shyly, and then looked away again.

"Were ever two human beings in such a situation before!"

"Everything has happened before," Malipieri answered. "There is nothing new."

"Does it hurt very much to die of starvation?" Sabina asked after a little pause.

"Not if one has plenty of water. It is thirst that drives people mad. Hunger makes one weak, that is all."

"And cold, I am sure."

"Very cold."

They were both silent. She looked steadily at the gleaming bronze statue before her, and Malipieri looked down at his hands.

"How long does it take to starve to death?" she asked at last.

"Strong men may live two or three weeks if they have water."

"I should not live many days," Sabina said thoughtfully. "It would be awful for you to be living on here, with me lying dead."

"Horrible. Do not think about it. We shall get out before morning."

"I am afraid not," she said quietly. "I am afraid we are going to die here."

"Not if I can help it," answered Malipieri.

"No. Of course not. I know you will do everything possible, and I am sure that if you could save me by losing your life, you would. Yes. But if you cannot break through the wall, there is nothing to be done."

"The water may go down to-morrow. It is almost sure to go down before long. Then we can get out by the way we came in."

"It will not go down. I am sure it will not."

"It is too soon to lose courage," Malipieri said.

"I am not frightened. It will not be hard to die, if it does not hurt. It will be much harder for you, because you are so strong. You will live a long time."

"Not unless I can save you," he answered, rising. "I am going back to work. It will be time enough to talk about death when my strength is all gone."

He spoke almost roughly, partly because for one moment she had made him feel a sort of sudden dread that she might be right, partly to make her think that he thought the supposition sheer nonsense.

"Are you angry?" she asked, like a child.

"No!" He made an effort and laughed almost cheerfully. "But you had better think about what you should like for supper in two or three hours! It is hardly worth while to put out that lamp," he added. "It will burn nearly twelve hours, for it is big, and it was quite full. There is a great deal of heat in it, too."

He went away again. But when he was gone, she drew the lamp over to her without leaving her seat, and put it out. She was very tired and a little faint, and by and by the distant sound of the crowbar brought back the drowsiness she had felt before, and leaning her head against the Aphrodite's curving waist, she lost consciousness.

He worked a good hour or more without result, came down to her, and found her in a deep sleep. As he noiselessly left her, he wondered how many men could have slept peacefully in such a case as hers.

Once more he took the heavy bar, and toiled on, but he felt that his strength was failing fast for want of food. He had eaten nothing since midday, and had not even drunk water, and in six hours he had done as much hard work as two ordinary workmen could have accomplished in a day. With a certain amount of rest, he could still go on, but a quarter of an hour would no longer be enough. He was very thirsty, too, but though he might have drunk his fill from the hollow of his hand, he could not yet bring himself to taste the water. He was afraid that he might be driven to it before long, but he would resist as long as he could.

Every stroke was an effort now, as he struggled on blindly, not only against the material obstacle, but against the growing terror that was taking possession of him, the hideous probability of having worked in vain after all, and the still worse certainty of what the end must be if he really failed.

Effort after effort, stroke after stroke, though each seemed impossible after the last. He could not fail, and let that poor girl die, unless he could die first, of sheer exhaustion.

If he were to stop now, it might be hours before he could go on again, and then he would be already weakened by hunger. There was nothing to be done but to keep at it, to strike and strike, with such half-frantic energy as was left in him. Every bone and sinew ached, and his breath came short, while the sweat ran down into his short beard, and fell in rain on his dusty hands.

But do what he would, the blows followed each other in slower succession. He could not strike twenty more, not ten, not five perhaps; he would not count them; he would cheat himself into doing what could not be done; he would count backwards and forwards, one, two, three, three, two, one, one, two—

And then, all at once, the tired sinews were braced like steel, and his back straightened, and his breath came full and clear. The blow had rung hollow.

He could have yelled as he sent the great bar flying against the bricks again and again, far in the shadow, and the echo rang back, louder and louder, every time.

The bar ran through and the end he held shot from his hands, as the resistance failed at last, and half the iron went out on the other side. He drew it back quickly and looked to see if there were any light, but there was none. He did not care, for the rest would be child's play compared with what he had done, and easier than play now that he had the certainty of safety.

The first thing to be done was to tell Sabina that the danger was past. He crept back with his light and stood upright. It hurt him to straighten himself, and he now knew how tremendous the labour had been; the last furious minutes had been like the delirium of a fever. But he was tough and used to every sort of fatigue, and hope had come back; he forgot how thirsty he had been, and did not even glance behind him at the water.

Sabina was still asleep. He stood before her, and hesitated, for it seemed cruel to wake her, even to tell her the good news. He would go back and widen the breach, and when there was room to get out, he could come and fetch her. She had put out the lamp. He lighted it again quietly, and was going to place it where it could not shine in her eyes and perhaps wake her, when he paused to look at her face.

It was very still, and deadly pale, and her lips were blue. He could not see that she was breathing, for his coat hung loosely over her slender figure. She looked almost dead. Her gloved hands lay with the palms upwards, the one in her lap, the other on the ground beside her. He touched that one gently with the back of his own, and it seemed to him that it was very cold, through the glove.

He touched her cheek in the same way, and it felt like ice. It would surely be better to wake her, and make her move about a little. He spoke to her, at first softly, and then quite loud, but she made no sign. Perhaps she was not asleep, but had fainted from weariness and cold; he knelt beside her, and took her hand in both his own, chafing it between them, but still she gave no sign. It was certainly a fainting fit, and he knew that if a woman was pale when she fainted, she should be laid down at full length, to make the blood return to her head. Kneeling beside her, he lifted her carefully and placed her on her back beside the Aphrodite, smoothing out his waistcoat under her head, not for a pillow but for a little protection from the cold ground.

Then he hesitated, and remained some time kneeling beside her. She needed warmth more than anything else; he knew that, and he knew that the best way to warm her a little was to hold her in his arms. Yet he would try something else first.

201

He bent over her and undoing one of the buttons of the coat, he breathed into it again and again, long, warm breaths. He did this for a long time, and then looked at her face, but it had not changed. He felt the ground with his hand, and it was cold; as long as she lay there, she could never get warm.

He lifted her again, still quite unconscious, and sat with her in his arms, as he had done before, laying her head against the hollow of his shoulder, and pressing her gently, trying to instil into her some of his own strong life.

At last she gave a little sigh and moved her head, nestling herself to him, but it was long before she spoke. He felt the consciousness coming back in her, and the inclination to move, rather than any real motion in her delicate frame; the more perceptible breathing, and then the little sigh came again, and at last the words.

"I thought we were dead," she said, so low that he could barely hear.

"No, you fainted," he answered. "We are safe. I have got the bar through the wall."

She turned up her face feebly, without lifting her head.

"Really? Have you done it?"

"Yes. In another hour, or a little more, the hole will be wide enough for us to get through it."

She hid her face again, and breathed quietly.

"You do not seem glad," he said.

"It seemed so easy to die like this," she answered.

But presently she moved in his arms, and looked up again, and smiled, though she did not try to speak again. He himself, almost worn out by what he had done, was glad to sit still for a while. His blood was not racing through him now, his head was not on fire. It seemed quite natural that he should be sitting there, holding her close to him and warming her back to life with his own warmth.

It was a strange sensation, he thought afterwards, when many other things had happened which were not long in following upon the events of that night. He could not quite believe that he was almost stupid with extreme fatigue, and yet he remembered that it had been more like a calm dream than anything else, a dream of peace and rest. At the time, it all seemed natural, as the strangest things do when one has been face to face with death for a few hours, and when one is so tired that one can hardly think at all.

CHAPTER XV

There was less consternation in the Volterra household than might have been expected when Sabina did not return before bedtime. The servants knew that she had gone out with an old gentleman, a certain Signor Sassi, at about five o'clock, but until Volterra came in, the Baroness could not find out who Sassi was, and she insisted on searching every corner of the house, as if she were in quest of his biography, for the servants assured her that Sabina was still out, and they certainly knew. She carefully examined Sabina's room too, looking for a note, a line of writing, anything to explain the girl's unexpected absence.

She could find nothing except the short letter from Sabina's mother to which reference has been made, and she read it over several times. Sabina received no letters, and had been living in something like total isolation. The Baroness had reached a certain degree of intimacy with her beloved aristocracy; but though she occasionally dropped in upon it, and was fairly well received, it rarely, if ever, dropped in upon her. It showed itself quite willing, however, to accept a formal invitation to a good dinner at her house.

She telephoned to the Senate and to a club, but Volterra could not be found. Then she went to dress, giving orders that Sabina was to be sent to her the moment she came in. She was very angry, and her sallow face was drawn into severe angles; she scolded her maid for everything, and rustled whenever she moved.

At last the Baron came home, and she learned who Sassi was. Volterra was very much surprised, but said that Sassi must have come for Sabina in connection with some urgent family matter. Perhaps some one of her family had died suddenly, or was dying. It was very thoughtless of Sabina not to leave a word of explanation, but Sassi was an eminently respectable person, and she was quite safe with him.

The Baron ate his dinner, and repeated the substance of this to his wife before the servants, whose good opinion they valued. Probably Donna Clementina, the nun, was very ill, and Sabina was at the convent. No, Sabina did not love her sister, of course; but one always went to see one's relations when they were dying, in order to forgive them their disagreeable conduct; all Romans did that, said the Baroness, and it was very proper. By and by a note could be sent to the convent, or the carriage could go there to bring Sabina back. But the Baron did not order the carriage, and became very thoughtful over his coffee and his Havana. Sabina had been gone more than four hours, and that was certainly a longer time than could be necessary for visiting a dying relative. He said so.

"Perhaps," suggested his wife, "it is the Prince who is ill, and Signor Sassi has taken Sabina to the country to see her brother."

"No," answered the Baron after a moment's thought. "That family is eccentric, but the girl would not have gone to the country without a bag."

"There is something in that," answered the Baroness, and they relapsed into silence.

Yet she was not satisfied, for, as her husband said, the Conti were all eccentric. Nevertheless, Sabina would at least have telegraphed, or sent a line from the station, or Sassi would have done it for her, for he was a man of business.

After a long time, the Baroness suggested that if her husband knew Sassi's address, some one should be sent to his house to find out if he had gone out of town.

"I have not the least idea where he lives," the Baron said. "As long as I had any business with him, I addressed him at the palace."

"The porter may know," observed the Baroness.

"The porter is an idiot," retorted the Baron, puffing at his cigar.

His wife knew what that meant, and did not enquire why an idiot was left in charge of the palace. Volterra did not intend to take that way of making enquiries about Sabina, if he made any at all, and the Baroness knew that when he did not mean to do a thing, the obstinacy of a Calabrian mule was docility compared with his dogged opposition. Moreover, she would not have dared to do it unknown to him. There was some good reason why he did not intend to look for Sassi.

"Besides," he condescended to say after a long time, "she is quite safe with that old man, wherever they are."

"Society might not think so, my dear," answered the Baroness in mild protest.

"Society had better mind its business, and let us take care of ours."

"Yes, my dear, yes, of course!"

She did not agree with him at all. Her ideal of a happy life was quite different, for she was very much pleased when society took a lively interest in her doings, and nothing interested her more than the doings of society. She presently ventured to argue the case.

"Yes, of course," she repeated, by way of preliminary conciliation. "I was only wondering what people will think, if anything happens to the girl while she is under our charge."

"What can happen to her?"

"There might be some talk about her going out in this way. The servants know it, you see, and she is evidently not coming home this evening. They know that she went out without leaving any message, and they must think it strange."

"I agree with you."

"Well, then, there will be some story about her. Do you see what I mean?"

"Perfectly. But that will not affect us in the least. Every one knows what strange people the Conti are, and everybody knows that we are perfectly respectable. If there is a word said about the girl's character, you will put her into the carriage, my dear, and deposit her at the convent under the charge of her sister. Everybody will say that you have done right, and the matter will be settled."

"You would not really send her to the convent!"

"I will certainly not let her live under my roof, if she stays out all night without giving a satisfactory account of herself."

"But her mother—"

"Her mother is no better than she should be," observed the Baron virtuously, by way of answer.

The Baroness was very much disturbed. She had been delighted to be looked upon as a sort of providence to the distressed great, and had looked forward to the social importance of being regarded as a second mother to Donna Sabina Conti. She had hoped to make a good match for her, and to shine at the wedding; she had dreamed of marrying the girl to Malipieri, who was such a fine fellow, and would be so rich some day that he might be trapped into taking a wife without a dowry.

These castles in the air were all knocked to pieces by the Baron's evident determination to get rid of Sabina.

"I thought you liked the girl," said the Baroness in a tone of disappointment.

Volterra stuck out both his feet and crossed his hands on his stomach, after his manner, smoking vigorously. Then, with his cigar in one corner of his mouth, he laughed out of the other, and assumed a playful expression.

"I do not like anybody but you, my darling," he said, looking at the ceiling. "Nobody in the whole wide world! You are the deposited security. All the other people are the floating circulation."

He seemed pleased with this extraordinary view of mankind, and the Baroness smiled at her faithful husband. She rarely understood what he was doing, and hardly ever guessed what he meant to do, but she was absolutely certain of his conjugal fidelity, and he gave her everything she wanted.

"The other people," he said, "are just notes, and nothing else. When a note is damaged or worn out, you can always get a new one at the bank, in exchange for it. Do you understand?"

"Yes, my dear. That is very clever."

"It is very true," said the Baron. "The Conti family consists chiefly of damaged notes."

He had not moved his cigar from the corner of his mouth to speak.

"Yes, my dear," answered the Baroness meekly, and when she thought of her last interview with the dowager Princess, she was obliged to admit the fitness of the simile.

"The only one of them at all fit to remain in circulation," he continued, "was this girl. If she stays out all night she will be distinctly damaged, too. Then you will have to pass her off to some one else, as one does, you know, when a note is doubtful."

"The cook can generally change them," observed the Baroness irrelevantly.

"I do not think she is coming home," said the Baron, much more to the point. "I hope she will! After all, if she does not, you yourself say that she is quite safe with this Signor Sassi—"

"I did not say that she would be safe from gossip afterwards, did I?"

It was perfectly clear by this time that he wished Sabina to leave the house as soon as possible, and that he would take the first opportunity of obliging her to do so. Even if his wife had dared to interfere, it would have been quite useless, for she knew him to be

208

capable of hinting to the girl herself that she was no longer welcome. Sabina was very proud, and she would not stay under the roof an hour after that.

"I did not suggest that you should bring her here," Volterra continued presently. "Please remember that. I simply did not object to her coming. That was all the share I had in it. In any case I should have wished her to leave us before we go away for the summer."

"I had not understood that," answered the Baroness resignedly. "I had hoped that she might come with us."

"She has settled the matter for herself, my dear. After this extraordinary performance, I must really decline to be responsible for her any longer."

It was characteristic of his methods that when he had begun to talk over the matter before dinner, she had not been able to guess at all how he would ultimately look at it, and that he only let her know his real intention by degrees. Possibly, he had only wished to gain time to think it over. She did not know that he had asked Malipieri to leave the Palazzo Conti, and if she had, it might not have occurred to her that there was any connection between that and his desire to get rid of Sabina. His ways were complicated, when they were not unpleasantly direct, not to say brutal.

But the Baroness was much more human, and had grown fond of the girl, largely because she had no daughter of her own, and had always longed to have one. Ambitious women, if they have the motherly instinct, prefer daughters to sons. One cannot easily tell what a boy may do when he grows up, but a girl can be made to do almost anything by her own mother, or to marry almost any one. The Baroness's regret for losing Sabina took the form of confiding to her husband what she had hoped to do for the girl.

"I am very sorry," she said, "but if you wish her to go, she must leave us. Of late, I had been thinking that we might perhaps marry her to that clever Malipieri."

The Baron smiled thoughtfully, took his cigar from his lips at last, and looked at his wife.

"To Malipieri?" he asked, as if not quite understanding the suggestion.

"Yes, I am sure he would make her a very good husband. He evidently admires her, too."

"Possibly. I never thought of it. But she has no dowry. That is an objection."

"He will be rich some day. Is he poor now?"

"No. Not at all."

"And she certainly likes him very much. It would be a very good match for her."

"Admirable. But I do not think we need trouble ourselves with such speculations, since she is going to leave us so soon."

"I shall always take a friendly interest in her," said the Baroness, "wherever she may be."

"Very well, my dear," Volterra answered, dropping the end of his cigar and preparing to rise. "That will be very charitable of you. But your friendly interest can never marry her to Malipieri."

"Perhaps not. But it might have been done, if she had not been so foolish."

"No," said the Baron, getting to his feet, "it never could have been done."

"Why not?" asked his wife, surprised by the decision of his tone.

"Because there is a very good reason why Malipieri cannot marry her, my dear."

"A good reason?"

"A very good reason. My dear, I am sleepy. I am going to bed."

Volterra rang the bell by the fireplace, and a man appeared almost instantly.

"You may put out the lights," he said. "We are going to bed."

"Shall any one sit up, in case Donna Sabina should come in, Excellency?" asked the servant.

"No."

He went towards the door, and his wife followed him meekly.

CHAPTER XVI

Sabina's strength revived in the warm night air, out in the courtyard, under the stars, and the awful danger from which Malipieri had saved her and himself looked unreal, after the first few moments of liberty. She got his watch out of her glove where it had been so many hours, and by the clear starlight they could see that it was nearly twenty minutes past two o'clock. Malipieri had put out the lamp, and the lantern had gone out for lack of oil, at the last moment. It was important that Sabina should not be seen by the porter, in the very unlikely event of his being up at that hour.

They had not thought that it could be so late, for it was long since Sabina had looked at the watch. The first thing that became clear to Malipieri was that it would be out of the question for him to take her home that night. The question was where else to take her. She was exhausted, too, and needed food at once, and her clothes were wet from the dampness. It would be almost a miracle if she did not fall ill, even if she were well taken care of at once.

There was only one thing to be done: she must go up to his apartment, and have something to eat, and then she must rest. In the meantime they would make some plan in order to explain her absence.

The porter's wife might have been of some use, if she could have been trusted with what must for ever remain a dead secret, namely, that Sabina had spent the night in Malipieri's rooms; for that would be the plain fact to-morrow morning. What had happened to Sassi and Masin was a mystery, but it was inconceivable that either of them should have been free to act during the past eight or nine hours and should have made no effort to save the two persons to whom they were respectively devoted as to no one else in the world.

Exhausted though he was, Malipieri would have gone down into the cellars at once to try and find some trace of them, if he had not felt that Sabina must be cared for first; and moreover he was sure that if he found them at all, he should find them both dead.

All this had been clear to him before he had at last succeeded in bringing her out into the open air.

"There is no help for it," he whispered, "you must come upstairs. Do you think you can walk so far?"

"Of course I can!" she answered, straightening herself bravely. "I am not at all tired."

Nevertheless she gladly laid her hand on his aching arm, and they both walked cautiously along the paved gutter that separated the wall from the gravel, for their steps would have made much more noise on the latter. All was quiet, and they reached Malipieri's door, by the help of a wax light. He led her in, still carrying the match, and he shut the door softly after him.

"At least," Sabina said, "no one can hear us here."

"Hush!"

He suspected that Toto must have got out, but was not sure. After lighting a candle, he led the way into his study, and made Sabina sit down, while he went back. He returned in a few moments, having assured himself that Toto had escaped by the window, and that Masin was not in, and asleep.

"Masin has disappeared," he said. "We can talk as much as we please, while you have your supper."

He had brought bread and wine and water, which he set before her, and he went off again to find something else. She ate hungrily after drinking a glass at a draught. He reappeared with the remains of some cold meat and ham.

"It is all I have," he explained, "but there is plenty of bread."

"Nothing ever tasted so good," answered Sabina gravely.

He sat down opposite to her and drank, and began to eat the bread. His hands were grimy, and had bled here and there at the knuckles where they had grazed the broken masonry. His face was streaked with dried perspiration and dust, his collar was no longer a collar at all.

As for Sabina, she had tried to take off the fawn-coloured hat, but it had in some way become entangled with her unruly hair, and it was hanging down her back. Otherwise, as she sat there her dress was not visibly much the worse for the terrible adventure. Her skirt was torn and soiled, indeed, but the table hid it, and the coat had kept the body of her frock quite clean. She did not look much more dishevelled than if she had been at a romping picnic in the country.

Nor did she look at all ill, after the wine and the first mouthfuls of food had brought all the warmth back to her. If anything, she was less pale than usual now, her lips were red again, and there was light in her eyes. There are little women who look as if they had no strength at all, and seem often on the point of breaking down, but who could go through a battle or a shipwreck almost without turning a hair, and without much thought of their appearance either; nor are they by any means generally the mildest and least reckless of their sex.

The two ate in silence for several minutes, but they looked at each other and smiled now and then, while they swallowed mouthful after mouthful.

"I wish I had counted the slices of bread I have eaten," said Sabina at last.

Malipieri laughed gaily. It did not seem possible that an hour or two earlier they had been looking death in the face. But his laughter died away suddenly, and he was very grave in a moment.

"I do not know what to do now," he said. "We shall have to make the Baroness believe that you have spent the night at Sassi's house. That is the only place where you can possibly be supposed to have been. I am not good at lying, I believe. Can you help me at all?"

Sabina laughed.

"That is a flattering way of putting it!" she answered. "It is true that I was brought up to lie about everything, but I never liked it. The others used to ask me why I would not, and whether I thought myself better than they."

"What are we to do?"

"Suppose that we tell the truth," said Sabina, nibbling thoughtfully at a last slice of bread. "It is much easier, you know."

"Yes."

Malipieri set his elbows on the table, leaned his bearded chin upon his scarred knuckles and looked at her. He wondered whether in her innocence she even faintly guessed what people would think of her, if they knew that she had spent a night in his rooms. He had no experience at all of young girls, and he wondered whether there were many like Sabina. He thought it unlikely.

"I believe in telling the truth, too," he said at last. "But when you do, you must trust the person to whom it is told. Now the person in this case will be the Baroness Volterra. I shall have to go and see her in the morning, and tell her what has happened. Then, if she believes me, she must come here in a cab and take you back. That will be absolutely necessary. You need say nothing that I have not said, and I shall say nothing that is not true."

"That is the best way," said Sabina, who liked the simplicity of the plan.

Her voice sounded sleepy, and she suppressed a little yawn.

"But suppose that she refuses to believe me," Malipieri continued, without noticing her weariness, "what then?"

"What else can she believe?" asked Sabina indifferently.

Malipieri did not answer for a long time, and looked away, while he thought over the very difficult situation. When he turned to her again, he saw that she was resting her head in her hand and that her eyes were closed.

"You are sleepy," he said.

She looked up, and smiled, hardly able to keep her eyes open.

"So sleepy!" she answered slowly. "I cannot keep awake a moment longer."

"You must go to bed," he said, rising.

"Yes—anywhere! Only let me sleep."

"You will have to sleep in my room. Do you mind very much?"

"Anywhere!" She hardly knew what she said, she hardly saw his face any longer.

He led the way with one of the lights, and she followed him with her eyes half shut.

"It seems to be in tolerably good order," he said, glancing round, and setting down the candle. "The key is in the inside. Turn it, please, when I am gone."

The room was scrupulously neat. Malipieri shut the window carefully. When he turned, he saw that she was sitting on the edge of the bed, nodding with sleep.

216

"Good-night," he said, in a low voice that was nevertheless harsh. "Lock your door."

"Good-night," she answered, with an effort.

He did not look at her again as he went out and shut the door, and he went quickly through the small room which divided the bedroom from the study, and in which he kept most of his clothes. He was very wide awake now, in spite of being tired, and he sat down in his armchair and smoked for some time. Suddenly he noticed the state of his hands, and he realized what his appearance must be.

Without making any noise, though he was sure that Sabina was in a deep sleep by this time, he went back through the first door and quietly got a supply of clothes, and took them with him to Masin's room, and washed there, and dressed himself as carefully as if he were going out. Then he went back to his study and sat down wearily in his armchair. Worn out at last, he was asleep in a few minutes, asleep as men are after a battle, whether the fight has ended in victory or defeat. Even the thought of Sabina did not keep him awake, and he would not have thought of her at all as he sat down, if he could have helped it.

After such a night as they had passed it was not likely that they should wake before ten o'clock on the following morning.

But the porter was up early, as usual, with his broom, to sweep the stairs and the paved entrance under the arch. When he had come back from the errand on which Malipieri had sent him, it had been already dusk. He had gone up and had rung the bell several times, but as no one opened he had returned to his lodge. It was not unusual for Malipieri and Masin to be both out at the same time, and he thought it likely that they were in the vaults. He cursed them both quietly for the trouble they had given him of mounting the stairs for nothing, and went to his supper, and in due time to bed.

He must go up again at eight o'clock, by which time Malipieri was always dressed, and as it was now only seven o'clock he had plenty of time to sweep. So he lit his pipe deliberately and took his broom, and went out of his lodge.

The first thing that met his eye was a dark stain on the stones, close to the postern. He passed his broom over it, and saw that it was dry; and it was red, but not like wine. Wine makes a purple stain on stones. He stooped and scratched it with his thick thumbnail. It was undoubtedly blood, and nothing else. Some one had been badly hurt there, or being wounded had stood some moments on the spot to open the door and get out.

The old man leaned on his broom awhile, considering the matter, and debating whether he should call his wife. His natural impulse was not to do so, but to get a bucket of water and wash the place before she could see it. The idea of going out and calling a policeman never occurred to him, for he was a real Roman, and his first instinct was to remove every trace of blood from the house in which he lived, whether it had been shed by accident or in quarrel. On the other hand, his wife might come out at any moment, to go to her work, and find him washing the pavement, and she would of course suppose that he had killed somebody or had helped to kill somebody during the night, and would begin to scream, and call him an assassin, and there would be a great noise, and much trouble afterwards. According to his view, any woman would naturally behave in this way, and as his views were founded on his own experience, he was probably right, so far as his wife was concerned. He therefore determined to call her.

She came, she saw, she threw up her hands and moaned a little about the curse that was on the house, and she helped him to scrub the stones as quickly as possible. When that was done, and when they had flooded the whole pavement under the arch, in order to conceal the fact that it had been washed in one place, it occurred to them that they should look on the stairs, to see if there were any blood there, and in the courtyard, too, near the entrance; but they could not find anything, and it was time for the woman to go to the place where she worked all day at ironing fine linen, which had been her occupation before she had been married. So she went away, leaving her husband alone.

He smoked thoughtfully and swept the stone gutter, towards the other end of the courtyard. He noticed nothing unusual, until he reached the door of the coach-house, and saw that it was ajar, whereas it was always locked, and he had the key in his lodge. He opened it, and looked in. The flood of morning light fell upon a little heap of broken brick and mortar, and he saw at a glance that a small breach had been made in the wall. This did not surprise him, for he knew that Malipieri and Masin had made holes in more than one place, and the architect had more than once taken the key of the coach-house.

What frightened him was the steady, roaring sound that came from the breach. He would as soon have thought of trusting himself to enter the place, as of facing the powers of darkness, even if his big body could have squeezed itself through the aperture. But he guessed that the sound came from the "lost water," which he had more than once heard in the cellar below, in its own channel, and he was instinctively sure that something had happened which might endanger the palace. The cellars were probably flooded.

On the mere chance that the door of the winding staircase might not be locked, he went out and turned into the passage where it was. He found it wide open. He had in his pocket one of those long wax tapers rolled into a little ball, which Roman porters generally have about them; he lit it and went down. There was water at the foot of the steps, water several feet deep. He retreated, and with more haste than he usually showed to do anything, he crossed the courtyard and went up to call Malipieri.

But Malipieri was asleep in his armchair in the inner room, and the bell only rang in the outer hall. The old man rang it again and again, but no one came. Then he stood still on the landing, took off his cap and deliberately scratched his head. In former times, it would have been his duty to inform Sassi, in whom centred every responsibility connected with the palace. But the porter did not know whether Sassi were dead or alive now, and was quite sure that the Baron would not approve of sending for him.

There was nothing to be done but to inform the Baron himself, without delay, since Malipieri was apparently already gone out. The Baron would take the responsibility, since the house was his.

The porter went down to his lodge, took off his old linen jacket and put on his best coat and cap, put some change into his pocket, went out and turned the key of the lock in the postern, and then stumped off towards the Piazza Sant' Apollinare to get a cab, for there was no time to be lost.

It was eight o'clock when he rang at the smart new house in the Via Ludovisi. Sabina and Malipieri had slept barely five hours.

A footman in an apron opened the door, and without waiting to know his business, asked him why he did not go to the servants' entrance.

"I live in a palace where there is a porter," answered the old man, assuming the overpowering manner that belongs to the retainers of really great old Roman houses. "Please inform the Baron that the 'lost water' has broken out and flooded the cellars of the Palazzo Conti, and that I am waiting for instructions."

CHAPTER XVII

220

Volterra went to bed early, but he did not rise late, for he was always busy, and had many interests that needed constant attention; and he had preserved the habits of a man who had enriched himself and succeeded in life by being wide awake and at work when other people were napping or amusing themselves. At eight o'clock in the morning, he was already in his study, reading his letters, and waiting for his secretary.

He sent for the porter, listened to his story attentively, and without expressing any opinion about what had happened, went directly to the palace in the cab which had brought the old man. He made the latter sit beside him, because it would be an excellent opportunity of showing the world that he was truly democratic. Half of Rome knew him by sight at least, though not one in twenty thousand could have defined his political opinions.

At the palace he paid the cabman instead of keeping him by the hour, for he expected to stay some time, and it was against his principles to spend a farthing for what he did not want. As he entered through the postern, he glanced approvingly at the damp pavement. He did not in the least believe that the porter washed it every morning, of course, but he appreciated the fact that the man evidently wished him to think so, and was afraid of him.

"You say that you rang several times at Signor Malipieri's door," he said. "Has he not told you that he is going to live somewhere else?"

"No, sir."

"Does he never leave his key with you when he goes out?"

"No, sir."

"Did you see him come in last night? Was he at home?"

"No, sir. I rang several times, about dusk, but no one opened. I did not hear him come in after that. Shall I go up and ring again?"

"No." Volterra reflected for a moment. "He has left, and has taken his key by mistake," he said. "But I should think that you must have seen him go. He would have had some luggage with him."

The porter explained that Malipieri had sent him on an errand on the previous afternoon, and had been gone when he returned. This seemed suspicious to Volterra, as indeed it must have looked to any one. Considering his views of mankind generally, it was not surprising if he thought that Malipieri might have absconded with something valuable which he had found in the vaults. He remembered, too, that Malipieri had been unwilling to let him visit the treasure on the previous day, and had named the coming afternoon instead.

"Can you get a man to open the door?" he asked.

"There is Gigi, the carpenter of the palace," answered the porter. "He is better than a locksmith and his shop is close by—but there is the water in the cellars—"

"Go and get him," said the Baron. "I will wait here."

The porter went out, and Volterra began to walk slowly up and down under the archway, breathing the morning air with satisfaction, and jingling a little bunch of keys in his pocket.

There was a knock at the postern. He listened and stood still. He knew that the porter had the key, for he had just seen him return it to his pocket after they had both come in; he did not wish to be disturbed by any one else just then, so he neither answered nor moved. The knock was repeated, louder than before. It had an authoritative sound, and no one but Malipieri himself would have a right to knock in that way. Volterra went to the door at once, but did not open it.

"Who is there?" he asked, through the heavy panel.

"The police," came the answer, short and sharp. "Open at once."

Volterra opened, and was confronted by a man in plain clothes, who was accompanied by two soldiers in grey uniforms, and another man, who looked like a cabman. On seeing a gentleman, the detective, who had been about to enter unceremoniously, checked himself and raised his hat, with an apology. Volterra stepped back.

"Come in," he said, "and tell me what your business is. I am the owner of this palace, at present. I am Baron Volterra, and a Senator."

The men all became very polite at once, and entered rather sheepishly. The cabman came in last, and Volterra shut the door.

"Who is this individual?" he asked, looking at the cabman.

"Tell your story," said the man in plain clothes, addressing the latter.

"I am a coachman, Excellency," the man answered in a servile tone. "I have a cab, number eight hundred and seventy-six, at the service of your Excellency, and it was I who drove the gentleman to the hospital yesterday afternoon."

"What gentleman?"

"The gentleman who was hurt in the house of your Excellency."

Volterra stared from the cabman to the man in plain clothes, not understanding. Then it occurred to him that the man in uniform might be wearing it as a disguise, and that he had to do with a party of clever thieves, and he felt for a little revolver which he always carried about with him.

"I know nothing about the matter," he said.

"Excellency," continued the cabman, "the poor gentleman was lying here, close to the door, bleeding from his head. You see the porter has washed the stones this morning."

"Go on." Volterra listened attentively.

"A big man who looked more like a workman than a servant came to call me in the square. When we got here, he unlocked the door himself, and made me help him to put the gentleman into the cab. It was about half-past five or a quarter to six, Excellency, and I waited at the hospital door till eight o'clock, but could not get any money."

"What became of the big man who called you?" asked Volterra. "Why did he not pay you?"

"He was arrested, Excellency."

"Arrested? Why? For taking a wounded man to the hospital?"

"Yes. You can imagine that I did not wish to be concerned in other people's troubles, Excellency, nor to be asked questions. So when I had seen the man and the doorkeepers take the gentleman in, I drove on about twenty paces, and waited for the man to come out. But soon two policemen came and went in, and came out again a few minutes later with the big man walking quietly between them, and they went off in the other direction, so that he did not even notice me."

"What did you do then?"

"May it please your Excellency, I went back to the door and asked the doorkeeper why the man had been arrested, and told him I had not been paid. But he laughed in my face, and advised me to go to the police for my fare, since the police had taken the man away. And I asked him many questions but he drove me away with several evil words."

"Is that all that happened?" asked Volterra. "Do you know nothing more?"

"Nothing, your Excellency," whined the man, "and I am a poor father of a family with eight children, and my wife is ill—"

"Yes," interrupted Volterra, "I suppose so. And what do you know about it all?" he enquired, turning to the man in plain clothes.

"This, sir. The gentleman was still unconscious this morning, but turns out to be a certain Signor Pompeo Sassi. His cards were in his pocket-book. The man who took him to the hospital was arrested because he entirely declined to give his name, or to explain what had happened, or where he had found the wounded gentleman. Of course all the police stations were informed during the night, as the affair seemed mysterious, and when this cabman came this morning and lodged a complaint of not having been paid for a fare from this palace to the hospital, it looked as if whatever had happened, must have happened here, or near here, and I was sent to make enquiries."

"That is perfectly clear," the Baron said, taking out his pocket-book. "You have no complaint to make, except that you were not paid," he continued, speaking to the cabman. "There are ten francs, which is much more than is owing to you. Give me your number."

The man knew that it was useless to ask for more, and as he produced his printed number and gave it, he implored the most complicated benedictions, even to miracles, including a thousand years of life and everlasting salvation afterwards, all for the Baron, his family, and his descendants.

"I suppose he may go now," Volterra said to the police officer.

The cabman would have liked to stay, but one of the soldiers opened the postern and stood waiting by it till he had gone out, and closed it upon his parting volley of blessings. The Senator reflected that they might mean a vote, some day, and did not regret his ten francs.

"I know Signor Sassi," he said to the detective. "He was the agent of Prince Conti's estate, and of this palace. But I did not know that he had been here yesterday afternoon. I live in the Via Ludovisi and had just come here on business, when you knocked."

He was very affable now, and explained the porter's absence, and the fact that a gentleman who had lived in the house, but had left it, had accidentally taken his key with him, so that it was necessary to get a workman to open the door.

"And it is as well that you should be here," he added, "for the big man of whom the cabman spoke may be the servant of that gentleman. I remember seeing him once, and I noticed that he was unusually big. He may have been here yesterday after his master left, and we may find some clue in the apartment."

"Excellent!" said the detective, rubbing his hands.

He was particularly fond of cases in which doors had to be opened by force, and understood that part of his business thoroughly.

The key turned in the lock of the postern, and the porter entered, bringing Gigi with him. They both started and turned pale when they saw the policeman and the detective.

"At what time did Signor Malipieri send you out on that errand yesterday afternoon?" asked Volterra, looking hard at the porter.

The old man drew himself up, wiped his forehead with a blue cotton handkerchief, and looked from the Baron to the detective, trying to make out whether his employer wished him to speak the truth. A moment's reflection told him that he had better do so, as the visit of the police must be connected with the stain of blood he had washed from the pavement, and he could prove that he had nothing to do with it.

"It was about five o'clock," he answered quietly.

"And when did you come back?" enquired the detective.

"It was dusk. It was after Ave Maria, for I heard the bells ringing before I got here."

"And you did not notice the blood on the stones when you came in, because it was dusk, I suppose," said the detective, assuming a knowing smile, as if he had caught the man.

"I saw it this morning," answered the porter without hesitation, "and I washed it away."

"You should have called the police," said the other severely.

"Should I, sir?" The porter affected great politeness all at once. "You will excuse my ignorance."

"We are wasting time," Volterra said to the detective. "The porter knows nothing about it. Let us go upstairs."

He led the way, and the others followed, including Gigi, who carried a leathern bag containing a few tools.

"It is of no use to ring again," observed Volterra. "There cannot be anybody in the apartment, and this is my own house. Open that door for us, my man, and do as little damage as you can."

Gigi looked at the patent lock.

"I cannot pick that, sir," he said. "The gentleman made me put it on for him, and it is one of those American patent locks."

"Break it, then," Volterra answered.

Gigi selected a strong chisel, and inserted the blade in the crack of the door, on a level with the brass disk. He found the steel bolt easily.

"Take care," he said to the Baron, who was nearest to him and drew back to give him room to swing his hammer.

He struck three heavy blows, and the door flew open at the third. The detective had looked at his watch, for it was his business to note the hour at which any forcible entrance was made. It was twenty minutes to nine. Malipieri and Sabina had slept a little more than five hours and a half.

Malipieri, still sleeping heavily in his armchair, heard the noise in a dream. He fancied he was in the vaults again, driving his crowbar into the bricks, and that he suddenly heard Masin working from the other side. But Masin was not alone, for there were voices, and he had several people with him.

Malipieri awoke with a violent start. Volterra, the detective, the two police soldiers, Gigi and the porter were all in the study, looking at him as he sat there in his armchair, in the broad light, carefully dressed as if he had been about to go out when he had sat down.

"You sleep soundly, Signer Malipieri," said the fat Baron, with a caressing smile.

Malipieri had good nerves, but for a moment he was dazed, and then, perhaps for the first time in his life, he was thoroughly frightened, for he knew that Sabina must be still asleep in his room, and in spite of his urgent request when he had left her, he did not believe that she had locked the door after all. The first thought that flashed upon him was that Volterra had somehow discovered that she was there, and had come to find her. There were six men in the room; he guessed that the Baron was one of those people who carry revolvers about with them, and two of the others were police soldiers, also armed with revolvers. He was evidently at their mercy. Short of throwing at least three of the party out of the window, nothing could avail. Such things are done without an effort on the stage by the merest wisp of a man, but in real life one must be a Hercules or a gladiator even to attempt them. Malipieri thought of what Sabina had said in the vault. Had any two people ever been in such a situation before?

For one instant, his heart stood still, and he passed his hand over his eyes.

"Excuse me," he said then, quite naturally. "I had dressed to go to your house this morning, and I fell asleep in my chair while waiting till it should be time. How did you get in? And why have you brought these people with you?"

He was perfectly cool now, and the Baron regretted that he had made a forcible entrance.

"I must really apologize," he answered. "The porter rang yesterday evening, several times, and again this morning, but could get no answer, and as you had told me that you were going to change your quarters, we supposed that you had left and had accidentally taken the key with you."

Malipieri did not believe a word of what he said, but the tone was very apologetic.

"The cellars are flooded," said the porter, speaking over Volterra's shoulder.

"I know it," Malipieri answered. "I was going to inform you of that this morning," he continued, speaking to the Baron. "I do not think that the police are necessary to our conversation," he added, smiling at the detective.

"I beg your pardon, sir," answered the latter, "but we are here to ask if you know anything of a grave accident to a certain Signor Sassi, who was taken from this palace unconscious, yesterday afternoon, at about a quarter to six, by a very large man, who would not give any name, nor any explanation, and who was consequently arrested."

Malipieri did not hesitate.

"Only this much," he replied. "With the authority of the Senator here, who is the owner of the palace, I have been making some archaeological excavations in the cellars. Signor Sassi was the agent—"

"I have explained that," interrupted the Baron, turning to the detective. "I will assume the whole responsibility of this affair. Signor Sassi shall be well cared for. I shall be much obliged if you will leave us."

He spoke rather hurriedly.

"It is my duty to make a search in order to discover the motive of the crime," said the detective with importance.

"What crime?" asked Malipieri with sudden sternness.

"Signor Sassi was very badly injured in this palace," answered the other. "The man who took him to the hospital would give no account of himself, and the circumstances are suspicious. The Baron thinks that the man may be your servant."

"Yes, he is my servant," Malipieri said. "Signor Sassi was trying to follow me into the excavations—"

"Yes, yes—that is of no importance," interrupted Volterra.

"I think it is," retorted Malipieri. "I will not let any man remain in prison suspected of having tried to murder poor old Sassi! I went on," he continued, explaining to the detective, "leaving the two together. The old gentleman must have fallen and hurt himself so badly that my man thought it necessary to carry him out at once. When I tried to get back, I found that the water had risen in the excavations and that the passage was entirely closed, and I had to work all night with a crowbar and pickaxe to break another way for myself. As for my man, if he refused to give any explanations, it was because he had express orders to preserve the utmost secrecy about the excavations. He is a faithful fellow, and he obeyed. That is all."

"A very connected account, sir, from your point of view," said the detective. "If you will allow me, I will write it down. You see, the service requires us to note everything."

"Write it down by all means," Malipieri answered quietly. "You will find what you need at that table."

The detective sat down, pulled back the cuff of his coat, took up the pen and began his report with a magnificent flourish.

"You two may go," said Malipieri to the porter and Gigi. "We shall not want you any more."

"As witnesses, perhaps," said the detective, overhearing. "Pray let them stay."

He went on writing, and the Baron settled himself in Malipieri's armchair, and lit a cigar. Malipieri walked slowly up and down the room, determined to keep perfectly cool.

"I hope the Baroness is quite well," he said after a time.

"Quite well, thank you," answered Volterra, nodding and smiling.

Malipieri continued to pace the floor, trying to see some way out of the situation in which he was caught, and praying to heaven that Sabina might still be sound asleep. If she were up, she would certainly come to the study in search of him before long, as the doors opened in no other direction. All his nerves and faculties were strung to the utmost tension, and if the worst came he was prepared to attempt anything.

"It is a very fine day after the rain," observed the Baron presently.

"It never rains long in Rome, in the spring," answered Malipieri.

The detective wrote steadily, and neither spoke again till he had finished.

"Of course," he said to Malipieri, "you are quite sure of your statements."

"Provided that you have written down exactly what I said," Malipieri answered.

The detective rose and handed him the sheets, at which he glanced rapidly.

"Yes. That is what I said."

"Let me see," Volterra put in, rising and holding out his hand.

He took the paper and read every word carefully, before he returned the manuscript.

"You might add," he said, "that I have been most anxious to keep the excavations a secret because I do not wish to be pestered by reporters before I have handed over to the government any discoveries which may be made."

"Certainly," answered the man, taking his pen again, and writing rapidly.

Volterra was almost as anxious to get rid of him as Malipieri himself. What the latter had said had informed him that in spite of the water the vaults could be reached, and he was in haste to go down. He had, indeed, noted the fact that whereas Sabina had left his house with Sassi at five o'clock, the latter had been taken to the hospital only three quarters of an hour later, and he wondered where she could be; but it did not even occur to him as possible that she should be in Malipieri's apartment. The idea would have seemed preposterous.

The detective rose, folded the sheets of paper and placed them in a large pocket-book which he produced.

"And now, gentlemen," he said, "we have only one more formality to fulfil, before I have the honour of taking my leave."

"What is that?" asked the Baron, beginning to show his impatience at last.

"Signor Malipieri—is that your name, sir? Yes. Signer Malipieri will be kind enough to let me and my men walk through the rooms of the apartment."

"I think that is quite unnecessary," Malipieri answered. "By this time Signor Sassi has probably recovered consciousness, and has told his own story, which will explain the accident."

"In the performance of my duty," objected the detective, "I must go through the house, to see whether there are any traces of blood. I am sure that you will make no opposition."

Fate was closing in upon Malipieri, but he kept his head as well as he could. He opened the door that led back to the hall.

"Will you come?" he said, showing the way.

The detective glanced at the other door, but said nothing and prepared to follow.

"I will stay here," said the Baron, settling himself in the armchair again.

"Oh, no! Pray come," Malipieri said. "I should like you to see for yourself that Sassi was not hurt here."

Volterra rose reluctantly and went with the rest. His chief preoccupation was to get rid of the detective and his men as quickly as possible. Malipieri opened the doors as he went along, and showed several empty rooms, before he came to Masin's.

"This is where my man sleeps," he said carelessly.

The detective went in, looked about and suddenly pounced upon a towel on which there were stains of blood.

"What is this?" he asked sharply. "What is the meaning of this?"

Malipieri showed his scarred hands.

"After I got out of the vault, I washed here," he said. "I had cut my hands a good deal, as you see. Of course the blood came off on the towels."

The detective assumed his smile of professional cunning.

"I understand," he said. "But do you generally wash in your servant's room?"

"No. It happened to be convenient when I got in. There was water here, and there were towels."

"It is strange," said the detective.

Even Volterra looked curiously at Malipieri, for he was much puzzled. But he was impatient, too, and came to the rescue.

"Do you not see," he asked of the detective, "that Signor Malipieri was covered with dust and that his clothes were very wet? There they are, lying on the floor. He did not wish to go to his bedroom as he was, taking all that dirt and dampness with him, so he came here."

"That is a sufficient explanation, I am sure," said Malipieri.

"Perfectly, perfectly," answered the detective, smiling. "Wrap up those towels in a newspaper," he said to the two soldiers. "We will take them with us. You see," he continued in an apologetic tone, "we are obliged to be very careful in the execution of our duties. If Signor Sassi should unfortunately die in the hospital, and especially if he should die unconscious, the matter would become very serious, and I should be blamed if I had not made a thorough examination."

"I hope he is not so seriously injured," said Malipieri.

"The report we received was that his skull was fractured," answered the detective calmly. "The hospitals report all suspicious cases to the police stations by telephone during the night, and of course, as your man refused to speak, special enquiries were made about the wounded gentleman."

"I understand," said Malipieri. "And now, I suppose, you have made a sufficient search."

"We have not seen your own room. If you will show me that, as a mere formality, I think I need not trouble you any further."

It had come at last. Malipieri felt himself growing cold, and said nothing for a moment. Volterra again began to watch him curiously.

"I fancy," the detective said, "that your room opens from the study in which we have already been. I only wish to look in."

"There is a small room before it, where I keep my clothes."

"I suppose we can go through the small room?"

"You may see that," said Malipieri, "but I shall not allow you to go into my bedroom."

"How very strange!" cried Volterra, staring at him.

Then the fat Baron broke into a laugh, that, made his watch-chain dance on his smooth and rotund speckled waistcoat.

"I see! I see!" he tried to say.

The detective understood, and smiled in a subdued way. Malipieri knit his brows angrily, as he felt himself becoming more and more utterly powerless to stave off the frightful catastrophe that threatened Sabina. But the detective was anxious to make matters pleasant by diplomatic means.

"I had not been told that Signor Malipieri was a married man," he said. "Of course, if the Signora Malipieri is not yet visible, I shall be delighted to give her time to dress."

Malipieri bit his lip and made a few steps up and down.

"I did not know that your wife was in Rome," Volterra said, glancing at him, and apparently confirming the detective in his mistake.

"For that matter," said the detective, "I am a married man myself, and if the lady is in bed, she might allow me merely to stand at the door, and glance in."

"I think she is still asleep," Malipieri answered. "I do not like to disturb her, and the room is quite dark."

"My time is at your disposal," said the detective. "Shall we go back and wait in the study? You would perhaps be so kind as to see whether the Signora is awake or not, but I am quite ready to wait till she comes out of her room. I would not put her to any inconvenience for the world, I assure you."

"Really," the Baron said to Malipieri, "I think you might wake her."

The soldiers looked on stolidly, the porter kept his eyes and ears open, and Gigi, full of curiosity, wore the expression of a smiling weasel. To the porter's knowledge, so far as it went, no woman but his own wife had entered the palace since Malipieri had been living in it.

Malipieri made no answer to Volterra's last speech, and walked up and down, seeking a solution. The least possible one seemed to be that suggested by the Baron himself. The latter, though now very curious, was more than ever in a hurry to bring the long enquiry to a close. It occurred to him that it would simplify matters if he and Malipieri and the detective were left alone together, and he said so, urging that as there was unexpectedly a lady in the case, the presence of so many witnesses should be avoided. Even now he never thought of the possibility that the lady in question might be Sabina.

The detective now yielded the point willingly enough, and the soldiers were sent off with Gigi and the porter to wait in the latter's lodge. It was a slight relief to Malipieri to see them go. He and his two companions went back to the study together.

The Baron resumed his seat in the armchair; he always sat down when he had time, and he had not yet finished his big cigar. The detective went to the window and looked out through the panes, as if to give Malipieri time to make up his mind what to do; and Malipieri paced the floor with bent head, his hands in his pockets, in utter desperation. At any moment Sabina might appear, yet he dared not even go to her door, lest the two men should follow him.

But at least he could prevent her from coming in, for he could lock the entrance to the small room. As he reached the end of his walk he turned the key and put it into his pocket. The detective turned round sharply and Volterra moved his head at the sound.

"Why do you do that?" he asked, in a tone of annoyance.

"Because no one shall go in, while I have the key," Malipieri answered.

"I must go in, sooner or later," said the detective, "I can wait all day, and all night, if you please, for I shall not use force where a lady is concerned. But I must see that room."

Like all such men, he was obstinate, when he believed that he was doing his duty. Malipieri looked from him to Volterra, and back again, and suddenly made up his mind. He preferred the detective, of the two, if he must trust any one, the more so as the latter probably did not know Sabina by sight.

"If you will be so kind as to stay there, in that armchair," he said to Volterra, "I will see what I can do to hasten matters. Will you?"

"Certainly. I am very comfortable here." The Baron laughed a little.

"Then," said Malipieri, turning to the detective, "kindly come with me, and I will explain as far as I can."

He took the key from his pocket again, and opened the door of the small room, let in the detective and shut it after him without locking it. He had hardly made up his mind what to say, but he knew what he wished.

"This is a very delicate affair," he began in a whisper. "I will see whether the lady is awake."

He went to the door of the bedroom on tiptoe and listened. Not a sound reached him. The room was quite out of hearing of the rest of the apartment, and Sabina, accustomed as she was to sleep eight hours without waking, was still resting peacefully. Malipieri came back noiselessly.

"She is asleep," he whispered. "Will you not take my word for it that there is nothing to be found in the room which can have the least connection with Sassi's accident?"

The detective shook his head gravely, and raised his eyebrows, while he shut his eyes, as some men do when they mean that nothing can convince them.

"I advise you to go in and wake your wife," he whispered, still very politely. "She can wrap herself up and sit in a chair while I look in."

"That is impossible. I cannot go in and wake her."

The detective looked surprised, and was silent for a moment.

"This is a very strange situation," he muttered. "A man who dares not go into his wife's room when she is asleep—I do not understand."

"I cannot explain," answered Malipieri, "but it is altogether impossible. I ask you to believe me, on my oath, that you will find nothing in the room."

"I have already told you, sir, that I must fulfil the formalities, whatever I may wish to believe. And it is my firm belief that Signor Sassi came by the injuries of which he may possibly die, somewhere in this apartment, yesterday afternoon. My reputation is at stake, and I am a government servant. To oblige you, I will wait an hour, but if the lady is not awake then, I shall go and knock at that door and call until she answers. It would be simpler if you would do it yourself. That is all, and you must take your choice."

Malipieri saw that he must wake Sabina, and explain to her through the door that she must dress. He reflected a moment, and was about to ask the detective to go back to the study, when a sound of voices came from that direction, and one was a woman's.

240

"It seems that there is another lady in the house," said the detective. "Perhaps she can help us. Surely you will allow a lady to enter your wife's room and wake her."

But Malipieri was speechless at that moment and was leaning stupidly against the jamb of the study door. He had recognized the voice of the Baroness talking excitedly with her husband. Fate had caught him now, and there was no escape. Instinctively, he was sure that the Baroness had come in search of Sabina, and would not leave the house till she had found her, do what he might.

CHAPTER XVIII

The Baroness had been called to the telephone five minutes after Volterra had gone out with the porter, leaving word that he was going to the Palazzo Conti and would be back within two hours. The message she received was from the Russian Embassy, and informed her that the dowager Princess Conti had arrived at midnight, was the guest of the Ambassador, and wished her daughter Sabina to come and see her between eleven and twelve o'clock. In trembling tones the Baroness had succeeded in saying that Sabina should obey, and had rung off the connection at once. Then, for the first time in her life, she had felt for a moment as if she were going to faint.

The facts, which were unknown to her, were simple enough. The Ambassador had been informed that a treasure had been discovered, and had telegraphed the fact in cipher to the Minister of Foreign Affairs in St. Petersburg, who had telegraphed the news to Prince Rubomirska, who had telegraphed to the Ambassador, who was his intimate friend, requesting him to receive the Princess for a few days. As the Prince and his sister were already in the country, in Poland, not far from the Austrian frontier, it had not

241

taken her long to reach Rome. Of all this, the poor Baroness was in ignorance. The one fact stared her in the face, that the Princess had come to claim Sabina, and Sabina had disappeared.

She had learned that the porter had come to say that the cellars of the Palazzo Conti were flooded, and she knew that her husband would be there some time. She found Sassi's card, on which his address was printed, and she drove there in a cab, climbed the stairs and rang the bell. The old woman who opened was in terrible trouble, and was just going out. She showed the Baroness the news of Sassi's mysterious accident shortly given in a paragraph of the Messaggero, the little morning paper which is universally read greedily by the lower classes. She was just going to the accident hospital, the "Consolazione," to see her poor master. He had gone out at half past four on the previous afternoon, and she had sat up all night, hoping that he would come in. She was quite sure that he had not returned at all after he had gone out. She was quite sure, too, that he had been knocked down and robbed, for he had a gold watch and chain, and always carried money in his pocket.

The Baroness looked at her, and saw that she was speaking the truth and was in real distress. It would be quite useless to search the rooms for Sabina. The old woman-servant had no idea who the Baroness was, and in her sudden trouble would certainly have confided to her that there was a young lady in the house, who had not been able to get home.

"For the love of heaven, Signora," she cried, "come with me to the hospital, if you know him, for he may be dying."

The Baroness promised to go later, and really intended to do so. She drove to the convent in which Donna Clementina was now a cloistered nun, and asked the portress whether Donna Sabina Conti had been to see her sister on the previous day. The portress answered that she had not, and was quite positive of the fact. The Baroness looked at her watch and hastened to the Palazzo Conti.

When she got there, the porter had already returned to his lodge, and he led her upstairs and to the door of the study.

Finding her husband alone, she explained what was the matter, in a few words and in a low voice. The Princess had come back, and wished to see Sabina that very morning, and Sabina could not be found. She sank into a chair, and her sallow face expressed the utmost fright and perplexity.

"Sassi left our house at five o'clock with Sabina," said the Baron, "and at a quarter to six he was taken from the door of this palace to the hospital by Malipieri's man. Either Malipieri or his man must have seen her."

"She is here!" cried the Baroness in a loud tone, something of the truth flashing upon her. "I know she is here!"

Volterra's mind worked rapidly at the possibility, as at a problem. If his wife were not mistaken it was easy to explain Malipieri's flat refusal to let any one enter the bedroom.

"You may be right," he said, rising. "If she is in the palace she is in the room beyond that one." He pointed to the door. "You must go in," he said. "Never mind Malipieri. I will manage him."

At that moment the door opened. Malipieri had recovered his senses enough to attempt a final resistance, and stood there, very pale, ready for anything.

But the fat Baron knew what he was about, and as he came forward with his wife he suddenly thrust out his hand at Malipieri's head, and the latter saw down the barrel of Volterra's revolver.

"You must let my wife pass," cried Volterra coolly, "or I will shoot you."

Malipieri was as active as a sailor. In an instant he had hurled himself, bending low, at the Baron's knees, and the fat man fell over him, while the revolver flew from his hand, half across the room, fortunately not going off as it fell on its side. While Malipieri was struggling to get the upper hand, the detective ran forward and helped Volterra. The two threw themselves upon the younger man, and between the detective's wiry strength and the Baron's tremendous weight, he lay panting and powerless on his back for an instant.

The Baroness had possibly assisted at some scenes of violence in the course of her husband's checkered career. At all events, she did not stop to see what happened after the way was clear, but ran to the door of the bedroom, and threw it wide open, for it was not locked. The light that entered showed her where the window was; she opened it in an instant, and looked round.

Sabina was sitting up in bed, staring at her with a dazed expression, her hair in wild confusion round her pale face and falling over her bare neck. Her clothes lay in a heap on the floor, beside the bed, Never was any woman more fairly caught in a situation impossible to explain. Even in that first moment she felt it, when she looked at the Baroness's face.

The latter did not speak, for she was utterly incapable of finding words. The sound of a scuffle could be heard from the study in the distance; she quietly shut the door and turned the key. Then she came and stood by the bed, facing the window. Sabina had sunk back upon the pillows, but her eyes looked up bravely and steadily. Of the two she was certainly the one less disturbed, even then, for she remembered that Malipieri had meant to go and tell the Baroness the whole truth, early in the morning. He had done so, of course, and the Baroness had come to take her back, very angry of course, but that was all. This was what Sabina told herself, but she guessed that matters would turn out much worse.

"Did he tell you how it happened that I could not get home?" she asked, almost calmly.

"No one has told me anything. Your mother arrived in Rome last night. She is at the Russian Embassy and wishes to see you at eleven o'clock."

"My mother?" Sabina raised herself on one hand in surprise.

"Yes. And I find you here."

The Baroness folded her arms like a man, her brows contracted, and her face was almost livid.

"Have you the face to meet your mother, after this?" she asked sternly.

"Yes—of course," answered Sabina. "But I must go home and dress. My frock is ruined."

"You are a brazen creature," said the Baroness in disgust and anger. "You do not seem to know what shame means."

Sabina's deep young eyes flashed; it was not safe to say such things to her.

"I have done nothing to be ashamed of," she answered proudly, "and you shall not speak to me like that. Do you understand?"

"Nothing to be ashamed of!" The Baroness stared at her in genuine amazement. "Nothing to be ashamed of!" she repeated, and her voice shook with emotion. "You leave my house by stealth, you let no one know where you are going, and the next morning I find you here, in your lover's house, in your lover's room, the door not even locked, your head upon your lover's pillow! Nothing to be ashamed of! Merciful heavens! And you have not only ruined yourself, but

245

you have done an irreparable injury to honest people who took you in when you were starving!"

The poor woman paused for breath, and in her horror, she hid her face in her hands. She had her faults, no doubt, and she knew that the world was bad, but she had never dreamt of such barefaced and utterly monstrous cynicism as Sabina's. If the girl had been overcome with shame and repentance, and had broken down entirely, imploring help and forgiveness, as would have seemed natural, the Baroness, for her own social sake, might have been at last moved to help her out of her trouble. Instead, being a person of rigid virtue and judging the situation in the only way really possible for her to see it, she was both disgusted and horrified. It was no wonder. But she was not prepared for Sabina's answer.

"If I were strong enough, I would kill you," said the young girl, quietly laying her head on the pillow again.

The Baroness laughed hysterically. She felt as if she were in the presence of the devil himself. She was not at all a hysterical woman nor often given to dramatic exhibitions of feeling, but she had never dreamt that a human being could behave with such horribly brazen shamelessness.

For some moments there was silence. Then Sabina spoke, in a quietly scornful tone, while the Baroness turned her back on her and stood quite still, looking out of the window.

"I suppose you have a right to be surprised," Sabina said, "but you have no right to insult me and say things that are not true. Perhaps Signor Malipieri likes me very much. I do not know. He has never told me he loved me."

The Baroness's large figure shook with fury, but she did not turn round. What more was the girl going to say? That she did not even care a little for the man with whom she had ruined herself? Yes. That was what she was going on to explain. It was beyond belief.

"I have only seen him a few times," Sabina said. "I daresay I shall be very fond of him if I see him often. I think he is very like my ideal of what a man should be."

The Baroness turned her face half round with an expression that was positively savage. But she said nothing, and again looked through the panes. She remembered afterwards that the room smelt slightly of stale cigar smoke, soap and leather.

"He wished me to see the things he has found before any one else should," Sabina continued. "So he got Sassi to bring me here. While we were in the vaults, the water came, and we could not get out. He worked for hours to break a hole, and it was two o'clock in the morning when we were free. I had not had any dinner, and of course I could not go with him to your house at that hour, even if I had not been worn out. So he brought me here and gave me something to eat, and his room to sleep in. As for the door not being locked, he told me twice to lock it, and I was so sleepy that I forgot to. That is what happened." After an ominous silence, the Baroness turned round. Her face was almost yellow now.

"I do not believe a word you have told me," she said, half choking.

"Then go!" cried Sabina, sitting up with flashing eyes. "I do not care a straw whether you believe the truth or not! Go! Go!"

She stretched out one straight white arm and pointed to the door, in wrath. The Baroness looked at her, and stood still a moment. Then she shrugged her shoulders in a manner anything but aristocratic, and left the room without deigning to turn her head. The instant she was gone Sabina sprang out of bed and locked the door after her.

Meanwhile, the struggle between Malipieri and his two adversaries had come to an end very soon. Malipieri had not really expected to prevent the Baroness from going to Sabina, but he had wished to try and explain matters to her before she went. He had upset Volterra, because the latter had pointed a revolver at his head, which will seem a sufficient reason to most hot-tempered men. The detective had suggested putting handcuffs on him, while they held him down, but Volterra was anxious to settle matters amicably.

"It was my fault," he said, drawing back. "I thought that you were going to resist, and I pulled out my pistol too soon. I offer you all my apologies."

He had got to his feet with more alacrity than might have been expected of such a fat man, and was adjusting his collar and tie, and smoothing his waistcoat over his rotundity. Malipieri had risen the moment he was free. The detective looked as if nothing had happened out of the common way, and the neatness of his appearance was not in the least disturbed.

"I offer you my apologies, Signor Malipieri," repeated the Baron cordially and smiling in a friendly way. "I should not have drawn my pistol on you. I presume you will accept the excuses I make?"

"Do not mention the matter," answered Malipieri with coolness, but civilly enough, seeing that there was nothing else to be done. "I trust you are none the worse for your fall."

"Not at all, not at all," replied Volterra. "I hope," he said, turning to the detective, "that you will say nothing about this incident, since no harm has been done. It concerns a private matter,—I may almost say, a family matter. I have some little influence, and if I can be of any use to you, I shall always be most happy."

The gratitude of so important a personage was not to be despised, as the detective knew. He produced a card bearing his name, and handed it to the Senator with a bow.

"Always at your service, sir," he said. "It is very fortunate that the revolver did not go off and hurt one of us," he added, picking up the weapon and handing it to Volterra. "I have noticed that these things almost invariably kill the wrong person, when they kill anybody at all, which is rare."

Volterra smiled, thanked him and returned the revolver to his pocket. Malipieri had watched the two in silence. Fate had taken matters out of his hands, and there was absolutely nothing to be done. In due time, Sabina would come out with the Baroness, but he could not guess what would happen then. Volterra would probably not speak out before the detective, who would not recognize Sabina, even if he knew her by sight. The Baroness would take care that he should not see the girl's face, as both Volterra and Malipieri knew.

The three men sat down and waited in silence after the detective had last spoken. Volterra lit a fresh cigar, and offered one to the detective a few moments later. The latter took it with a bow and put it into his pocket for a future occasion.

The door opened at last, and the Baroness entered, her face discoloured to a blotchy yellowness by her suppressed anger. She stood still a moment after she had come in, and glared at Malipieri. He and the detective rose, but Volterra kept his seat.

"Were you right, my dear?" the latter enquired, looking at her.

"Yes," she answered in a thick voice, turning to him for an instant, and then glaring at Malipieri again, as if she could hardly keep her hands from him in her righteous anger.

He saw clearly enough that she had not believed the strange story which Sabina must have told her, and he wondered whether any earthly power could possibly make her believe it in spite of herself. During the moments of silence that followed, the whole situation rose before him, in the only light under which it could at first appear to any ordinary person. It was frightful to think that what had been a bit of romantic quixotism on his part, in wishing Sabina to see the statues which should have been hers, should end in her social disgrace, perhaps in her utter ruin if the Baroness and her husband could not be mollified. He did not know that there was one point in Sabina's favour, in the shape of the Princess's sudden return to Rome, though he guessed the Baroness's character well enough to have foreseen, had he known of the new complication, that she would swallow her pride and even overlook Sabina's supposed misdeeds, rather than allow the Princess to accuse her of betraying her trust and letting the young girl ruin herself.

"I must consult with you," the Baroness said to her husband, controlling herself as she came forward into the room and passed Malipieri. "We cannot talk here," she added, glancing at the detective.

"This gentleman," said Volterra, waving his hand towards the latter, "is here officially, to make an enquiry about Sassi's accident."

"I shall be happy to wait outside if you have private matters to discuss," said the detective, who wished to show himself worthy of the Baron's favour, if he could do so without neglecting his duties.

"You are extremely obliging," Volterra said, in a friendly tone.

The detective smiled, bowed and left the room by the door leading towards the hall.

"It seems to me," the Baroness said, still suppressing her anger, as she turned her face a little towards Malipieri and spoke at him over her shoulder, "it seems to me that you might go too."

It was not for Malipieri to resent her tone or words just then, and he knew it, though he hated her for believing the evidence of her senses rather than Sabina's story. He made a step towards the door.

"No," Volterra said, without rising, "I think he had better stay, and hear what we have to say about this. After all, the responsibility for what has happened falls upon him."

"I should think it did!" cried the Baroness, breaking out at last, in harsh tones. "You abominable villain, you monster of iniquity, you snake, you viper—"

"Hush, hush, my dear!" interposed the Baron, realizing vaguely that his wife's justifiable excitement was showing itself in unjustifiably vulgar vituperation.

"You toad!" yelled the Baroness, shaking her fist in Malipieri's face. "You reptile, you accursed ruffian, you false, black-hearted, lying son of Satan!"

She gasped for breath, and her whole frame quivered with fury, while her livid lips twisted themselves to hiss out the epithets of abuse. Volterra feared lest she should fall down in an apoplexy, and he rose from his seat quickly. He gathered her to his corpulent side with one arm and made her turn away towards the window, which he opened with his free hand.

"I should be all that, and worse, if a tenth of what you believe were true," Malipieri said, coming nearer and then standing still.

He was very pale, and he was conscious of a cowardly wish that Volterra's revolver might have killed him ten minutes earlier. But he was ashamed of the mere thought when he remembered what Sabina would have to face. Volterra, while holding his wife firmly against the window sill, to force her to breathe the outer air, turned his head towards Malipieri.

"She is quite beside herself, you see," he said apologetically.

The Baroness was a strong woman, and after the first explosion of her fury she regained enough self-control to speak connectedly. She turned round, in spite of the pressure of her husband's arm.

"He is not even ashamed of what he has done!" she said. "He stands there—"

The Baron interrupted her, fearing another outburst.

"Let me speak," he said in the tone she could not help obeying. "What explanation have you to offer of Donna Sabina's presence here?" he asked.

As he put the question, he nodded significantly to Malipieri, over his wife's shoulder, evidently to make the latter understand that he must at least invent some excuse if he had none ready. The Baron did not care a straw what became of him, or of Sabina, and wished them both out of his way for ever, but he had always avoided scandal, and was especially anxious to avoid it now.

Malipieri resented the hint much more than the Baroness's anger, but he was far too much in the wrong, innocent though he was, to show his resentment.

He told his story firmly and coolly, and it agreed exactly with Sabina's.

"That is exactly what happened last night," he concluded. "If you will go down, you will find the breach I made, and the first vaults full of water. I have nothing more to say."

"You taught her the lesson admirably," said the Baroness with withering scorn. "She told me the same story almost word for word!"

"Madam," Malipieri answered, "I give you my word of honour that it is true."

"My dear," Volterra said, speaking to his wife, "when a gentleman gives his word of honour, you are bound to accept it."

"I hope so," said Malipieri.

"Any man would perjure himself for a woman," retorted the Baroness with contempt.

"No, my dear," the Baron objected, trying to mollify her. "Perjury is a crime, you know."

"And what he has done is a much worse crime!" she cried.

"I have not committed any crime," Malipieri answered. "I would give all I possess, and my life, to undo what has happened, but I have neither said nor done anything to be ashamed of. For Donna Sabina's sake, you must accept my explanation. In time you will believe it."

"Yes, yes," urged Volterra, "I am sure you will, my dear. In any case you must accept it as the only one. I will go downstairs with Signor Malipieri and we will take the porter to the cellars. Then you can go out with Sabina, and if you are careful no one will ever know that she has been here."

"And do you mean to let her live under your roof after this?" asked the Baroness indignantly.

"Her mother is now in Rome," answered Volterra readily. "When she is dressed, you will take her to the Princess, and you will say that as we are going away, we are reluctantly obliged to decline the responsibility of keeping the young girl with us any longer. That is what you will do."

"I am glad you admit at least that she cannot live with us any longer," the Baroness answered. "I am sure I have no wish to ruin the poor girl, who has been this man's unhappy victim—"

"Hush, hush!" interposed Volterra. "You must really accept the explanation he has given."

"For decency's sake, you may, and I shall have to pretend that I do. At least," she continued, turning coldly to Malipieri, "you will make such reparation as is in your power."

"I will do anything I can," answered Malipieri gravely.

"You will marry her as soon as possible," the Baroness said with frigid severity. "It is the only thing you can do."

Malipieri was silent. The Baron looked at him, and a disagreeable smile passed over his fat features. But at that moment the door opened, and Sabina entered. Without the least hesitation she came forward to Malipieri, frankly holding out her hand.

"Good morning," she said. "Before I go, I wish to thank you again for saving my life, and for taking care of me here."

He held her hand a moment.

"I ask your pardon, with all my heart, for having brought you into danger and trouble," he answered.

"It was not your fault," she said. "It was nobody's fault, and I am glad I saw the statues before any one else. You told me last night that you were probably going away. If we never meet again, I wish you to remember that you are not to reproach yourself for anything that may happen to me. You might, you know. Will you remember?"

She spoke quite naturally and without the least fear of Volterra and his wife, who looked on and listened in dumb surprise at her self-possession. She meant every word she said, and more too, but she had thought out the little speech while she was dressing, for she had guessed what must be happening in the study. Malipieri fixed his eyes on hers gratefully, but did not find an answer at once.

"Will you remember?" she repeated.

"I shall never forget," he answered, not quite steadily,

By one of those miracles which are the birthright of certain women, she had made her dress look almost fresh again. The fawn-coloured hat was restored to its shape, or nearly. The mud that had soiled her skirt had dried and she had brushed it away, though it had left faint spots on the cloth, here and there; pins hid the little rents so cleverly that only a woman's eye could have detected anything wrong, and the russet shoes were tolerably presentable. The Baroness saw traces of the adventure to which the costume had been exposed, but Volterra smiled and was less inclined than ever to believe the story which both had told, though he did not say so.

"My wife and I," he said cordially, "quite understand what has happened, and no one shall ever know about it, unless you speak of it yourself. She will go home with you now, and will then take you to the Russian Embassy to see your mother."

Sabina looked at him in surprise, for she had expected a disagreeable scene. Then she glanced at the Baroness's sallow and angry face, and she partly understood the position.

"Thank you," she said proudly, "but if you do not mind, I will go to my mother directly. You will perhaps be so kind as to have my things sent to the Embassy, or my mother's maid will come and get them."

"You cannot go looking like that," said the Baroness severely.

"On the contrary," Volterra interposed, "I think that considering your dangerous adventure, you look perfectly presentable. Of course, we quite understand that as the Princess has returned, you should wish to go back to her at once, though we are very sorry to let you go."

Sabina paused a moment before answering. Then she spoke to the Baroness, only glancing at Volterra.

"Until to-day, you have been very kind to me," she said with an effort. "I thank you for your kindness, and I am sorry that you think so badly of me."

"My dear young lady," cried the Baron, lying with hearty cordiality, "you are much mistaken! I assure you, it was only a momentary misapprehension on the part of my wife, who had not even spoken with Signor Malipieri. His explanation has been more than satisfactory. Is it not so, my dear?" he asked, turning to the Baroness for confirmation of his fluent assurances.

"Of course," she answered, half choking, and with a face like thunder; but she dared not disobey.

"If my mother says anything about my frock, I shall tell her the whole story," said Sabina, glancing at her skirt.

"If you do," said the Baroness, "I shall deny it from beginning to end."

"I think that it would perhaps be wiser to explain that in some other way," the Baron suggested. "Signor Malipieri, will you be so very kind as to go down first, and take the porter with a light to the entrance of the cellars? He knows Donna Sabina, you see. I will come down presently, for I shall stay behind and ask the detective to look out of the window in the next room, while my wife and Donna Sabina pass through. In that way we shall be quite sure that she will not be recognized. Will you do that, Signor Malipieri? Unless you have a better plan to suggest, of course."

Malipieri saw that the plan was simple and apparently safe. He looked once more at Sabina, and she smiled, and just bent her head, but said nothing. He left the room. The detective was sitting in a corner of the room beyond, and the two men exchanged a silent nod as Malipieri passed.

Everything was arranged as the Baron had planned, and ten minutes later the Baroness and Sabina descended the stairs together in silence and reached the great entrance. The two soldiers were standing by the open door of the lodge, and saluted in military fashion. Gigi, the carpenter, sprang forward and opened the postern door, touching his paper cap to the ladies.

They did not exchange a word as they walked to the Piazza Sant' Apollinare to find a cab. Sabina held her head high and looked straight before her, and the Baroness's invisible silk bellows were distinctly audible in the quiet street.

"By the hour," said the Baroness, as they got into the first cab they reached on the stand. "Go to the Russian Embassy, in the Corso."

CHAPTER XIX

"So you spent last night in the rooms of a man you have not seen half a dozen times," said the Princess, speaking with a cigarette in her mouth. "And what is worse, those dreadful Volterra people found you there. No Conti ever had any common sense!"

What Sabina had foreseen had happened. Her mother had looked her over, from head to foot, to see what sort of condition she was in, as a horse-dealer looks over a promising colt he has not seen for some time; and the Princess had instantly detected the signs of an accident. In answer to her question Sabina told the truth. Her mother had watched her face and her innocent eyes while she was telling the story, and needed no other confirmation.

"You are a good girl," she continued, as Sabina did not reply to the last speech. "But you are a little fool. I wonder why my children are all idiots! I am not so stupid after all. I suppose it must have been your poor father."

The white lids closed thoughtfully over her magnificent eyes, and opened again after a moment, as if she had called up a vision of her departed husband and had sent it away again.

"I suppose it was silly of me to go at all," Sabina admitted, leaning back in her chair. "But I wanted so much to see the statues!"

She felt at home. Her mother had brought her up badly and foolishly, and of late had neglected her shamefully. Sabina knew that and neither loved her nor respected her, and it was not because she was her mother that the girl felt suddenly at ease in her presence, as she never could feel with the Baroness. She did not wish to be at all like her mother in character, or even in manner, and yet she felt that they belonged to the same kind, spoke the same language, and had an instinctive understanding of each other, though these things implied neither mutual respect nor affection.

"That horrible old Volterra!" said the Princess, with emphasis. "He means to keep everything he has found, for himself, if he can. I have come only just in time."

Sabina did not answer. She knew nothing of the law, and though she fancied that she might have some morally just claim to a share in the treasure, she had never believed that it could be proved.

"Of course," the Princess continued, smoking thoughtfully, "there is only one thing to be done. You must marry this Malipieri at once, whether you like him or not. What sort of man is he?"

The faint colour rose in Sabina's cheeks and not altogether at the mere thought of marrying Malipieri; she was hurt by the way her mother spoke of him.

"What kind of man is he?" the Princess repeated, "I suppose he is a Venetian, a son of the man who married the Gradenigo heiress, about the time when I was married myself. Is he the man who discovered Troy?"

"Carthage, I think," said Sabina.

"Troy, Carthage, America, it is all the same. He discovered something, and I fancy he will be rich. But what is he like? Dark, fair, good, bad, snuffy or smart? As he is an archaeologist, he must be snuffy, a bore, probably, and what the English call a male frump. It cannot be helped, my dear! You will have to marry him. Describe him to me."

"He is dark," said Sabina.

"I am glad of that. I always liked dark men—your father was fair, like you. Besides, as you are a blonde, you will always look better beside a dark husband. But of course he is dreadfully careless, with long hair and doubtful nails. All those people are."

"No," said Sabina. "He is very nice-looking and neat, and wears good clothes."

The Princess's brow cleared.

"All the better," she said. "Well, my dear, it is not so bad after all. We have found a husband for you, rich, of good family—quite as good as yours, my child! Good-looking, smart—what more do you expect? Besides, he cannot possibly refuse to marry you after what has happened. On the whole, I think your adventure has turned out rather well. You can be married in a month. Every one will think it quite natural that it should have been kept quiet until I came, you see."

"But even if I wanted to marry him, he will never ask for me," objected Sabina, who was less surprised than might be expected, for she knew her mother thoroughly.

The Princess laughed, and blew a cloud of smoke from her lips, and then showed her handsome teeth.

"I have only to say the word," she answered. "When a young girl of our world has spent the night in a man's rooms, he marries her, if her family wishes it. No man of honour can possibly refuse. I suppose that this Malipieri is a gentleman?"

"Indeed he is!" Sabina spoke with considerable indignation.

"Precisely. Then he will come to me this afternoon and tell his story frankly, just as you have done—it was very sensible of you, my dear—and he will offer to marry you. Of course I shall accept."

"But, mother," cried Sabina, aghast at the suddenness of the conclusion, "I am not at all sure—"

She stopped, feeling that she was much more sure of being in love with Malipieri than she had been when she had driven to the palace with Sassi on the previous afternoon.

"Is there any one you like better?" asked the Princess sharply. "Are you in love with any one else?"

"No! But—"

"I had never seen your father when our marriage was arranged," the Princess observed.

"And you were very unhappy together," Sabina answered promptly. "You always say so."

"Oh, unhappy? I am not so sure, now. Certainly Hot nearly so miserable as half the people I know. After all, what is happiness, child? Doing what you please, is it not?"

Sabina had not thought of this definition, and she laughed, without accepting it. In one way, everything looked suddenly bright and cheerful, since her mother had believed her story, and she knew that she was not to go back to the Baroness, who had not believed her at all, and had called her bad names.

"And I almost always did as I pleased," the Princess continued, after a moment's reflection. "The only trouble was that your dear father did not always like what I did. He was a very religious man. That was what ruined us. He gave half his income to charities and then scolded me because I could not live on the other half. Besides, he turned the Ten Commandments into a hundred. It was a perfect multiplication, table of things one was not to do."

Poor Sabina's recollections of her father had nothing of affection in them, and she did not feel called upon to defend his memory. Like many weak but devout men, he had been severe to his children, even to cruelty, while perfectly incapable of controlling his wife's caprices.

"I remember, though I was only a little girl when he died," Sabina said.

"Is Malipieri very religious?" the Princess asked "I mean, does he make a fuss about having fish on Fridays?" She spoke quite gravely.

"I fancy not," Sabina answered, seeing nothing odd in her mother's implied definition of righteousness. "He never talked to me about religion, I am sure."

"Thank God!" exclaimed the Princess devoutly.

"He always says he is a republican," Sabina remarked, glad to talk about him.

"Really?" The Princess was interested. "I adore revolutionaries," she said thoughtfully. "They always have something to say. I have always longed to meet a real anarchist."

"Signor Malipieri is not an anarchist," said Sabina.

"Of course not, child! I never said he was. All anarchists are shoemakers or miners, or something like that. I only said that I always longed to meet one. People who do not value their lives are generally amusing. When I was a girl, I was desperately in love with a cousin of mine who drove a four-in-hand down a flight of steps, and won a bet by jumping on a wild bear's back. He was always doing those things. I loved him dearly." The Princess laughed.

"What became of him?" Sabina asked.

"He shot himself one day in Geneva, poor boy, because he was bored. I was always sorry, though they would not have let me marry him, because he had lost all his money at cards." The Princess sighed. "Of course you want a lot of new clothes, my dear," she said, changing the subject rather suddenly. "Have you nothing but that to wear?"

Sabina's things had not yet come from the Via Ludovisi. She explained that she had plenty of clothes.

"I fancy they are nothing but rags," her mother answered incredulously. "We shall have to go to Paris in any case for your trousseau. You cannot get anything here."

"But we have no money," objected Sabina.

"As if that made any difference! We can always get money, somehow. What a child you are!"

Sabina said nothing, for she knew that her mother always managed to have what she wanted, even when it looked quite impossible. The girl had been brought up in the atmosphere of perpetual debt and borrowing which seemed natural to the Princess, and nothing of that sort surprised her, though it was all contrary to her own instinctively conscientious and honourable nature.

Her mother had always been a mystery to her, and now, as Sabina sat near her, she crossed her feet, which were encased in a pair of the Princess's slippers, and looked at her as she had often looked before, wondering how such a reckless, scatter-brained, almost penniless woman could have remained the great personage which the world always considered her to be, and that, too, without the slightest effort on her part to maintain her position.

Then Sabina reflected upon the Baroness's existence, which was one long struggle to reach a social elevation not even remotely rivalling that of the Princess Conti; a struggle in which she was armed with a large fortune, with her husband's political power, with the most strictly virtuous views of life, and an iron will; a struggle which could never raise her much beyond the point she had already reached.

Sabina's meditations were soon interrupted by the arrival of her belongings, in charge of her mother's maid, and the immediate necessity of dressing more carefully than had been possible when she had been so rudely roused by the Baroness. She was surprised to find herself so little tired by the desperate adventure, and without even a cold as the result of the never-to-be-forgotten chill she had felt in the vaults.

In the afternoon, the Princess declared that she would not go out. She was sure that Malipieri would present himself, and she would receive him in her boudoir. The ambassador had given her a very pretty set of rooms. He was a bachelor, and was of course delighted to have her stay with him, and still more pleased that her pretty daughter should join her. It was late in the season, he was detained in Rome by an international complication, and he looked upon the arrival of the two guests as a godsend, more especially as the Princess was an old acquaintance of his and the wife of an intimate friend. Nothing could have been more delightful, and everything was for the best. The Princess herself felt that fortune was shining upon her, for she never doubted that she could lay hands on some of the money which the statues would bring, and she was sure, at least, of marrying Sabina extremely well in a few weeks, which was an advantage not to be despised.

During the hours that followed her first conversation with her mother, Sabina found time to reflect upon her own future, and the more she thought of it, the more rosy it seemed. She was sure that Malipieri loved her, though he had certainly not told her so yet, and she was sure that she had never met a man whom she liked half so much. It was true that she had not met many, and none at all in even such intimacy as had established itself between him and her at their very first meeting; but that mattered little, and last night she had seen him as few women ever see a man, fighting for her life and his own for hours together, and winning in the end. Indeed, had she known it, their situation had been really desperate, for while Masin was in prison and in ignorance of what had happened, and Sassi lying unconscious at the hospital after a fall that had nearly killed him outright, it was doubtful whether any one else could have guessed that they were in the vaults or would have been able to get them out alive, had it been known.

She had always expected to be married against her will by her mother, or at all events without any inclination on her own part. She had been taught that it was the way of the world, which it was better to accept. If the proposed husband had been a cripple, or an old man, she would have been capable of rebellion, of choosing the convent, of running away alone into the world, of almost anything. But if he had turned out to be an average individual, neither uglier, nor older, nor more repulsive than many others, she would probably have accepted her fate with indifference, or at least with the necessary resignation, especially if she had never met Malipieri. Instead of that, it was probably Malipieri whom she was to marry, the one of all others whom she had chosen for herself, and in place of a dreary existence, stretching out through endless blank years in the future, she saw a valley of light, carpeted with roses, opening suddenly in the wilderness to receive her and the man she loved.

It was no wonder that she smiled in her sleep as she lay resting in the warm afternoon, in her own room. Her mother had made her lie down, partly because she was still tired, and partly because it would be convenient that she should be out of the way if Malipieri came.

He came, as the Princess had expected, and between two and three o'clock, an hour at which he was almost sure to find her at home. From what Sabina had said to the Baroness in his presence, and from his judgment of the girl's character, he felt certain that she would tell her mother the whole story at once. As they had acknowledged to each other in the vaults, they were neither of them good at inventing falsehoods, and Sabina would surely tell the truth. In the extremely improbable case that she had not been obliged to say anything about the events of the night, his visit would not seem at all out of place. He had seen a good deal of Sabina during her mother's absence, and it was proper that he should present himself in order to make the Princess's acquaintance.

He studied her face quickly as he came forward, and made up his mind that she expected him, though she looked up with an air of languid surprise as he entered. She leaned forward a little in her comfortable seat, and held out her plump hand.

"I think I knew your mother, and my daughter has told me about you," she said. "I am glad to see you."

"You are very kind," Malipieri answered, raising her hand to his lips, which encountered a large, cool sapphire. "I have had the pleasure of meeting Donna Sabina several times."

"Yes, I know." The Princess laughed. "Sit down here beside me, and tell me all about your strange adventure. You are really the man I mean, are you not?" she asked, still smiling. "Your mother was a Gradenigo?"

"Yes. My father is alive. You may have met him, though he rarely leaves Venice."

"I think I have, years ago, but I am not sure. Does he never come to Rome?"

266

"He is an invalid now," Malipieri explained gravely. "He cannot leave the house."

"Indeed? I am very sorry. It must be dreadful to be an invalid. I was never ill in my life. But now that we have made acquaintance, do tell me all about last night I Were you really in danger, as Sabina thinks, or is she exaggerating?"

"There was certainly no exaggeration in saying that we were in great danger, as matters have turned out," Malipieri answered. "Of the two men who knew that we were in the vault, one is lying insensible, with a fractured skull, in the hospital of the Consolazione, and the other has been arrested by a mistake and is in prison. Besides, both of them would have had every reason to suppose that we had got out."

"Sabina did not tell me that. How awful! I must know all the details, please!"

Malipieri told the whole story, from the time when Volterra had first invited him to come and make a search. The Princess nodded her energetic approval of his view that Sabina had a right to a large share in anything that was found. The poor girl's dowry, she said, had been eaten up by her father's absurd charities and by the bad administration of the estates which had ruined the whole family. Malipieri paid no attention to this statement, for he knew the truth, and he went on to the end, telling everything, up to the moment when Volterra had at last quitted the palace that morning and had left him free.

"Poor Sassi!" exclaimed the Princess, when he had finished. "He was a foolish old man, but he always seemed very willing. Is that all?"

"Yes. That is all. I think I have forgotten nothing."

The Princess looked at him and smiled encouragingly, expecting him to say something more, but he was grave and silent. Gradually, the smile faded from her face, till she looked away, and took a cigarette from the table at her elbow. Still he said nothing. She lit the cigarette and puffed at it two or three times, slowly and thoughtfully.

"I hope that Donna Sabina is none the worse for the fatigue," Malipieri said at last. "She seemed quite well this morning. I wondered that she had not caught cold."

"She never caught cold easily, even as a child," answered the Princess indifferently. "This affair may have much more serious consequences than a cold in the head," she added, after a long pause.

"I think the Volterra couple will be discreet, for their own sakes," Malipieri answered.

"Their servants must know that Sabina was out all night."

"They do not know that poor Sassi did not bring her to you here, and the Baroness will be careful to let them understand that she is here now, and with you. Those people dread nothing like a scandal. The secret is between them and us. I do not see how any one else can possibly know it, or guess it."

"The fact remains," said the Princess, speaking out, "that my daughter spent last night in your rooms, and slept there, as if she had been in her own home. If it is ever known she will be ruined."

"It will never be known, I am quite sure."

"I am not, and it is a possibility I cannot really afford to contemplate." She looked fixedly at him.

268

Malipieri was silent, and his face showed that he was trying to find some way out of the imaginary difficulty, or at least some argument which might quiet the Princess's fears.

She did not understand his silence. If he was a man of honour, it was manifestly his duty at least to offer the reparation that lay in his power; but he showed no inclination to do so. It was incomprehensible.

"I cannot see what is to be done," he said at last.

"Is it possible that I must tell you, Signer Malipieri?" asked the Princess, and her splendid eyes flashed angrily.

Malipieri's met them without flinching.

"You mean, of course, that I should offer to marry Donna Sabina," he said.

"What else could an honourable man do, in your position?"

"I wish I knew." Malipieri passed his hand over his eyes in evident distress.

"Do you mean to say that you refuse?" the Princess asked, between scorn and anger. "Are you so little one of us that you suppose this to be a question of inclination?"

Malipieri looked up again.

"I wish it were. I love your daughter with all my heart and soul. I did, before I saved her life last night."

The Princess's anger gave way to stupefaction.

"Well—but then? I do not understand. There is something else?"

"Yes, there is something else. I have kept the secret a long time, and it is not all my own."

"I have a right to know it," the Princess answered firmly, and bending her brows.

"I never expected to tell it to any one," Malipieri said, in a low voice, and evidently struggling with himself. "I see that I shall have to trust you."

"You must," insisted the Princess. "My daughter has a right to know, as well as I; and you say that you love her."

"I am married."

"Good heavens!"

She sank back in her chair, overwhelmed with surprise at the simple statement, which, after all, need not have astonished her so much, as she reflected a moment later. She had never heard of Malipieri until that day, and since he had never told any one of his marriage, it was impossible that her daughter should have known of it. She was tolerably sure that the latter's adventure would not be known, but she had formed the determination to take advantage of it in order to secure Malipieri for Sabina, and had been so perfectly sure of the result that she fell from the clouds on learning that he had a wife already.

On his part, he was not thinking of what was passing in her mind, but of what he should have thought of himself, had he, with his character, been in her position. The bald statement that he was married and his confession of his love for Sabina looked badly side by side, in the clear light of his own honour; all the more, because he knew that, without positively or directly speaking out his heart to the girl, he had let her guess that he was falling in love with her.

He had said so, though in jest, on that night when he had been alone with her in Volterra's house; his going there, on the mere chance of seeing her alone, and the interest he had shown in her from their first meeting, must have made her think that he was in love. Moreover, he really was, and like most people who are consciously in love where they ought not to be, he felt as if everybody knew it; and yet he was a married man.

"I am legally married under Italian law," he said, after a pause. "But that is all. My wife bears my name, and lives honourably under it, but that is all there has ever been of marriage in my life. I can honestly say that not even a word of affection ever passed between us."

"How strange!" The Princess listened with interest, wondering what was coming next.

"I never saw her but once," Malipieri continued. "We met in the morning, we were married at noon, at the municipality, we parted at the railway station twenty minutes later, and have never met again."

"But you are not married at all!" cried the Princess. "The Church would annul such a marriage without making the least trouble."

"We were not even married in church," said Malipieri. "We were married at the municipality only."

"It is not a marriage at all, then."

"Excuse me. It is perfectly valid in law, and my wife has a certified copy of the register to prove that she has a right to my name."

"Were you mad? What made you do it? It is utterly incomprehensible—to bind yourself for life to a woman you had never seen! What possible motive—"

"I will tell you," said Malipieri. "It all happened long ago, when I was little more than twenty-one. It is not a very long story, but I beg you not to tell it. You do not suppose me capable of keeping it a secret in order to make another marriage, not really legal do you?"

"Certainly not," answered the Princess. "I believe you to be an honourable man. I will not tell your story to any one."

"You may tell Donna Sabina as much of it as you think she need hear. This is what happened. I served my time in a cavalry regiment—no matter where, and I had an intimate friend, nearly of my own age, and a Venetian. He was very much in love with a young girl of a respectable family, but not of his own station. Of course his family would not hear of a marriage, but she loved him, and he promised that he would marry her as soon as he had finished his military service, in spite of his own people. He would have been of age by that time, for he was only a few months younger than I, and he was willing to sacrifice most of his inheritance for love of the girl. Do you understand?"

"Yes. Go on."

"He and I were devotedly attached to each other, said I sympathized with him, of course, and promised to help him if he made a runaway match. He used to get leave for a couple of days, to go and see her, for she lived with her parents in a small city within two hours of our garrison town. You guess what happened.—They were young, they were foolish, and they were madly in love."

The Princess nodded, and Malipieri continued.

"Not long afterwards, my friend was killed by a fall. His horse crushed him. It was a horrible accident, and he lived twelve hours after it, in great pain. He would not let the doctors give him morphia. He said he would die like a man, and he did, with all his senses about him. While he lay dying, I was with him, and then he told me all the truth. The girl would not be able to conceal it much longer. There was no time to bring her to his bedside and marry her while he still breathed. He could not even leave her money, for he was a minor. He could do nothing for her and her parents would turn her into the street; in any case she was ruined. He was in frightful agony of mind for her sake, he was dying before my eyes, powerless to help her and taking his suffering and his fault with him to the next world, and he was my friend. I did what I could. I gave him my word of honour that I would marry her legally, give her and her child my name, and provide for them as well as I could. He thanked me—I shall never forget how he looked—and he died quietly, half an hour afterwards. You know now. I kept my word. That is all."

The Princess looked at his quiet face a moment in silence, and all that was best in her rose up through all that was artificial and worldly, and untruthful and vain.

"I did not know that there were such men," she said simply.

CHAPTER XX

"So he got out," said Gigi to Toto, filling the latter's glass to the brim.

"May he die assassinated!" answered Toto. "I will burn a candle to the Madonna every day, in order that an apoplexy may seize him. He is the devil in person, this cursed engineer. Even the earth and the water will not have him. They spit him out, like that."

Toto illustrated the simile with force and noise before drinking. Gigi's cunning face was wreathed in smiles.

"You know nothing," he observed.

"What is it?" asked Toto, with his glass in his hand and between two sips.

"There was old Sassi, who was hurt, and the engineer's gaol-bird mason-servant. They were with him. It was all in the Messaggero this morning."

"I know that without the newspaper, you imbecile. It was I that told you, for I saw all three pass under the window while I was locked in. Is there anything else you know?"

"Oh, yes! There was another person with them."

"I daresay," Toto answered, pretending blank indifference. "He must have been close to the wall as they went by. What difference does it make since that pig of an engineer got out?"

"The other person was caught with him when the water rose," said Gigi, who meant to give his information by inches.

"Curse him, whoever he was! He helped the engineer and that is why they got out. No man alone could have broken through that wall in a night, except one of us."

"The other person was only a woman, after all," answered Gigi. "But you do not care, I suppose."

"Speak, animal of a Jesuit that you are!" cried Toto. "Do not make me lose my soul!"

Gigi smiled and drank some of his wine.

"There are people who would pay to know," he said, "and you would never tell me whether the sluice gate of the 'lost water' is under number thirteen or not."

"It is under number thirteen, Master Judas. Speak!"

"It was the little fair girl of Casa Conti who was caught with the engineer in the vaults."

Even Toto was surprised, and opened his eyes and his mouth at the same time.

"The little Princess Sabina?" he asked in a low voice.

Gigi shrugged his shoulders with a pitying air and grinned.

"I told you that you knew nothing," he observed in triumph. "They were together all night, and she slept in his room, and the Senator's wife came to get her in the morning. The engineer took the porter off to the cellars before they came down, so that he should not see her pass; but he forgot me, the old carpenter of the house, and I opened the postern for the two ladies to go out. The little Princess's skirt had been torn. I saw the pins with these eyes. It was also spotted with mud which had been brushed off. But thanks be to heaven I have still my sight. I see, and am not blind."

"Are you sure it was she?" asked Toto, forgetting to curse anybody.

"I saw her as I see you. Have I not seen her grow up, since she used to be wheeled about in a baby carriage in Piazza Navona, like a flower in a basket? Her nurse made love with the 'woodpecker' who was always on duty there."

The Romans call the municipal watchmen "woodpeckers," because they wear little pointed cocked hats with a bunch of feathers. They have nothing to do with police soldiers, nor with the carabineers.

Toto made Gigi tell him everything he knew. At the porter's suggestion Volterra had sent for the mason, as the only man who knew anything about the "lost water," and Toto had agreed, with apparent reluctance, to do what he could at once, as soon as he had satisfied himself that Malipieri had really made another opening by which the statues could be reached. Toto laid down conditions, however. He pretended that he must expose himself to great danger, and insisted upon being paid fifty francs for the job. Furthermore, he obtained from Volterra, in the presence of the porter as witness, a formal promise that his grandfather's bones should have Christian burial, with a fine hearse and feathers, and a permanent grave in the cemetery of Saint Lawrence, which latter is rather an expensive luxury, beyond the means of the working people. But the Baron made no objection. The story would look very well in a newspaper paragraph, as a fine illustration of the Senator's liberality as well as of his desire to maintain the forms of religion. It would please everybody, and what will do that is cheap at any price, in politics.

The result of these negotiations had of course been that the water had subsided in the vaults within a few hours, and Toto even found a way of draining the outer cellars, which had been flooded to the depth of a couple of feet, because the first breach made by Malipieri had turned out to be an inch or two lower than the level of the overflow shaft.

When the two workmen had exchanged confidences, they ordered another half litre of wine, and sat in silence till the grimy host had set it down between them on the blackened table, and had retired to his den. Then they looked at each other.

"There is an affair here," observed Gigi presently.

"I suppose you mean the newspapers," said Toto nodding gravely. "They pay for such stories."

"Newspapers!" Gigi made a face. "All journalists are pigs who are dying of hunger."

Toto seemed inclined to agree with this somewhat extreme statement, on the whole, but he distinguished. There were papers, he said, which would pay as much as a hundred francs for a scandalous story about the Roman princes. A hundred francs was not a gold mine, it was not Peru. But it was a hundred francs. What did Gigi expect? The treasure of Saint Peter's? A story was a story, after all, and anybody could deny it.

"It is worth more than a hundred francs," Gigi answered, with his weasel smile, "but not to the newspapers. The honour of a Roman princess is worth a hundred thousand."

Toto whistled, and then looked incredulous, but it began to dawn upon him that the "affair" was of more importance than he had supposed. Gigi was much cleverer than he; that was why he always called Gigi an imbecile.

The carpenter unfolded his plan. He knew as well as any one that the Conti were ruined and could not raise any such sum as he proposed to demand, even to save Sabina's good name. It would apparently be necessary to extract the blackmail from Volterra by some means to be discovered. On the other hand, Volterra was not only rich, he also possessed much power, and it would be somewhat dangerous to incur his displeasure.

Toto, though dull, had a certain rough common sense and pointed this out. He said that the Princess must have jewels which she could sell to save her daughter from disgrace. She and Donna Sabina were at the Russian Embassy, for the Messaggero said so. Gigi, who could write, might send her a letter there.

"No doubt," assented the carpenter with a superior air. "I have some instruction, and can write a letter. But the jewels are paste. Half the Roman princesses wear sham jewellery nowadays. Do you suppose the Conti have not sold everything long ago? They had to live."

"I do not see why," observed Toto. "Princes without money might as well be dead, an apoplexy on them all! Well, what do you propose to do? That old franc-eater of a Senator will not pay you for the girl's reputation, since she is not his daughter."

"We must think," said Gigi. "Perhaps it would do no harm to write a letter to the Princess. The engineer is poor, of course. It is of no use to go to him."

"All engineers are starving to death," Toto answered cheerfully. "I have seen them eat bread and onions and drink water, like us. Would they eat onions and dry bread if they could have meat? It is when they become contractors that they get money, by cheating the rich and strangling the poor. I know them. They are all evil people."

"This is true," assented Gigi, "I have seen several, before this one."

"This one is the eternal father of all assassins," growled Toto. "He talked of walling me up alive."

"That was only a joke, to frighten you into holding your tongue," said Gigi. "And you did."

"A fine joke! I wish you had been down there, hiding beside the gold statue instead of me, while two murderers sat by the little hole above and talked of walling it up for a week or ten days! A fine joke. The joke the cat makes to the mouse before eating it!"

"I can tell the Princess that the money must be sent In thousand-franc notes," said Gigi, who was not listening. "It cannot go to the post-office registered, because it must be addressed to a false name. Somebody must bring it to us."

"And bring the police to catch us at the same time," suggested Toto contemptuously. "That will not do."

"She must bring it herself, to a safe place."

"How?"

"For instance, I can write that she must take a cab and drive out of the city on the Via Appia, and drive, and drive, until she meets two men—they will be you and me—one with a red handkerchief hanging out of his coat pocket, and the other with an old green riband for a band to his hat. I have an old green riband that will do. She must come alone in the cab. If we see any one with her, she shall not see us. She will not know how far out we shall be, so she cannot send the police to the place. It may be one mile from the gate, or five. I will write that if she does not come alone, the story will be printed in all the papers the next morning."

Toto now looked at his friend with something almost like admiration.

"I did not know that you had been a brigand," he remarked pleasantly. "That is well thought. Only the Princess may not be able to get the money, and if she does, she had better bring it in gold. We will then go to America."

Neither of the men had the least idea that a hundred thousand francs in gold would be an uncommonly awkward and heavy load to carry. They supposed it would go into their pockets.

"If she does not come, we will try the Senator before we publish the story," said Gigi. "By that time we shall have been able to think of some way of putting him under the oil-press to squeeze the gold out of him."

"In any case, this is a good affair," Toto concluded, filling his pipe. "Nothing is bad which ends well, and we may both be gentlemen in America before long."

So the two ruffians disposed of poor little Sabina's reputation in the reeking wine shop, very much to their own imaginary advantage; and the small yellow-and-blue clouds from their stinking pipes circled up slowly through the gloom into the darkness above their heads, as the light failed in the narrow street outside.

Then Gigi, the carpenter, bought two sheets of paper and an envelope, and a pen and a wretched little bottle of ink, and a stamp, all at the small tobacconist's at the corner of Via della Scrofa, and went to Toto's lodging to compose his letter, because Toto lived alone, and there were no women in the house.

Just at the same time, Volterra was leaving the Palazzo Madama, where the Senate sits, not a couple of hundred yards away. And the two workmen would have been very much surprised if they could have guessed what was beginning to grow in the fertile but tortuous furrows of his financial and political intelligence, and that in the end their schemes might possibly fall in with his.

CHAPTER XXI

As it had become manifestly impossible to keep the secret of the discovery in the Palazzo Conti any longer, Volterra had behaved with his accustomed magnanimity. He had not only communicated all the circumstances to the authorities at once, offering the government the refusal of the statues, which the law could not oblige him to sell if he chose to keep them in the palace, but also publicly giving full credit to the "learned archaeologist and intrepid engineer, Signer Marino Malipieri, already famous throughout Europe for his recent discoveries in Carthage." In two or three days the papers were full of Malipieri's praises. Those that were inclined to differ with the existing state of things called him a hero, and even a martyr of liberty, besides a very great man; and those which were staunch to the monarchy poked mild fun at his early political flights and congratulated him upon having descended from the skies, after burning his wings, not only to earth, but to the waters that are under the earth, returning to the upper air laden with treasures of art which reflected new glory upon Italy.

All this was very fine, and much of it was undoubtedly true, but it did not in the least help Malipieri to solve the problem which had presented itself so suddenly in his life. The roads to happiness and to reputation rarely lead to the same point of the compass when he who hopes to attain both has more heart than ambition. It is not given to many, as it was to Baron Volterra, to lead an admiring, submissive and highly efficient wife up the broad steps of political power, financial success and social glory. Neither Caesar nor Bonaparte reached the top with the wife of his heart, yet Volterra, more moderately endowed, though with almost equal ambition, bade fair to climb high with the virtuous helpmeet of his choice on his arm.

Malipieri slept badly and grew thinner during those days. His devotion to his dying friend had been absurdly quixotic, according to ordinary standards, but it had never seemed foolish to him, and he had never regretted it. He had always believed that a man of action and thought is freer to think and act if he remains unmarried, and it had never occurred to him that he might fall in love with a young girl, without whom life would seem empty. He was quixotic, generous and impulsive, but like many men who do extremely romantic things, he thought himself quite above sentimentality and entirely master of his heart. Hitherto the theory had worked very well, because he had never really tried to practise it. Nothing had seemed easier than not to fall in love with marriageable young women, and he had grown used to believing that he never could.

With that brutality to his own feelings of which only a thoroughly sentimental man is capable, he left the Palazzo Conti on the day following the adventure, and took rooms in a hotel in the upper part of the city. Nothing would have induced him to spend a night in his room since Sabina's head had lain upon his pillow. With Volterra's powerful help, Masin had been released, though poor Sassi had not returned to consciousness, and Malipieri learned that the old man had changed his mind at the last minute, had insisted upon trying to follow Sabina after all, and had fallen heavily upon his head in trying to get down into the first chamber; while Masin, behind him, implored him to come back, or at least to wait for help where he was. The rest needs no explanation.

Malipieri took a few things with him to the hotel, and left Masin to collect his papers and books on the following day, instructing him to send the scanty furniture, linen and household belongings to the nearest auction rooms, to be sold at once. Masin, none the worse for a night and day in prison, came back to his functions as if nothing had happened. He and his master had been in more than one adventure together. This one was over and he was quite ready for the next.

There was probably not another man in Italy, and there are not many alive anywhere, who would have done what Malipieri did, out of pure sentiment and nothing else. To him, it seemed like a natural sacrifice to his inward honour, to refuse which would have been cowardly. He had weakly allowed himself to fall in love with a girl whom he could not possibly marry, and whom he respected as much as he loved. He guessed, though he tried to deny it, that she was more than half in love with him, since love sometimes comes by halves. To lie where she had lain, dreaming of her with his aching eyes open and his blood on fire, would be a violation of her maiden privacy, morally not much less cowardly in the spirit than it could have been in the letter, since he could not marry her.

The world laughs at such refinements of delicate feeling in a man, but cannot help inwardly respecting them a little, as it respects many things at which it jeers and rails. Moreover, Malipieri did not care a fig for the world's opinion, and if he had needed to take a motto he would have chosen "Si omnes, ego non"; for if there was a circumstance which always inclined him to do anything especially quixotic, it was the conviction that other people would probably do the exact opposite. So Masin took the furniture to an auction room on a cart, and Malipieri never saw it again.

While the press was ringing his praises, and he himself was preparing a carefully written paper on the two statues, while the public was pouring into the gate of the Palazzo Conti to see them, and Volterra was driving a hard bargain with the government for their sale, he lived in a state of anxiety and nervousness impossible to describe. He was haunted by the fear that some one might find out where Sabina had been on the night after she had left Volterra's house, and the mere thought of such a possibility was real torment, worse than the knowledge that he could never marry her, and that without her his life did not seem worth living. Whatever happened to Sabina would be the result of his folly in taking her to the vaults. He might recover from any wound he had himself received, but to see the good name of the innocent girl he loved utterly ruined and dragged through the mud of newspaper scandal would be a good deal worse than being flayed alive. It was horrible to think of it, and yet he could not keep it out of his thoughts. There had been too many people about the palace on the morning when Sabina had left it with the Baroness. Especially, there had been that carpenter, of whom no one had thought till it was too late. If Gigi had recognized Sabina, that would be Malipieri's fault too, for Volterra had not known that the man had been employed about the house for years. A week passed, and nothing happened. He had neither seen Sabina nor heard of her from any one. He was besieged by journalists, artists, men of letters and men of learning, and the municipal authorities had declared their intention of giving a banquet in his honour and Volterra's, to celebrate the safe removal of the two statues from the vault in which they had lain so long. He, who hated noisy feasting and speech-making above all things, could not refuse the public invitation. All sorts of people came to see him, in connection with the whole affair, and he was at last obliged to shut himself in during several hours of the day, in order to work at his dissertation. Masin alone was free to reach him in case of any urgent necessity.

One morning, while he was writing, surrounded by books, drawings and papers, Masin came and stood silently at his elbow, waiting till it should please him to look up. Malipieri carefully finished the sentence he had begun, and laid down his pen. Then Masin spoke.

"There is a lady downstairs, sir, who says that you will certainly receive her upon very important business. She would not give her name, but told the porter to try and get me to hand you this note."

Malipieri sighed wearily and opened the note without even glancing at the address. He knew that Sabina would not write to him, and no one else interested him in the least. But he looked at the signature before reading the lines, and his expression changed. The dowager Princess Conti wrote a few words to say that she must see him at once and was waiting. That was all, but his heart sank. He sent Masin to show her the way, and sat resting his forehead in his hand until she appeared.

She entered and stood before him, softly magnificent as a sunset in spring; looking as even a very stout woman of fifty can, if she has a matchless complexion, perfect teeth, splendid eyes, faultless taste, a wonderful dressmaker and a maid who does not hate her.

Malipieri vaguely wondered how Sabina could be her daughter, drew an armchair into place for her, and sat down again by his writing-table. The windows were open and the blinds were drawn together to keep out the glare, for it was a hot day. A vague and delicious suggestion of Florentine orris-root spread through the warm air as the Princess sat down. Malipieri watched her face, but her expression showed no signs of any inward disturbance.

"Are you sure that nobody will interrupt us?" she asked, as Masin went out and shut the door.

"Quite sure. What can I do to serve you?"

"I have had this disgusting letter."

She produced a small, coarse envelope from the pale mauve pocket-book she carried in her hand, and held it out to Malipieri, who took it and read it carefully. It was not quite easy for him to understand, as Gigi wrote in the Roman dialect without any particular punctuation, and using capitals whenever it occurred to him, except at the beginning of a sentence. To Malipieri, as a Venetian, it was at first sight about as easy as a chorus of Aeschylus looks to an average pass-man.

As the sense became clear to him, his eyelids contracted and his face was drawn as if he were in bodily pain.

"When did you get this?" he asked, folding the letter and putting it back into the envelope.

"Five or six days ago, I think. I am not sure of the date, but it does not matter. It says the money must be paid in ten days, does it not? Yes—something like that. I know there is some time left. I have come to you because I have tried everything else."

"Everything else?" cried Malipieri, in sudden anxiety. "What in the world have you tried?"

"I sent for Volterra the day after I got this."

"Oh!" Malipieri was somewhat relieved. "What did he advise you to do? To employ a detective?"

"O dear, no! Nothing so simple and natural. That man is an utter brute, and I am sorry I left Sabina so long with his wife. She would have been much better in the convent with her sister. I am afraid that is where she will end, poor child, and it will be all your fault, though you never meant any harm. You do not think you could divorce and marry her, do you?"

Malipieri stared at her a moment, and then bit his lip to check the answer. He had no right to resent whatever she chose to say to him, for he was responsible for all the trouble and for Sabina's good name.

"There is no divorce law in Italy," he answered, controlling himself. "Why do you say that Volterra is an utter brute? What did he advise you to do?"

"He offered to silence the creature who wrote this letter if I would make a bargain with him. He said he would pay the money, if I would give Sabina to his second son, who is a cavalry officer in Turin, and whom none of us has ever seen."

Malipieri's lips moved, but he said nothing that could be heard. A vein that ran down the middle of his forehead was swollen, and there was a bad look in his eyes.

"I would rather see the child dead than married to one of those disgusting people," the Princess said. "Did you ever hear of such impertinence?"

"You let her live with them for more than two months," observed Malipieri.

"I know I did. It was simply impossible to think of anything better in the confusion, and as they offered to take charge of her, I consented. Yes, it was foolish, but I did not suppose that they would let her go off in a cab with that old dotard and stay out all night."

Malipieri felt as if she were driving a blunt nail into his head.

"Poor Sassil" he said. "He was buried yesterday."

"Was he? I am not in the least sorry for him. He always made trouble, and this was the worst of all Sabina almost cried because I would not let her go and see him at the hospital. You know, he never spoke after he was taken there—he did not feel anything."

Malipieri wondered whether the Princess, in another sense, had ever felt anything, a touch of real pity, or real love, for any human being. He did not remember to have ever met a woman who had struck him as so utterly heartless; and yet he could not forget the look that had come into her face, and the simple word she had spoken, when he had told her his story.

"I understand that you refused Volterra's proposal," he said, returning to the present trouble. "Do you mean to say that he declined to help you unless you would accept it?"

"Oh, no! He only said that as I was not disposed to accept what would make it so much easier, he would have to think it over. I have not seen him since."

"But you understand what he had planned, do you not?" Malipieri asked. "It is very simple."

"It is not so clear to me. I am not at all clever, you know." The Princess laughed carelessly. "He must have a very good reason for offering to pay a hundred thousand francs in order that his son may marry Sabina, who has not a penny. I confess, if it were not an impertinence, it would look like a foolish caprice. I suppose he thinks it would be socially advantageous."

Her lip curled and showed her even white teeth.

"His wife is a snob," Malipieri answered, "but Volterra does not care for anything but power and money, except perhaps for the sort of reputation he has, which helps him to get both." "Then of what possible use could it be to him to marry his son to Sabina, and to throw all that money away for the sake of getting her?"

Malipieri hesitated, not sure whether it would be wise to tell her all he thought.

"In the first place," he said slowly, "I do not believe he would really pay the blackmail, or if he did, he would catch the man, get the money back, and have him sent to penal servitude. He is very clever, and in his position he can have whatever help he asks from the government, especially in a just cause, as that would be. Perhaps he thinks that he has guessed who the man is."

"Have you any idea?" asked the Princess, glancing down at the dirty little letter she still held.

"In the second place," Malipieri continued, without heeding the question, "I am almost sure that when you were in difficulties, two or three months ago, he got the better of you, as he gets the better of every one. With the value of these statues, he has probably pocketed a couple of million francs by the transaction."

"The wretch!" exclaimed the Princess. "I wish you were my lawyer! You have such a clear way of putting things."

Even then Malipieri smiled.

"I have always believed what I have just told you," he answered. "That was the reason why I hoped that Donna Sabina might yet recover what she should have had from the estate. Volterra is sure that if you can take proper steps, you will recover a large sum, and that is why he is so anxious to marry his son to your daughter. He thinks the match would settle the whole affair."

"The idiot! As if I did not need the money myself!"

Again Malipieri smiled.

"But you will not get it," he answered. "You will certainly not get it if Volterra is interested in the matter, for it will all go to your daughter. Your other two children have had their share of their father's estate, and that of the daughters should have amounted to at least two millions each. But Donna Sabina has never had a penny. Whatever is recovered from Volterra will go to her, not to you."

"It would be the same thing," observed the Princess carelessly.

"Not exactly," Malipieri said, "for the court will appoint legal guardians, and the money will be paid to her intact when she comes of age. In other words, if she marries Volterra's son, the little fortune will return to Volterra's family. But of course, if you consented to the marriage, he would compromise for the money, before the suit was brought, by settling the two millions upon his daughter-in-law, and if he offered to do that, as he would, no respectable lawyer in the world would undertake to carry on the suit, because Volterra would have acted in strict justice. Do you see?"

"Yes. It is very disappointing, but I suppose you are right."

"I know I am, except about the exact sum involved. I am an architect by profession, I know something of Volterra's affairs and I do not think I am very far wrong. Very good. But Volterra has accidentally got hold of a terrible weapon against you, in the shape of this blackmailer's letter."

"Then you advise me to accept his offer after all?"

"He knows that you must, unless you can find something better. You are in his power."

"But why should I, if I am to get nothing by it?" asked the Princess absent-mindedly.

"There is Donna Sabina's good name at stake," Malipieri answered, with a little sternness.

"I had forgotten. Of course! How stupid of me!" For a moment Malipieri knew that he should like to box her ears, woman though she was; then he felt a sort of pity for her, such as one feels for half-witted creatures that cannot help themselves nor control their instincts.

"Then I must accept, and let Sabina marry that man," she said, after a moment's silence. "Tell me frankly, is that what you think I ought to do?"

"If Donna Sabina wishes to marry him, it will be a safe solution," Malipieri answered steadily.

"My dear man, she is in love with you!" cried the Princess in one of her sudden fits of frankness. "She told me so the other day in so many words, when she was so angry because I would not let her go to see poor old Sassi die. She said that you and he and her schoolmistress were the only human beings who had ever been good to her, or for whom she had ever cared, You may just as well know it, since you cannot marry her!"

In a calmer moment, Malipieri might have doubted the logic of the last statement; but at the present moment he was not very calm, and he turned a pencil nervously in his fingers, standing it alternately on its point and its blunt end, upon the blotting-paper beside him, and looking at the marks it made.

"How can she possibly wish to marry that Volterra creature?" asked the Princess, by way of conclusion. "She will have to, that is all, whether she likes it or not. After all, nobody seems to care much, nowadays," she added in a tone of reflection. "It is only the idea I always heard that Volterra kept a pawnshop in Florence, and then became a dealer in bric-a-brac, and afterwards a banker, and all sorts of things. But it may not be true, and after all, it is only prejudice. A banker may be a very respectable person, you know."

"Certainly," assented Malipieri, wishing that he could feel able to smile at her absurd talk, as a sick man wishes that he could feel hungry when he sees a dish he likes very much, and only feels the worse for the mere thought of touching food.

"Nothing but prejudice," the Princess repeated. "I daresay he was never really a pawnbroker and is quite respectable. By the bye, do you think he wrote this letter himself? It would be just like him."

"No," Malipieri answered. "I am sure he did not. Volterra never did anything in his life which could not at least be defended in law. The letter is genuine."

"Then there is some one who knows, besides ourselves and Volterra and his wife?"

"Yes. I am sure of it."

"You are so clever. You must be able to find out who it is."

"I will try. But I am sure of one thing. Even if the money is not paid on the day, the story will not be published at once. The man will try again and again to get money from you. There is plenty of time."

"Unless it is a piece of servants' vengeance," the Princess said. "Our servants were always making trouble before we left the palace, I could never understand why. If it is that, we shall never be safe. Will you come and see me, if you think of any plan?"

She rose to go.

"I will go to the Embassy to-morrow afternoon, between three and four."

"Thanks. Do you know? I really cannot help liking you, though I think you are behaving abominably. I am sure you could get a divorce in Switzerland."

"We will not talk about that," Malipieri answered, a little harshly.

When she was gone, he called Masin, and then, instead of explaining what he wanted, he threw himself into an armchair and sat in silence for nearly half an hour. Masin was used to his master's ways and did not speak, but occupied himself in noiselessly dusting the mantelpiece at least a hundred times over.

CHAPTER XXII

Volterra had not explained to the Princess the reason why her acceptance of his offer would make it so much easier for him to help her out of her difficulty. He had only said that it would, for he never explained anything to a woman if an explanation could be avoided, and he had found that there are certain general ways of stating things to which women will assent rather than seem not to understand. If the Princess had asked questions, he would have found plausible answers, but she did not. She refused his offer, saying that she had other views for her daughter. She promptly invented a rich cousin in Poland, who had fallen in love with Sabina's photograph and was only waiting for her to be eighteen years old in order to marry her.

She had gone to Malipieri as a last resource, not thinking it probable that he could help her, or that he would change his mind and try to free himself in order to marry Sabina. She came back with the certainty that he would not do the latter and could not give any real assistance. So far, she had not spoken to Sabina of her interview with the Baron, but she felt that the time had come to sound her on the subject of the marriage, since there might not be any other way. She had not lost time since her arrival, for she had at once seen one of the best lawyers in Rome, who looked after such legal business as the Russian Embassy occasionally had; and he had immediately applied for a revision of the settlement of the Conti affairs, on the ground of large errors in the estimates of the property, supporting his application with the plea that many of the proceedings in the matter had been technically faulty because certain documents should have been signed by Sabina, as a minor interested in the estate, and whose consent was necessary. He was of opinion that the revision would certainly be granted, but he would say nothing as to the amount which might be recovered by the Conti family. As a matter of fact, the settlement had been made hastily, between Volterra, old Sassi and a notary who was not a lawyer; and Volterra, who knew what he was about, and profited largely by it, had run the risk of a revision being required. For the rest, Malipieri's explanation of his motives was the true one.

At the first suggestion of a marriage with Volterra's son Sabina flatly refused to entertain the thought. She made no outcry, she did not even raise her voice, nor change colour; but she planted her little feet firmly together on the footstool before her chair, folded her hands in her lap and looked straight at her mother.

"I will not marry him," she said. "It is of no use to try to make me. I will not."

Her mother began to draw a flattering though imaginary portrait of the young cavalry officer, and enlarged upon his fortune and future position. Volterra was immensely rich, and though he was not quite one of themselves, society had accepted him, his sons had been admirably brought up, and would be as good as any one. There was not a prince in Rome who would not be glad to make such a match for his daughter.

"It is quite useless, mother," said Sabina. "I would not marry him if he were Prince Colonna and had the Rothschilds' money."

"That is absurd," answered the Princess. "Just because you have taken a fancy to that Malipieri, who cannot marry you because he has done the most insane thing any one ever heard of."

"It was splendid," Sabina retorted.

"Besides," her mother said, "you do not know that it is true."

Sabina's eyes flashed.

"Whatever he says, is true," she answered, "and you know it is. He never lied in his life!"

"No," said the Princess, "I really think he never did."

"Then why did you suggest such a thing, when you know that I love him?"

"One says things, sometimes," replied the Princess vaguely. "I did not really mean it, and I cannot help liking the man. I told him so this morning. Now listen. Volterra is a perfect beast, and if you refuse, he is quite capable of letting that story get about, and you will be ruined."

"I will go into a convent."

"You know that you hate Clementina," observed the Princess.

"Of course I do. She used to beat me when I was small, because she said I was wicked. Of course I hate her. I shall join the Little Sisters of the Poor, or be a Sister of Charity. Even Clementina could not object to that, I should think."

"You are a little fool!"

To this observation Sabina made no reply, for it was not new to her, and she paid no attention to it. She supposed that all mothers called their children fools when they were angry. It was one of the privileges of motherhood.

The discussion ended there, for Sabina presently went away and shut herself up in her room, leaving her mother to meditate in solitude on the incredible difficulties that surrounded her.

Sabina was thinking, too, but her thoughts ran in quite another direction, as she sat bolt upright on a straight-backed chair, staring at the wall opposite. She was wondering how Malipieri looked at that moment, and how it was possible that she should not even have seen him since she had left his rooms with the Baroness a week ago, and more; and why, when every hour had dragged like an age, it seemed as if they had parted only yesterday, sure to meet again.

She sat still a long time, trying to think out a future for herself, a future life without Malipieri and yet bearable. It would have been easy before the night in the vaults; it would have seemed possible a week ago, though very hard; now, it was beyond her imagination. She had talked of entering a sisterhood, but she knew that she did not mean to do it, even if her reputation were ruined.

She guessed that in that event her mother would try to force her into a convent. The Princess was not the sort of woman who would devote the rest of her life to consoling her disgraced daughter, no matter how spotlessly blameless the girl might be. She would look upon her as a burden and a nuisance, would shut her up if she could, and would certainly go off to Russia or to Paris, to amuse herself as far as possible from the scene of Sabina's unfortunate adventure.

"Poor child!" she would say to her intimate friends, "She was perfectly innocent, of course, but there was nothing else to be done. No decent man would have married her, you know!"

And she would tell Malipieri's story to everybody, too, to explain why he had not married Sabina. She had no heart at all, for her children or for any one else. She had always despised her son for his weaknesses and miserable life, and she had always laughed at her elder daughter; if she had been relatively kind to Sabina, it was because the girl had never given any trouble nor asked for anything extravagantly inconvenient. She had never felt the least sympathy with the Roman life into which she had been brought by force, and after her husband had died she had plainly shown his quiet Roman relatives what she thought of them.

She would cast Sabina off without even a careless kind word, if Sabina became a drag on her and hindered her from doing what she pleased in the world. And this would happen, if the story about the night in the Palazzo Conti were made public. Just so long, and no longer, would the Princess acknowledge her daughter's existence;

and that meant so long as Volterra chose that the secret should be kept.

At least, Sabina thought so. But matters turned out differently and were hurried to an issue in a terribly unexpected way.

Both Volterra and Malipieri had guessed that the anonymous letter had been written by Gigi, the carpenter, but Volterra had seen it several days before the Princess had shown it to Malipieri. Not unnaturally, the Baron thought that it would be a good move to get the man into his power. Italy is probably not the only country where men powerful in politics and finance can induce the law to act with something more than normal promptitude, and Volterra, as usual, was not going to do anything illegal. The Minister of Justice, too, was one of those men who had been fighting against the Sicilian "mafia" and the Neapolitan "camorra" for many years, and he hated all blackmailers with a just and deadly hatred. He was also glad to oblige the strong Senator, who was just now supporting the government with his influence and his millions. Volterra was sure of the culprit's identity and explained that the detective who had been sent to investigate the palace after Sassi's accident had seen the carpenter and would recognize him. Nothing would be easier than to send for Gigi to do a job at the palace, towards evening, to arrest him as soon as he came, and to take him away quietly.

This was done, and in twenty-four hours Gigi was safely lodged in a cell by himself, with orders that he was on no account to be allowed any communication with other prisoners.

Then Volterra went to see him, and instead of threatening him, offered him his help if he would only tell the exact truth. Gigi was frightened out of his wits and grasped at the straw, though he did not trust the Baron much. He told what he had done; but with the loyalty to friends, stimulated by the fear of vengeance, which belongs to the Roman working man, he flatly denied that he had an accomplice. Yes, he had spoken in the letter of two men who would be walking on the Via Appia, and he had intended to take his brother-in-law with him, but he said that he had not meant to explain why he took him until the last minute. It was a matter for the galleys! Did his Excellency the Senator suppose that he would trust anybody with that, until it was necessary?

The consequence was that Gigi was kept quietly in prison for a few days before any further steps were taken, having been arrested at the instance of the Ministry of Justice for trying to extract blackmail from the Conti family, and being undoubtedly guilty of the misdeed. Volterra's name did not even appear in the statement.

Malipieri had not Volterra's influence, and intended to try more personal methods with the carpenter; but when he appeared at the palace in the afternoon, and asked the porter to go and call Gigi, the old man shook his head and said that Gigi had been in prison three days, and that nobody knew why he had been arrested. The matter had not even been mentioned by the Messaggero.

Malipieri had never connected Toto with Gigi, and did not even know that the two men were acquainted with each other. He had not the slightest doubt but that it was Toto who had caused the water to rise in the well, out of revenge, but he knew that it would now be impossible to prove it. Strange to say, Malipieri bore him no grudge, for he knew the people well, and after all, he himself had acted in a high-handed way. Nevertheless, he asked the porter if the man were anywhere in the neighbourhood.

But Toto had not been seen for some time. He had not even been to the wine shop, and was probably at work in some distant part of Rome. Perhaps he was celebrating his grandfather's funeral with his friends. Nobody could tell where he might be.

Malipieri went back to his hotel disconsolately. That evening he read in the Italie that after poor Sassi had been buried, the authorities had at once proceeded to take charge of his property and effects, because the old woman-servant had declared that he had no near relations in the world; and the notary who had served the Conti family had at once produced Sassi's will.

He had left all his little property, valued roughly at over a hundred thousand francs, to Donna Sabina Conti. Had any one known it, the date of the will was that of the day on which he had received her little note thanking him for burying her canary, out on Monte Mario.

The notary's brother and son, notaries themselves, were named as guardians. The income was to be paid to Sabina at once, the capital on her marriage. The newspaper paragraph recalled the ruin of the great family, and spoke of the will as a rare instance of devotion in an old and trusted servant.

Sabina and the Princess learned the news at dinner that evening from a young attache of the Embassy who always read the Italie because it is published in French, and he had not yet learned Italian. He laughingly congratulated Sabina on her accession to a vast fortune. To every one's amazement, Sabina's eyes filled with tears, though even her own mother had scarcely ever seen her cry. She tried hard to control herself, pressed her lids hastily with her fingers, bit her lips till they almost bled, and then, as the drops rolled down her cheeks in spite of all she could do, she left the table with a broken word of excuse.

"She is nothing but a child, still," the Princess explained in a tone of rather condescending pity.

The young attache was sorry for having laughed when he told the story. He had not supposed that Donna Sabina knew much about the old agent, and after dinner he apologized to his ambassador for his lack of tact.

"That little girl has a heart of gold," answered the wise old man of the world.

The Princess had a profoundly superstitious belief in luck, and was convinced that Sabina's and her own had turned with this first piece of good fortune, and that on the following day Malipieri would appear and tell her that he had caught the writer of the letter and was ready to divorce his wife in order to marry Sabina. Secure in these hopes she slept eight hours without waking, as she always did.

But she was destined to the most complete disappointment of her life, and to spend one of the most horribly unpleasant days she could remember.

Long before she was awake boys and men, with sheaves of damp papers, were yelling the news in the Corso and throughout Rome.

"The Messaggero! The great scandal in Casa Conti! The Messaggero! One sou!"

CHAPTER XXIII

Toto had done it. In his heart, the thick-headed, practical fellow had never quite believed in Gigi's ingenious scheme, and the idea of getting a hundred thousand francs had seemed very visionary. Since Gigi had got himself locked up it would be more sensible to realize a little cash for the story from the Messaggero, saying nothing about the carpenter. The only lie he needed to invent was to the effect that he had been standing near the door of the palace when Sabina had come out. The porter, being relieved from the order to keep the postern shut against everybody had been quite willing to gossip with Toto about the detective's visit, the closed room and Malipieri's refusal to let any one enter it. As for what had happened

300

in the vaults, Toto could reconstruct the exact truth much more accurately than Gigi could have done, even with his help. It was a thrilling story; the newspaper paid him well for it and printed it with reservations.

There was not a suggestion of offence to Sabina, such as might have afforded ground for an action against the paper, or against those that copied the story from it. The writer was careful to extol Malipieri's heroic courage and strength, and to point out that Sabina had been half-dead of fatigue and cold, as Toto knew must have been the case. It was all a justification, and not in the least an accusation. But the plain, bald fact was proved, that Donna Sabina Conti had spent the night in the rooms of the now famous Signor Malipieri, no one else being in the apartment during the whole time. He had saved her life like a hero, and had acted like a Bayard in all he had done for the unfortunate young lady. It was an adventure worthy of the middle ages. It was magnificent. Her family, informed at once by Malipieri, had come to get her on the following morning. Toto had told the people at the office of the Messaggero, who it was that had represented the "family," but the little newspaper was far too worldly-wise to mention Volterra in such a connection. Donna Sabina, the article concluded, was now with her mother at the Russian Embassy.

The evening papers simply enlarged upon this first story, and in the same strain. Malipieri was held up to the admiration of the public. Sabina's name was treated with profound respect, there was not a word which could be denied with truth, or resented with a show of justice. And yet, in Italy, and most of all in Rome, it meant ruin to Sabina, and the reprobation of all decent people upon Malipieri if he did not immediately marry her.

It was the ambassador himself who informed the Princess of what had happened, coming himself to the sitting-room as soon as he learned that she was visible. He stayed with her a long time, and they sent for Sabina, who was by far the least disturbed of the

301

three. It was all true, she said, and there was nothing against her in the article.

Masin brought the news to Malipieri with his coffee, and the paper itself. Malipieri scarcely ever read it, but Masin never failed to, and his big, healthy face was very grave.

Malipieri felt as if he were going to have brain fever, as his eye ran along the lines.

"Masin," he said, when he had finished, "did you ever kill a man?"

"No, sir," answered Masin. "You have always believed that I was innocent, though I had to serve my seven years."

"I did not mean that," said Malipieri.

Then he sat a long time with his untasted coffee at his elbow and the crumpled little sheet in his hand.

"Of course, sir," Masin said at last, "I owe you everything, and if you ordered me—"

He paused significantly, but his master did not understand.

"What?" he asked, starting nervously.

"Well, sir, if it were necessary for your safety, that somebody should be killed, I would risk the galleys for life, sir. What am I, without you?"

Malipieri laughed a little wildly, and dropped the paper.

"No, my friend," he said presently, "we would risk our lives for each other, but we are not murderers. Besides, there is nobody to be killed, unless you will have the goodness to put a bullet through my head."

And he laughed again, in a way that frightened the quiet man beside him. What drove him almost mad was that he was powerless. He longed to lay his hands on the editor of the paper, yet there was not a word, not a suggestion, not an implied allusion for which any man in his senses could have demanded an apology. It was the plain truth, and nothing else; except that it was adorned by fragmentary panegyrics of himself, which made it even more exasperating if that were possible. He had not only wrecked Sabina's reputation by his quixotic folly; he was to be praised to the skies for doing it.

His feverish anger turned into a dull pain that was much worse. The situation looked utterly hopeless. Masin stood still beside him watching him with profound concern, and presently took the cup of coffee and held it to his lips. He drank a little, like a sick man, only half consciously, and drew back, and shook his head. Masin did not know what to do and waited in mute distress, as a big dog, knowing that his master is in trouble, looks up into his face and feebly wags his sympathetic tail, just a little, at long intervals, and then keeps quite still.

Malipieri gradually recovered his senses enough to think connectedly, and he tried to remember whether he had ever heard of a situation like his own. As he was neither a novelist nor a critic, he failed, and frankly asked himself whether suicide might not be a way out of the difficulty for Sabina. He was not an unbeliever, and he had always abhorred and despised the idea of suicide, as most thoroughly healthy men do when it occurs to them; but if at that time he could have persuaded himself that his death could undo the harm he had brought upon Sabina he would not have hesitated a moment. Neither his body nor his soul could matter much in comparison with her good name. Hell was full of people who had got there because they had done bad things for their own advantage; if he went there, it would at least not be for that. He did not think of hell at all, just then, nor of heaven or of anything else that was very far off. He only thought of Sabina, and if he once wished himself dead for his own sake, he drove the cowardly thought away. As long as he was alive, he could still do something for her—surely, there must be something that he could do. There must be a way out, if he could only use his wits and his strength, as he had made a way out of the vaults, for her to pass through, ten days ago.

There was nothing, or at least he could think of nothing, that could help her. To try and free himself from the bond he had put upon himself would be to break a solemn promise given to a dying man whom he had dearly loved. The woman he had seen that once, to marry her and leave her, had been worthy of the sacrifice, too, as far as lay in her. He had given her a small income, enough for her and her little girl to live on comfortably. She had not only kept within it, but had learned to support herself, little by little, till she had refused to take the money that was sent to her. At regular times, she wrote to him, as to a benefactor, touching and truthful letters, with news of the growing child. He knew that it was all without affectation of any sort, and that she had turned out a thoroughly good and honest woman. The little girl knew that her father was dead, and that her own name was really and legally Malipieri, beyond a doubt. Her mother kept the copy of her certificate of birth together with the certificate of marriage. The Signora Malipieri lived as a widow in Florence and gave lessons in music and Italian. She had never asked but one thing of Malipieri, which was that he would never try to see her, nor let her daughter know that he was alive. It was easy to promise that. He knew that she had been most faithful to her lover's memory, cherishing the conviction that in the justice of heaven he was her true husband, as he would have been indeed had he lived but a few months longer. She was bringing up her child to be like herself, save for her one fault. Malipieri had settled a sufficient dowry on the girl, lest anything should happen to him before she was old enough to marry.

The mere suggestion of divorcing a woman who had acted as she had done since his friend's death, was horrible to him. It was like receiving a blow in the face, it was mud upon his honour, it was an insult to his conscience, it was far worse than merely taking back a gift once given in a generous impulse. If he had felt himself capable of such baseness he could never again have looked honest men fairly in the eyes. It would mean that he must turn upon her, to insult her by accusing her of something she had never done; he knew nothing of the divorce laws in foreign countries, except that Italians could obtain divorce by a short residence and could then come back and marry again under Italian law. That was all he knew. The Princess had not asked of him a legal impossibility, but he had felt, when she spoke, that it would be easier to explain the dogma of papal infallibility to a Chinese pirate than to make her understand how he felt towards the good woman who had a right to live under his name and had borne it so honourably for many years.

Sabina would understand. He wished now, with all his heart, that in the hours they had spent together he had told her the secret which he had been obliged to confide to her mother. He wondered whether she knew it, and hoped that she did. She would at least understand his silence now, she would know why he was not at the Embassy that morning as soon as he could be received by her mother. She might not forgive him, because she knew that he loved her, but she would see why he could not divorce in order to marry her.

An hour passed, and two hours, and still he sat in his chair, while Masin came and went softly, as if his master were ill. Then reporters sent up cards, with urgently polite requests to be received, and he had to give orders that he was not to be disturbed on any account. He would see no one, he would answer no questions, until he had made up his mind what to do.

At last he rose, shook himself, walked twice up and down the room and then spoke to Masin.

"I am going out," he said. "I shall be back in an hour."

He had seen that there was at least one thing which he must do at once, and after stopping short, stunned to stupor by what had happened, his life began to move on again. It was manifestly his duty to see the Princess again, and he knew that she would receive him, for she would think that he had changed his mind after all, and meant to free himself. He must see her and say something, he knew not what, to convince her that he was acting honourably.

He was shown to her sitting-room, as if he were expected. It was not long since the ambassador had left her and her daughter had gone back to her room, and she was in a humour in which he had not seen her before, as he guessed when he saw her face. Her wonderful complexion was paler than usual, her brows were drawn together, her eyes were angry, there was nothing languid or careless in her attitude, and she held her head high.

"I expected you," she said. "I sent word that you were to come up at once."

She did not even put out her hand, but there was a chair opposite her and she nodded towards it. He sat down, feeling that a struggle was before him.

"The ambassador has just been here," she said. "He brought the newspaper with him, and I have read the article. I suppose you have seen it."

Malipieri bent his head, but kept his eyes upon her.

"I have told the ambassador that Sabina is engaged to marry you," she said calmly.

Malipieri started and sat upright in his chair. If he had known her better, he might have guessed that what she said was untrue, as yet; but she had made the statement with magnificent assurance.

"Your engagement will be announced in the papers this evening," she continued. "Shall you deny it?"

She looked at him steadily, and he returned her gaze, but for a long time he could not answer. She had him at a terrible advantage.

"I shall not deny it publicly," he said at last. "That would be an injury to your daughter."

"Shall you deny it at all?" She was conscious of her strong position, and meant to hold it.

"I shall write to the lady who is living under my name, and I shall tell her the circumstances, and that I am obliged to allow the announcement to be made by you."

"Give me your word that you will not deny your engagement to any one else. You know that I have a right to require that. My daughter knows that you are married."

Malipieri hesitated only a moment.

"I give you my word," he said.

She rose at once and went towards one of the doors, without looking at him. He wondered whether she meant to dismiss him rudely, and stood looking after her. She stopped a moment, with her hand on the knob of the lock, and glanced back.

"I will call Sabina," she said, and she was gone.

He stood still and waited, and two or three minutes passed before Sabina entered. She glanced at him, smiled rather gravely, and looked round the room as she came forward, as if expecting to see some one else.

"Where is my mother?" she asked, holding out her hand.

"She said she was going to call you," Malipieri answered.

"So she did, and she told me she was coming back to you, because I was not quite ready."

"She did not come back."

"She means us to be alone," Sabina said, and suddenly she took both his hands and pressed them a little, shaking them up and down, almost childishly. "I am so glad!" she cried. "I was longing to see you!"

Even then, Malipieri could not help smiling, and for a moment he forgot all his troubles. When they sat down, side by side, upon a little sofa, the Princess was already telling the ambassador that Malipieri had come and that they were engaged to be married. She had carried the situation by a master stroke.

"She has told you all about me," Malipieri said, turning his face to Sabina. "You know what my life is. Has she told you everything?"

"Yes," Sabina answered softly, but not meeting his look, "everything. But I want to hear it from you. Will you tell me? Will it hurt you to tell me about what you did for your friend? You know my mother is not always very accurate in telling a story. I shall understand why you did it."

He had known that she would, and he told her the story, a little less baldly than he had told her mother, yet leaving out such details as she need not hear. He hesitated a little, once or twice.

"I understand," she repeated, watching him with innocent eyes. "She felt just as if they were really married, and he could not bear to die, feeling that she would be without protection, and that other men would all want to marry her, because she was beautiful. And her father and mother were angry because she loved him so much."

"Yes," Malipieri answered, smiling, "that was it. They loved each other dearly."

"It was splendid of you," she said. "I never dreamt that any man would do such a thing."

"It cannot be undone." He was at least free to say that much, sadly.

There was a pause, and they looked away from each other. At last Sabina laid her hand lightly upon his for a moment, though she did not turn her face to him.

"I should not like you so much, if you wished to undo it," she said.

"Thank you," he answered, withdrawing the hand she released when she had finished speaking, and folding it upon his other. "I should love you less, if you did not understand me so well."

"It is more than understanding. It is much more."

He remembered how he had taken her slender body in his arms to warm her when she had been almost dead of the cold and dampness, and a mad impulse was in him to press her to him now, as he had done then, and to feel her small fair head lay itself upon

309

his shoulder peacefully, as it surely would. He sat upright and pressed one hand upon the other rather harder than before.

"You believe it, do you not?" she asked. "Why is your face so hard?"

"Because I am bound hand and foot, like a man who is carried to execution."

"But we can always love each other just the same," Sabina said, and her voice was warm and soft.

"Yes, always, and that will not make it easier to live without you," he answered rather harshly.

"You need not," she said, after an instant's pause.

He turned suddenly, startled, not understanding, wondering what she could mean. She met his eyes quite quietly, and he saw how deep and steady hers were, and the light in them.

"You need not live without me unless you please," she said.

"But I must, since I cannot marry you, and you understand that I could not be divorced—"

"My mother has just told me that no decent man will marry me, because all the world knows that I stayed at the palace that night. She must be right, for she could have no object in saying it if it were not true, could she? Then what does it matter how any one talks about me now? I will go with you. We cannot marry, but we shall always be together."

Malipieri's face expressed his amazement.

"But it is impossible!" he cried. "You cannot do that! You do not know what you are saying!"

"Oh, yes, I do! That poor, kind old Sassi has left me all he had, and I can go where I please. I will go with you. Would you rather have me shut up in a convent to die? That is what my mother will try to do with me, and she will tell people that I was 'mad, poor girl'! Do you think I do not know her? She wants this little sum of money that I am to have, too, as if she and the others had not spent all I should have had. Do you think I am bound to obey my mother, if she takes me to the convent door, and tells me that I am to stay there for the rest of my life?"

The gentle voice was clear and strong and indignant now. Malipieri twisted his fingers one upon another, and sat with his head bent low. He knew that she had no clear idea of what she was saying when she proposed to join her existence with his. Her maiden thoughts could find no harm in it.

"You do not know what your mother said to me, before you came in," he answered. "She told me that she would announce our engagement at once, and made me give my word that I would not deny it to any one but my legal wife."

"You gave your word?" Sabina asked quickly, not at all displeased.

"What could I do?"

"Nothing else! I am glad you did, for we can see each other as much as we like now. But how shall we manage it in the end, since we cannot marry?"

"Break the imaginary engagement, I suppose," Malipieri answered gloomily. "I see nothing else to be done."

"But then my mother says that no decent man will marry me. It will be just the same, all over again. It was very clever of her; she is trying to force you to do what she wants. In the meantime you can

311

come and see me every day—that is the best part of it. Besides, she will leave us alone together here, for hours, because she thinks that the more you fall in love with me the more you will wish to get a divorce. Oh, she is a very clever woman! You do not know her as I do!"

Malipieri marvelled at the amazing combination of girlish innocence and keen insight into her mother's worldly and cynical character, which Sabina had shown during the last few minutes. There never yet was a man in love with girl or woman who did not find in her something he had never dreamt of before.

"She is clever," he assented gravely, "but she cannot make me break that promise, even for your sake. I cannot help looking forward and thinking what the end must be."

"It is much better to enjoy the present," Sabina answered. "We can be together every day. You will write to your—no, she is not your wife, and I will not call her so! She would not be really your wife if she could, for she made you promise never to go and see her. That was nice of her, for of course she knew that if she saw you often, she must end by falling in love with you. Any woman would; you know it perfectly well. You need not shake your head at me, like that. You will write to her, and explain, and she will understand, and then we will let things go on as long as they can till something else happens."

"What can possibly happen?"

"Something always happens. Things never go on very long without a change, do they? I am sure, everything in my life has changed half a dozen times in the last fortnight."

"In mine, too," Malipieri answered.

"And if things get worse, and if worse comes to worst," Sabina answered, "I have told you what I mean to do. I shall come to you, wherever you are, and you will have to let me stay, no matter what people choose to say. That is, if you still care for me!"

She laughed softly and happily, and not in the least recklessly, though she was talking of throwing the world and all connection with it to the winds. The immediate future looked bright to her, since they were to meet every day, and after that, "something" would happen. If nothing did, and they had to face trouble again, they would meet it bravely. That was all any one could do in life. She had found happiness too suddenly after an unhappy childhood, to dream of letting it go, cost what it might to keep it.

But she saw how grave he looked and the hopeless expression in his loving eyes, as he turned them to her.

"Why are you sad?" she asked, smiling, and laying her hand on his. "We can be happy in the present. We love each other, and can meet often. You have made a great discovery and are much more famous than you were a few days ago. A newspaper has told our story, it is true, but there was not a word against either of us in it, for I made them let me read it myself. And now people will say that we are engaged to be married, and that we got into a foolish scrape and were nearly killed together, and that we are a very romantic couple, like lovers in a book! Every girl I know wishes she were in my place, I am sure, and half the men in Rome wish that they could have saved some girl's life as you did mine. What is there so very dreadful in all that? What is there to cry about—dear?"

Half in banter, half in earnest, she spoke to him as if he were a child compared with her, and leaned affectionately towards him; and the last word, the word neither of them had spoken yet, came so softly and sweetly to him on her breath, that he caught his own, and turned a little pale; and the barriers broke all at once, and he kissed her. Then he got hold upon himself again, and gently pushed her a

313

little further from him, while he put his other hand to his throat and closed his eyes.

"Forgive me," he said, in a thick voice. "I could not help it."

"What is there to forgive? We are not betraying any one. You are not breaking a promise to any other woman. What harm is there? You did not give your friend your word that you would never love any one, did you? How could you? How could you know?"

"I could not know," he answered in a low voice. "But I should not have kissed you."

He knew that she could not understand the point of honour that was so clear to him.

"Let me think for you, sometimes," she said.

Her voice was as low as his, but dreamily passionate, and the strange young magic vibrated in it, which perfect innocence wields with a destroying strength not even guessed at by itself.

The door opened and the Princess entered the room in a leisurely fashion, wreathed in smiles. She had successfully done what it would be very hard for Malipieri to undo. He rose.

"Have you told Sabina what I said?" she enquired.

"Yes."

She turned to the girl, who was leaning back in the corner of the sofa.

"Of course you agree, my child?" she said, with a question in her voice, though with no intonation of doubt as to the answer.

314

"Certainly," Sabina answered, with perfect self-possession. "I think it was by far the most sensible we could do. Signor Malipieri will come to see us, as if he and I were really engaged."

"Yes," assented the Princess. "You cannot go on calling him Signor Malipieri when we are together in the family, my dear. What is your Christian name?" she asked, turning to him.

"Marino."

"I did not know," Sabina said, with truth, and looking at him, as if she had found something new to like in him. "Is he to call me Sabina, mother?"

"Naturally. Well, my dear Marino—"

Malipieri started visibly. The Princess explained.

"I shall call you so, too. It looks better before people, you know. You must leave a card for the ambassador, at the porter's, when you go downstairs, He is going to ask you to dinner, with a lot of our relations, to announce the engagement. I have arranged it all beautifully—he is so kind!"

CHAPTER XXIV

Masin was very much relieved when his master came home, looking much calmer than when he had gone out and evidently having all his senses about him. Malipieri sent to ask at what time the mails left Rome for Florence, and he sat down to his table without remembering that he had eaten nothing that day.

It was not easy to write out in a concise form the story of all that has here been told in detail. Besides, he had not the habit of writing to the Signora Malipieri, except such brief acknowledgments of her regular letters to him as were necessary and kind. For years she had been to him little more than a recollection of his youth, a figure that had crossed his life like a shadow in a dream, taking with it a promise which he had never found it hard to keep. He remembered her as she had been then, and it had not even occurred to him to consider how she looked now. She sometimes sent him photographs of the pretty little girl, and Malipieri kept them, and occasionally looked at them, because they reminded him of his friend, of whom he had no portrait.

He found it very hard to tell this half-mythical woman and wholly mythical wife of all that had happened, while scrupulously avoiding the main fact, which was that he and Sabina loved each other. To have told that, too, would have seemed like a reproach, or still worse, like a request to be set at liberty.

He wrote carefully, reading over his sentences, now and then correcting one, and even entertaining a vague idea of copying the whole when he had finished it. The important point was that she should fully understand the necessity of announcing his engagement to marry Donna Sabina Conti, together with his firm intention of breaking it off as soon as the story should be so far forgotten as to make it safe to do so, having due regard for Donna Sabina's reputation and good name.

He laid so much stress on these points, and expressed so strongly his repentance for having led the girl into a dangerous scrape, that many a woman would have guessed at something more. But of this he was quite unaware when he read the letter over, believing that he could judge it without prejudice, as if it had been written by some one else. The explanation was thorough and logical, but there was a little too much protest in the expressions of regret. Besides, there were several references to Sabina's unhappy position as the daughter of an abominably worldly and heartless woman, who would lock her up in a convent for life rather than have the least trouble about her. He could not help showing his anxious interest in her future, much more clearly than he supposed.

The consequence was that when the Signora Malipieri read the letter on the following morning, she guessed the truth, as almost any woman would, without being positively sure of it; and she was absent-minded with her pupils all that day, and looked at her watch uneasily, and was very glad when she was able to go home at last and think matters over.

It was not easy to decide what to do. She could not write to Malipieri and ask him directly if he was in love with Sabina Conti and wished to marry her. She answered him at once, however, telling him that she fully understood his position, and thanking him for having written to her before she could have heard the story from any other source.

He showed the letter to Sabina, and it pleased her by its frank simplicity, and perfect readiness to accept Malipieri's statement without question, and without the smallest resentment. Somehow the girl had felt that this shadowy woman, who stood between her and Malipieri, would make some claim upon him, and assert herself in some disagreeable way, or criticise his action. It was hateful to think she really had a right to call herself his wife, and was therefore legally privileged to tell him unpleasant truths. Sabina always connected that with matrimony, remembering how her father and mother used to quarrel when he was alive, and how her brother and sister-in-law continued the tradition. If the Volterra couple were always peaceful, that was because the Baroness was in mortal awe of her fat husband, a state of life to which Sabina did not wish to be called. It was true that Malipieri's position with regard to his so-called wife had nothing to do with a real marriage, but Sabina had felt the disapproving presence of the woman she had never seen, and whom she imagined to be perpetually shaking a warning finger at Malipieri and reminding him sourly that he could not call his soul his own. The letter had destroyed the impression.

317

Meanwhile Malipieri was appalled by the publicity of a betrothal which was never to lead to marriage. The Princess took care that as much light as possible should be cast upon the whole affair, and to the Baroness Volterra's stupefaction and delight, told every one that the match had been made under her auspices, and that the Conti family owed her eternal gratitude for it and for her care of Sabina during nearly three months. The Princess told the story of the night in the vaults again and again, to her friends and relations, extolling everything that Malipieri had done, and especially his romantic determination to show the girl he was going to marry the treasures which should have belonged to her, before any one else should see them.

The Princess told Volterra, laughingly and quite frankly, that her lawyer would do everything possible to get for her a share in the value of the statues discovered, and Volterra, following her clever cue, laughed with her, and said it should be a friendly suit, and that the lawyers should decide among themselves how it should be settled, without going into court. Volterra was probably the only man in Rome who entertained a profound respect for the Princess's intelligence; yet he was reckoned a good judge in such matters. He himself was far too wise to waste regrets upon the failure of his tactics, and the stake had not been large, after all, compared with his great fortune. Magnanimity was a form of commodity which could be exchanged for popularity, and popularity was ready money. A thousand votes were as good as two million francs, any day, when one was not a senator for life, and wished to be re-elected; and a reputation for spotless integrity would cover a multitude of financial sins. Since it had been impossible to keep what did not belong to him, the next best thing was to restore it to the accompaniment of a brass band and a chorus of public approval. The Princess, clever woman, knew exactly how he felt and helped him to do the inevitable in a showy way; and it all helped her to carry her daughter and herself out of a difficult position in a blaze of triumph.

"My dear," she said to the girl, "you may do anything you please, if you will only do it in public. Lock your door to say your prayers, and the world will shriek out that you have a scandal to conceal."

It dawned upon Sabina that her cynical, careless, spendthrift, scatter-brained mother had perhaps after all a share of the cunning and the force which rule the world to-day, and which were so thoroughly combined in Volterra's character. That would account for the way in which she sailed through storms that would have wrecked the Baroness and drowned poor little Sabina herself.

Meanwhile a hundred workmen had dug down to the vault under the courtyard of the Palazzo Conti, the statues had been lifted out intact, with cranes, and had been set upon temporary pedestals, under a spacious wooden shed; and the world, the flesh and the devil, including royalty, went to see them and talked of nothing else. All Europe heard the story of Malipieri's discovery, and of his adventure with his betrothed wife, and praised him and called him and her an "ideal couple."

Sabina's brother came up from the country to be present at the Embassy dinner, and of course stopped at the Grand Hotel, and made up his mind to have an automobile at once. His wife stayed in the country with the delicate little child, but sent Sabina a note of congratulation.

Clementina, writing from her convent, said she hoped that Sabina might redeem the follies of her youth in a respectable married life, but the hope was not expressed with much conviction. Sabina need not disturb the peace of a religious house by coming to see her.

The Princess boldly gave out that the marriage would take place in the autumn, and confided to two or three gossips that she really meant to have a quiet wedding in the summer, because it would be so much more economical, and the young couple did not like the idea of waiting so long. As for a dowry, everybody knew that Sassi, dear, kind-hearted old man, had left Sabina what he had; and there were the statues.

Prince Conti came to the Embassy as soon as he arrived, and met Malipieri, to whom he was overpoweringly cordial in his weak way. On the whole, at their first interview, he judged that it would not be easy to borrow money of him, and went away disappointed.

Society asked where Malipieri's father was, and learned that he was nearly seventy and was paralysed, and never left his house in Venice, but that he highly approved of his son's marriage and wished to see his future daughter-in-law as soon as possible. The Princess said that Sabina and Malipieri would live with him, but would come to Rome for the winter.

Prince Rubomirsky, Sabina's uncle, sent her a very handsome diamond necklace, which the Princess showed to all her friends, and some of them began to send wedding presents likewise, because they had been privately informed that the marriage was to take place very soon.

Sabina lived joyously in the moment, apparently convinced that fate would bring everything right, and doing her best to drive away the melancholy that had settled upon Malipieri. Something would happen, she said. It was impossible that heaven could be so cruel as to part them and ruin both their lives for the sake of a promise given to a man dead long ago. Malipieri wished that he could believe it.

He grew almost desperate as time went on and he saw how the Princess was doing everything to make the engagement irrevocable. He grew thin, and nervous, and his eyes were restless. The deep tan of the African sun was disappearing, too, and sometimes he looked almost ill. People said he was too much in love, and laughed. Little by little Sabina understood that she could not persuade him to trust to the future, and she grew anxious about him. He wondered how she could still deceive herself as to the inevitable end.

"We can go on being engaged as long as we please," she said hopefully. "There are plenty of possible excuses."

"You and I are not good at lying," he answered, with a weary smile. "We told each other so, that night."

"But it is perfectly true that I am almost too young to be married," said she; "and really, you know, it might be more sensible to wait till I am nineteen."

"We should not think it sensible to wait a week, if there were no hindrance. You know that."

"Of course! But when there is a hindrance, as you call it, it is very sensible indeed to wait," retorted Sabina, with a truly feminine sense of the value of logic. "I shall think so, and I shall say so, if I must. Then you will have to wait, too, and what will it matter, so long as we can see each other every day? Have people never waited a year to be married?"

"You know that we may wait all our lives."

"No. I will not do that," Sabina said with sudden energy. "If nothing happens, I will make something happen. You know what I told you. Have you forgotten? And I am sure your father will understand."

"I doubt it," Malipieri answered, smiling in spite of himself.

To tell the truth, since her mother had cleared away so many dangers, and showed no intention of shutting her up in a convent, Sabina had begun to see that it would be quite another matter to run away and follow Malipieri to the ideal desert island, especially after they had been openly engaged to be married and the engagement had been broken. The world would have to know the story of his marriage then, and it would call him dishonourable for having allowed himself to be engaged to her when he was not free. It would say that she had found out the truth, and that he was a villain, or something unpleasant of that sort. But she meant to keep up the illusion bravely, as long as there was any life in it at all, and then "something must happen."

"It seems so strange that I should be braver than you," she said.

He did not wonder at that as much as she did. Her reputation was saved now, but his honour was in the balance, and at the mercy of a worldly and unscrupulous woman. When he broke the engagement, the Princess would tell the story of his marriage and publish it on the housetops. He told Sabina so.

"You are safe," he added; "but when I lose you, I shall lose my place among honourable men."

"Then I shall tell the truth, and the whole truth, to every one I know," Sabina answered, in the full conviction that truth, like faith, could perform miracles, and that a grain of it could remove mountains of evil. "I shall tell the whole world!" she cried. "I do not care what my mother says."

He was silent, for it was better, after all, that she should believe in her happiness as long as she could. She said nothing more for some time and they sat quite still, thinking widely opposite thoughts. At last she laid her hand on his; the loving little way had become familiar to her since it had come instinctively the first time.

"Marino!"

"Yes?"

"You know that I love you?"

"Indeed I know it."

"And you love me? Just as much? In the same way?"

"Perhaps more. Who knows?"

"No, that is impossible," she answered. "Now listen to me. It is out of the question that we should ever be parted, loving each other as we do, is it not?"

The door opened and a servant entered, with a card.

"The lady told me to inform your Excellency that she is a connection of Signor Malipieri," said the man. "She hopes that she may be received, as she is in Rome for only a few hours."

Sabina looked at the card and handed it silently to Malipieri, and her fingers trembled.

"Angelica Malipieri."

That was the name and there was the address in Florence, in Via del Mandorlo.

"Ask the lady to come here," said Sabina, quietly; but her face was suddenly very white.

CHAPTER XXV

Sabina and Malipieri sat in silence during the minutes that followed. From time to time, they looked at each other. His self-possession and courage had returned, now that something decisive was to take place, but Sabina's heart was almost standing still. She felt that the woman had come to make a scene, to threaten a scandal and utterly to destroy the illusion of happiness. If not, and if she had merely had something of importance to communicate, why had she not gone to Malipieri first, or written to ask for this interview with Sabina? She had come suddenly, in order to take advantage of the surprise her appearance must cause. For once, Sabina wished that her mother were with her, her high and mighty, insolent, terrible mother, who was afraid of nobody in the world.

The door opened, and the footman admitted a quiet little woman, about thirty years old, already inclined to be stout. She was very simply but very well dressed, she had beautiful brown hair, and when she came forward Sabina looked into a pair of luminous and trustful hazel eyes.

"Donna Sabina Conti?" asked the Signora Malipieri in a gentle voice.

"Yes," Sabina answered.

She and Malipieri had both risen. The Signora made a timid movement with her hand, as if she expected that Sabina would offer hers, which Sabina did, rather late, when she saw that it was expected. The lady glanced at Malipieri and then at Sabina with a look of enquiry, as he held out his hand to her and she took it. He saw that she did not recognize him.

"I am Marino Malipieri," he said.

"You?" she cried in surprise.

Then a faint flush rose in her smooth cheeks, and Sabina, who was watching her, saw that her lip trembled a little, and that tears rose in her eyes.

"Forgive me," she said, in an unsteady voice. "I should have known you, after all you have done for me."

324

"I think it is nearly thirteen years since we met," Malipieri answered. "I had no beard then."

She looked at him long, evidently in strong emotion, but the tears did not overflow, and the clear light came back gradually in her gaze. Then the three sat down.

"I thought I had better come," she said. "It seemed easier than to write."

"Yes," Sabina answered, not knowing what to say.

"You see," said the Signora, "I could not easily write to you frankly, as I had never seen you, and I did not like to write to Signor Malipieri about what I wanted to know."

"Yes," said Sabina, once more, but this time she looked at Malipieri.

"What is it that you wish to know, Signora?" he asked kindly, "Whether it is all exactly as my letter told you? Is that it?"

She turned to him with a look of reproach.

"Does a woman doubt a man who has done what you have done for me?" she asked. "I wanted to know something more—a little more than what you wrote to me. It would make a difference, perhaps."

"To you, Signora?" asked Sabina quickly.

"No. To you. Perhaps it would make a great difference in the way I should act." She paused an instant. "It is rather hard to ask, I know," she added shyly.

She seemed to be a timid little woman.

"Please tell us what it is that you wish to know, Signora," said Malipieri, in the same kind tone, trying to encourage her.

"I should like to ask—I hardly know just how to say it—if you would tell me whether you are fond of each other—"

"What difference can that make to you, Signora?" Malipieri asked with sudden hardness. "You know that I shall not break my word."

She was hurt by the tone, and looked down meekly, as if she had deserved the words.

"We love each other with all our hearts," said Sabina, before either of the others could say more. "Nothing shall ever part us, in this world or the next."

There was a ring of clear defiance to fate in the girl's voice, and Signora Malipieri turned to her quickly, with a look of sympathy. She knew the cry that comes from the heart.

"But you think that you can never be married," she said, almost to herself.

"How can we? You know that we cannot!" It was Malipieri who answered.

Then the timid little woman raised her head and looked him full in the face, and spoke without any more hesitation.

"Do you think that I have never thought of this possibility, during all these years?" she asked. "Do you really believe that I would let you suffer for me, let your life be broken, let you give up the best thing that any life holds, after you have done for me what perhaps no man ever did for a woman before?"

"I know you are grateful," Malipieri answered very gently. "Do not speak of what I have done. It has not been at any sacrifice, till now."

But Sabina leaned forward and grasped the Signora Malipieri's hands. Her own were trembling.

"You have come to help us!" she cried. "It is so easy, now that I know that you love each other."

"How?" asked Sabina, breathless. "By a divorce?"

"Yes."

"I shall never ask for that," Malipieri said, shaking his head.

"You are the best and truest gentleman that ever protected a woman in trouble, Signor Malipieri," said the little woman quietly. "I know that you will never divorce me. I know you would not even think of it."

"Well, but then—" Malipieri stopped and looked at her.

"I shall get a divorce from you," she said, and then she looked happily from one to the other.

Malipieri covered his eyes with his hand. He had not even thought of such a solution, and the thought came upon him in his despair like a flood of dazzling light. Sabina was on her knees, and had thrown her arms wildly round the Signora Malipieri's neck, and was kissing her again and again.

"But it is nothing," protested the Signora, beaming with delight. "It is so simple, so easy, and I know exactly what to do."

"You?" cried Sabina between laughing and crying.

"Yes. I once gave lessons in the house of a famous lawyer, and sometimes I was asked to stay to luncheon, and I heard a great case discussed, and I asked questions, until I thoroughly understood it all. You see, it was what I always meant to do. There is a little fiction about the way it is managed, but it is perfectly legal. Though Italians may naturalize themselves in a foreign country, they can regain their own nationality by a simple declaration. Now, Signor Malipieri and I must be naturalized in Switzerland. I know a place where it can be done easily. Then we can be divorced by mutual consent at once. We come back to Italy, declare our nationality wherever we please, and we are free to be married to any one else, under Italian law. The fiction is only that by paying some money, it can all be done in three months, instead of in three years."

Malipieri had listened attentively.

"Are you positively sure of that?" he asked.

"I have the authority of one of the first lawyers in Italy."

"But the Church?" asked Sabina anxiously. "I should not think it a marriage at all, if I were not married in church."

"I have asked a good priest about that," answered the Signora. "I go to confession to him, and he is a good man, and wise too. He told me that the Church could make no objection at all, since there has really been no marriage at all, and since Signor Malipieri will present himself after being properly and legally married to you at the municipality. He told me, on the contrary, that it is my duty to do everything in my power to help you."

"God bless you!" Sabina cried. "You are the best woman in the world!"

Malipieri took the Signora's hand and pressed it to his lips fervently, for he could not find any words.

"I shall only ask one thing," she said, speaking timidly again.

"Ask all I have," he answered, her hand still in his.

"But you may not like it. I should like to keep the name, if you do not mind very much, on account of my little girl. She need never know. I can leave her with a friend while we are in Switzerland."

"It is yours," he said. "Few of my own people have borne it as worthily as you have, since I gave it to you."

Here, therefore, ends the story of Sabina Conti and Marino Malipieri, whose marriage took place quietly during the autumn, as the Princess had confidently said that it should. It is a tale without a "purpose" and without any particular "moral," in the present appalling acceptation, of those simple words. If it has interested or pleased those who have read it, the writer is glad; if it has not, he can find some consolation in having made two young people unutterably blissful in his own imagination, whereas he manifestly had it in his power to bring them to awful grief; and when one cannot make living men and women happy in real life, it is a harmless satisfaction to do it in a novel. If this one shows anything worth learning about the world, it is that a gifted man of strong character and honourable life may do a foolish and generous thing whereby he may become in a few days the helpless toy of fate. He who has never repented of a good impulse which has brought great trouble to other people, must be indeed a selfish soul.

As for the strange circumstances I have described, I do not think any of them impossible, and many of them are founded upon well-known facts. I have myself seen, within not many years, a construction like the dry well in the Palazzo Conti, which was discovered in the foundations of a Roman palace, and had been used as an oubliette. There were skeletons in it and fragments of weapons of the sixteenth century and even of the seventeenth.

There was also a communication between the cellars of the palace and the Tiber.

I read George Sand's fantastic novel Consuelo many years ago, and I am aware that she introduced a well, in an ancient castle, in which the water could be made to rise and fall at will, in order to establish or interrupt communication with a secret chamber. I do not know whether she imagined the construction or had seen a similar one, for such wells are said to be found in more than one old fortress in Europe. The "lost water" really exists at many points under Rome; its rising and falling are sometimes unaccountable; and I know at least one old palace in which it has been used and found pure, within the memory of man. So far, the explanations suggested by engineers have neither satisfied those who have propounded them, nor those who have had practical experience of the "lost water." The subject is extremely interesting but is one of very great difficulty, as it is generally quite impossible to make explorations in the places where the water is near the surface. The older part of modern Rome was built haphazard, and often upon the enormous substructures of ancient buildings, of which the positions can be conjectured only, and of which the plans and dimensions are very vaguely guessed by archaeologists. All that can be said with approximate certainty of the "lost water" is that it must run through long-forgotten conduits, that it rises here and there in wells, and that it is mostly uncontaminated by the river.

Those familiar with the Vatican museum will have at once recognized the colossal statue of gilt bronze which now stands in the circular hall known as the "Rotonda." It was accidentally found, when I was a boy, in the courtyard of the Palazzo Righetti in the Campo dei Fiori, carefully and securely concealed by a well-built vault, evidently constructed for the purpose, in the foundations of the Theatre of Pompey. I went to see it, when only a portion of the vault had been removed, and I shall never forget the vivid impression it made upon me. So far as I know, there has not been any explanation of its having been hidden there, but among the lower classes in Rome there are traditions of great treasure supposed to be buried in other parts of the city. I have taken the liberty of making the discovery over again at a point some distance from the Palazzo Righetti, and in the present time. The statue was really found in 1864, and the gem in the ring was stolen. The marble Venus which Malipieri saw with it is imaginary, but I was also taken to see the beautiful statue of Augustus, now in the Braccio Nuovo of the Vatican, on the spot where it came to light in the Villa of Livia, in 1863.

The great mediaeval family of Conti became extinct long ago. The palace to which I have given their name would stand on the site of one now the property of the Vatican, but would be of a somewhat different construction.

Finally, I wish to protest that there are no so-called "portraits" in this story of the heart of old Rome. Many Romans were ruined by the financial crisis of 1888 and its consequences, either at the time or later. The family to which Sabina belonged is wholly imaginary, and its fall was due to other causes. I trust that no ingenious reader will try to trace a parallel where none exists. I would not even have a certain young and famous architect and engineer, for whom I entertain the highest admiration and esteem, recognize a "portrait" of himself in Marino Malipieri, if these pages should ever come to his notice, and I have purposely made my imaginary hero as unlike him as possible, in appearance, manner and speech.

Those who have noticed the increasing tendency of modern readers to bring accusations of plagiarism against novels that deal partly with facts will understand why I have said this much about my own work. To others, the few details I have given may be of some interest.

F. Marion Crawford – A Short Biography

Francis Marion Crawford was born in Bagni di Lucca, Italy on 2nd August, 1854, the only son of the American sculptor Thomas Crawford and Louisa Cutler Ward. His aunt was Julia Ward Howe, the American poet, most famous for the words to 'The Battle Hymn of the Republic'.

After his father's death in 1857, his mother remarried to Luther Terry, with whom she had Crawford's half-sister, Margaret Ward Terry.

Crawford's education began at St Paul's School, Concord, New Hampshire and then went on to Cambridge University, the University of Heidelberg and finally the University of Rome.

In 1879, Crawford went to India to study the ancient language of Sanskrit and to edit Allahabad, The Indian Herald.

Returning to America in February 1881, he enrolled at Harvard University for a year to continue his studies in Sanskrit. Crawford had no real career path at this time although for two years he contributed to various periodicals, mainly The Critic.

Early in 1882, Crawford established a close, lifelong friendship with Isabella Stewart Gardner, a noted and eccentric heiress from Boston who over the years built up a large and eclectic collection of art.

Crawford lived most of his time in Boston with his Aunt Julia and Uncle Sam. The family were concerned by his lack of ambition, prospects in general, and his financial ones in particular.

His mother had hoped he might train in Boston for a career as an operatic baritone based on his private renditions of Schubert lieder. With that in mind it was, in January 1882, that George Henschel, the conductor of the Boston Symphony Orchestra, was called in to assess young Crawford's talents. Henschel was direct and to the point. Crawford would 'never be able to sing in perfect tune'. His Uncle Sam, knowing that Crawford was keen on literary pursuits, proposed that his years in India might be good source material to write about. Crawford agreed. He set to work. Uncle Sam also set about developing contacts with a number of New York publishers.

Events moved very quickly. By December of that year Crawford had completed his first novel, 'Mr Isaacs', based on modern Anglo-Indian life flavoured with a touch of Oriental mystery. It was an immediate success. Crawford set about writing a second novel and the result was 'Dr Claudius' in 1883.

In October 1884 he married Elizabeth Berdan, the daughter of the Civil War Union General Hiram Berdan. The marriage would produce two sons; Harold and Bertram, and two daughters; Eleanor and Clara.

Crawford, buoyed by his excellent start, now decided to return to Italy and to live there permanently.
The couple initially went to Sorrento and lived at the historic Hotel Cocumella during 1885 before moving permanently to Sant' Agnello, where the purchase of the Villa Renzi would now be rededicated as Villa Crawford.

As a writer Crawford had more than his fair share of detractors but, perhaps due to the physical distance between author and these detractors, they did not distract from his prolific output.

Each year seemed to bring a new F. Marion Crawford novel. His popularity was evident although some works, such as 1896's offering 'Adam Johnstone's Son', was described by his left-wing English contemporary, George Gissing, as "rubbish". Over half of his novels are set in Italy. He also wrote three long historical studies of Italy and was nearing completion on a history of Rome in the Middle Ages when he died.

His 'Saracinesca' series are considered his best works. The third in the series, 'Don Orsino' (1892) was told against the background of a real estate bubble and is especially effective. The volume immediately after was 'Corleone' (1897), and the first major treatment of the Mafia in literature.

Crawford himself was fondest of 'Khaled: A Tale of Arabia' (1891), a story of a genie who becomes human. 'A Cigarette-Maker's Romance' (1890) was dramatized, and had considerable popularity on the stage as well as in its novel form.

Towards the end of the 1890's Crawford ventured down another path with his writing. He began his historical works. 'Ave Roma Immortalis' was published in 1898, followed by 'Rulers of the South' (1900), and 'Gleanings from Venetian History' (1905). Most were re-titled with longer more explanatory titles for the American market. Within them all his careful and precise knowledge of the local Italian history together with his literary talents combined to great effect.

Whilst on an American Lecture tour in the winter of 1897-1898 Crawford was researching and gathering technical information for his historical work 'Marietta' (published 1901), that describes glass-making in late medieval Venice. Whilst visiting a glass-smelting plant in Colorado he suffered a severe lung injury when he inhaled toxic gasses. This would eventually contribute to his death a decade or so later.

Crawford's commercial popularity and appeal at the time was such that in 1901, the American Macmillan firm began a deluxe uniform edition of his novels as his works came up for re-printing. In 1904 the P. F. Collier Company in New York was authorized to publish a 25-volume edition (which was later expanded to 32 volumes).

In 1902 he wrote a stage play 'Francesca da Rimini', that was produced in Paris by his friend and legendary actress Sarah Bernhardt.

Towards the end of his life Hollywood had begun to realise that his works were a valuable source of stories and ideas and several were turned into movies and continued to be so for decades after his death.

Crawford also had a gift for pulling off excellent short stories. Several, such as 'The Upper Berth' (1886), 'For the Blood Is the Life' (1905, a vampiress tale), 'The Dead Smile' (1899), and 'The Screaming Skull' (1908), are among the most anthologized classics of the horror genre. After his death several collected volumes were published from various sources.

After most of his fictional works had been published, most had the view that he was a gifted narrator; and his books of fiction, were full of historic vitality and energy as well as dramatic characterization. He was widely popular among readers to whom literature was more for escapism than a confrontation with reality or pages of subjective analysis. In 'The Novel: What It Is' (1893), Crawford was both resolute and disarming in defending his literary approach, self-conceived as a combination of romanticism and realism, defining the art form in terms of its marketplace and audience. The novel, he wrote, is "a marketable commodity" and "intellectual artistic luxury" that "must amuse, indeed, but should amuse reasonably, from an intellectual point of view .... Its intention is to amuse and please, and certainly not to teach and preach; but in order to amuse well it must be a finely-balanced creation ...."

Francis Marion Crawford died at Sorrento on Good Friday 1909 at Villa Crawford of a heart attack.

Novels

Mr. Isaacs: A Tale of Modern India (1882)
Dr. Claudius (1883)
To Leeward (1884)
A Roman Singer (1884)
An American Politician (1884)
Zoroaster (1885)
A Tale of a Lonely Parish (1886)
Saracinesca (1887)
Marzio's Crucifix (1887)
Paul Patoff (1887)
With the Immortals (1888)
Greifenstein (1889)
Sant' Ilario (1889); sequel to Saracinesca
A Cigarette-Maker's Romance (1890)
Khaled: A Tale of Arabia (1891)
The Witch of Prague (1891)
The Three Fates (1892)
Don Orsino (1892); sequel to Sant' Ilario
The Children of the King (1893)
Pietro Ghisleri (1893)
Marion Darche (1893)
Katharine Lauderdale (1894)
The Upper Berth (1894); with "By the Waters of Paradise"
Love in Idleness (1894)
The Ralstons (1894); sequel to Katharine Lauderdale
Casa Braccio (1895); related to Katharine Lauderdale and The Ralstons.
Adam Johnstone's Son (1896)
Taquisara (1896)
A Rose of Yesterday (1897)
Corleone (1897)

Via Crucis (1899)
In the Palace of the King (1900)
Marietta (1901)
Cecilia (1902)
Man Overboard! (1903)
The Heart of Rome (1903)
Whosoever Shall Offend (1904)
Soprano (1905); U.S. title: Fair Margaret.
A Lady of Rome (1906)
Arethusa (1907)
The Little City of Hope (1907)
The Primadonna (1908); sequel to Soprano/Fair Margaret
The Diva's Ruby (1908); sequel to The Primadonna
The White Sister (1909)
Stradella (1909)
The Undesirable Governess (1910)
Wandering Ghosts; British title: Uncanny Tales.

Non-fiction

Our Silver (1881)
The Novel: What It Is (1893)
Constantinople (1895)
Bar Harbor (1896)
Ave Roma Immortalis (1898)
Rulers of the South (1900; 1905 in the U.S. as Southern Italy and Sicily and The Rulers of the South)
Gleanings from Venetian History (1905; in the U.S. as Salvae Venetia and in 1909 as Venice; the People and the Place)

Drama

In the Palace of the King (1900) with Lorrimer Stoddard.

Francesca da Rimini (1902) The piece was adapted into an opera by Franco Leoni in 1904.

Evelyn Hastings (1902) Unpublished typescript discovered in 2008.

The White Sister (1909) with Walter C. Hackett.

Filmography

A Cigarette-Maker's Romance, directed by Frank Wilson (UK, 1913, based on the novella)

The White Sister, directed by Fred E. Wright [it] (1915, based on the novel)

In the Palace of the King [it], directed by Fred E. Wright [it] (1915, based on the novel)

Whosoever Shall Offend, directed by Arrigo Bocchi (UK, 1919, based on the novel)

Il cuore di Roma, directed by Edoardo Bencivenga (Italy, 1919, based on the novel)

A Cigarette-Maker's Romance, directed by Tom Watts (UK, 1920, based on the novella)

Saracinesca [it], directed by Gaston Ravel (Italy, 1921, based on the novel)

Sant' Ilario [it], directed by Henry Kolker (Italy, 1923, based on the novel)

The White Sister, directed by Henry King (1923, based on the novel)

In the Palace of the King, directed by Emmett J. Flynn (1923, based on the novel)

Son of India, directed by Jacques Feyder (1931, based on the novel Mr. Isaacs)

The White Sister, directed by Victor Fleming (1933, based on the novel)

The Screaming Skull, directed by Alex Nicol (1958, named after the short story)

The White Sister, directed by Tito Davison (Mexico, 1960, based on the novel)

www.ingramcontent.com/pod-product-compliance
Lightning Source LLC
Chambersburg PA
CBHW021216260626
47172CB00002B/463